STEALING THUNDER

D1352962

STEALING THUNDER

PETER MILLAR

BLOOMSBURY

First published in Great Britain 1999
This paperback edition published 1999

Bloomsbury Publishing plc
38 Soho Square, London W1V 5DF

Copyright © 1999 by Peter Millar

The moral right of the author has been asserted

A CIP catalogue record for this book
is available from the British Library

ISBN 0 7475 4583 9

10 9 8 7 6 5 4 3 2 1

Typeset by Hewer Text Ltd, Edinburgh
Printed and bound in Great Britain by Clays Ltd, St Ives plc

To my mother and father, time after time.

How can I save my little boy from Oppenheimer's deadly toy? . . .
There is no monopoly of common sense,
on either side of the political fence.

Sting, 'Russians'

To betray, you must first belong; I never belonged.

Kim Philby, 1963

Acknowledgements

Many people have been helpful in finishing this book. For their help at the research stage I would like to thank Carson Marks and John Gustafson at Los Alamos, Nick Hance at Harwell, and Lorna Arnold for her historical insights. Also Svein Saemunsson of Icelandair who introduced me to the extraordinary phenomenon that is his country. David Reynolds at Bloomsbury for his tolerance and Pascal Carris for his enthusiasm and care, Julian Coman for listening in the pub, and my wife, Jackie, for being there when needed, as always.

Contents

Author's Note

This is a work of fiction, but much of it is based on facts drawn from the most important episode in the history of the Second World War. The Manhattan Project was an extraordinary achievement. Its results, for better or worse, shaped the rest of the twentieth century. The Cold War, which grew out of the nuclear standoff, arguably maintained peace for fifty years until the last legacy of the old dictatorships had faded; but at a human price which many still believe was far too high.

Most of the details of Klaus Fuchs's personality, family history and activities at Los Alamos are true, down to his love of Charles Dickens, his Buick and the fact that the British mission used him to fetch drinks for parties. Similarly, the details of Harry Gold's exploits are substantially accurate. As for the other main historical dramatis personae, I have taken liberties with their actions, but rarely with their expressed beliefs.

Prologue

The Legacy

Alamogordo Desert, 16 July 1945

The men who were afraid put on suntan lotion in the dark. They smeared it over their faces by lamplight. Out there beneath the ominously empty sky was one of the world's great wildernesses: flat and cracked by the noonday sun; and at night, as cold as an empty tomb. It was known as the *Jornado del Muerto*, the Dead Man's Journey. The only living things were scorpions, rattlesnakes, fire ants and tarantula spiders.

A few hours earlier an improbable electric storm had raked the parched earth, drowning it in torrential rain, while forked lightning ripped the night sky and great cannon roars of thunder cracked above them.

In the small concrete rooms where the men waited and watched, those with religious inclinations said silent prayers. The tall, lean, aesthetic-looking American in a porkpie hat – an amateur Sanskrit scholar and the individual on whom the matter of the moment weighed heaviest, was an atheist. None the less, he muttered to himself, 'Lord, these affairs are heavy on the heart.' Edward Teller, the Hungarian with the Groucho Marx eyebrows, fiddled with his dark glasses. Enrico Fermi, the stocky little Italian, reworked his mental arithmetic. And Klaus Fuchs, the quiet, academic German with the horn-rimmed glasses, closed his eyes, asking himself silently if what he really hoped for was failure.

Then, at precisely 5.29 and 45 seconds, the darkness disappeared. In its place was the light of a thousand suns: an artificial sunrise that cast a shadow over the future of humanity.

*   *   *

Half a century later, as grey slanting November rain fell on the Berlin cobbles, an indigo Opel glided to the edge of the pavement and stopped. The driver's door opened and the substantial shape of Hermann Dickel climbed out. 'Stinking bloody city, stinking bloody weather – and stinking bloody people,' he added for good measure to a group of street urchins kicking stones in the gateway of one of the six-storey, nineteenth-century tenement blocks that dominated the Berlin cityscape.

Dickel was a Bavarian by birth; he would never forgive Helmut Kohl, the self-styled 'Chancellor of German Unity', for moving the capital back. Old virtues indeed? Prussian order? The city was a quagmire of lawlessness and vice. He noticed the eldest of the three boys eye his car and shot him a ferocious warning glare: 'Polizei,' he lied in his best imitation of a Berliner plainclothes cop with a sore head. 'Understand? One mark on that car and I'll hang you all out to dry.' He pulled up the collar of his raincoat and stomped off into the courtyard of what had once been the most feared building in central Europe.

Normannenstrasse, an unremarkable backstreet in the district of Friedrichshain, runs parallel to the great avenue that leads out of Berlin towards the Polish border. Until 1989 it had housed the secret city that had been the headquarters of the Staatssicherheits-dienst, the state security service of the German Democratic Republic: Stasi for short. But since then the flats that had housed the families of the men sworn – KGB-style – to serve as the 'sword and shield of the party' had been turned over to the local housing authorities. The 'élite' shop which never ran out of bananas was now a supermarket, while the gatehouse where the armed guards had sat was a snack bar serving Berliner Kindl pils, advertised by a tousle-haired moppet peering out of the top of a frothy beer stein.

In the far corner a closed circuit television camera, its eye now turned blindly to the ground, marked the entrance to the Office of the Federal Representative for the Documentation of the State Security Service of the Former German Democratic Republic. Berliners called it simply the *Gauck-behörde* or Gauck's business, after the Lutheran pastor appointed to supervise admission to the inheritance of rumour-mongering, blackmail and betrayal. People in Dickel's line of work were not strictly welcome, though no one really imagined they could be completely excluded.

He selected the relevant identity card from his wallet and walked through to the lobby where Marthe Brunbacker was waiting for him. She led him into an antiquated paternoster lift, its cabins continuously rising and falling on a loop – an experience Dickel always found disconcerting. Two floors higher, they stepped on to terra firma and walked down a hospital-like corridor to a small office. On the desk was a folder marked, in thin pencil which Dickel had to strain to read upside down, with a single word: 'Donnerstag'.

'Donnerstag? Thursday?' Dickel looked at her questioningly.

'Perhaps. It's a codeword. For the file. Under the circumstances I think our Stasi friends were being unusually whimsical.'

The big man squinted. Uncomprehending.

'Donners-tag,' she repeated slowly, separating the two component parts of the word. 'The day of thunder. Appropriate, don't you think?'

Dickel frowned. 'No one else has seen this?' he asked, sharply.

'That's the only copy. Quite how it got lost is another question. I suspect there may have been disagreements about the course of action taken. It was all so close to the end, closer than any of us knew, of course. It's everything I said, providing it all stands up. But I suspect there may be problems.'

Dickel raised an eyebrow. 'Yes, so do I. But that's what we pay these youngsters for.'

He put the file in his briefcase, nodded curtly and took his leave.

Outside the rain had turned to a steady drizzle in the dismal early dusk. Dickel returned to the Opel only to find a jagged white line, like a dying patient's heart rate, scraped by a stone on the driver's door.

'Fucking brats,' Dickel cursed under his breath.

As he turned the key in the ignition he thought he heard the sound of jeering giggles.

But the street was empty.

Two weeks later, several hundred miles to the north-west, Gundar Peterson pulled on his boots, zipped up his down jacket and tied back the flaps on his fur hat. Outside, he stood still for a few seconds to let his eyes adjust to the flat light. The landscape was an almost featureless vista of unbroken white, dotted only with the distant shapes of his shaggy-haired ponies as they nosed around the edge of the frozen lake. The wisps of steam rising from the dark surface of the water bore testimony to the volcanic heat that kept it from freezing. He plodded across the snow to the barn. Inside,

Freya was tethered to a rail, shivering. His eyes moistened as he stroked her thinning mane. He could scarcely bring himself to look at the bare patches of flesh on her flanks. He cursed himself silently for having attracted the wrath of the true God by naming his little herd after the old pagan deities.

Killing was not something that came easily to him. It was with sadness that he loaded his double-barrelled shotgun and took aim at the suffering animal's fragile skull. Out across the snowfields, two explosions sounded in quick succession. A few of the ponies by the lakeside whinnied and set off at a brisk canter to nowhere.

The neighbours who came calling two days later found man and beast together on the barn floor, bone and brain so intermingled that is was impossible to tell which had belonged to the rational being and which to the dumb animal.

PART ONE

Initiation

1

Burke's Law

It was a Tuesday evening and El Vino's wine bar in Fleet Street was nearly empty. For more years than Eamonn Burke had had liquid lunches, EV's had been the traditional watering hole for the two most self-obsessed professions on British soil: journalism and the law. It served wine and spirits exclusively, and in large quantities.

'What's up with your lot, then? All taken the pledge, have they?' said Derek, the head barman. He looked to Burke like a Guards officer who had never quite lost the puppy fat around his chin. 'Our little establishment no longer grand enough for Her Majesty's press corps, hmmm?'

'Ambition, Derek, the scourge of the drinking classes. Perrier and planning meetings. Where have all the old hacks gone? Gone to be executives every one.'

Derek leaned across the counter to join in the inevitable refrain. Burke did the harmonies: 'When will they ever learn, when will they ehhhv-er leaaarn?'

Burke had been disappointed to find the bar empty but for a few tired lawyers. Tuesday were normally a good night. The hacks who worked on the Sundays traditionally regarded it as a lost day anyway: one for filling out expense forms and then renewing the necessity for them with a long lunch that stretched into an evening of gossip-mongering, character assassination and old war-horse anecdotes over EV claret or the stuff George Prosset of *The Times* called 'cooking whisky'. Also, any decision taken at the supposedly crucial editorial conference on a Tuesday morning stood as much chance as an ice-cube in a gin-and-tonic of making it to the weekend. Tuesday was a day for voicing disagreements, a token gesture before the editorial meetings reverted to the 'nodding dog' format (a nickname born in the sweat shop of the *Daily Mail*). The tough newspaper executives of Hollywood melodrama were in real life more like the little plastic canines that sit in the back window of Nissan Sunnys. But given half a chance, most of these docile bastards would murder each other for a pat on the head from the editor. Burke was deeply disenchanted with his chosen career.

Now approaching forty, he had already made it to the top, as a foreign correspondent in Washington and Moscow, first for the *Guardian* and latterly as a successful freelance. Burke was good, the word on the street went, bloody good, in fact: could turn a sow's ear into a silk purse in less time than it took most of the tossers to turn in their expenses. But he was a tad too left, the old school said, for the mainstream Murdoch empire. The legend was that Burke might be the best fireman from Belfast to Burundi when it came to covering a blaze, but there was always a risk that the wanker might start one of his own. George Prosset, one of his oldest drinking buddies and closet admirers, though seldom a hirer, repeatedly recounted in mock-astonishment that Eamonn Burke allegedly didn't even fiddle his expenses.

The problem was that there weren't many stories that interested him these days. The political world had turned squeaky clean, the intrigue of the Cold War had disintegrated into small wars, mostly rather dirty. But even they did not fire his imagination. For him, the only reason for going back out there was the fag of having to make money.

Burke knew the consequences of concentrating more on somebody else's spurious excitements than on the things that mattered: his marriage had effectively ended acrimoniously six months earlier. There were no children. He and Caroline had not even argued long over money. The house had been sold and they had both moved into one-bedroomed flats.

The relationship had foundered on the sharp rocks of their own incompatible ambitions – he constantly on assignment overseas, she working late with a view to promotion even when he was back in the UK.

On his side, there had been the girl in Bosnia, of course, but then everyone had had girls in Bosnia. Human comfort to take away the bad taste of too much reality. But Caroline had her own reality, by the name of Georgie, a new-wave émigré Russian. He was a producer with an independent television production company, fond of chess, late-night philosophical conversations and oral sex; the kind you did without making physical contact. Burke had found a message one day on the answering machine. It was just a reminder of an appointment and could have been perfectly innocent – Caroline was a rising executive in the BBC and met programme-makers all the time – but Burke knew it wasn't. He had recognized the tones, the studied formality inadequately camouflaging complicity. That offhand, 'Give me a call then, if there's a problem of any, hmmm, sort.' In other words, if Burke arrived back unannounced from his latest foreign jaunt.

At the beginning of the summer, they had had their last full-blooded row. She had actually drawn his blood, with the sharp edge of a floppy disk she had hurled at him. She had been remorseful, administered antiseptic and they had patched it up with a tumultuous night in bed and woken up with sore heads and the irrevocable feeling that the marriage was over. Burke had moved out in August. All that remained was the routine sitting out of the legally required waiting time before filing for divorce.

'Steady astern, madame.' Derek had emerged from behind the counter to help two male barristers manhandling a well-lubricated lady judge ten years their junior into her Burberry despite her obvious intention to sit on a half-finished glass of Chablis. 'Thank you, and good night,' he beamed facetiously. 'Can't have you sitting on the Queen's Bench in wet knickers, then, can we?' he delivered between clenched teeth *sotto voce* as the door closed behind the swaying threesome.

Burke ordered another claret, took a packet of Marlboro from his pocket and lit up. He was slightly embarrassed by the act, but only because of the brand. He had come to think of Marlboro as rather vulgar, the poor man's Americana. But then that was why he had started them in the first place, to reclaim a token of his identity in an alien environment. Although no one could have told by his accent, Eamonn Burke was an American citizen, an American by birth; Irish–American, his father would have proudly insisted, though the fact was he had accidentally grown up to be something altogether more rare – an English–American. The old man would have turned in his grave in the cold earth of County Mayo. As a first secretary at the embassy to the court of St James's with a watching brief on the Ulster situation, Mickey Burke had sent back a series of pessimistic – and ultimately extremely prescient – reports to the State Department at Foggy Bottom. There had been hints, from grey-haired men who still kept an open door for Burke, that it was not just 'State' that the old man had been reporting to. Langley, Virginia, loomed unmentioned in the background of every conversation.

The old man had died of a heart attack in his late forties. Burke had been ten years old, a happy-go-lucky kid who attended the American School in London and played baseball. Within two years his life had been transformed out of all recognition. His mother remarried, to a man who was 'something in the City'. Burke was sent to boarding school, 'to get a proper English education.' He had, too, once he got past the jibes about his accent, the bullying, and learned not to hold a cricket bat as if he was about to hit a home run. They had been difficult years, but, as generations of English gentlemen before him would have agreed, they had made him what he was. Whatever that was.

'Time now, ladies and gentlemen. Let's be having your glasses, please.' Derek's voice rang out across the bar.

Burke put his hand in his pocket to check that he still had his car keys, though he was well aware that driving was the last thing he should be considering. Instead of the keys, however, his hand closed on a folded envelope, one that had thunked on his doormat two days ago and been shoved into a jacket pocket to be read later.

He pulled it out, noticing in passing the German stamp with an impression of Norman Foster's restored Reichstag in Berlin. The letterhead shouted *Eon* with a smaller strapline beneath that announced itself as '*Das neue Heft für das neue Jahrtausend*', the new magazine for the new millennium. Burke had never heard of it. But these days there were more new magazines opening and closing than there were readers to buy them. The German market in particular seemed to have gone on a fertility binge. Recession or no recession; D-mark, euro, no matter what you called it, the Germans still had more money. From a jobbing hack's point of view, their magazines still knew how to pay properly, very properly indeed, he noted, scanning the letter in front of him.

The fee on offer was extraordinary: full expenses plus DM6,000/ Euro4,500 per week – about £2,000 at current exchange rates, he quickly calculated – to work on an article with one of their staff reporters. The letter was signed Hermann Dickel, commissioning editor, features. The name meant nothing to Burke.

If he had been sober, of course, he would have realized that the absence of any mention of the article's subject matter was most unusual. Normally, there was, at the very least, an agreed outline on the table before any money. Burke loathed incompetent commissioning: an ambiguous brief inadequately explained so that two weeks' research and a week's writing ended up with some overpaid bimbo simpering down the telephone that 'that is not what we meant at all'.

'Come along, squire. Even the idle rich have to go to bed sometimes.' Derek was smiling sarcastically across the counter, sublimely aware that it was still only 8.30p.m., but equally determined that one El Vino tradition that would not die under his stewardship was the one that got him home in time to go down to the local pub himself.

Burke drained the dregs of his claret, looked at the letter again and put it back in his pocket, not quite certain what to make of it. A decent contract for little more than playing minder to some kraut reporter might be just what he needed to get his life out of the doldrums. God knows, he could do with the money, what with the inequitable division of the spoils of their brief marriage that Caroline's lawyer was insisting on wringing out of him. Ah well, sleep on it. He threw on his raincoat and lurched for the door. Burke's law, really, he thought: just when you think it's time to give up the whole business and go into something honest, like running an estate agency, along comes a *deus ex machina* to save the day.

Or in this case, he wryly reflected, for it was the point that had persuaded him to accept the commission, a *dea ex machina*. The letter had given a woman's name for the reporter they were sending him to wetnurse: Sabine Kotzke. Well he would nurse her okay. What was that the Romans did to the Sabines, Burke mused. Then the macho balloon popped; it occurred to him that he was unlikely to be a match for some butch Brunnhilde.

Anyhow, the Germans pronounced it differently: Sa-bee-na, like the Belgian airline. Probably look like one, he thought, as he weaved into the damp night air in search of a taxi. He had, mercifully, quite forgotten his car.

2

A Package from Berlin

When he staggered out of El Vino's at 8.40 on the Tuesday evening, Burke fully intended to send the fax from his home computer first thing the next morning. But, mildly elated by the job offer, he had dropped in at another Fleet Street pub and, having fallen into a long and meaningful conversation with a doe-eyed legal secretary with a witching Edinburgh accent, had consumed four pints of London Pride. He returned home in such gloriously self-confident mood – despite being alone, the secretary having pleaded a pressing engagement early next morning – that he had failed to clamber out of bed before 11.30, which gave him just under thirty-five minutes to arrive an unacceptable five minutes late for an editor's meeting at Wapping.

The rest of the day had therefore been spent in muttered condemnation of the old bastard in the cellar bar of The Vineyard, and in concocting reasons why he should not go home and ferret around for the scraps of paper which his accountant was demanding to prevent his being persecuted by the tax inspector. It was in the middle of this orgy of self-pity that he remembered where he had left his car the night before. Inspired to a new fit of self-loathing, he set off to fetch it only to find the vehicle had been immobilized by a wheel clamp. Its release required lengthy negotiations plus the payment of a substantial penalty – with the result that it was not released into his care until the following morning.

Thus it was a distinctly jaded Eamonn Burke who, almost seventy-two hours later, caught sight of the jacket he had worn on Tuesday evening lying on the back of a kitchen chair, and remembered the short-lived euphoric enthusiasm of that night. Somewhat to his own surprise, he sent the fax anyway.

*　　*　　*

It had not helped that she began by complaining. She had left four messages on a particularly curt answering machine, without getting any reply, she said. Burke remembered vaguely seeing the flashing light the night before and turning it off rather than playing the messages. He cursed himself. It was precisely this sort of call that the damn thing was supposed to pre-empt. Trying to keep the annoyance out of his voice, he had suggested a meeting at 4.30 in the afternoon in a pub called The Harp, on Chandos Place, close to Charing Cross station.

He had set out, therefore, early, and surprised himself by examining his reflection in the bathroom mirror before leaving, as if wondering what sort of an impression he made these days. It was not as good as it might have been: tall, gangly, with the slight stoop that came from forever having to bend down to hear shorter people talking. His trademark lopsided grin was still there. From one profile, George Prosset had once declared that he looked like an angelic choirboy, but from the other side he appeared more like a down-and-out who'd just suffered a stroke. Caroline had said it was the combination that made him sexy, sort of innocent and dangerous at the same time. These days, he thought, the down-and-out was getting the upper hand.

He caught a bus, got off at Leicester Square and strolled down towards Charing Cross. For once he was disinclined to curse the crowds of tourists and street artists. He arrived at The Harp just after four o'clock; time enough for a pint or two, he thought happily.

At the back of Burke's mind had been the fact that The Harp was a passable pub with decent beer but also easy to escape from if she turned out to be a middle-aged Teutonic dragon or teenage workaholic bore. He had asked how they would recognize each other, and she replied that she was familiar with his picture by-line. He grimaced. That particular picture had been shot by a snapper with a grudge because Burke had left his light-meter in a Belgrade bar, and made him look like a dangerous lunatic. The editor liked it. But then, Burke thought, that was how he felt about him.

He was just raising a second London Pride to his lips when the door opened at the far end of the bar and in walked the woman he had been waiting for. Improbably, he thought afterwards, Burke recognized her immediately. After all, not only Germans wore leather trousers in London nowadays, although somehow English girls in their tight black leather rarely managed such a lack of self-consciousness. Hers were a natural-looking hide colour, not stretched tight, but comfortable-looking, functional yet a fashion statement at the same time. The French had a word for her: gamine. Short, but not boyish, auburn hair that hung in a mock fringe over big bright eyes. She was wearing a loose shirt and a shawl thrown carelessly around her shoulders. Yet the very way the clothes hung on her frame managed to suggest the litheness of the body underneath, athletic yet slight. The way she moved suggested indifference to men's eyes; he wondered if it was studied.

'Eamonn Burke, I presume. So pleased to meet you,' she said in the same faultless English he had been surprised by on the telephone, coupled with an elfin grin. Burke beamed back.

'Delighted, I'm sure. Can I get you a drink?'

She scanned the bar with a flash of sharp brown eyes and asked for a small Guinness. He smiled. In his experience, few Germans knew enough to avoid the fizzy coloured water that passed for continental-style beer in England, while good, honest bitter was beyond them. Burke fetched the drinks and they retreated to a quiet corner.

His first impression was that Sabine Kotzke had a self-assurance that bordered on the arrogant, and that it only added to her attraction. Her hair, he noticed, matched her eyes almost perfectly without either feature looking as if it had been artificially altered, and she had that typically German complexion that results from a healthy carnivorous diet and long skiing holidays.

Those, at least, were the lines he thought of the next day, rehearsing the story for his next encounter in The Vineyard with Prosset. At that precise moment, however, Burke found his usual facility with words had deserted him. The last thing he wanted to talk about with any young woman was the bloody newspaper business. She thought differently. So they talked about *Eon*. She told him it had been a relatively small-circulation magazine that had recently been taken over by a new entrepreneurial management who were determined to turn it into a German-language equivalent of *National Geographic* and *The Economist* rolled into one. He said he could imagine the product.

'Ecology stuff still big in Germany, then?' he ventured, agonizingly conscious of the dullness of their conversation.

'In the end, ecology is the only story that matters. How many habitable worlds do you know?'

14

Burke groaned internally and decided to go easy on the irony. He'd tried a few Fleet Street jokes on 'greenies' in the past. Few enough of them had a sense of humour; there was no point in pushing it, least of all with a German.

The moment was relieved by two drunks in pinstripes careering towards them, miscalculating the direction of the door. Burke corrected their course, but one of them flung an arm wide and knocked him backwards. Sabine put out her hand to prevent him toppling into her, and to his surprise she held him up.

'Impressive,' he said, when they had recovered their equilibrium and seen the drunks lurching off towards the station.

Kotzke surprised him by blushing.

It was the moment that broke the ice. So it was with unimaginable horror that Burke heard himself accidentally doing the one thing he had been intending to delay as long as possible: he popped the question.

'So what's this piece we're supposed to work on, then?'

To his immense relief, Kotzke broke into a broad smile and said it was too long a tale to start standing in a bar, but perhaps she could tell him about it over dinner.

They ate in a noodle place in Lisle Street. Burke was an enthusiastic lover of Chinese food. Sabine surprised him with an un-German characteristic: she handled chopsticks perfectly. She also did the right thing in expecting to order several dishes and share them. Burke had always assumed an instinctive affinity for Asian food to be a legacy of empire in the Brits' case. But then he had no idea what legacies Sabine Kotzke might be carting around in her psychological baggage.

He tried to find out. To be honest, he thought, anything would be better than talking shop. She had been to London several times before, she said. The first was in 1990, just after the Wall came down. She was eighteen at the time and had spent her whole life on the wrong side of it. She had gone through the whole Communist youth organization bit, been a Young Pioneer with a red scarf around her neck and watched dubbed Soviet TV series about the adventures of baby Lenin.

She had gone through the 'Jugendweihe' – farewell to youth – induction into the ranks of the FDJ, the Free German Youth that actually had more in common with the Hitler Youth, except that the shirts were blue instead of brown. She laughed and said it was terrible, but not that bad. Rather a good place, in fact, for boys and girls to get together, if he knew what she meant.

'And were you ever a Communist? Did you believe all that?'

'No.' Her answer was brusque. She changed the subject. How easy was it, she wanted to know, to earn a living in England without a steady job? Touché, thought Burke. He had spent most of his adult life trying to duck the answer. He waffled blithely about tax breaks and even narrated the old chestnut that freelance journalism was the worst job in the world but better than working. He told her about the old Fleet Street prohibition against making 'that extra phone call', the one that blows your whole story up in your face, and was surprised when she laughed. He had thought she wouldn't quite have understood the degree of moral pragmatism involved.

Against his better judgment Burke went over the bones of his impending divorce. The last thing he had wanted to do was spend the evening talking about Caroline, turning the most promising date he had had in months into a marriage-guidance counselling situation. He tried to shift the conversation to Sabine's own private life, the question of a boyfriend, but, she parried all his probes.

Sabine got the bill and pocketed the receipt. Burke made no pretence of objecting. It was her show, after all, though he reflected that the waiter would not exactly be out celebrating on her tip.

Her hotel was along Lancaster Gate, with the inestimable advantage, as far as Burke was concerned, that it meant they were going the same way. She was going to get a cab, but as it was still early and unusually springlike, he suggested they walk. Walking in London was a better option than most people realized. Burke hated the Tube and gridlocked traffic equally. Besides, he thought, if you lived in Notting Hill and put up with the carnival, the car thefts and the burglaries, you might as well get the advantage of being able to stroll to the West End. He reckoned he could get home from Soho in half an hour, and most of it through the park. Since they had not yet discussed business, Burke was not wholly surprised when he suggested a nightcap and she accepted.

It was only when he opened the door of his half-basement flat that it occurred to him his domestic circumstances were hardly suited to receiving visitors. Mrs Konopka, his Polish cleaning lady, came on Wednesdays; five days later it usually looked like a dosshouse for homeless alcoholics who collected newsprint for bedding value rather than information or literary merit. He kicked a pile of accumulated newspapers out of the way. Sabine, he noticed, took a few seconds before following; he thought he saw her cast a dubious glance along the street. But whether she was looking for something or just summing up the neighbourhood, he couldn't tell.

Burke turned on the light. There was no need to pull the curtains; he could not remember the last time he had got around to opening them. He threw some junk mail, telephone bills and a credit card statement off a battered sofa on to the floor.

'Have a seat.'

Sabine Kotzke looked around her. Piles of paper lay on the floor, and there were books, dozens of them, stacked in untidy heaps on the carpet. A shelf on top of the radiator, by contrast, contained only a few empty beer bottles and some souvenirs of Burke's career. She lifted one, a Russian matryoshka doll painted in an unmistakable grinning caricature of the British Prime Minister, Tony Blair. She opened it. Inside was an equally clever depiction of his predecessor, John Major, who in turn contained a mini-Margaret Thatcher. Inside her, like a fat baby, was a solid little Winston Churchill.

'Right, what do you fancy?' Burke called from the kitchen. 'Gin without tonic, vodka without orange or whiskey without ice? Brandy? It's only Spanish but it's fairly decent.'

He poked his head back around the door frame.

'Thanks.' 'Brandy would be great.' He disappeared again.

'I like your matryoshka doll. Where did you get it? Moscow?'

'Sort of,' Burke called back from the kitchen. 'An old friend of mine sent it. He and I had been through some rough times under the Soviets together, there and in Afghanistan. He thought it was funny. It was interesting, he said, that the real expression of Russian freedom was not that they should have got round to parodying their own rulers but foreigners too. Curiously Communism made for better manners.'

'At least your history is not such a problem.'

'What do you mean?' Burke emerged carrying a half-empty bottle of Fundador and two tumblers.

'I have a doll like this too. Also bought in Moscow a few years ago. It has Helmut Kohl outside – at least he was the right size.'

'And inside?'

'Helmut Schmidt, then Willy Brandt and Konrad Adenauer . . . and Adolf Hitler.'

'Ouch! I see what you mean.'

'That's how they still think of us. Rotten at the core.'

Burke was about to say the expression was '*to* the core' but thought better of it. He poured a large measure into a whiskey tumbler and handed it to her.

'Perhaps we should talk business,' she said.

Burke moved another heap of papers from a worn leather armchair opposite her and sat down.

'I suppose so, really. You're the boss. What's the story? And why me?'

Kotzke stayed standing. Burke was conscious of her eyes wandering around the room, taking in the dishevelled state of his existence. He guessed she was wondering if it had been like this when he was married – no wonder the woman walked out, she probably thought.

'You have quite a reputation.'

'I'm flattered.'

'You don't need to be. You exposed ministers from your own government giving the okay to arms deals with Iraq before the Gulf War, despite an international embargo. If it hadn't been for you, Declan Conway would have spent twenty years in a Belfast jail for a crime he didn't commit, and all because a group of unscrupulous Protestant policemen had decided they could fill in the "missing bits" of evidence.'

'That wasn't all me. I had a lot of help.' Some of it, he still suspected, at times when the lazy beast that passed for his conscience stirred, probably from the IRA itself.

'Don't play down your own work. You were uncovering the hypocrisy of the Soviet war in Afghanistan when I was a teenager being told our "fraternal allies" were protecting socialism at the request of the people. But when you were in Moscow you still embarrassed Washington by revealing the CIA thought the Soviets' persecution of the dissident Andrei Sakharov was "useful". You have a reputation for being tenacious, and for not being easily frightened by governments and bullies.'

Just by women, Burke thought.

'I don't know what to say.'

'You don't need to say anything. We have done our homework. Believe me: you are just the man for the job.'

Burke shrugged helplessly. If she had wanted to win his co-operation by appealing to his professional vanity she had done her stuff.

'First of all,' she continued, 'I am assuming the money as mentioned in Dickel's letter is agreed. Secondly, we work together and whatever comes out is our copyright in Germany. But you can do what you want with it abroad. Including England of course.'

Burke nodded. It all seemed more than generous to him.

'Since you ask, we are particularly hoping that your contacts in Moscow will be useful.' Burke raised an eyebrow involuntarily. The time he had spent in Moscow had not been the happiest of his memories. 'And also, I think, you have intelligence contacts in England.'

Burke almost laughed out loud. He never ceased to be amazed by the way in which editors liked to believe those who worked for them had a key to secret places.

'Quite frankly,' she said, as if bringing a speech to its conclusion, 'I am glad – I hope – to be working with you.'

Burke was sitting back in his tatty chair grinning broadly. Kotzke had managed to do something the jaded man of the day before would have deemed impossible: made him feel like a twenty-year-old trainee again seeing his name in print for the first time.

'What can I say? That's quite a testimonial. But perhaps now you'd like to tell me just what this story's about.'

She began with a question.

'You have heard of a man called Klaus Fuchs?'

'You mean the atom spy?'

She nodded.

'Sure. He was the bloke who stole the secret of the atom bomb, virtually handed Stalin on a plate the produce of the best collected minds of the Western world and more or less started the Cold War single-handed.'

'That's him. But do you know what happened to him?'

'More or less. He got thrown in jail, for a dozen years or so, then went back home, your home, Germany's home-grown commie-land. As far as I know he disappeared into well-rewarded obscurity as a dutiful son of the state and died happy and contented, of old age, just in time to avoid seeing it all collapse in ruins. Right?'

'Up to a point.'

'What's the point?'

'The point is, that he didn't die as happy and contented as you might think. The obituaries were disinformation. I'm afraid Herr Professor Doktor Fuchs did not die of old age. He was murdered. I want to know why.'

3

P.O. Box 1663, Santa Fe, New Mexico

July 1944

'It was the best of times, it was the worst of times, it was the age of wisdom, it was the age of foolishness, it was the epoch of belief, it was the epoch of incredulity, it was the season of Light, it was the season of Darkness, it was the spring of hope, it was the winter of despair, we had everything before us, we had nothing before us.' Emil Julius Klaus Fuchs repeated in his head the opening words of *A Tale of Two Cities* as he turned the ignition key and his Buick added its exhaust fumes to the dry air of the Santa Fe.

There were scholars who thought *A Tale of Two Cities* was not Charles Dickens's best book. But to Klaus Fuchs none seemed more apposite to the day and age, to his own situation and the plight of humanity in the middle of the twentieth century. In particular, that rambling prose ode to ambiguity was singularly suited to the German scientist's present state of mind.

Fuchs had loved Dickens ever since he had arrived in England as a twenty-one-year-old refugee from Hitler's Germany in 1933. Almost eleven years had passed since then. This was another world again, he thought, breathing in the dry desert air, a world on the cusp. Of heaven or hell.

From the relative comfort of his vehicle, Fuchs watched the scene at the little office known only by its street number, 109 East Palace: the staging post for the 'Special' to The Hill. Women were as usual struggling with shopping and children on to the big green army bus. Fuchs had come into town on the first shuttle bus that morning and gone to Santa Fe's single used-car lot. He was no haggler and had handed over what seemed an extravagantly large sum in cash for the gunmetal grey Buick he had been assured would 'run like a coyote chasin' chickens', even out on those hot desert roads. But a car was necessary. Also, it would allow him to be helpful, and he liked that. Making friends was not one of his key attributes. However, he was not offering any free lifts today: much as he liked being popular, he could not have people relying on 'good ol' Klaus' for a lift every time they wanted to go into town. There would be times when he would have to make the journey on his own. In that respect, he reflected pragmatically, his social incompetence could sometimes be a boon.

The bus was still standing by the roadside as Fuchs put the Buick into gear and pulled away. Most of his colleagues liked Santa Fe. It represented an idealized remnant of the romantic Wild West legend that for so many Americans, he had discovered, was a substitute for history. The strong late afternoon sunlight emphasized the warm sandstone colours of the adobe buildings against the deep unbroken blue of the New Mexico sky. Fuchs could see the superficial romance of the place that had made it a Mecca for creative types, just as, he reflected grimly, the pretty Bavarian town of Dachau had been before the Nazis built a concentration camp there. Fuchs had thought a lot about Dachau. He had almost ended up there.

He took the now familiar route out along the Taos highway before turning off on to the dirt road up into the mountains. 'Injun country,' he mused, smiling to himself. He had soaked up a bit of the Wild West mythology in New York, had even watched a western for the first time. He had quite enjoyed it. The morality was so simplistic. Was that, he wondered, how Americans really saw the world?

He was passing the San Ildefonso Indian pueblo village. More adobe buildings, superficially less well-kept than the white men's, but with neat rows of dried red chilli peppers hanging in strings from the protruding wooden beams by each doorway: the darkest, deepest red in a landscape dominated by that end of the visible spectrum. The desert sand was an orange ochre, the colour of the rust that had eaten away the paintwork on a pickup truck by the side of the main dirt road through the Indian pueblo. Rust, he thought, was a defining motif of the pueblos, an unmistakable symptom of the cancer that eroded the Indians' existence: poverty.

Even the dirt was red here, as red as the great outcrops of sun-scorched rock, chiselled by the wind and the sand into strange craggy shapes. This was how the surface of Mars might look, Fuchs thought. From what he could tell, the whole of the northern half of this great empty desert state was the same, rising to the jagged crimson mountain range that, three hundred years earlier, the Spaniards had dubbed the Sangre de Cristo, the Blood of Christ. Only in the distance did a single natural structure, like some giant's basalt tombstone, alter the monotone: the great bulk of the Black Mesa, the local San Ildefonso Indians' sacred mountain.

The Buick rattled and emitted strange squeaking noises above the rear axle as Fuchs turned on to the dirt road. He felt the suspension complain, bumping him from side to side on the rutted track. He wondered how long even a big Buick could take this sort of punishment. To Fuchs, American cars – even the older models – were strange, exciting mechanical animals. He had not the faintest idea if he had paid a fair price or whether the machine he had purchased would last only a few months in this inhospitable climate. Santa Fe represented the only outpost of what passed for civilization in a thousand kilometres or more. Unless, of course, you counted Albuquerque, the state's only other big town. And Fuchs most definitely did not. He had been there.

Up ahead was the bridge over the Rio Grande, which saved at least half an hour on the trip. One of the bus drivers had felt the entire structure sag as he attempted to cross from Santa Fe with thirty women and children, and since then, it had been declared off-limits to heavier vehicles. Fuchs held his breath as the Buick trundled over the boards, noticing that more had broken recently. Sooner or later, he thought, the general would have to divert some of his men to a repair detail. They were supposed to be the Corps of Engineers, after all. Bridge-building ought to have been right up their street.

Fuchs smiled to himself at the inappropriateness of the idiom. He smiled primarily at the fact of having noticed it. Perhaps he was thinking in English at last. Even after all this time, Fuchs knew he still had a German accent. He had been surprised initially to find that the Americans were even less happy than the English at dealing with obvious foreigners. So much for the great mixing bowl, he thought. It was different on The Hill, of course; there it was a real multinational community, even if most of them had become American citizens through the necessity of fleeing Europe.

Even the British team, he reflected, was more Saxon than Anglo. Apart from himself there was Otto Frisch, the Viennese physicist whose aunt Lise had first identified nuclear fission. He had shared a cabin with Frisch on the ship to New York and they had talked music as much as physics, for Frisch was almost as accomplished a pianist as he was a scientist. It was he who had inspired Fuchs to purchase a violin and take up playing again.

And then there were Rudolf and Eugenia Peierls who had been his sponsors ever since he had returned to England from his first trip to North America: five uncomfortable months as an enemy alien at a camp overlooking the St Lawrence river in Canada. Those months of exile had been important for Fuchs. He had met a lot of interesting people. But he had been delighted when he was given security clearance and was going back to England. He suspected Rudi Peierls had had a hand in it. They had met the year before at a scientific conference and got on well. Rudi had seen his talent and was not about to let it go to waste. On his return he had been given a job at Birmingham University working in the great man's laboratory. Rudi and Genia became like a family to him, inviting him round to their cosy home for Sunday lunch: typical hunks of British roast beef, even though Rudi was as German as Fuchs and Genia was Russian. But like Frisch, they had something in common. They were Jewish. Fuchs was different. That was not the reason he had been forced to flee Germany.

Already he could see The Hill ahead of him. Never, it occurred to him, had a nickname been more misleading. Particularly when he thought of it in German: *der Hügel* was something quintessentially rounded, something one rolled up and over. This was *ein Fels* – a cliff, a great forbidding rocky escarpment. That was why the general had given it the thumbs up. It could have been the prototype for Conan Doyle's *Lost World*. But instead of a vivarium of the primeval past, it had become the cradle of the future.

The Buick strained as it began the steep, winding ascent up the narrow road that climbed from the valley floor. The road twisted, carving its way up the face of the red rock, an improbable ascent that even with the amount of traffic that now used it was not so much a highway as a dirt track. The very definition of inaccessibility, Fuchs thought, but then that was the point.

It had been Oppenheimer's idea originally. A sickly New York child from a well-off Jewish family, J. Robert Oppenheimer had been sent west in the hope that a frontier lifestyle would make him more robust. It had worked, better than the family doctor could ever have dreamed. The family had a ranch in the Sangre de Cristo Mountains and he was fond of riding there. He had once confided in a letter to a friend: 'My two great loves are physics and desert country. It's a pity that they can't be combined.' When he had been plucked from his laboratory at the University of California's campus in Berkeley and appointed to head up the country's most secret physics project, his dream came true. His first task was to find a location. There was one brief: it should be as isolated as possible.

In the Jemez mountains a series of jutting mesas, the eroded remnants of a great prehistoric volcano, spread out like tentacles from the grassed-over volcanic caldera which still lay high above them. On one of these rocky spurs in 1917 an east coast philanthropist who, like Oppenheimer himself, had been sent west to be toughened up, had founded a ranch school for boys. He had called it after the deep canyon to the south which was itself named for the cottonwood trees clumped along the stream which flowed through it. It was an innocent derivation for a name which was to become synonymous with deadly weapons in a future Cold War: Los Alamos.

When Oppenheimer first showed the site to General Leslie Groves, the military commander of the operation, he was delighted. Secrecy was paramount. It had been Grove's idea to obscure all traces of the project and its location by giving it a codename that related solely to the headquarters site of his engineers corps – an office in downtown Manhattan. Whatever the Manhattan Project might have meant to an unauthorized person who by some accident came across the name, it was unlikely to conjure up an image of a laboratory in a converted boys' school in northern New Mexico.

Fuchs ground the Buick to a halt by the guardpost, took out his security pass, complete with photograph and the print of his left index finger and thumb, and handed it to the military policeman. The East Gate was the main entrance to and from The Hill. It was the one official way through the ring of barbed wire and sentry posts that had been Groves's first priority on the site, put up even before the first prefabricated houses for the scientific staff.

Despite the security, however, the MP examined Fuchs's card only cursorily. Like most of the regulars he prided himself on knowing most of the technical staff by sight. No one really believed that some Nazi spy was going to find his way out to this god-forsaken corner of the desert and try to get in disguised as one of the scientists. Besides, for a few dollars any of the Indians would show him the hole in the fence which they kept open with an almost religious zeal, no matter how many times the General's men closed it up. Fuchs knew all about the hole; his room-mate in the single men's dormitory, an American called Richard Feynmann, a bright young physicist with an offbeat sense of humour and a reputation as a bongo-drummer and prankster, used to sneak back in through it, throwing the books – if not the guards themselves – into total confusion by leaving the site twice in a row without having officially re-entered.

'Thank you, sir,' the MP drawled in a Louisiana accent as he returned Fuchs's pass. 'You'll need to report to administration, sir, to get yourself a pass for this vehicle. Sure must be nice to have your own wheels out here.' Fuchs smiled his thin smile and drove on.

The East Gate was at the very end of the mesa, where the single-track road wound up along the only accessible route from the canyon. From the gate it was another three miles to the centre of the 'city'. Fuchs laughed at the American idea that every settlement was a budding metropolis. All Los Alamos had in common with any city he knew was overcrowding. When the idea of a secret laboratory had first been mooted, the initial estimate was that it might house some 100 scientists with their families and associated technical and military personnel, perhaps 250 to 300 at most. The construction work at Los Alamos had begun on that scale. But very quickly it became apparent that more people than anyone had imagined would be needed if the site was to take the project all the way from theory through design to manufacture and testing. Already the population was in excess of 4,000. One thing the military men had apparently failed to budget for was the proclivity of an enclosed human community to reproduce at alarming rates. The average age at Los Alamos was twenty-five and falling fast: almost all the hospital space had been turned over to crêche facilities. But even the birth certificates were governed by the rules of secrecy; 'place of birth' carried only the oblique official designation 'P.O.Box 1663, Santa Fe, New Mexico'.

And no metropolis had unmetalled roads. Wheels and caterpillar treads ground up the dust in summer and turned them to mud when the rains came. Apart from the mud and the dust, green was the predominant colour. There was the summer green of the aspens that rose up the mountainside beyond the mesa, here and there decimated by the mad Pole, George Kistiakowsky, head of the explosives testing team, who had cleared space for a ski slope by taping high explosive around the base of the trees. But the most all-pervasive green was of nature's crude imitation: military paint, camouflage green. It defined Los Alamos; it was the colour of the vehicles, the hospital, the houses and the PX shop; it was even the colour of the water tower that stood on stilts and served as the focal point for the sprawling makeshift town.

Fuchs pulled the Buick in a wide loop around the water tower and past the new two-storey houses, married quarters for scientists and senior technicians with families. The GIs – those who served as guards, drivers, cooks, bottle-washers – were billeted in cramped barracks intended for half as many men. There were separate quarters for those draftees who had useful technical skills: mathematicians, physics graduates, young men with brains who had thought the war would mean danger and action, and had instead ended up posted to a shanty town to crunch numbers for no apparent purpose. The military, at the General's own insistence, were told as little as possible about what Los Alamos was really for.

That was until Oppenheimer had insisted on changing the rules. He did as he had done with the civilian scientists, whom Groves had wanted organized in cells, sharing information purely on a need-to-know basis. 'Oppie' had arranged for a lecture to be given by Fuchs's dormitory-mate, Feynmann, who had a gift for explaining even the most abstract scientific concepts. The result had been staggering: when the men found out that rather than working on some administration matter they were involved in the design of a superweapon that could win the war, productivity and enthusiasm doubled overnight. The General had muttered, but even he had been impressed by the results.

Fuchs hoped Feynmann was in. He wanted to show him the new car. Perhaps he would offer to lend it to him. He knew the young American's wife was seriously ill in a hospital in Albuquerque and it was not easy to requisition transport to go that sort of distance, even in an emergency.

Of course, Fuchs would have to have first priority when the need arose. And he was sure it would. The owl-faced man would find him, or someone else would. What was happening at Los Alamos was too important to allow security risks, too important to ignore the only sort of security that in the long term mattered to the world: mutual security. In the meantime, he would get on with his work, and wait.

As Fuchs was driving through the East Gate at Los Alamos, a pudgy man with glasses was standing on the hot pavement outside the Bell

Cinema in Brooklyn. He had been there for half an hour, studying the poster for Humphrey Bogart in *The Treasure of the Sierra Madre*. At one point he walked as far as the hot-dog stall a block away, purchased a frankfurter in a bun with mustard and relish and ate it as he sauntered slowly back towards the cinema. The casual observer would have assumed he had been stood up. But a more trained eye might have noticed that the man had been looking at his watch with more than a passing interest, and that at precisely 6.15 he crossed the road, put a dime in a public telephone, spoke for a few seconds and then turned on his heel and left without a glance back at the cinema.

4

The Invisible Man

New York, July 1944

For Harry Gold, standing outside the Brooklyn movie theatre, it was the moment he had been dreading. When he had realised his tame German professor was not going to show for their scheduled meeting, he made a brief telephone call to the man he knew only as 'John'. The response had been simple: 'I'll be in touch.' For the past year Gold had felt like a champion angler, playing the big fish on a long line, regularly landing him to the applause of the spectators and yet, every time he turned back to his rod, there he was still on the end of the line, ready and eager for a repeat performance. Now, suddenly, the line had snapped.

It was on the Monday of the following week that the telephone rang at his home in Philadelphia. It was John. The voice, calm, unemotional, with just the slightest trace of an accent, betrayed none of the excitement that Gold felt. His colleagues, he said, had come up with an address for his doctor. They should meet at the usual place and he would pass it on.

The two men met on Saturday morning next to the stone lions on the crowded steps of the New York Library. John handed Gold a slip of paper with a typewritten address. He said he did not expect Fuchs still to be living there, but there was the remote possibility that he had left a forwarding address. Gold should call, but be careful not to draw attention to himself. It was possible – though unlikely – that the address was under surveillance. If nothing came of it, then they would have no alternative but to follow Fuchs's advice, and rely on his own makeshift fallback plan.

As John melted into the anonymity of Manhattan, Gold headed

for a second-hand bookshop on 41st Street. He had intended to buy a book on physics, the sort of thing that a boffin would read. But on second thoughts he felt it would be unwise to draw attention to Fuch's occupation. People were so suspicious these days. Instead, Gold wandered over to a small section of books in foreign languages. German – unsurprisingly, he thought, given the large number of Jewish traders in the district – was well represented. Without much consideration, Gold picked up a book by Thomas Mann. He was one of the few German authors he had heard of. *Der Zauberberg*: he wondered what it meant. It would never dawn on Harry Gold that *The Magic Mountain* was, given the location Fuchs had moved to, a singularly appropriate choice.

He took his purchase into a nearby coffee shop, pulled out a deliberately unsharpened pencil and on the flyleaf copied out carefully, in as neutral block capitals as he could, the address John had given him: 'Dr Klaus Fuchs, Apartment 38, 128 West 77th Street'. Then he went back out and hailed a cab.

The building at 128, West 77th was a typical Manhattan brownstone, home to the sort of people who believed the world's fastest-growing metropolis would one day make them rich. The doorman, eyeing Gold's unpressed suit, nodded cautiously and asked if he could be of service.

'Hi there. Could be.' Gold had put on his most ingratiating smile. 'I found this here book in a coffee shop over by Times Square. Said some fella had left it behind. This place is kind of on my way home, so I thought I'd just drop by and leave if off. Guess the fella who forgot it might be grateful to get it back if you know what I mean.'

The doorman took the book, read the name and address, and smirked. Gold took a long shot. 'The sort of guy who might only get remembered because of his name, eh?' It was the sort of crude comment that he hoped might break the ice. It did.

'Yeah, sure thing. Old Barney the janitor here kept on about it. "Still no broads, Fuch?" he used to say. "I guess Mr Fuchs just don't live up to that name of his. Heh, heh.' Tell you the truth, pal, I got to feel sorry for the guy. Must have been hell even introducing himself. But I can't help you. He doesn't live here any more. Moved out about a month ago.'

'Oh, that's sure a shame. I don't suppose he left a forwarding address? A phone number or anything?'

'Sorry. Can't help you. I heard he left on a boat.'

Gold caught the evening train back to Philadelphia and planned a trip to Boston. The professor had a sister there. He had foreseen all this. At their last meeting he had told Gold that when the time came for him to be moved, it would be sudden. The link would be his sister. It was the one time they had almost become close during the nine months of occasional meetings.

That time they had met outside a movie theatre and, fearing that they were being stared at by a man in the crowd, had gone in. They sat apart throughout some dreary film, and afterwards went off to an Italian restaurant in the Bronx. Fuchs had been almost garrulous, for him. He had told him about his brother Gerhardt, a devoted Communist who had taken refuge in Switzerland and lived in fear of Nazi agents; about his father who had been a pastor back in Germany and then taught theology. He was still there but Fuchs had not heard from him in years. To make contact would put him in danger. The Gestapo still had files on his own student activities at Kiel before he escaped to England. He mentioned briefly his mother, said she was dead. And he talked of his sister, Kristel, who was married to a businessman called Heinemann, an American of German extraction, and lived in Cambridge, Massachusetts, just across the Charles river from Boston.

The man Gold knew as John took the call on his private phone in a Manhattan office block. The chief task now was to find their precious German again as soon as possible. The Russian was fairly certain he would be at the secret new laboratory in New Mexico. The man had come to them of his own volition. Everything he had supplied so far had been in his own hand, much of it in fact his own work which he clearly felt he had the right to share with whomsoever he wished. It was not an ideal state of affairs. Moscow had been happy, although it was a happiness that betrayed deep-seated worries about American progress. The latest communiqué had contained several questions for Fuchs. John was not unhappy; he had been allocated huge sums in American dollars, should he need to encourage his source financially. But so far the German had not even raised the question of money. Perhaps he should let Gold raise it with him. There was no harm in the motherland showing its appreciation. Besides, accepting a little offering often hooked people for life. He had given Fuchs a nickname of his own: Prometheus. He hoped Gold would be lucky in Boston.

As it turned out, Gold was extremely unlucky. Kristel Heinemann told him she had heard nothing of her brother for several weeks. On a second visit, she showed him a postcard from her brother. It said little and gave as a return address only P.O. Box 1663, Santa Fe, New Mexico. It meant nothing to Gold though John had nodded with apparent satisfaction when he passed it on. The Russian gave Gold a plain postcard to leave with Kristel to be passed on to her brother whenever he might show up for a visit. It gave a New York telephone number where he could leave a message that he had arrived and would be staying a few days; no need to mention a name or a place. It was the same number that Gold used to contact John, and he feared he was being cut out of the operation.

In fact, John was equally anxious. It was six months now since he had been able to pass to Moscow one of the thick brown envelopes crammed with tight, neat writing and mathematical formulae. This was not the way these things were meant to work. He was the controller, but the agent was out of control.

5

Pandora's Box

Burke was sitting on the edge of his chair, sipping his brandy and looking into the earnest eyes of the young woman opposite him.

'What makes you so sure this man was murdered? This is all a long time ago. Fuchs confessed and went to jail in 1950, and was released and sent back to East Germany nine years later. Who do you think murdered him, and why?'

'The obvious suspects are the Stasi, the East German secret police. We have come across some documents. Things that suggest Fuchs may have been thinking of defecting again, or at least leaving a testament. Something that someone didn't want to come out.

'Not least the British and American governments, though he'd already done his worst by them, one presumes. I wonder what else Dr Fuchs might have signed up to for his "get out of jail free" card back in 1959?' Burke raised his eyebrows. 'I'm assuming that this testament didn't survive him.'

'Hardly. In the chaos of 1989–90 it's remarkable anything survived at all. Assuming that it wasn't destroyed earlier.'

'I think you'd better fill me in.'

'It seems that in his confession when he was arrested, all those years ago, Dr Fuchs told the truth, but not the whole truth. Either that,' she paused for effect, 'or your British secret service submitted less than the whole truth to the court.'

'Good heavens, can't imagine that.' Burke wondered if she picked up the irony in his voice.

'I don't know quite where to begin.'

'How about the beginning? Where did you come by this stuff in the first place and what does it say?' Burke reached for the bottle and refilled her glass.

'About six weeks ago,' she began, 'Günther Eckberg, one of our science correspondents, was trying to put together a piece about the extent to which the old East German scientific establishment had been reduced to a tool of the Soviet military machine. He talked to some well-known Stasi men in Leipzig and Dresden. Over a few beers one evening, this old stager who had been the party's eyes and ears in the Dresden research establishment offers him a pile of "top secret" papers.

'At first our man wants nothing to do with it. Mostly, what you get for your money is details of a few researchers' private lives. But these days Germany has enough on her conscience without airing more dirty washing in public; and it doesn't sell magazines.'

Burke nodded. He had always believed there was a moral background to his journalism, but in a society like Germany, ripped apart twice in two generations, could that mean sometimes ignoring certain issues for the greater good of the community's mental health? Sabine must have to deal with that question every day. What sort of compromises did that involve?

'But,' she continued, 'when the guy cuts his price and starts almost pleading with him for the sake of the starving grandchildren, Eckberg agrees to take a look. A routine skim reveals that ninety per cent of the material is the usual stuff. Much of it isn't even classified: requisition forms in triplicate for new valves for bunsen burners, a whole ream of correspondence on the subject of getting a single new 286 series computer – and this is supposed to be the cutting edge of the communist bloc's top secret scientific research. It was pathetic. Believe me.'

'I believe you. I once met a Russian cosmonaut who told me the most important piece of equipment on board the early Soyuz craft was the spanner.'

'Anyway, eventually our man, mainly to keep his contact sweet, and partly because he thinks there just might be a whimsical piece to be done about the appalling conditions GDR scientists worked under, buys the lot for DM1,000 and ships it to Berlin where it lies around in various in-trays until my features editor, on a boring afternoon, decides to sift through it. What does he come up with? A couple of old maths jotters filled with complicated formulae and notes, apparently unrelated, scribbled down the sides of the pages. It was like fragments of a diary. The sort of book that its owner carried around with him, to jot things down as they occurred to him. Someone who was methodical but also slightly absent-minded.'

'An absent-minded professor.'

'Exactly. Though at that stage, of course, we had no idea who it belonged to. A few of the notes were connected to the mathematical formulae, though not many. This was a man for whom mathematics was a language in its own right. Others were notes about his financial situation, problems with his cars – he ran two apparently, an extraordinary privilege even for the privileged in the GDR – a red Wartburg and, would you believe, an ageing British MG, for which it was almost impossible to get parts. Anyhow, the editor was going to throw it out, but he tossed it to me to take a look, primarily because I have a degree in physics.'

'I hadn't figured you for a boffin.'

'A what?'

'A boffin, an egg-head, a mad scientist.'

'Oh. No, you're right. I'm not – at least not in that league. The maths was over my head, and meaningless out of context. But with a little concentration, I realized these were calculations used only in particle physics. Whoever our "diary" writer was, he knew his stuff. Just for fun I compared the scribbles against some of the published orthographs by better-known GDR scientists. It only took a few minutes to be pretty certain that this was the work of Klaus Fuchs . . .'

'Sums can be that identifiable?'

'At a certain level, you don't even need to distinguish the handwriting. Fuchs was not just a spy; he was a world-class physicist. For most of his later life he was involved in top-notch research connected to the Soviet weapons programme. Once I suspected it might be Fuchs everything started to make more sense. He had spent his last years at the Dresden research plant, though nobody knew what the place was supposed to be doing. Those were the sort of questions you just didn't ask.

'When I started to pay attention to more of the words, any doubts vanished. There were whole chunks that read like notes for an autobiography: reminiscences, going back to a time spent in prison in England, and then, crucially, to Los Alamos. Suddenly, quite out of the blue, Fuchs drops in a reference to some great secret which he is about to reveal. You can imagine it caught my interest.'

Burke nodded.

'What I was reading, I gathered quite quickly, was the rough draft for a last testament. There was something quite extraordinary that this old man – who, you have to remember, never really considered himself a spy – wanted to get off his chest.'

Kotzke put down her glass and reached for her bag. She took out a sheaf of papers and handed them to Burke.

'I photocopied a few of the relevant pages.'

Burke took another swig of brandy and glanced at the first sheet. It showed a page from a small notebook, about A5 size he estimated, squared like the sort of paper that continental children used for maths. It was covered with writing in a small, neat, precise hand. But the writer had clearly been brought up to use the old Gothic script.

'I'm sorry. I can't make head or tail of this. I had the same trouble with Goebbels's diaries once.'

'Don't worry, I understand. But as a little girl I learned to decipher my grandfather's handwriting. He lived in the West and sent us presents. I'm afraid there was self-interest in the correspondence.'

Burke liked the apologetic easterner in her; it was a softer, less aggressive personality.

'The crucial details are here.' She pointed to a paragraph about halfway down the third sheet which had been highlighted in yellow. Burke handed it back and sat down on the sofa next to her to follow the text. She began to read, drawing an elegantly pointed fingernail under the tight, precise handwriting.

'"*The thing to do is to put the record straight: the efforts men went to in order to ensure that the world might be a better place. Now I am not so sure that it is*" – you have to remember that it seems he was writing this in 1987, when East Germany was really going to the devil and there was no sign of the reforms in Moscow spreading to us.'

Burke nodded. She continued reading.

'"*Not many people still alive know the whole story. Perhaps only two or three at most. But sooner or later there will be a reckoning. The important element, the material evidence, remains frozen. But one day there will be a thaw . . . nothing stays hidden for ever . . . it is time to speak out, I can do no more harm than keeping quiet.*"'

'Good stuff so far. Go on.'

Kotzke kept her eyes on the paper. 'That's it. There is more but nothing specific.'

'I don't believe you. You're having me on.'

Kotzke took a deep breath and looked up. Burke's face, only inches from hers, displayed his scepticism only too clearly. She pulled away to the end of the sofa. The voice was offended, defensive, using anger for a shield: 'Look, Mr Burke. My magazine has approached you with a business proposition. More than that, we might just be giving you a handle on the best story of your life. If you really think we are a bunch of fools and you know so much better, then there's really no point in wasting any more of each other's time.'

Burke took the point, in his own way. What was he trying to prove, for heaven's sake? If some mad German rag wanted to pay him handsomely for a couple of weeks trawling around on a dead man's trail, who was he to spoil it all by nitpicking. But time-wasting was against his nature. And he found himself feeling protective towards this rather stroppy young woman who was, after all, just a kid reporter hoping for a scoop. The least he could do was let her down gently.

'Okay, I'm sorry. I just don't see what sort of lead that gives us. Help me here for a moment: I mean, what are we supposed to be looking for and where do we start? There's not very much there to go on.'

'That is why you are involved.' The hostile stare metamorphosed into a smile. With an edge.

'Fuchs does not leave us completely high and dry.' She turned to another sheet. 'Look here in the margin. He has written, "*Wer weiß noch? wußte?*" Who else knows? And then he has second thoughts and changes the verb to the past tense.'

Burke looked. Underneath there was a list of names, some with question-marks or place-names next to them.

Arnold Skardon – MI5 London. *Tot. Wer sonst?*
John – Moskau.
Washington? *überhaupt jemand??*
der Mönch . . . !

The last line had been added like a postscript, possibly later, indented and noticeably lower than the others.

'Well, it's something, I suppose: some bloke called Arnold Skardon, apparently an MI5 man in London, now dead, however, and maybe someone else, a bloke called John in Moscow. Washington? Obviously he means someone in the State Department or the Pentagon, or more likely someone who was there fifty years ago! Which brings us to "the monk", who merits an exclamation mark in my book too.'

Burke could see only two possibilities: either her colleague Eckberg was being fed a calculated drip by an ex-Stasi man determined to eke out his pension with a few selectively edited pieces of ambiguous archive material from his bottom drawer, or – just conceivably, though he doubted it – some item of genuine interest had escaped the CIA hoover (an in-house joke at Langley, that). The American spooks had gone through most of the Stasi archives, electronic or otherwise, while the West Germans' own intelligence service, the Bundesnachrichtendienst, was still trying to come to terms with its chief espionage target folding like a house of cards. Not a few politicians in Bonn were wanting to know why they hadn't been warned. Since then stuff had filtered through to the press in dribs and drabs. But much of it was deliberately targeted, leaked, it was widely suspected, by Stasi men determined to poison the system that had beaten theirs.

'We thought you had contacts, within your British intelligence? And also in Moscow. You spent some time there and I, for one, Mr Burke, was very impressed with what you wrote.

'Also, that part of it at least is not as hopeless as it sounds. We know who John in Moscow is: a man who called himself Yakovlev. He was an official at the Soviet consulate in New York back in the 1950s. He was also an agent of the NKVD, a predecessor of the KGB. He was ultimately responsible for transmitting Fuchs's intelligence from Los Alamos back to the Kremlin. He was last heard of in Moscow in 1991. If he is still alive, if we can find him, then at least we have a starting point.'

Heading for bed some hours later, Eamonn Burke was still wondering what he was doing and why. The story intrigued him, it was true, but even with the dubious lead in Moscow, he was not convinced that it would work out to be anything as interesting as Kotzke thought.

If he was honest with himself, the diary fragments seemed inconclusive. And then there was the question of how they had survived. Most top-secret Stasi files had been shredded in the panicky house-cleaning the East German secret police had begun after the Berlin Wall had fallen, when Gorbachev refused to honour Honecker's request for tanks to crush the workers' protests in

Leipzig and it had become clear, to everyone except the Western intelligence services, that the old order was over.

Sabine said she had dipped into the magazine's slush fund, and paid one of the semi-illegal 'burrowers' who specialized in flushing out details from the officially inaccessible Stasi records that remained – the CIA trawl had been almost as devastating as the Stasi clearout – for any references to the Dresden institute in 1987 or '88. The man had found nothing specific, but had offered her a brief set of surveillance notes on a target in Dresden called 'Lunte', a relatively unusual codename: it was German for a fox's brush. Given that 'Fuchs' was German for 'fox', she had thought it was too ridiculous to be linked, but equally too obvious to neglect. She had spent long hours comparing the surveillance reports, the details in the physicist's diary and other agenda from the institute. They matched. Not only that, they gave a picture of a man who in the last few months of his life was obviously under in-depth investigation.

Fuchs had been due to give a lecture in West Berlin. It would have been the first time he had been back on the western side of the Iron Curtain since he was flown out of London aboard a Polish airliner in 1959, following his release from Wakefield prison. The diary suggested he had been looking forward to it immensely. It was to be a quick in-out, across through Checkpoint Charlie in the afternoon, and back that same evening as soon as the conference had ended. The references in the diary to this upcoming event were blandly factual, excessively so, in fact. 'As if Fuchs was wary of admitting even to himself the opportunity it offered,' Kotzke had observed. And in a margin of the partially complete document 'legacy', she had come across the date of the conference. Had the scientist secretly intended to abandon his planned speech on the night and read out his 'secret' instead? Did the Stasi suspect? And if so, did they decide to pre-empt him? At any rate, in December 1988, less than a year before the fall of the Berlin Wall, but potentially more importantly, only three days before he was due to go West, Fuchs died. Suddenly. Apparently of a heart attack.

'It could have just been convenient,' Kotzke had admitted, 'except for one little thing.'

'Which was?' Burke was tiring of the tease.

'That the surveillance operation on "Lunte" was closed down the night before. The file mark said simply: operation terminated.'

It was convincing, Burke had agreed, though not exactly proof. 'The truth is out there,' he mused. The question was: where to start looking for it?

What the hell? It was worth going through the motions, if only to earn his fee from Berlin. There was always Dickie Boston, his tame 'service' contact. A decent lunch might screw something out of the old school. There were worse ways of spending a few days and a few German marks. And he still had friends in Washington, friends of his father to be accurate, for whatever that was worth, given that they had no idea where to start. Meanwhile, perhaps most importantly, there was Valery Korkin in Moscow. If anyone could find ex-comrade Yakovlev, Korkin was the man. It had always struck Burke as bizarre that the man who had turned out to be his best friend and most reliable ally had been born a citizen of a country that was supposedly an enemy. Even if Burke scarcely thought of himself as American nowadays, Korkin was unquestionably a Russian. It was one of the few scattered pieces of evidence that Burke could muster for belief in God that his friend was now extremely successful; and relatively rich, for an honest man in the new Russia.

Burke checked the time difference – it was gone 3.00a.m. in Moscow now; too late to ring Korkin. The big man would not be asleep but almost certainly in the arms of a floozy or drinking the night away in some den. Burke made a mental note to call him around lunchtime the next day, when he would be in full command of his facilities.

It was not just Sabine Kotzke's story, however, that had intrigued him. The woman herself was a beguiling mixture of arrogance and vulnerability, intelligence and credulity. She had reawakened something in him, he thought, as he dropped his trousers to join the other heaps of clothes on the bedroom floor for Mrs Konopka to deal with on Wednesday morning.

To his surprise, however, he did not go to sleep immediately. His brain, fuelled rather than addled by the alcohol, refused to grant him rest.

As he expected, his offer had been politely, and firmly, turned down. She was a big enough girl to get around town on her own, thank you very much. But she pecked him on both cheeks at the door. Delighted to have you on board, Mr Burke. I hope our little German story will not prove too boring for you, or too challenging – this last with a sting in it. Burke had watched her trip lightly up his steps, then hesitate and suddenly no longer seem quite as confident. Just getting her bearings, she had said. Left at the end, then second right and straight on to the main road. Yes, of course, she had replied hurriedly. Thanks. Goodbye. See you tomorrow.

At the end of the road, barely fifty yards away, she stopped briefly and looked around. At first he thought she was looking for a taxi, but two passed with their 'For hire' lights on. A middle-aged couple, arguing, obviously on their way home from the pub, passed her. Only when the street was completely empty did Sabine cross over and head towards the Bayswater Road.

6

Kiva

'Klaus, *Schätzchen*, come with us. You really must.'

Fuchs was polishing the Buick outside the Big House, as the main building of the old ranch school – now the single men's domitory – was called. It was the Russian-accented voice of Genia Peierls, calling him 'treasure' in her husband's language, German.

Fuchs would have thought anyone else was being sarcastic. But with Genia, he knew it was genuine. She was always trying to make up for having been the one, back in England, who first dubbed him 'penny-in-the-slot' on the grounds that if you asked him a question, he gave an answer, but 'put nothing in and you get nothing out'. Fuchs found it harmless enough, but Genia now seemed embarrassed. She and Rudolf had, after all, a genuine affection for their protégé.

Genia was a great organizer. Best of all, she liked organising hiking trips into the extraordinary landscape that surrounded Los Alamos. 'Here we are,' she would proclaim, 'in the midst of some of the most fascinating country on God's earth and you men just want to spend your time off playing poker in a stuffy room.'

She was referring chiefly to George Kistiakowsky, the Polish munitions expert who had taught his fellow scientists the joys of playing cards for money. 'The thing about a good poker player is that he always believes he can't lose as long as he keeps a grip on the mathematics.' The trouble was that Los Alamos was not exactly short on good mathematicians. One of the keenest poker novices was 'Johnny' von Neumann, the man who worked on the computers. But the only man who really worried 'Kisty' was Isidor Rabi.

He was not part of the project as such but a frequent visitor from Chicago. Rabi had grown up in a Yiddish-speaking family so orthodox that he had had to discover for himself that the earth revolved around the sun. He had ended up as one of the foremost physicists of his generation. But that was no excuse, in Kisty's eyes, for being a card-sharp too.

Fuchs, despite his own prodigious flair for mathematics, had never been tempted to join the poker schools. It was assumed that his reluctance was just another aspect of his generally reclusive shyness. But he was a sucker for Genia's expeditions. Today she had organized a full day's excursion, complete with picnic baskets, through the aspen forests around the end of the canyon, over the next mesa and down into Frijoles canyon, which 500 years earlier had been the centre of a flourishing Indian civilization. There were still cave homes, ruins of stone buildings including an ancient kiva, the stone circle at the centre of the most sacred rituals and the spiritual heart of any tribe. One particular aspect of today's adventure was irresistible to Fuchs: the party included the most famous of Los Alamos's occasional visitors, Niels Bohr.

The Dane's arrival had been a psychological boost to everyone on The Hill. It was he who had defined the modern concept of the structure of the atom, for which he had been awarded the Nobel Prize in 1922. Without his ground-breaking work, the Manhattan Project might never have been conceived. But, almost more importantly, he was a living reminder of the evil that justified an enterprise which one or two had grumbled was not what they had entered a career in science for.

Bohr was one of Denmark's estimated 7,500 Jews. On 29 September 1943, only days before the Nazis planned to round them all up for transport to Germany, Bohr and his wife Margarethe had escaped to neutral Sweden in a fishing boat which threaded its way through German minefields. From here he was taken first to England and then to Los Alamos. He had not volunteered to be a full member of the team – Fuchs assumed that at fifty-eight he was probably too old for the privations – but he had established a role as a visiting godfather, a universal figure of respect.

Fuchs had met Bohr briefly, and had heard him speak, slowly, with great deliberation. Einstein had regarded the Dane as a spiritual son and had put his ponderous speech down to an exaggerated, but wholly natural modesty. He had memorably described him as 'uttering his opinions like one perpetually groping and never like one in the possession of definite truth'. But Bohr was far from the stereotype of a weedy academic; he was a big man, who had been a spectacular athlete in his university days. Even now he was a physically as well as intellectually impressive figure.

Fuchs did not want to bore or embarrass his famous companion by asking him to rehearse once again the story of his dramatic escape from Copenhagen, and it was the Dane who broke the ice. To Fuchs's surprise, he raised the one issue he had no wish to talk about.

'So, Klaus. Do you think this weapon will ever be used? What do you feel, as a German, about dropping such a device, with such unknown power, on your fellow countrymen? Please, I do not wish to disconcert you, but it is something we have to think about.'

Fuchs had heard rumours that Bohr was becoming increasingly worried about the morality of using a superweapon, particularly when he had – albeit indirectly – contributed so crucially to its origins. But the last thing Fuchs wanted was to be drawn into a conversation on the moral implications of a bomb that could alter for ever the global balance of power. He knew what had to be done. He was doing it. It was not betrayal. It was how science was meant to be. There should be no secrets between allies. But to get involved in a discussion of the topic would be to risk expressing his opinions too freely, and that might raise security questions, particularly in the mind of the ever-suspicious General Groves. He parried Bohr with a standard response used on The Hill : 'If it ends the war, then it will be worthwhile.'

'Precisely.' The big man fixed Fuchs with the steady gaze of an apostle in search of a convert. 'But it must end not just this war, but all wars. You know they have no idea exactly what force this bomb may yield. You yourself are engaged on the calculations, so I do not need to tell you that it is a highly speculative endeavour: we have little frame of reference. I suspect that it will be tremendous. It will set history on to a new track.'

Fuchs noticed an intensity in his eyes, which in anyone else would have been mistaken for a psychological disorder. In Niels Bohr it was a window on to an intellect that never slept.

'What will be the result if one country alone has this bomb?' the Dane continued.

Fuchs told himself he was not hearing this.

'The very reason for the work we are doing here was the fear that the first country to achieve it might be Nazi Germany. But should any one country, no matter how benevolent it may seem to us today, be allowed mastery of human destiny? This work will not be secret for ever. If we are successful, then others will be too – sooner or later. How much should we be telling our allies?'

Fuchs studied the ground before him as they marched down the dusty trail. Could it be that Bohr thought as he did? Was it not more plausible that the Dane had been primed to test him? Scientists at Los Alamos talked openly, but it was also no secret that the General was becoming increasingly paranoid and putting pressure on Oppenheimer to report any doubts about the reliability of his people.

'There is an agreement with Britain,' Fuchs began. 'They, I mean we,' he found the word strange in his own mouth even though he had been a British citizen for the past two years, 'we will share in the weapon.'

Bohr swept aside the statement. 'Of course, the British will be in on it. I too am here thanks to them. But I doubt if they or their empire will wield as much influence in the world that emerges from this bloody conflict. I am thinking of the Russians.'

Fuchs felt the mild sweat he had worked up on the walk turn suddenly cold. He said nothing.

But Bohr was not looking at him. 'Look,' he was saying. The canyon wall was pitted with dark holes, like dovecotes carved out of the living ochre rock: the precursors of the pueblo villages, the remnants of a genuine trogolodyte civilization worshipped as a mythical golden age when the conquistadors were building their first church in Albuquerque. Bohr had stopped and was standing in the centre of a roughly marked-out stone circle.

'You know what this is?' he asked.

The German had no idea.

'Genia explained to me earlier. I believe it is the *kiva*, the Indians' sacred place. This is where they performed their mysteries.'

Fuchs looked around at the stones and thought it not unlike similar circles he had seen in England. There was one, he recalled, not far from Banbury: the Rollright Stones, it was called. He had driven there as a diversion, on the way back to Birmingham, one afternoon after meeting 'her'. Even at the thought of the young woman who had called herself Sonja he felt a dry tickling in the back of the throat, the beginning of his familiar rasping cough. He had begun to fear it was a nervous reaction. It had begun back then, when he first started passing information to the Russian at the Embassy in London, and later to the strange girl who spoke perfect German, but could still pass for an English country girl. Things had been simpler then: the stakes smaller, the betrayal less obvious. Science had no natural frontiers, and all he had been sharing was his own work. To what nation did that belong anyway? Certainly not the abomination that his own had become. Pure science was about channelling mankind's knowledge out of such narrow boundaries.

It was in New York that the cough had started in earnest, just as the game had become more elaborate. He had woken early and choked like a heavy smoker, he remembered, the morning he was due to walk down 42nd Street to Times Square holding a baseball in one hand. Fine for some American teenager, but the thin German professor with the receding hairline and the sober suit had felt ridiculously obvious, as if they had told him to wear a placard around his neck announcing 'Secrets for sale'. But he had not reckoned on New York. No one paid the slightest notice, no more to him than they did to the pudgy-faced man who came up to him on the corner of the square, wearing gloves and holding a spare pair in his hand. Fuchs had felt like a bit-part actor in a bad movie. He had gone home that evening and coughed over the lavatory bowl until his lungs heaved in his chest. Then he had lain back on the sofa in the brownstone apartment building, poured himself a whiskey and laughed quietly to himself. Sadly.

'But you know what was the greatest mystery to them?' Fuchs was jolted back to the present by the sound of Bohr's powerful voice as he stood in the midst of the ancient Indian *kiva*.

'Hmm?' Bohr looked at Fuchs questioningly, but answered before the German could respond.

'The gun. They did not have it. The Spaniards did. A new technology that gave complete mastery to the invaders. Do we know that Western culture was so much better than theirs? How can we tell? Theirs has not survived. Superior technology obliterated it. That is what we are building at Los Alamos: the power to obliterate. I have no doubts that it has to be built. Even that it might have to be used. But I wonder, sometimes, does humanity have a death wish?'

'Well, look. Here are our great physicists about to master archaeology.' Bernice Brode had caught up with them while the others were setting out picnic things. The women had prepared southern-fried chicken, dusted in flour and pepper and deep-fried;

46

there was potato salad, a cold ham and even a strange green paste that Genia said was called guacamole, a Mexican thing, made with avocados, chilli peppers and onion. She served it with some flat Indian corn bread. Bohr seemed to enjoy it. Fuchs found the texture too bland and the taste too spicy. It was the sort of thing Oppenheimer would love, with his taste for Mexican food.

'Acch,' the Dane suddenly sighed and for a moment Fuchs thought he was about to lapse into German, which he spoke at least as well as he did English. To his relief, however, Bohr showed no inclination to continue the conversation. He leaned back, closed his eyes and let the sunshine fall on his pale forehead. When he did speak, the language was not what Fuchs was expecting at all.

'*Che sera, sera.*'

In his office back at Los Alamos Robert Oppenheimer was reclining in his chair, sucking on an unlit pipe. Before him, the hulking figure of Niels Bohr paced the room.

'It all depends, inevitably,' Oppenheimer was saying, 'on the General.'

'I know.'

'Groves is naturally paranoid. That's his job and if he was any way different, he wouldn't be doing it. Security is the military brass's top priority. You can see it from their point of view. If the Nazis got the bomb . . .'

'Yes, of course. You don't need to tell me.'

'So what do you think?'

'I just don't know. He is so quiet, even for a scientist. We discussed the moral issue, the problem of use. But I could not draw him out. But then one would expect that.' He sighed again. 'Anything is possible, of course. Anything.'

'Even that.' It was not exactly a question. But Bohr took it as one, stopping in his relentless stride to look Oppenheimer in the eye.

'So we agree. We think there is a chance, just a chance, that our friend Klaus Fuchs is a spy?'

The Dane nodded, almost imperceptibly.

Oppenheimer took another suck on his pipe, pursed his lips for a second, then, staring into the middle distance, added:

'The question is: what do we do about it?'

7

The Snowman

New York/Boston, February 1945

The message from Moscow, when it came, was brief and to the point. The only trouble was that he had not received it.

Fuchs had not been able to make Christmas 1944 at his sister's. The work at Los Alamos was intensifying and he was putting in some eighteen hours a day. When he arrived in early February, Kristel had told him that an old friend of his called Raymond had been to see her back in November. He should have been expecting it. It was, after all, what he had told the man to do. But somehow the news that he had actually been here, intruded on a more personal part of his life, seemed to Klaus Fuchs like an uninvited intrusion.

Almost immediately the cough came back, sending Kristel rushing into the kitchen for a glass of water. He had explained that it was a reaction to the dry desert air and she told him, as he knew she would, to take care of his chest. Then she was back to the topic.

'Here,' she said, 'he left this for you.'

Fuchs snatched the envelope from her hand and pocketed it. Only late that evening did he sit on his bed and open it. Inside was an anonymously typewritten card with a New York telephone number and the instruction to call, leaving no name or address, but saying simply that he had arrived and how long he would be staying.

Harry Gold was preparing his supper when the telephone rang and he heard the unmistakable tones of John. The man was calling, it appeared, from a gasoline station. Gold found it hard to make him out as he was clearly in a state of some excitement. The doctor had called, he repeated three times. It was urgent that Raymond return his visit. Could he meet John at the usual place, in the park. He had a package for the doctor that he would like him to take.

On a cold New England afternoon, three days after the call from John, Gold found himself tramping through the snow to the Heinemanns' home. Fuchs himself answered the door and invited him in. The two went upstairs to his room, 'like two naughty schoolboys', Kristel Heinemann was to recall.

Gold later remembered that Fuchs had seemed genuinely pleased to see him and talked in detail about the conditions at Los Alamos, which he described as primitive in the extreme, but intellectually the most stimulating environment he had ever worked in. He had lots of important information to pass on. But he would need time to collate it. He had not known when Gold would arrive.

It was snowing heavily as Harry Gold made his way to the steps of Boston's imposing State House as arranged. In the gathering gloom even the glow of the street lights against the marble seemed cold. There was little traffic about. On the corner a policeman looked him up and down. 'Hey, pal. Don't hang out too long in the open tonight. They say it's gonna be a cold one.'

'Thanks, officer. I'm just waiting for someone,' he said, cursing Fuchs for choosing such a conspicuous meeting place. He understood, of course. The man did not want to implicate his sister. As if that could be avoided. But meeting here was so much more obvious.

'Well, I sure hope she doesn't stand you up. I wouldn't put a dog out on a night like this.'

Gold smiled and shuffled his feet, scarcely able to feel his toes. The policeman turned up the collar of his cape against the snow and walked off slowly, leaving Gold alone in the yellow pool of lamplight. A few minutes later he saw the gangly figure of Fuchs turn the corner, unmistakable even in a heavy overcoat and with a small black beret on his head.

'Good to see you, doctor. I was beginning to think you'd left me to freeze.'

Fuchs looked him sharply in the eye, as if the fact that 'Raymond' was a human being had not until that moment occurred to him.

'Sorry,' he said. 'I was delayed.' He was clearly not in the mood for small-talk.

At times like these Harry Gold felt he hated the man, though he knew he loved him. He gave his life meaning. He was a genius, of course; Gold genuinely believed that. He had had just enough time on two occasions now to glance at the contents of the papers he handed over to John. He knew he understood far more of what was in them than the Russian did. And when he had been given a list of technical questions to pass to Fuchs at their last meeting he had felt sure they made little sense. There were errors in the translation, as if whoever was responsible for putting them into English had been deliberately kept in the dark about the subject matter. Which was, of course, exactly the case. Naturally, he had simply done what he was supposed to: passed them on. But he had seen Fuchs sneer when he read them, and felt somehow that the German thought him responsible. He had even tried to talk to Fuchs about his work, to discuss the problems of separating the necessary uranium isotopes, a subject to which he felt he could genuinely contribute, but Fuchs had brushed his comments aside as if he had been a lavatory attendant instead of a trained chemist.

The pair were walking as briskly as the conditions would allow, down the hill. Occasionally a car would pass them, tyres squelching through grey slush. Fuchs put his hand inside his overcoat and pulled out a thick manila envelope.

'Take this. It is the most important thing I have ever given you. Now, we must discuss our next meeting.' The tone was business-like. 'It will not be possible for me to come here again soon. The pace is accelerating. You must come to Santa Fe.'

Gold could see the logic in what Fuchs was saying, but was not sure when he could get the time off work. Fuchs had suggested a meeting in April, but reluctantly settled for June.

'I just hope that when you come, it will not be too late.'

The war in Europe was moving into a decisive phase. No one knew how long Germany could last. In the east the Russian advance seemed unstoppable, something both men naturally welcomed, but what it would mean for the Manhattan Project was uncertain. The bomb had been designed for use against Germany; would it be used against Japan? And Soviet Russia was not at war with Japan.

Reaching again into his overcoat Fuchs produced a Santa Fe street map. Pulling Gold into the shelter of a store doorway, he opened it, indicating in the glow of the streetlight two parallel lines on the edge of the city.

'That is the Castillo Street bridge. It crosses the Santa Fe river.

There is a bench there. People often sit on it to pass the time of day. I shall meet you there at 4.00p.m. on the fourteenth of June.'

Gold opened his mouth and then closed it again. He would have to make the arrangements. Perhaps he could bring forward his summer vacation. The German nodded and made as if to go.

'Wait.' Gold stopped him. 'I was asked to give you this.' He handed Fuchs an envelope. The German looked at it curiously and opened it. Inside was a slim wallet, of the type carried by gentlemen wearing evening dress.

Nice, thought Harry. Not the sort of thing they would offer me. But then the doctor is class. 'A present, from Moscow,' he said, as John had instructed him. Fuchs looked bemused, but put the wallet in his pocket.

'There's also this.' Harry Gold, with his heart in his mouth, took out the other envelope he had been given to hand over. In it, he knew, was $1,500, almost a year's wages. 'In case you need anything, they said.'

Fuchs opened it and almost dropped it as if he had been handed something unclean. He looked at Gold with an expression the little chemist would remember all his life. If he had already formed the opinion that his admiration for Fuchs was unrequited, now he felt as if he had defiled himself further. Like the look on Adam's face encountering the serpent after it had tempted Eve, was how he would tell it to unsympathetic FBI ears.

Fuchs stood there in front of him, his face showing scorn mingled with pity. He knew, surely, that it was not Harry's doing. This was more money than they had ever given Harry. Surely he knew that. Fuchs thrust it back at him, abruptly, said two words, 'Till June,' then turned crisply on his heel and walked off into the falling snow.

Gold stared after him for a few minutes, the envelope containing a small fortune limp in his hand. He would return it to John. He would try to imitate the German's gesture, he thought. Such scorn. At that moment he felt he despised himself almost as much as Klaus Fuchs did. He looked for a second at the wad of notes inside the open envelope, then put it back into his breast pocket. In the bigger pocket of his raincoat he put the map Fuchs had given him. It was a move he would spend long years of his life regretting. The map would be crucial evidence at his trial.

It was Saturday night down at the big hall. It had been built as the boys' school assembly, but now served as the general mess, dance hall, bar and social centre. Tonight it was a theatre. Posters had gone up all over the ramshackle collection of prefab army billets, clapboard houses and barbed wire fences that passed for a town: 'The Los Alamos Amateur Dramatic Society proudly presents *Arsenic and Old Lace*.' Fuchs had heard the head of civilian administration, a big Texan with a broad smile and even broader accent, boasting about the atmosphere he credited himself with creating up on The Hill: 'Just one big happy family, like a summer camp except that all these here folks are doing work that could win us the war.'

There were all sorts of rumours circulating about some 'surprise' or other, even suggestions that a few of the project's more eminent figures had been prevailed upon to take part.

Over a beer Richard Feynmann had persuaded Fuchs to go and see the play with him.

'Do you good, Klaus,' Feynmann had quipped. 'Take you out of yourself, get a bit more of the Anglo-Saxon sense of humour.'

Now Fuchs found himself sitting in the makeshift theatre, wondering for just how much of the performance the two large GIs in front were going to munch popcorn and shift around in their seats. Feynmann, next to him, was also eating popcorn.

'Hey, Klaus, have some. It's good.'

Fuchs found the stuff dry and unpalatable, and it had an alarming ability to bring on the cough he dreaded. But he declined Feynmann's offer as gracefully as he could. He liked the young American, indeed recognized in him an extraordinary talent, though he found his irreverent, almost anarchic manner disconcerting. He was touched by Feynmann, too. The man's wife, Arlene, was in hospital dying of tuberculosis. As Fuchs had one of the few private cars among the scientists – an astounding number of them were unable to drive, he had discovered – Feynmann had embarrassedly prevailed on him more than once to drive him to Albuquerque. He had suggested that Klaus lend him the car, but Fuchs had seen it as an opportunity and volunteered to take him. In his long-term plans an excuse for visiting Albuquerque was vital. He made a bit of a fuss about it being no bother, but had contrived to let the American believe it was simply because he was such a fuss-pot he would let no one else drive his precious car. Feynmann had thought Oppenheimer would be reluctant to let both of them go at once, and had been surprised when the boss had okayed it. Fuchs saw it as proof once again of the basic humanity of his colleagues.

It had been Feynmann's sense of anarchy that had finally persuaded Fuchs to accompany him to the play, though he feared his English might let him down on some of the jokes. His command of the language was generally excellent, but better in scientific terminology than colloquialisms, particularly when uttered in some of the stranger American accents. Feynmann dismissed his fears. He couldn't think of an occasion, he insisted, when Fuchs had missed something. In the end Fuchs was delighted he had come; the performance was a huge success. The young lieutenant playing Mortimer turned out to have a gift for mimicry, and caused as much amusement with his impersonations of Cary Grant in the movie version as with the lines he had been given.

But there was no doubt that the *pièce de résistance* was the much treasured 'surprise'. When Mortimer finally realizes that his demonic aunts have been murdering their lodgers and decides to help get rid of the evidence, the window seat was opened to reveal a succession of stored corpses. Last to emerge, covered in flour to give his suntanned skin a deathly pallor, was the suitably skeletal body of J. Robert Oppenheimer himself, director of the Manhattan Project. The audience erupted in laughter.

Afterwards, as they joined the crowds bustling out of the hall, Feynmann asked him what he had thought of the scene. Fuchs was almost as surprised by the question as he had been by the grotesque event itself. 'Very typical,' he replied, 'very American. And, I suppose, very funny. Quite apt really. In the midst of life, we are in death. Here above all, at Los Alamos, we should know that.'

Feynmann, of course, knew it only too well. And Fuchs knew that he did. To what extent, he wondered, did personal tragedy shape a man's philosophy. He had his own answer. Feynmann, slapping him on the shoulder in that infuriating American manner as they parted company, had a different one. Fuchs wondered how he reconciled it with the world he lived in, and decided he would never know the answer.

Neutral Switzerland, 1 April 1945

The man who occasionally called himself Mr Harper sat lost in thought as he looked through the train window at the fields already turning green as the last of the winter meltwater was absorbed by the fertile soil. Busy housewives waved to one another from their balconies as they started on the lengthy business of spring cleaning, beating the carpets, scrubbing the brightly painted chalet shutters and planting the hanging baskets.

It was hard to imagine that out there, beyond this artificial island, protected by its invisible walls of secret diplomacy, cynicism and pragmatic greed, a war was being fought to its bitter conclusion. But the eventual outcome of the cataclysm would depend on the urgent report he would send in top secret cipher to Washington the instant he reached the Embassy in Bern. There was also the report sent by his counterpart, the Englishman known as Colonel White. And – in theory more important – the reply that the men with whom they had spent four hours in a Geneva hotel room would deliver. And once the document was agreed, the 'protocol' as it was technically known, there could be no going back.

Ever since his early career as a diplomat in Vienna, watching the Hapsburg empire collapse around him, and subsequently at Versailles, where he witnessed President Wilson's naïve but well-intentioned plans for a new, fairer Europe based on self-determination become swallowed up by the same old short-sighted self-interest, Allen Dulles had been increasingly convinced that the great powers should use more than the obvious channels of war and diplomacy to shape history. Only by acting behind the scenes could catastrophes be pre-empted. Britain had been too late in 1939. The former British prime minister Neville Chamberlain had sullied his hands and ruined his reputation, to no avail.

Dulles had watched the smelting of the opportunistic alliance between Hitler and Stalin with the cynical eye of the professional, and had laughed out loud when the Nazis launched their attack on Russia in June 1941. But it was not only the Russians who had been caught cat-napping. America too had been behind-hand, entering the war only as an afterthought, in 1941, when anyone with sense might have foreseen that by then it had long been inevitable. Pearl Harbor was the wrong reason. And the result of wrong reasoning.

The OSS, Office of Strategic Services, had been set up partly to make sure Uncle Sam was never again caught with his pants down in quite such embarrassing circumstances. But to fulfil its real purpose, Dulles knew, it would have to do more than that. It would not just have to pre-empt history, but make it. Even if on occasion it had to get its hands dirty.

The meeting he had just concluded in Geneva might be viewed in a hostile light by public opinion at the moment, and possibly even by history, if things went wrong. But history, as any fool knew – even Adolf Hitler – depended on the future. And the future depended on the present. And the present was never without risk. And the risks were what he lived for. A new dawn was about to break over the world. A brand new sunrise. Sunrise. Yes, he liked the word.

8

Unearthing the Fox

Eamonn Burke stood by the window of his Ladbroke Grove flat watching a taxi depositing a fare by the pedestrian crossing. The driver clicked the cab light from blue to orange as he moved off from the kerb, leaving his former passenger struggling with an umbrella on the pavement. Burke watched her fight against a gust of wind that threatened to blow the umbrella inside out, smiled to himself at the comedy of her misfortune and then thought better of it. *Schadenfreude*, he mused, one of the most basic of human emotions. And one of the most base, he added.

'How come your lot invented a word for it?' he asked of Sabine Kotzke, who lay on Burke's floor, before her a pile of photocopies and an open folder with pages of careful notes in her neat script.

'What?' She looked up.

'Oh, nothing,' Burke parried. 'I was just wondering what the point of it all was.'

'The point of what?'

'To hell with the story. Life, the universe and everything. To what purpose disturbing the dust on a bowl of rose petals, and so on.'

'Rose petals? I am sorry, Eamonn, if you are going to talk about flowers I will think you are being romantic.'

'I beg your pardon?'

'I'm only joking.'

She was, too. Ms Kotzke was sexually inscrutable. The thought flickered through his mind that perhaps she didn't like men at all.

He was interested to see what she had dug up. He had sent her to the News International library, courtesy of George Prosset, who had been delighted to show off the extent of his empire to an attractive young foreign journalist. At Burke's request, Prosset had allowed her to delve into the *Times* obituaries and cuttings. She told him what Burke had told her to: that she was working on a piece of historical reconstruction that might form the basis of a non-fiction book in Germany. He knew that would be enough to bore the pants off his drinking partner who, despite his upmarket pretensions, had a basically tabloid approach to foreign news. Disasters and football hooligans were what Prosset really liked best. On no account was she to mention that she was working with Burke, he had insisted.

His brief had been specific: to get as much of the original material as possible from contemporary reports of Fuchs's trial, to add to this the gleanings from her own German sources and try to paint a picture of the ghost they were chasing. Burke wanted to know whether there was any correlation between the oblique references in the diary snippets and what was on the record about the atom spy's life. He had spent most of the day at the Public Record Office in Kew, looking through the few publicly available official papers relating to the espionage scandal and the damage it did to relations between London and Washington. Right now, he was more convinced than ever that they were scrabbling in the shadows.

'What's on the record here and in Germany is the same, not too complicated,' she said. 'Fuchs's father was a pastor who lost the faith and found socialism, at least the Social Democrat type. He moved the family from Leipzig to Kiel. Fuchs went that bit further when the politics in Germany began to get bad. He worked for the Communist party at Kiel university. Then the Nazis got on his trail, and he left. His cousin was engaged to a girl working for a family in Somerset. An "au pair". A French term, isn't it?'

'Yes, it means a sort of live-in babysitter. Never mind.'

'This family were also English fellow-travellers of the party. You know in Russian the word is *"sputniki"*, like the satellites?' She smirked, pleased to have got her own back in the linguistic stakes. Burke gave an appreciative nod. Actually he had known, but there was no point in telling her.

'Fuchs gets himself out of Germany and goes to stay with this English family. There he goes to university in Bristol, but the trouble starts with a Pole. Doesn't it always? Jürgen Kuczynski, a half-Polish German whose sister Ursula was a sex pussy.'

'Kitten.'

'What?'

'Sex kitten, is the expression.'

Sabine shrugged. 'Yeah okay, some cat. I mean she used it, you know, like a spy, like in the first big war: Mata Hari?'

Burke had begun pacing the room. Outside the light had all but gone.

'Okay. War breaks out,' Sabine continued. 'Fuchs gets put in prison. Suddenly all Germans are the same again, yeah? Everyone is a Nazi.'

'It was an instinctive reaction. They didn't really put them in jail.'

'No, worse. They sent them to *camps*,' the word was pregnant in her mouth, 'in Canada,' as if somehow the location made it worse.

'They weren't the same sort of camp. And at least it was out of the way.'

'Like in South Africa, where the British invented the concentration camp, for the Boers?'

'Invented, perhaps. But like so many British inventions, it wasn't developed to its full potential. Are you sure you want to have this argument.'

'No.' It was said quietly.

'Anyhow, Fuchs wasn't there long, was he?'

'No. He had a charmed life and another German friend who was not a suspect, a Herr Peierls. He has been living here and is part of the upper class already; it can make such a difference to be . . . *vornehm*?'

'Establishment.'

'He is working at a university in Birmingham and says Fuchs is what he needs so he gets him, all the way back from Canada. What he is working on is Tube Alloys' – she stumbled over the pronunciation: 'toob alloees' – 'what does this mean?'

'It doesn't mean anything. That was the point. It was designed to sound boring, I imagine, like some sort of plumber's supplies. There were probably all sorts of strange minor ministries back then, thousands of men in drab regulating rationing of everything from wrought-iron railings to bus tickets.'

'So perhaps it is a good name after all. To conceal the atomic bomb project. But it does not fool the Pole. Kuczynski gets back in touch. Tells Fuchs he must do his bit for the party. Soon he is passing notes – just on his own work, however – straight to a Russian attaché at the Soviet Embassy in Kensington Gardens. Hey, that is close to here, yeah?'

'Yeah.'

Burke smiled and sank into the tattered leather armchair. Secretly he was rather impressed with the quality of her homework. But then perhaps he was just playing to his own stereotypes, thinking of her as some junior reporter.

'He met the Russian at a secret house . . .'

'A safe house.'

'This was also near here. In Kensington Park Road. He meets him three times in '41. Then he gets transferred, to Mata Hari. The joke is that she is Kuczynski's sister, but Fuchs does not know.

'Her codename at the time was Sonja. She later calls herself Ruth and turns up everywhere, spying in all sorts of places before finally disappearing behind the Iron Curtain in the fifties. She meets him at a cafe near the railway station at a town called Banbury and out in the country – near some monument called the Rollright Stones, maybe Mick Jagger comes from there – miles away from anywhere, but maybe not so far from Birmingham. And Fuchs has a car.

'But then, as always, you English give everything to the Americans. This "Tube Alloys" is moved to New York. Fuchs is now a British citizen. A mistake, huh? That is how he got tried for treason in the end. His control switched to New York too, a man called Harry Gold, codenamed "Raymond". He in his turn is reporting to a Russian. This must be our "John" – Yakovlev. I suppose he's in New York because he is really at the United Nations.'

'Do you?'

'Why else in New York instead of Washington?'

'Except that the United Nations didn't exist until after the war. And America was never a member of the League of Nations.'

Sabine put her hand to her mouth, embarrassed at the mistake. Burke couldn't help rubbing it in. He had done his own homework and saw no harm in her knowing it:

'Yakovlev was the Soviet consul in New York. He was one of the new breed of Soviet spook, not just a patriot but a guy who actually believed Communism was the future. They'd thrown him in at the deep end after a three-month English course. When he arrived in New York he must have sounded like Boris Karloff and been almost as inconspicuous. He reported direct to the NKVD, Stalin's so-called People's Commissariat for Internal Affairs.'

'Proof if ever we needed it that the old bastard knew his chief enemy was the common sense of his own people.'

'Said with feeling.'

'Consider it experience.'

Burke nodded. There had been even less love lost than he had imagined between Ms Kotzke and the regime she grew up under.

'Anyway, Yakovlev's predecessor in New York had latched on to Gold years earlier when the Soviets were mainly into industrial espionage. Gold was willing to leak information on the manufacturing processes at the Philadelphia chemical plant where he worked. Hardly first-division stuff.

'Comrade Yakovlev gave him a dream – the great fraternalism of the Red Flag which would save America from the boom-bust cycle of capitalism, stop another depression like the one that had turned all his parents' dreams of a brave new world to dust. He was Jewish and the family was originally called Golodetsky – from the Russian for hunger rather than the German for precious metal – but the racist thugs who processed immigrants on Ellis Island weren't concerned with complications like that. As far as they were concerned, another load of kikes had to have some sort of name connected with money. You Germans weren't the only anti-Semites, you know?'

Burke glanced down to see if he had provoked a reaction, but her face was a mask of passivity. He continued:

'The FBI were on to Yakovlev, but they didn't bother to tail him on a regular basis. They intercepted his telex traffic, but it was all in code. It was only in 1948 when a bunch of spooks at the US Army Signals Corps headquarters at Fort Meade got their hands on some Soviet one-time pads and began reading their old mail. One of these included a document written by Fuchs.'

'That was what led to his arrest?'

'Yes, but not immediately.' Burke flicked over the page of his notepad. 'In itself that wasn't proof. Yakovlev could have got hold of it without him knowing. But when they found another signal from Yakovlev referring to an agent in the British mission, the FBI put two and two together and talked to M15, who leaned on Fuchs's current bosses at Harwell.'

'Where's Harwell?'

'Just outside Oxford. It's not very important now, but back in the late forties it was Britain's nuclear weapons establishment. Fuchs had ended up as head of the theoretical division. You can imagine how enthusiastic Whitehall was to hear that he might be a Soviet agent.'

Sabine whistled softly.

'They spent time trying to find alternatives. The trouble was there weren't any. When the Russians exploded their first atomic bomb in September 1949, years before anyone thought they'd be ready, someone decided it was time to find out just how much help they'd had. When they put it to him, Fuchs apparently just cracked. It seems he was way out of tune with reality.'

'His family were probably quite used to extremes,' Sabine suggested. 'His sister later committed suicide, as had his grandmother and his mother. Fuchs was the one who found his mother. He was nineteen years old. He comes home from his studies and there she is lying on the floor, with this horrible look on her face. She'd swallowed hydrochloric acid.'

'Christ, what a way to go.'

'I wonder how much that influenced his ability to block things out, to lead a double life. In his confession he described it as "kind of controlled schizophrenia". No wonder.'

'So what about the man who took the confession?' she enquired. 'Any chance of getting through to him?'

'Not unless you have a ouija board. Arnold Skardon, it turns out, isn't one man but two. William Skardon, the interrogator, and Henry Arnold, who was head of security at Harwell, someone Fuchs seems to have become quite friendly with. Anyway, it seems Skardon was one of MI5's hotshot interrogators. But he retired from the service and died in 1988. Gold's gone too. The FBI put him away for thirty years after turning state's evidence against the Rosenbergs, the American Jewish couple who were Communist fellow-travellers and ended up in the electric chair.

'When he came out after sixteen years, Gold went into medical research but died during open-heart surgery back in 1972. Same story with Arnold. Fuchs wrote to him a couple of times from prison. He felt he'd let him down. But he's been pushing up the daisies for years.'

'Really.' Kotzke narrowed her eyes. 'All of them. Dead? Something of a coincidence, don't you think?'

Burke shrugged. 'This all happened a long time ago. Arnold was eighty-eight when he died. I think trying to hatch conspiracy theories might be stretching our evidence here, don't you?'

'Maybe.' Kotzke was straight-faced. 'But you forget the incident back in '49, just before they arrested Fuchs.'

'What incident?'

'Someone tried to kill him. That is what he thought.'

'You mean that night when he was driving home from Harwell

with another of the scientists? The other man said a stone shattered the windscreen.'

'Do you think that's what it was?'

'Maybe. Maybe not. Look, by then our man must have been getting pretty paranoid. The other bloke said afterwards Fuchs hit the deck as if someone was shooting at the car and took ages to calm down. At the time they all thought he was just neurotic as hell. But surely it was just his guilt complex. Maybe he thought the KGB was coming for him; I can see his point. If they'd got him before he was arrested, he would never have been able to confess his espionage. But no bullet was ever found, nothing to prove it was anything more than his own imagination.

'Unless . . .' Burke's mind was wandering ahead of his words, down the dark corridors that existed in secret places '. . . unless there were people who'd already done the digging. People who thought putting Klaus Fuchs on trial would be a big mistake, and wouldn't get the right result. People worried about dirty washing.'

9

Fellow Travellers

The dining room of the Travellers' Club in London's Pall Mall is one of the finer examples of Victorian style to be found in the British capital. The club itself, on the elegant thoroughfare that leads from the Foreign Secretary's official residence in Carlton House Terrace down towards St James's Palace, bears only a street number on the brass plaque. It was, of course, known to the taxi-driver who deposited Eamonn Burke there just before lunchtime on Thursday. If he had to rattle the bars of the spooks' cages, there was no better moment than feeding time.

Burke often thought the Travellers was one of those English anachronisms which his real father would not have understood. In its day it had cultivated a reputation as the hangout of spies and adventurers. But the world he had grown up in had prepared him for membership of a gentlemen's club. And the Travellers these days at least was prepared to extend that definition even to the gentlemen of the press. He had become a member in his mid-twenties and had found the place a bit of a bore, but of inestimable use for quiet lunches with the sort of contact who liked to be considered hard to come by.

Dickie Boston prided himself on being the new breed of spook, the product of a Midlands comprehensive who had taken a first-class honours degree in history at Cambridge – 'the school for spooks, old bean', as he referred to it in his parody of the old school tie generation that 'people like him' regarded as responsible for the Philby-Burgess-Maclean conspiracy. Ever since Burke had come across him in Peshawar during the Afghan affair, Boston's parodies had increasingly come to replace whatever personality might have been there in the first place.

He entered the downstairs bar as if he had been born to a viceroy of the Raj rather than a Renault dealer in Nottingham, thought Burke. 'Eamonn, begorrah! Good to see you. How's the revolution?'

Burke smiled wearily. It had become one of Boston's many affectations to treat Burke as some sort of Noraid fund-raiser for Sinn Fein.

Today Boston was full of his own news. He had been moving flats, leaving girlfriends, struggling with mortgage repayments and cursing the civil service pay structure. It was one of their private jokes that James Bond never complained about his overdraft. He sank a fino sherry and insisted they have another before Burke could persuade him upstairs to the dining room.

Burke selected a table near the great high windows. There was a guffawing from the other end of the room; half a dozen hacks sycophantically over-reacting to some dirty joke from a minor minister. About two-thirds of the tables were occupied, but they were far enough apart for it to be difficult to overhear. Most members in any case gave the impression that their own conversations were far more important than anyone else's could possibly be.

Boston chose smoked salmon with scrambled egg followed by roast rack of lamb. Burke opted for quails' eggs and rare calf's liver with bacon.

'So, what's it all about, Eamonn?

'Oh, nothing very exciting. Just an old anniversary that I'm trying to put some spin on. To be specific, one of your lot's more celebrated catches, Klaus Fuchs.'

'Going back a bit, aren't you?'

'That's the point of anniversaries. It's fifty years since he was arrested: I thought you might be able to give me a new angle. There must be all sorts of bits and pieces that got salted away for convenience's sake and will never come out under the thirty-, fifty- or whatever-year-rule because they've dropped off the edge of the table . . . You know the sort of stuff I mean.'

'God, can't say I do, really. Surely it's all in the cuts somewhere. Just dig it up and rehash it for Joe Public. Good for us, right enough, I suppose. Not often we get our praises sung these days. Ought to be all out for it I suppose in this age of transparency . . . 'Bottle of Sancerre, d'you fancy for starters? Never have found a wine that works well with smoked salmon. Tried Alsace Gewürztraminer – y'know for the spicy side of it – but still ended up tasting like silver polish. The advantage of a Sancerre is simply that it tastes so good when you slurp it down afterwards with the brown bread and butter. Still, life's a party, eh, old man?'

Burke pressed on relentlessly. 'What I was wondering is if there was any snippet you could dig out of the dead men's files that might give the story a bit of a twist. There were all sorts of rumours at one stage. I seem to recall reading somewhere that Fuchs was paranoid about being attacked when he was at Harwell after the war. And then something about a diary or papers of some sort hidden in a hollow bedleg in his cell?

'Perhaps there was something in his confession that didn't make the newspapers at the time. Too sensitive then but no problem now. You know the sort of thing. By the way, whatever happened to the bloke who did his interrogation? An interview with him might just make it sing.' Would Boston admit Skarden was dead?

Boston took out a large white handkerchief and blew his nose loudly into it, then began to tuck heartily into his salmon. Burke waited a moment and then decided his lunch guest was deliberately missing his cue.

'So, what do you think?'

Boston looked up as if the topic of their conversation had momentarily slipped his mind.

'Eh? Oh, dunno. Can't tell you, old bean. Must've been one of the other lot, obviously. Domestic, I mean.'

He used the word much as if he were talking about his family's ancestral cook.

'Their cock-up in the first place of course, clearing the bugger. Retired long ago, I suspect. The interrogator, I mean. Probably still hung up by the Official Secrets Act anyway if he hasn't turned up his tootsies by now. Not that I can imagine there's anything much that wasn't let out at the time. Embarrassing enough I should have thought. God knows the poor buggers didn't know what they had to come, particularly my lot. Mind you, I suppose Maclean would have been one of "our men" – if you'll pardon the phrase – in Washington at the time. God, what a shambles.'

Burke dipped a quail's egg in celery salt and ate it.

'Still, I could a shuftie round the antiquities department – if they haven't lost half of it in our move to Caesar's Palace – have I told you that's the latest nickname for the jolly green giant?'

Burke smiled. Inventing new names for the latter-day glass pyramid that housed the Secret Intelligence Service on the south bank of the Thames was a well established Fleet Street game; as was the competition among the inmates to make sure the one that passed into legend was one they had invented themselves. He suspected Dickie was better placed than he pretended to find out any secret lurking in Fuchs's past; at their last meeting he had dropped broad hints about his appointment to the new Joint Steering Committee which was supposed to end the old rivalry and ensure co-operation between both branches of British intelligence.

'Not sure I can see your point, though. Thought you might be targeting something more up to date. Bit of a bore, the old Fuchs thing, surely? Why not get on to something more recent? Might be easier to help you there. Less history to trawl through, and all that.'

'I thought that would have made it easier, being so long ago. Who did you think I meant? Gordievsky?'

'Why not? Bit of a coup old Oleg was, you know. You should know. I gave you the best bits. A good story, us spiriting him out in a fridge and all that.'

'Sure, sure, Dickie. Much appreciated, as you know. But right now I'm interested in older stuff. Would have thought you'd have been delighted. After all, as you say, it wasn't SIS who cocked up the initial vetting, was it . . . was it?' Burke suddenly wondered just how much faith he could put in anything his companion Boston told him.

Boston shook his head in that dismissively definitive way he had that always made Burke suspect he was lying. But he decided to take it at face value, for the moment.

'Anyway, all I'm after is a bit of really deep background: access to some of the stuff that never made the papers of the day, the sort of stuff somebody decided to sit on because they thought it wasn't what the great British reader needed to know – and the public was still very much treated on a "need to know" basis back then.'

Boston gave him a reproving schoolmaster look, then lowered his gaze again. Burke watched him.

'I mean, there must be somebody, not in the service, somebody on the fringe even, in the grey area between the scientists and the suits, who kept track of it all, somebody who has a shrewd idea of what went on at all those conversations and meetings when they were playing God with the biggest weapon in history.'

'Hmm . . . nuclear winter,' Boston muttered.

'Sorry?'

Boston looked momentarily taken aback, as if he had been

interrupted on a totally different train of thought. 'You know, nuclear winter: what they thought would happen if there was a serious exchange, black clouds over the sun, that sort of thing.'

It was an uncharacteristically reflective note for Boston to strike. Just then the main courses arrived. Boston eyed the wine list thirstily before ordering up a bottle of '84 Margaux.

'Just the thing, and the second bottle'll go down swimmingly with the Bleu de Bresse, eh? Sure your rag'll run to it, are you? Highly placed anonymous sources, all that.'

Burke glanced at his own list – which included the prices – and thought it was just as well he was working on a German budget. Not, he reminded himself, something he would broadcast in Dickie's presence. There were people even now at Vauxhall Cross who hadn't forgiven the Hun.

10

Sins of Omission

It was towards six o'clock in the evening and Eamonn Burke was sitting in the back bar of the Nag's Head just off Oxford Street waiting for Sabine. After the frustrating lunch with Boston he had made his way to El Vino's in search of the left-over-from-lunchtime mob. He had found George Prosset leaning on the bar, staring into the dregs of a glass of claret.

'Eamonn, good to see you,' Prosset had declared with genuine enthusiasm, and ordered another bottle. Burke found himself, against his better judgment, launching into the subject of Fuchs. Happily, Prosset's mind was more on his own matters, the labyrinthine intrigues woven in the corridors of Wapping, where he worried he had lost the thread, and the perennial sniping of his own foreign correspondents from their safe bolt-holes overseas. After a while, Burke had found himself tiring of his company and realized he needed to be alone.

Now he was, and was annoyed with himself for not making more of it. To some people, beer on top of claret might have seemed like suicide; to Burke it acted more like a brain tonic. Ideally, he thought, he would have liked to go to sleep and wake in the middle of the night shouting 'Eureka!'. In reality, he knew, all he would surface with would be a hangover.

He pulled out a notepad and a pen and began to draw a somewhat erratic flow diagram. It took him a minute to see it was flowing nowhere. He lifted his head and surveyed his surroundings. Classic Victorian gone slowly to seed, by way of flock wallpaper and a fruit machine. A man with a hooked nose and a distracted air talking to himself over a glass of lager reminded him of Fagin in *Oliver Twist*. Funny, he thought, how some human types lingered in the landscape, looking as if they might have been more at home in earlier generations. A wizened old man with a strong Irish accent and a chin like a worn wire brush asked if he could borrow his *Evening Standard*. Burke handed it to him, telling him to keep it. He looked at his empty glass, wondered about a refill, decided against it and turned once again to his notepad.

He was deeply annoyed with the fudge they seemed to be floating in. Fuchs's murder was a story in itself. Not front-page material – at least not in England, though possibly in Germany – but still a good yarn, depending, of course, on the identity of the culprit and the motive. But what intrigued him was something in Kotzke's manner that hinted at a much bigger story.

On the spur of the moment, Burke decided to take a piece of Prosset's disinterested advice and ring the *Times*'s former science correspondent, Edgar Morris, whom he had always considered a doddery old tosser. But Prosset had assured him the old boy had been a bit of a whizz on the atom stuff in his day. Back when everybody really thought nuclear energy was a goer.

To his surprise, the number answered almost immediately. Burke was relieved when Morris not only remembered him but showed no antipathy despite the lack of courtesy which he had – as he now regretted – always shown the older man.

'An old story, eh? Well, you've come to the right person.'

Burke smiled at the self-deprecation, but was disappointed to find him not the mine of information Prosset had promised.

'Klaus Fuchs? Well, that takes me back. Caused one hell of a stink, he did. A right slap in the face for the national ego, and in front of the Yanks, too. I wrote his obituary, of course, you know. One of the last things they let me do. But I'm not really the expert. No, not at all. Got most of my information second hand.'

'Well, I'd be most grateful,' Burke continued in his most obsequious voice, hating himself for it, 'if you could point me in any direction that might prove useful. I daresay the magazine I'm working for could be persuaded to cough up a few bob, you being a freelance now and all that . . .'

'Don't be silly. I'm not deluding myself that I'm anything other than retired these days. Glad to be shot of the business, to tell you the truth.

'Well, as I said, I'd be very grateful . . .'

'Yes, yes. No problem. No, old Nora's who you want to speak to. Must be getting on a bit now. Over eighty, I reckon.'

'I'm sorry?'

'The archivist, she was down at Harwell in the heyday of the project. Knew everybody, she did. Had access to all the records, more or less the official historian. No, I don't think you'll find anybody knows more about it than she does. Lives in Oxford these days. A word of warning, though, don't mention the war.'

'What do you mean?'

'Well, don't mention the filthy Hun, really. She was married to a German. Think he might have knocked her about a bit. Anyhow, it all ended in tears. Left a bit of a bad taste, I gather. Not to worry though, not as if you're working for *Stern* magazine, is it?'

'I'm sorry, I didn't quite catch her full name.'

'That's because I didn't quite give it to you. Nora, Nora Winter. Nuclear Winter, they used to call her. Here's the number.'

Burke scribbled it down and thanked Morris profusely, promising to remember him to her. Then he put the phone down.

'You canny old bastard, Boston,' he muttered under his breath. He lifted the receiver again and began to dial.

11

Thunder

Sabine arrived at 6.37, Burke noticed, looking at his watch. Seven minutes late. Not very Teutonic. He smiled. Punctuality was a vice he had little time for.

'Hi, there. How was your spy?'

'Deceptive. But I've got something out of it, one way or another. I've found someone who remembers Fuchs, and she's willing to talk.'

'She? One of your British Mata Haris?' Sabine looked jealous, Burke thought. He found the idea seductive, even as he dismissed it.

'Not exactly. She's a little old for me.'

'I thought you liked the mature woman?'

'The lady in question is in her eighties, though frankly it took all the charm I could muster to get her to see me.'

'Great. So when do we go and where?'

'Oxford, but not "we", just me.'

'A liaison after all, then.' She looked at him obliquely, teasingly, so he let her have it.

'Sort of. She just doesn't like Germans. She had a bad experience, I'm afraid. Her husband.'

'In the war.'

'No, in matrimony. She married a fat chemist from Düsseldorf. Turned out to be a right bastard.'

'That, Mr Burke, is not exclusive to German men.'

'Touché. Anyhow. I'm going to see her tomorrow. You'll just have to trust me.'

'Do I have a choice?'

'Only one, actually. Your place or mine? . . . For dinner, I mean.'

Sabine looked at him for a few seconds, then delivered an answer he hadn't quite expected:

'Actually neither, if you don't mind.'

He didn't mind; he saw what she meant. A good line was one thing, but in reality, the idea of cooking a meal in the shambles of his domestic accommodation appealed to him even less than the prospect of sitting down in a soulless hotel dining room.

'I know a decent place, not far from either of us, in Notting Hill. Do you fancy an Italian?'

'Maybe. I haven't had one for a while,' she replied. Eamonn Burke found himself laughing at the double entendre. Served him right. After all, he had started it. But he couldn't help wondering, not for the first time in the seventy-two hours he'd known her, just how much of a come-on Ms Kotzke really was. Perhaps somewhere, some day, he would run into a woman who did not want to tease pricks. But then maybe he should stop acting like one.

It was late-night shopping every Thursday in central London. Burke had forgotten the fact when he had arranged the Nag's Head as a meeting place, and again when he had suggested walking to the restaurant. After they had shouldered their way through the heaving crowds and reached the relatively deserted Bayswater Road, Burke felt an immense sense of relief and slowed his stride. Sabine, he realized, had been almost running to keep up with him. The drizzle had evolved into a slow steady rain and her hair hung in limp strands across her forehead. She was not in the best of humours.

'We might have caught a taxi, especially considering I'm paying the bills.'

'I'm sorry,' Burke said blandly. 'I just wasn't thinking about you. It's a failing.'

'You bet. No wonder your wife left you.'

Burke stopped dead in his tracks. Her voice had been matter-of-fact, almost light-hearted; he wondered if she really had any idea how fragile even the biggest men could be. And decided she hadn't.

Sabine kept pace easily now, by his side, but the banter they had exchanged in the pub had evaporated. That was it, he thought, he had been a fool to think anything else. This was just another woman who saw him as an emotional failure, cold and unsympathetic. And maybe they were right. Eamonn Burke silently cursed the world.

And the world cursed him back. The concussion struck him like a hammer blow to the side of the head. The blast seared his skin. The horribly familiar roar pummeled his inner ear, like being thrust into a 747's engine on take-off. For a terrifying instant Burke was back on the Shankill Road, Belfast, 1991. The harsh stink of cordite in cold air, the sickening barbecue smell of charred human flesh. The 'bits in bags' as the snappers had called the shots no newspaper could publish.

He opened his eyes and saw, hurtling towards him through the dark cloud of smoke the unmistakable black shape of a London taxi. Behind the taxi's wheel, James Carterton, forty-nine, from Ladywell, licensed London cabby number 45324, married with two kids who would never see him again, fought to control his vehicle, standing on the squealing brakes as the pain in his chest jackhammered the last fragment of life out of his body.

12

The Wild West

The Santa Fe Trail, 14 June 1945

Harry Gold had never been so far west in his life. The heat oppressed him. On the interminable overcrowded bus journey from Albuquerque to Santa Fe he had leaned against the window, eyes closed, trying hard not to be sick. Flies, involuntarily taken along for the ride, buzzed against the glass.

The bus was full. In fact, full was a serious understatement, even by New York rush hour subway standards. A large Navajo woman was squeezed next to Gold, beaming at him whenever he looked her way, silver feather earrings nodding as her vast bulk was rocked to and fro each time the bus's rickety suspension was challenged by another pothole. An old man with a ripped straw hat and a face the colour and texture of an old well-worn donkey saddle hung to one of the overhead straps and stared constantly at Gold for, it seemed to him, the one and a half life-times it took for the bus to reach its destination.

Santa Fe was not all he had hoped for, either. The name had a romantic ring, but it looked like just another hick town with no proper buildings and sanitary facilities he didn't care to think about. Gold checked into an overpriced room at the La Fonda Hotel and got out the street map Fuchs had given him. It was already two o'clock. The journey from Albuquerque had taken nearly four hours. What depressed him most was the prospect of the return trip the next day.

He went downstairs and headed for the bar. At least, the barman was white. Everybody else in the goddamn place looked like they had just stepped out of some Wild West Rodeo show. He was sure he had spotted Geronimo and Sitting Bull on the back of the bus, while the driver had looked and talked like Wyatt Earp's long lost grandson. At least he had spoken English, after a fashion. How long were the Spaniards supposed to have been gone? Clearly not long enough, or far enough, come to that. Gold had the new immigrant's instinctive prejudice against any deviations from the culture he had been pushed so hard to assimilate. If there was one thing he knew, it was what a real American was. He was proud of his patriotism. In a funny sort of way.

The barman recommended a margarita. Gold had never had one before, but as he sloshed down the potent tequila cocktail and licked the salt from his lips, his opinion of the south-west began to alter slightly. He was sorry he hadn't time for a second. But this was a strange town and, despite the map, he wanted to be sure of getting his bearings. After all this time, it would be a bit rich if he and Fuchs just failed to connect.

In fact, it took Gold less than twenty minutes to locate the spot Fuchs had indicated. To kill time he spent a half-hour wandering around the town's small historical museum, looking at Indian artefacts and exhibits relating to the old Santa Fe Trail, when this little town was the gateway to the rich pickings of southern California. The original Spanish settlement had functioned like an oasis. For the few souls who stopped here on the route north out of Mexico, he reflected, this crude little shanty town with its babbling brook that ran under the trees must have seemed like the celestial city after the bleak, waterless desert trail.

Shortly after 3.30 Gold left the museum and made for Castillo Street bridge. There, exactly as Fuchs had promised, was a little wooden bench in the shade. Gold suddenly wished he had bought a newspaper. He wondered what stories from the secret laboratory in that baking red sand furnace percolated into the local press. There would not be much, he decided. Probably nothing. He wondered how the locals felt about so much obvious activity on their doorstep. He would have liked to ask, but he saw no point in drawing unnecessary attention to himself.

At 3.52 the daily shuttle bus to The Hill passed by bulging with passengers and luggage, and Gold thought perhaps the trip from Albuquerque hadn't been so bad after all. Was that really indicative of the conditions in which the military's top secret project was being conducted? It could not be anything else. The dark green of the army bus was unmistakable. Gold laughed to himself: perhaps they should have had 'Secret Service' on a destination card in the cab.

Apart from that, a couple of pickups and a bright red battered Dodge saloon that appeared to contain half an entire Navajo reservation crammed together silently while the radio blasted out foxtrot music, there was little on the roads. Harry settled down. Fuchs would be punctual.

Klaus Fuchs had woken twice during the night. The first time it had been because of the heat, and because he needed to pee. He had spent the evening drinking beer in the mess hall with Feynmann and Frisch, watching the Austrian do his increasingly eccentric impersonations of the 'Injuns'. He had pulled a marine's forage cap down over his head, pushed out his bottom lip, stuck a cigarette to it, pulled out his shirt tail and borrowed a string of beads from one of the women sipping dry martinis in the corner. Feynmann and he had been in stitches as the man who had defined the principle of nuclear fission sloped around the floor performing an approximation of a Jemez fertility dance while humming 'The Blue Danube'.

Fuchs had lost track of the number of beers they had knocked back. He had become quite fond of American beer. It was gassy and relatively weak, but they managed to keep it cool even up here. At first he had worried about his drinking. He thought he might say something foolish, be goaded into a political discussion or, worst of all, become maudlin and reveal his doubts. In fact, to his own surprise, he found drink had the opposite effect. It was as if the alcohol temporarily erased everything but the superficial. Beer brought him as close as he had ever known to sharing a genuine spirit of camaraderie.

But it did not help him sleep. Once awakened by the insistent pressure on his bladder, he found he drifted into a more uneasy repose. That was when the dream came back to him. He was with his parents, returning to the house after his father's sermon, hot, bored and thirsty. A few of the townsfolk would come by to share a beer with the pastor. But there was nothing for young Klaus to drink. The thirst got worse and worse, until he felt his throat crinkle inside like dried parchment. The men were laughing, telling jokes, paying no attention as he screamed in their faces. Round and round and round the little room. And then out, down some dark, echoing hallway that had no existence in any place he had ever called home. His throat still drying until hairs began to grow out of the red raw

76

membranes, hairs that stood erect like needles as they became the points of great globular cacti growing to fill his mouth. He tried to call for his mother but the cactus spines already pierced his cheeks from the inside. Then the ground gave way before him and there in a pool of light lay his mother on the floor, her eyes wide and staring, an empty glass by her side and a great green, suppurating cactus bursting out of her ripped-open mouth.

He awoke in a sweat. Then breathed a sigh of relief that at least he had not woken Feynmann, asleep only feet away through the thin partition. He had cautiously – or perhaps incautiously – broached with the young American the topics Bohr had raised. Fuchs had been suspicious about the Dane: had he been testing him? How did Feynmann, a relatively junior member of the team, feel, he wondered? He had led the conversation gradually around to the power that the bomb, if it worked, would give to whichever country possessed it, and was grateful when the young physicist had instantly leaped to the topic. Feynmann's reaction, however, had been radically different: 'The only way this weapon will prove a defence is if we can keep a monopoly on it. No monopoly, no defence, if everybody can do it, then no city will be safe. It may be the stupidest thing humanity has done to invent this bomb, but it's too late to go back, and if we get it, we sure as hell don't want to share it.' Fuchs had agreed, of course. He always did. It was how he survived, he told himself. But somehow, it made the cough worse, as he crept out, while Feynmann, a man he liked intensely, yet knew now was a danger to his very existence, lay asleep so close by. Outside, he gave vent to it: dry, rough, lung-wracking. By tonight, he knew, it would be worse, much worse.

It was barely dawn: a rosy glow creeping across the sky and turning the Sangre de Cristo range to an even more spectacular shade of crimson. He decided to take a stroll before breakfast. It was not often that the ramshackle little town looked so peaceful. He thought of going over to the Tech-area and settling down to a few hours' work. One of the projects he had become involved in was compiling the 'Los Alamos Encyclopedia', a bold attempt to bring together all the research being done on The Hill. It was fascinating work. It was also, from Fuchs's point of view, extremely useful. There was nothing like having an overview.

Trying to keep to the wooden boards that served as sidewalks around the Big House – the thing Fuchs hated most about Los Alamos was the dust – he set off at a brisk pace towards the water tower, then turned left and walked up past the line of bigger houses which had survived from the Ranch School days. The street had become known as Bathtub Row, for these few houses were the only ones to enjoy that private amenity. The Oppenheimers lived in one, and the others were taken by similarly senior scientists with families.

Fuchs noticed the curtains were still drawn in the upstairs half of the house occupied by Rudolf and Genia Peierls and their boys. The Fermis lived downstairs: Enrico, the brilliant little Italian who had been awarded the Nobel Prize in 1938 for his pioneering work into radioactive substances, and his Jewish wife Laura, for whose sake they had fled a Rome that was enthusiastically taking on the Nazis' anti-Semitism. Fermi had been drafted into the Manhattan Project at an early stage and had lived up to expectations by producing the world's first controlled and sustained nuclear chain reaction. And he had done it in a wooden-framed graphite and uranium reactor built in the squash courts of the west stands of Stagg Field, the University of Chicago's football ground. Knowing what they now knew about just how successful the process could be – only after it was proved possible, did the concept of 'nuclear meltdown' enter the scientific vocabulary – Fuchs wondered if Fermi would still have gone ahead, there, in one of America's most populous cities. He decided that he would have done. It was Fermi, Fuchs had heard Oppenheimer mention discreetly, who the previous year had suggested fast-breeding strontium-90 – one of the most deadly of radioactive isotopes, absorbed by the body instead of calcium into the bone – and using it to poison Germany's food supplies. It was one of those occasions when Fuchs had found his natural poker face a boon. He had thought of his father, and all the other millions of innocent civilians in Germany who had never supported the Nazis but had been too weak to stand against them. Fuchs despised them, but did not feel they deserved to have their bone structure destroyed from within. Winning the war against the Nazis was one thing; but to do so at the cost of human values seemed pointless.

Within a couple of hours the sun would be mercilessly high in the sky. Fuchs wanted to be on his way by then. He crossed over to Fuller Lodge and found Kistiakowsky already in the line for breakfast.

'Morning, Klaus. You up with the birds again? I didn't even hear you rise.'

'I did not sleep well. Also, today I must go into Santa Fe. Is there anything I can get for you?'

Kistiakowsky turned down the offer and the two sat together through a breakfast of eggs and homefries at the long mess table.

'Have a nice day, Klaus. Don't goof off too much. We need that brain of yours.'

Fuchs smiled and headed for the labs. He had decided to spend the morning in his role as liaison between Kisty's explosives men and the theoretical division. Apart from anything else, it would serve to refresh his memory.

It was about 12.30, therefore, when Klaus Fuchs finally pulled his Buick out of the parking lot and headed towards the East Gate and the road that in his own mind was now firmly established as the Santa Fe Trail. The MP checked his pass cursorily as usual and waved him through. 'Drive safely now, sir. Hate you to mess up that fine machine of yours.'

Forty minutes later, Fuchs pulled his 'fine machine' off the dirt road and took a detour on to a little-used track. There, under the shade of a spreading Joshua tree, Fuchs took out a thick wad of foolscap paper and in his neat, careful hand began to write, from memory, complete with relevant equations and calculations which had become so much part of his life that they were burned into his unconscious, the memo to Moscow that would change the fate of the postwar world and ensure that the Cold War became reality.

13

Lightning

Numbed as a rabbit in headlights, Burke gaped as the cab swerved across the road inches from his head. It careered into the kerb and came to an abrupt halt, belching black diesel from its rear end. Burke coughed as he inhaled, and took in the improbable fact that he was still alive. Blood dripped into his eye.

He tried to stand, but stumbled to his knees. On the pavement a young woman stood as if electrocuted, open-mouthed and screaming as she stared at the blood that trickled down her thighs. In the distance Burke could hear the insane Red Indian war whoop of a police car siren.

Then, through the pall of smoke, he made out the slight figure of Sabine lurching towards him from the doorway of the Oriental Carpet Centre, whose wares now lay exposed to the cordite-ridden air. Shards from the plate-glass window now lay like a dully glittering minefield crunching under her feet. The blast that had hurled him into the middle of the road had thrown her the other way. Which meant it must have been dangerously close.

'*Scheisse*! Are you all right?' She crouched beside him, and cradled his head. Burke nodded as he put his arm around her neck and allowed himself to be helped to his feet, all the time achingly aware of the softness of her breasts. Glass dust sparkled in her hair. Strangely beautiful, he thought, like powdered diamonds.

Burke could see the lifeless body of the taxi driver against the windscreen. A policeman came running up to them. 'Are you okay, sir? The young lady? There'll be an ambulance along any minute. Bloody bastards.' His radio crackled unintelligibly and he turned away to talk into it. 'Best move to the pavement, sir. You'll be looked after shortly.' In the doorway, where Sabine had been thrown, the girl with the cut legs now lay slumped. There were two people beside her. Someone had folded a coat as a pillow.

Burke surveyed the scene. For all his experiences from Afghanistan to Belfast, he had never been quite that close to an explosion. Only afterwards. His mind raced back to Frizell's chip shop on the Shankill Road where a young man had walked in with a badly made bomb and massacred nine people, including himself. Burke had been on the scene only minutes after it happened, and been sick at the sight of charred and bloody flesh amid the glass and rubble. But this time, he realized with relief, the bomb had been relatively minor. The taxi driver was the only obvious fatality.

A police Rover had pulled across the road, its flashing red-and-blue lights now dominating the night, like a disco without the music. An officer with a megaphone was directing cars into side streets and warning pedestrian ghouls not to gather. There could be another device.

Most took heed. So did Burke. It was an old IRA stunt. A little bomb first, to summon the emergency services, then hit them with the biggy. A second blue light flashed in the distance: an ambulance, trapped in the traffic. Burke wondered where the bomb had been planted. It had not been that big, after all, his professional eye estimated bleakly. Five pounds maybe. A classic wastepaper bin device. But it had been close, bloody close. What had been its target? Not that the IRA needed one. Or was it the IRA? Within a hundred yards in either direction were the old offices of Aeroflot, now Russian airlines, and of Libyan Arab Airlines. Both had enough enemies. Chechens? Anti-Gaddaffi freedom fighters? London was too convenient a stage for other people's quarrels.

'Come on, let's get out of here.'

'Eamonn, are you sure you shouldn't go to hospital?'

Burke wasn't sure. But he knew he didn't want to.

'No. I'm all right, honestly. I'm not really hurt. This is more mess than damage.'

Sabine was dabbing the blood on his forehead with a handkerchief. His ears were still ringing. He could sense a headache coming on. He knew he ought to go to hospital, have a brain scan even. Except they would be there all night, kept in for observation like laboratory mice. With a lack of suspects, the interrogators would work on them instead.

It was Sabine who took the decision. 'Eamonn, come on. Let's go. Your flat is not too far from here. The old Communist youth organization trained us all in first aid, you know. That and some more of your terrible brandy is all we need.'

The matter was sealed by the sight of an officious-looking woman police constable approaching them. He put his arm around Sabine and walked into the small crowd of sightseers, who parted for them as if they had the plague.

'Excuse me, sir, madam? Wait a minute, please. The ambulance is just here.' The policewoman had broken into a modest trot but the crowd closed behind them. Only injury provoked awe and respect, and the policewoman wasn't bleeding. Burke allowed Sabine to steer him into the side-streets. A cab rounded the corner in front of them, the driver puzzled by the obvious commotion ahead.

'You free?' asked Burke, shielding his head wound with his hand. No cab-driver wanted to risk getting blood on his seats.

The man glanced at them. 'Yeah. As long as you don't want to go that way. What's going on anyway. Bleedin' bomb or something?'

'Think so, mate,' Burke replied, giving the man his address.

'Fucking paddies. Scum, that's what I say. Send them all home. Tow it out into the Atlantic and sink it. Nothing personal, though. Not Irish yourself, are you, guv?'

'No.' Burke breathed deeply. Like Peter denying Christ, his father would have said. Not really, he thought. Not really anything at all.

'Here, let me deal with that.'

Burke looked down at the woman holding what appeared to be a wad of cotton wool soaked in antiseptic from the debris of his medical chest. Sabine had been clearly dismayed by its contents – the average BMW car first-aid kit was a fully equipped emergency ward in comparison, she lost no time in telling him.

In the background Burke could hear the evening news on the living-room television. The explosion was the main item. No one had yet claimed responsibility. The police had found evidence of a small Semtex device planted in a wastepaper bin on a lamp-post. There was worried discussion about the possibility of some new Irish Republican offensive, but other, Middle Eastern terrorist organizations were not being ruled out. The total number of injured was given as seven, though not all, the newscaster added, had been admitted to hospital. Police appealed for witnesses to come forward, especially a man and woman who were believed to have been among the injured but left the scene immediately. Christ, Burke thought, with my luck we'll end up on the wanted list. He wondered who the injured were that he had not noticed. The taxi driver was listed as the sole fatality. A heart attack, possibly caused by shock.

His cut looked worse than it was, Burke had decided: a jagged laceration running for about an inch and a half above the left eye. Luckily, there did not appear to be any glass fragments imbedded. His head had scraped along the tarmac. Sabine had been more at risk from flying glass. She might have lost an eye; instead he would probably get away with a black one.

'Where did you get the dressing?' he inquired.

'It's not a dressing. Not a proper one. But it will have to do.'

'What is it?'

She looked up sharply into his open eye. 'A tampon.'

'A . . . ?' Burke jerked his head back, not certain if he was more surprised or embarrassed.

'Tch, don't move,' she tutted, and looked up at him with that witching smile. And they both laughed.

He had had to bend to let her fix the dressing with plasters. She had bitten her lip as if worried about causing him pain, and raised herself on tiptoes to meet him. He had put his left hand on her shoulder to steady her. His fingers spread out beneath her hair to support her head as she tilted her face upwards. She brushed a strand of his hair tenderly back from the wound. Pain, he thought, was so dangerously like pleasure.

Then, before he had really appreciated it, let alone taken advantage of it, she pulled away. The moment was gone, if it had ever been there.

14

Rude Awakening

Eammon Burke woke up feeling like he had been blind drunk for six weeks, the gash over his eye like it had been stitched with a leather thong. The events of the previous night came back like a bad dream. He could hear the screams, taste the blood, smell the cordite, the diesel and the burned tyre rubber. The crowds, the commotion, the sirens all played through his head on a loop. And then the aftermath. The strange sensation of being ministered to gently by a woman he hardly knew. He lifted his head painfully and looked around him, and saw with a shock that Sabine Kotzke's head lay barely a foot away from his.

Trying not to wake her, Burke eased himself up on to his elbows. The evidence was nowhere near as incriminating as he had hoped. Whereas Burke in his jockey shorts was under the quilt, she lay on top of it, covered by her green raincoat. Just what state of undress she was in he could not tell, though a pair of Levi's and her blue jumper draped across the chair in the corner suggested she had made some compromise between comfort and modesty. Burke raised his eyebrows with the sudden realization that she must have put him to bed. The fact that he was still wearing his shorts was proof enough. Her consideration of his own modesty made him smile.

Christ, he thought with embarrassment: I must have passed out on her. The brandy? No, they had not had that much. Or had they? They had sat talking in the living-room, watching the late news broadcast's uninstructive repeat of the report on the bomb, followed by some studio speculation that was, if anything, even less intelligent or informed than their own. Though somewhere along the line, he vaguely recalled thinking that it was what he and Sabine were not saying that was more important.

His head started to throb again. In the distance he could hear the sounds of traffic, a low rumble with the intermittent squeal of brakes on buses. He looked at Sabine again, moved to touch her shoulder, to waken her. After all, who knew what might develop if she found herself next to him on a bed. But then again, how many times in his life, Burke asked himself, had he spoiled not even a relationship, but the merest chance of one, by making casual presumptions. He blew a silent kiss at her sleeping forehead and eased himself as surreptitiously as possible out of bed.

From his wardrobe he selected one of several crumpled, unironed shirts and padded into the kitchen in his bare feet, with the intention of putting the kettle on to make coffee. Which was when he remembered Nora Winter. He had said he would be at the old lady's house in Oxford by 10.30.

Shit. He looked at his watch. Given that it was already gone 9.00, there was little enough chance of that. He would have to ring her *en route*. Burke found the chinos he had worn the day before, along with the rest of his clothes, neatly folded on the sofa in the living-room. He pulled them on quickly, dragged a comb across his head and winced painfully. He dashed into the bathroom and could hardly suppress a titter at the sight of Sabine's makeshift dressing, though at the same time he was impressed by its efficiency. Gritting his teeth, he pulled away the plasters and the stained cotton wadding. Not too bad, he thought, In time, it might even add a Clint Eastwood dimension to his craggy features. For the moment, however, another plaster would be a more practical solution.

A quick glimpse into the bedroom revealed that Sabine was still asleep. He ripped a page from his battered Filofax and scribbled on it quickly:

Good morning. I hope you slept well. You looked too sweet to waken. Have gone to Oxford as arranged. Thought it might be unwise to put off in case she changed her mind. If a mad Russian calls, take a message and tell him I'll call back. Dinner this evening? Somewhere less exciting. I should be back about 7.00. See you here? Keys are by the telephone. Have a nice day. E.
    P.S. Apologies for my behaviour, or lack of it.

Burke thought it a bit wordier than he had intended, but had no time to compose a shorter version. He propped it on the kitchen table against a coffee jar, grabbed his cellphone and car keys and left.

15

Gold Dust

Santa Fe, June 1945

In the eight-page document Fuchs had passed to Gold the previous Christmas, he had made clear that the future of the atomic bomb, as far as the Americans were concerned, no longer lay with uranium. General Groves had set up huge factories in a semi-wilderness called Oak Ridge along the banks of the Clinch River in eastern Tennessee, designed to extract the rare uranium-235 from raw ore using the latest electromagnetic and gaseous diffusion techniques. It was a wasteful, complicated and hideously expensive business.

But twentieth-century science had already discovered its philosopher's stone: nuclear fission. Bombarding uranium with radiation could induce its atoms to split, turning it into known but uncommon elements called 'rare earths'. And in 1940, two scientists at the University of California in Berkeley had realized that the uranium was not only splitting but also capturing nuclei from the bombardment. The result was a completely new element: a substance that could be separately identified by its chemistry.

Uranium had been named after the planet Uranus. So they called the new element after the next planet out from the sun: neptunium. It turned out to be highly unstable, quickly decomposing into more common elements. Inspired by the achievement, however, another pair of scientists, the Italian Emilio Segrè and the Swedish-American Glenn Seaborg, had taken the logic further. The element they had produced was relatively stable. Continuing the trend, they named it after the solar system's furthest known planet: plutonium. The unofficial historian of the atomic bomb project, Richard Rhodes, would later dub it 'the element God had not welcomed at the creation'.

The important thing was that plutonium was highly fissile. In other words, much smaller quantities were needed to reach the crucial 'critical mass': the density at which an element transformed its matter into energy at the rate of the heart of a burning star. It could also be produced relatively cheaply by a simple reactor powered by ordinary uranium. Plutonium had what was needed if the atomic bomb was to become a permanent feature of the armories of the future: a production-line capability.

Fuchs suspected that Igor Kurchatov – the Soviets' only sensible choice to head up their own research into an atomic bomb – would have already come to the same conclusion. But in the report he had given Gold in Boston, he had revealed what the Russians barely dreamed of: that the United States had already built and was operating a plutonium production facility. A half-abandoned village called Hanford with a population of barely one hundred souls next to a ferry-crossing on the Columbia river in the sparsely populated sheep-grazing country of south-eastern Washington state had been bought up by Groves on behalf of the government. Overnight it had been transformed – in an overstated echo of the military camp that Los Alamos had become – into a giant nuclear reactor complex employing tens of thousands of workers.

Fuchs had also revealed the problems that beset the plutonium project. The new material was so fissile that unless it could be thrown together from a sub-critical to a critical mass in an incredibly brief instant of time, it would already have decayed beyond the level needed to produce a nuclear explosion. The plutonium bomb might be cheap, but it might also be a damp squib.

The solution which the Los Alamos team were working on, and which George Kistiakowsky's explosives group was specifically in charge of, was an 'implosion' bomb. This meant engineering explosives in a much more precise way than anything previously attempted. Fuchs had scribbled down within those eight sheets of paper something of phenomenal strategic importance – the fact that the critical mass of plutonium needed for an explosion had been estimated at around eleven pounds – and he had also given away the Ukrainian's ingenious idea of creating explosive 'lenses' to focus the blast precisely on the radioactive core.

Now, sitting in his Buick, as the hands of his watch moved relentlessly towards the long-planned meeting with Gold, Fuchs was filling in the rest. For the first time, he included a detailed diagram of the plutonium bomb that was now almost ready for testing. It consisted of two hemispheres of plutonium, each weighing slightly over five pounds and coated with nickel, no larger than an orange. This in turn was packed within an eight-pound tamper of natural uranium, designed to serve as a shield that would hold the assembly together for the microseconds in which the chain reaction started. Finally this whole core would be surrounded by a precision-engineered assembly of a hundred or so pieces of interlocked wedge-shaped high explosives. In its casing it stood about five-feet high, like a slightly elongated egg. But the hardest part to perfect had been a tiny device about the size and shape of a golf ball that lay between the dual hemispheres: the initiator. Oppenheimer called it 'the heart of the matter'.

The crucial fact in the new design was that the two plutonium hemispheres could be placed in such dangerous proximity because they weighed in total less than critical mass. The scientists were gambling on playing a trick on nature. Critical mass had been worked out for all conceivable conditions on earth. But at the heart of the explosion, the pressure would be unlike anything on earth. It would be closer to that at the centre of a burning star. Under those conditions, the plutonium would be compressed and therefore less mass would be needed to trigger the critical phase of its self-annihilation.

Almost by way of a postscript, Fuchs added the calculations he himself had done as part of his work with Kistiakowsky, roughly estimating the potential yield of the bomb. Out of natural modesty he also included the estimates of Feynmann and Hans Bethe. The best guess, he summed up, was that one bomb would have an explosive force equivalent to 10,000 tonnes of TNT. But by the time of his next meeting with Gold, there would be real figures. By then the big balloon would finally have gone up. Or burst.

Gold breathed a sigh of relief when he saw Fuchs pull up in the grey Buick. He got in and they drove off past the gas station and out on to the Albuquerque road, exchanging pleasantries. After a few miles, Fuchs pulled over. When could Gold make it out west again, he needed to know? Things were moving fast. He estimated the plutonium bomb would be ready to test within weeks. A decision on whether or not to use the uranium bomb against Japan was imminent. Targets were already under discussion. Although the scientists were not involved, little was kept from them. He believed part of the decision might depend on what happened at the summit in Potsdam, and whether or not Russia would invade Japanese-occupied Manchuria. But Gold had no opinion to offer, and to Fuchs it seemed as if he had little interest. He was anxious to take his parcel and be gone.

'Be careful,' he said handing over the foolscap envelope. 'This is your most important package yet.'

Gold had said he would be catching the next bus back to Albuquerque. Fuchs dropped him near the bus station, and said goodbye. He wanted to meet in August, but Gold said he could not easily get more leave from work that soon. They agreed on 19 September. As Fuchs turned the wheel and headed back out to The Hill, he wondered, not for the first time, how much Gold really understood. The science, he knew, was way over the man's head. But the science was not all that mattered in the information he was passing back this time. A month's delay in their next meeting could be critical. The fate of the world might depend on it.

From the viewpoint of Allen Dulles, staring out of his window in the American Embassy in Bern at Swiss burghers in their Sunday best, the fate of the world looked as if it had already been decided.

The war in Europe was ending in a stampede. That idiot Eisenhower had headed for the Alps in the politically inept belief that the Führer had hidden himself away in some mountain fastness, but the Russians had taken Berlin, and the capital remained the key. Now the real power game was beginning. The inevitable aftermath of an alliance of necessity.

Dulles walked over to his filing cabinet and unlocked it. He removed a sealed envelope, ripped it open and took out a densely typed document. He glanced at it, smiled ruefully and then crossed the room to the tiled stove. It was unlit, for summer had already begun. But Dulles opened the little iron door, put the document inside, struck a match and lit it. For a few minutes he watched it burn, then poked at it to destroy the ash. Then, for good measure, he added the brown envelope and watched as it too reduced to grey powder.

They would be doing something similar in Washington, he assumed, and in London. And . . . he shrugged his shoulders. Some things had to be left to the gods.

16

Winter's Tale

Burke had called from his cellphone in the car to rearrange his meeting with Nora Winter, apologizing profusely that he had not been able to get to Oxford by 10.30, but blaming the London traffic. He had offered to take her to lunch but she had declined. 'I only take a light snack, you know,' she had informed him in a cultured, high-pitched voice.

So it was nearly 2.00 p.m., after a pint and a sandwich on his own, when Burke found himself opening the wrought-iron gate to Nora Winter's house and walking up the paved path past a couple of bare, neglected-looking rose bushes.

After hearing her voice, Burke half expected her to look like matron too, as he stood in the porch, with its neatly swept black and white chequered tile floor, and watched the unclear figure approaching through the frosted, dimpled glass panels in a door painted hospital-corridor green.

'Good afternoon, can I help you?'

It was Miss Marple, in a shocking purple jump-suit. She was only half his height and Burke had to resist the urge to crouch down to talk to her.

'Ms Winter? Eamonn Burke, I spoke to you on the phone.'

'Ah yes, the young man interested in history. And it's Miss, by the way. I attempt to eradicate all vestiges of my former marriage.'

He wasn't sure if it was the sort of remark that required a reply or an apology, but before he could manage either she had disappeared back into the house, without inviting him in. Burke was uncertain whether he was supposed to follow her. He had just decided that he was, when she returned wearing a green jacket.

'Well, what are we waiting for?' She banged the door behind her and scurried past him. Burke looked on, surprised. Old ladies were supposed to be frail.

'Sorry, where are we going?'

'Harwell, of couse. I thought we might as well talk *in situ*, as it were. Nothing going on there now, of course. All closed down in 1990. Just an awful lot of spent nuclear fuel. But a visit will stimulate the mental processes. Anyhow, I like to turn up unannounced occasionally, just to show the buggers I'm still alive . . . And do stop saying "sorry" all the time.'

'Sorry. I mean, right.'

'Your car or mine? Better be mine, less problem at the gate. They can be funny about strange number plates sometimes. You drive, though. I hate it.'

Burke realized, as she pulled a set of keys from her pocket and shepherded him towards the ageing Mini Metro parked outside, that he was going to hate it too.

Twenty minutes later, feeling that he might never walk again after driving with his knees next to his ears, Burke slowed down as he spotted the sign that indicated Harwell village and asked if he should turn off.

'No, no. Don't be silly. Keep going.'

Burke scanned the countryside ahead for signs of a nuclear research institute. It occurred to him that he hadn't a clue really. The giant cooling towers of Didcot power station squatted on the horizon, an ugly stereotyped image of nuclear power, though Burke knew they were a red herring: Didcot burned coal.

'Slow down, we're nearly at the gate.'

It wasn't what he had been expecting. Harwell looked more like a housing estate than a scientific facility. Even the security precautions were less than intimidating: a low office building and a neatly painted white gate. Only the barrier across the road and the policeman emerging from his cubicle suggested anything out of the ordinary.

He clearly recognized the little car, as she had said he would. He was about to wave them through when he realized that the man behind the wheel was not its usual diminutive driver.

'My nephew,' Nora leaned across from the passenger seat to explain. 'He's helping me clear out junk from my old office.'

'Sweet,' Nora said, as they drove past the barrier. 'Totally ineffectual, of course, even if he is supposed to be armed to the teeth. Now, what was it you wanted to see first?'

Burke had told her over the telephone that he was researching a book about the parallel development of the Soviet and Western nuclear deterrents. Her reply had been disconcerting.

'Rather like Richard Rhodes's *Dark Sun*. Hasn't it been done?'

'Yes, well, I hope I've got a new angle,' he had replied, cursing himself for not realizing the old lady would have read everything on the subject if she were as well informed as Morris had implied. But she had agreed to see him anyway. Burke suspected she revelled in any chance to make use of a lifetime of research that was probably seriously under-exploited. He had talked it over with Sabine and decided he would fence delicately around the topic of their inquiry. Winter had had access, in theory at least, to cabinet papers in compiling her official history of the British nuclear project. She admitted there were two versions: the one which had seen the light of day as a publication of Her Majesty's Stationery Office, and the other which would in all probability be kept for ever under the cast-iron lid of the Official Secrets Act. Burke was mindful that she had obviously had to sign the act too. There was no question, therefore, of her telling him all she knew, certainly not as the result of direct questioning. But then sometimes, the best way to score a goal was to come at the keeper obliquely.

'Well, perhaps if we could see whatever remains of those days.'

'Park there,' she barked, pointing to a space in front of a metal-framed building that looked like a vintage aircraft hangar.

'Used to be an RAF base, Harwell. Good flat land like most of south Oxfordshire.'

Burke followed her through a small door to the right of the main hangar entrance. Inside it looked more like a scrapyard than the home of Britain's mid-century hopes for an atom-powered future. Great hunks of unidentifiable machinery stood in neglected heaps, ironwork with transistors, valves, bits of yesterday's high-technology looking crude, antique, outsized, like toddlers' building bricks.

'Well, what do you think?' The old lady was gesturing towards a great cube that occupied fully one corner of the hangar. It was perhaps thirty feet high and painted – a long time ago – dark blue, though it appeared to be made out of concrete. As a structure it was wholly unremarkable, save for one word spelled out in big white letters high on the wall facing them: GLEEP.

'That's what it was all about, initially at least. Ought to be preserved as a national monument, really. Instead they'll probably tear it down, as soon as they can.'

93

'What is it?'

'Gleep, you silly boy. The Graphite Low Energy Experimental Pile. Europe's very first nuclear reactor. Produced about enough power to heat an electric kettle. But it was a great scientific achievement in its day. Went critical in 1946. Old GLEEP here is the real father-figure of the European atomic energy programme. All the other British reactors are directly descended from it. It and its big brother BEPO anyway. Got their plutonium from here. The first fast reactors, Zephyr, Zeus, then Pluto, Dido and Lido, were all built here. Old Gleep ran longest of them all: forty-three years.'

'But not all involved in weapons production?'

'Good grief, no. That barely outlived Fuchs at Harwell. In 1951 they closed down the weapons programme here, transferred all the dodgy stuff to Aldermaston. You remember the marches? No, probably too young. Lots of pacifist people. Come on.'

Burke found himself striding after the little figure as she scuttled off to another exit.

'Come on. I've got a little office in a broom cupboard in here.' She gestured towards a nondescript brick building in front of them. 'Used to be the RAF corporals' mess, back in the thirties. Ridgeway House looked a bit like that.'

'Ridgeway?'

'I'll show you in a minute.'

The building's lobby was filled with an exhibition about Harwell's future as a science park for high-technology companies, but the walls were lined with big photographs of how it had looked in the 1940s. The outline of the former airfield was immediately apparent. The straight road they had driven down had, Burke realized, been the main runway. Where there were now trees and car parks, there had then been prefabricated housing, little make-shift laboratories, and a sea of mud where building contractors laboured on the great 200-foot-high chimney that now dominated the site: the stack which had once pushed the 'hot' air from the BEPO reactor out over the Oxfordshire countryside.

Nora pointed to a building on the map that looked very similar to the one they were in.

'There we are: Ridgeway House. Demolished a couple of years ago. That was where Fuchs lived when he first came here. Must have been a bit like that out in New Mexico, I imagine. Dormitory halls, everyone sleeping in little cubicles. Anyhow, they moved the top brass out a bit later. Fuchs got one of the little prefab homes they brought in: over there on 9th street.

Burke followed her as she led the way up a flight of stairs into a tiny, messy office. Nora plonked herself unapologetically on to the single chair. Burke pushed a few books back and sat on the edge of the desk.

'Are all the streets like American streets, I mean with just numbers instead of names?'

'No. Used to be more. Got names after some of the physicists now. You saw Fermi Avenue. Makes it all rather silly if you ask me, like one of those theme park thingies. Nothing wrong with numbers, especially on a site full of mathematicians.'

Burke seized the opportunity. 'That was Fuchs's real speciality wasn't it? Number-crunching?'

'Absolutely. He was head of the Theoretical Physics division here. Started up the whole idea of site-wide computing. Most calculations were still done with hand-cranked machines in his day. He never saw the results of the changes he put in place. Don't suppose they got very good computers in East Germany.'

'Do you remember what the reaction was when Fuchs was arrested?'

'It was a shock to the whole country; it was truly traumatic. But especially here. You have to understand what this place was like: a sort of hard-working holiday camp. Everyone living in rather primitive conditions, but with a great sense of camaraderie. Not as intense as it had been at Los Alamos, I dare say, but not that different, I imagine. There was a determination not to let Britain be left behind, you know. Hah.'

Burke thought it was rather a bitter little laugh.

'Fuchs was an upstanding member of the Harwell community, the sort of person you had round to tea. People looked up to him. After his arrest, morale was down to rock bottom. Very depressing. The idea that Fuchs might have been a Soviet spy had simply never occurred to the other scientists. Look at this.'

Winter began rummaging on the over-stacked shelves. From a pile of old magazines she extracted one called *ECHO* and handed it to him. It turned out to be the house journal of the United Kingdom Atomic Energy Authority, the residual body left after privatization of the rest: the main business bits of the nuclear research programme.

'Fiftieth anniversary edition. Came out back in 1996. Turn to page sixteen.'

Burke opened it at a spread of black-and-white photographs from the 1940s and '50s. Nora directed his attention to one of a collection of middle-aged men in glasses and shabby coats.

'That's Sir John Cockroft in the centre, Harwell's first director.'

Burke glanced at the figure, who looked like an older Bill Gates. But it was the figure next to him that immediately seized Burke's attention: a taller man with thick-rimmed spectacles and a distinctive domed forehead. Unquestionably, it was Klaus Fuchs.

'Read the caption. Coy, isn't it.'

The words below the photograph identified only Cockroft. The others were referred to simply as 'early Harwell heroes, 1946'. Early, indeed. Before one of the heroes was unmasked as a villain.

'It was a particular blow to Cockcroft. Fuchs had been very much his blue-eyed boy, you know. He was really pleased to get him back from the Americans. Thought they would have tried to hold on to him. Fuchs had been working with Edward Teller, you know, on the hydrogen bomb. He had even taken out a patent on the initiator, I'm sorry – tut, now you've got me at it – part of the detonation system, though it's hardly a patent you'll find on the shelves of the Science Reference section in the British Library, or the Library of Congress, for that matter. Still highly classified, which is a bit of a joke really since the Russians have presumably had it since 1946. I dare say it's easier to get access in Moscow these days.'

'You don't seem to bear him any malice.'

'No. Why should I?'

'Because he was a traitor. If there has to be a villain of your history, surely it's Fuchs?'

'I suppose so. But not by his own lights. He never really understood the idea of nationalism, you know. Of course, it was a particular shock for the émigré community; they all came under suspicion. Think of people like poor Rudi Peierls. He had sponsored Fuchs, and now here he was, himself a German and with a Russian wife, for goodness' sake. Genia wrote a nasty letter to Fuchs in prison, laying into him for letting the side down. I heard he was very cut up about it. Hadn't really understood whom he was letting down. But then he never was very good with women.'

'You speak from experience?'

Burke tried to imagine this prim old lady flirting in her youth.

'Not with Fuchs, believe me; he wasn't exactly a lady-killer. The women who did take to him always wanted to mother him. Let me ask *you* a question, Mr Burke. Have you ever been married?'

Burke flinched. Any moment now and she would be raising the topic he'd been warned to avoid at all costs.

'Yes.'

'But now it's over?'

'Yes.'

He wondered how she knew, and how it had come about that the interrogation roles had been switched.

'Hmmm.' Nora Winter pursed her thin lips and furrowed her wrinkled brow.

'Did one of you "betray" the other?'

He could hear the inverted commas in her voice.

'Yes.'

'Which?'

'Both, I suppose. In the end.'

'Do you feel guilt?'

'Yes. I mean "no".'

'No, you mean yes. Morris put you on to me. Did he tell you about my marriage?'

'No.'

'You mean yes. But I doubt if he told you the truth. I doubt if he knows it.'

'He said you were married to a German. He said . . . he . . . er might have hit you.'

To Burke's astonishment she threw back her head and laughed.

'Dieter? He was a lamb. No, more of a sheep really. About the most spineless man I've ever encountered. That was the problem. Did Morris tell you I'm Jewish?'

'No. I mean, why would he? Was that part of the problem?' Burke wondered why he was not finding it absurd to be sitting discussing marital problems with a woman twice his age. But somehow Nora Winter had a way of making age seem more an accident of history than a barrier between generations. 'Was he anti-Semitic?'

'Hardly. He was wracked by guilt. To listen to him you'd have thought he'd been a guard at Auschwitz, instead of a poor sap who nearly died in Dachau for the heinous crime of having been a junior member of the Social Democratic Party in the thirties. He was the living conscience of Germany. Sometimes I think he married me to make amends. He'd been a chemist by profession and after the war got a job offer from ICI. He was only too keen to leave Germany. We met up at a party in London. He proposed almost the minute he heard I was Jewish.'

'What happened?'

'I betrayed him. Repeatedly, I'm afraid. Dieter and I were living in the accommodation they'd built at Abingdon for Harwell staff. I'd just been drafted in as a deputy archivist. I fell for one of the young scientists. Nobody important, I'm afraid, and it didn't last. Dieter found out by accident.'

'What did he do?'

'He forgave me, of course. Said it was the least he could do. I'd forgiven him the sins of his countrymen.'

'Generous.'

'Ridiculous. What was the link between the Holocaust and my infidelity? Nothing at all. Was I to have a licence to shag half the eligible population of England on account of the fact that Hitler had murdered six million Jews? What sort of moral equivalence was that? I told him to go back to Germany.'

'You were harsh.'

She shrugged. 'Perhaps. Cruel to be kind, you might say. It was never going to work. Betrayal is a terrible thing, Mr Burke. But it comes easier than you think. And there are many different ways of defining it.'

Burke wasn't quite sure if she was trying to make a point.

'To understand Klaus Fuchs, you need to understand the climate at Los Alamos back in the forties. It was a lot more complicated than most people think.'

Burke wondered if Nora Winter was keen to say more than she could. He decided to try to press her, gently.

'Was there something, do you think, that never came out? Something Fuchs might have felt tempted to reveal.'

She looked at him sharply. 'Mr Burke, there are always things that never "come out", as you put it. History isn't fact, just the currently prevailing version of events. You might have heard the old joke that God tolerates historians only because they do the one thing he can't: they have the power to alter the past.'

'But could Fuchs have had a secret?' He decided it was worth a gamble. 'One that he might have been killed for?' Or one that someone might now kill to protect. The thought came to him unbidden; he put his hand to the plaster on his forehead.

'Are you serious?' The old lady's eyes narrowed perceptibly.

Burke nodded.

'So that's what this is about. Some lame-brained conspiracy theory.'

Burke cursed himself inwardly. Had he overplayed the hand? If so, there was no harm to be done by exposing the rest of it.

'What happened to Arnold, the Harwell security man, the one who arrested Fuchs?'

'He died of old age, as far as I know.'

'And William Skardon, the M15 interrogator?'

'He's dead too, as I imagine you know or you would not be asking.'

'So?'

'So what? I am not. They were old men, Mr Burke. This all happened a very long time ago. I strongly suggest you are letting your imagination run away with you.'

Burke said nothing. Nora Winter met his gaze unblinkingly, then turned and lifted the receiver on a telephone half-submerged beneath the papers on her desk.

'I'll call you a taxi, Mr Burke. I'm afraid I shan't be going back to Oxford immediately. Like I told the policeman, I really must tidy this place. They expect me to give up the space any day now. I'm sure whoever you work for can afford the taxi fare.'

She spoke into the receiver.

'This is Nora Winter. In the archive section. Yes, thank you, still going strong. Can I have a car, please. To Oxford. It's for my nephew. Straight away. Thank you.'

They walked in silence down the stairs. Winter drove to the main gate, surprisingly capably, Burke noticed, despite her professed dislike. The policeman by the barrier gave a friendly wave. She ignored it. In the car-park outside, a dark green Ford Sierra with a roof sign that said 'Cumnor Cars. 24-hour service' was waiting. Winter let Burke out. He stooped to say good-bye, and held out his hand. But she wasn't looking at him. From her handbag she had taken a ball-point pen and a small notebook. She tore a page out, folded it over and placed it in his hand.

'Just in case you ever find yourself in Los Alamos, Mr Burke. Goodbye, and good luck.'

Burke unfolded the piece of paper. There was a name on it: 'Dr Hiram Carter' and a ten-digit US telephone number. He pocketed it and walked over to the taxi.

As the driver turned out of the Harwell car-park and on to the Oxford road, a blue BMW overtook them and settled to a steady speed in front. Burke thought nothing of it.

17

Quis Custodiet . . . ?

Los Angeles, California, 27 June 1945

The men in the Pontiac sat and smoked, staring up at the lighted window with drawn curtains.

'How long do you reckon he's been in there now?' said the older one, a sallow-skinned man with thinning hair.

'About three hours, I guess. Got here just before dusk.'

'Reckon he's fixin' to stay the night.'

'Could be.'

'Can't say I blame him. Nice bit of ass. Even if it is Commie ass.'

'Yup. Guy like him's gotta watch where he plays ball, though. Catch him too far in the left field and he'll find himself back in the dug-out with his tail between his legs before you can say Babe Ruth.'

'Yeah. But right now I guess that babe's got more than his tail between her legs.' The older man took a slow draw on his cigarette and settled down further in the passenger seat, his eyes fixed on the closed curtains as if visualizing the scene on the other side.

'How long we gonna stick this out?'

'All night if we have to. The general wants this boy cleared or nailed to rights. God knows why but I reckon he's up to more than his balls in somethin' top secret. War work, I guess.'

Across the road a few drunks weaved uncertainly out of a corner bar, dodged a passing pickup truck and disappeared down the dark street.

Behind the curtains J. Robert Oppenheimer lay naked on his back on the broad bed, staring at the ceiling. Beside him, the woman with the closely cropped dark hair lay curled almost into a foetal position. There would have been hot tears in her eyes, he knew, were Jean Tatlock the sort of woman who could cry. Sex between them had been as good as it had ever been, passionate, intense, physically and emotionally exhausting. But there were other exhaustions taking their toll on her. His life had changed, in ways he himself had never imagined. Their youthful idealism had been overtaken in his case by a hard, challenging and cruel necessity. What still fired her soul had been devoured in his.

The early days of their affair – before he had been married – were like a dream now. He had not meant to sleep with her tonight. He had not meant to betray Kitty. But this was not so much betrayal as a reprise of an old melody, he lied to himself. There was still something about her that he could not easily reject. Now he would have to. She knew it. He wondered how she would survive in the real America. He wondered how he would.

He left before dawn. It was a long drive back to The Hill. It would take most of the day. The men in the Pontiac watched him climb into his car, noted the time and headed home to bed.

Klaus Fuchs sat back with an iced lemonade on the veranda of the Big House, watching the summer sun dip low over the pines. It was a landscape both familiar and alien, at times eerily reminiscent of the Thuringian forests, at others still echoing with the war whoops of the long-departed Jemez Indians.

He watched as Oppenheimer's big, low-slung Chevy turned the corner by the water-tower. The chief was back, back from one of his high-octane, low-profile meets in Los Angeles, the sprawling super-annuated shanty-town that they said would one day overtake venerable San Francisco as the metropolis of California. Fuchs suspected the chief's regular meetings dealt with more than funding. They had to be talking about targets, particularly now that the war which most of The Hill's inhabitants had signed up to fight was over and done. He felt sorry for Germany. No, he corrected himself, not for Germany, but for the Germans: his own folk – *Volk* had been one of Hitler's favourite words; the American fondness for it represented an older, decent understanding, derived from the German of earlier settlers, the people who had made America great, but whose contributions today were glossed over.

'Hi, Klaus. How are you?' He sat up. Oppenheimer's voice was unmistakable.

Fuchs fought the impulse to spring to his feet. It was not the American way. Back in Leipzig, he would have jumped to attention, bowed to Herr Professor Direktor Doktor Oppenheimer and then the two of them, having observed the ritual their society dictated, would have lapsed into an unspoken yet agreed familiarity. Here the familiarity was superficially immediate which left him suspecting it was really a lie.

'Hello.' He heard the awkwardness in his voice, searching for a form of address with which he felt comfortable, while all too painfully aware that his striving for acceptability was, in the eyes of his American colleagues, his most alienating characteristic.

'How's it going?'

He knew this question was rhetorical, a figure of speech. On the occasions when he had attempted to give a considered answer, he had been regarded as eccentric. Now he just nodded. But he felt Oppenheimer was looking at him strangely, with a direct gaze that went straight through to his soul.

For a brief, terrifying moment, Fuchs felt the familiar dryness start to clog his throat. But Oppenheimer was not even looking at him any more. The lean, tanned face was staring into the middle distance, somewhere out beyond the tree line. An American would have jumped in, asked the director what was on his mind. Fuchs knew that. But he didn't do it. There were leaps he simply could not make. It was a terrible thing, he thought to himself, the space between men.

'Are you happy here, Klaus?'

The question caught him off-guard. It was not what he had expected. Americans worked at being happy, or at least thought they ought to. Klaus Fuchs did not. Happiness, as far as he understood it, was a sort of visitation, something that happened and often was only understood afterwards. Long afterwards, in Wakefield prison, when he also, to his surprise, decided he was at least not unhappy, he would reflect that the time at Los Alamos had been perhaps the happiest of his life. At least, until that evening when Oppenheimer accosted him on the veranda of the Big House.

But once again, the director had not waited for an answer. The question was as much a reflection of his own state of mind as a genuine inquiry about his colleague's.

'You know, the project's going well, at last. We may be within range of a test of the implosion gadget.'

Despite General Groves, Oppie believed in openness. But now

they were in endgame. The scientists would not be consulted about how, where and when their work would be put to practical use – like a mother, the ever-perceptive Isidor Rabi had said, being allowed no say in what happened to her child.

'I am aware that there are still some wrinkles to be sorted out with Kisty's explosive lenses. But I think he is confident,' said Fuchs.

'Oh, yeah. But there are going to be wrinkles right up until the moment we press that button. The only sure and certain way we'll know that baby will go is by trying her. The only thing is, we've kind of missed the boat.'

'Boat?' Fuchs was unaware that plans to ship the bomb overseas were already so advanced. This was something he had not passed on to John.

'Just an expression, Klaus.'

Fuchs felt a moment of intense irritation with his own stupidity. English idioms were a minefield.

'The war in Germany's over,' Oppenheimer continued. 'Hitler was the main inspiration for this bomb. It was only Einstein's warning that the Nazis might get there first that got Roosevelt up and running. God only knows what might have happened if he'd been right. Given what we're starting to hear out of Germany now, we would have been right to use the damn thing on them as soon as possible . . . I'm sorry, Klaus, I know it's your countrymen I'm talking about. But then that's why you're here. Right?'

'Absolutely, Robert. The Nazis were never my countrymen, except in a racial sense which only they would acknowledge. They disgraced Germany.' Already in the thirties, he had heard rumours of horrors being perpetrated in the Nazi camps against his fellow Communists. He had suspected even then that it was probably worse for the Jews. Just how much worse had become evident as the allied troops, from east and west, entered Ravensbrück, Belsen, Auschwitz. Fuchs had no doubts at all. 'They disgraced humanity.'

It was said with a passion. Oppenheimer turned and looked for a moment straight into the pale eyes behind the horn-rimmed spectacles. There was not the slightest possibility of doubt that the young German scientist was sincere. No wonder he had passed the vetting procedure. Okay, he was not Jewish like so many of the others. He did not have an inbuilt reason for hating the Nazis. Except maybe that he was a decent human being.

Oppenheimer smiled. 'What do we do now? Eh?'

'There is a problem?' But it was more a statement than a

question. Fuchs knew there was a problem. For the majority of his fellow scientists on The Hill, the war in Europe had been virtually all of the war. But not for the Americans. The enemy that had attacked them first was still fighting. On the defensive, but still fighting, in places with a determination that defied common sense, and strategic logic. But for a thousand reasons, many of them more cultural than tactical, Japan was not about to give up. And seen from Los Alamos, that bred a logic all of its own.

'You know.' Oppenheimer sucked on the stem of his pipe. 'In a way I wouldn't mind one hell of a lot if we never had to use this baby. Perhaps just proving to the world that it works will be enough.'

'But surely we will not announce the test in advance?'

'Hell, no. To tell the truth, I'm not even sure they'll announce it afterwards. Not even to our allies.'

'You mean . . .' Fuchs let the sentence trail, secretly sorry he had started it. What Oppenheimer was saying was obvious. It just wasn't a topic he felt he ought to be initiating.

Fuchs got up to go. He was flattered that the man appeared to be confiding in him, but worried about what his true agenda was. Fuchs felt a wave of affection for this American who had done so much to bring one of mankind's most fearsome, yet inevitable, scientific projects so close to its conclusion. But the conversation was still one of those best avoided. In his circumstances, too much honesty could be fatal.

'Hey, Klaus.' Oppenheimer stood too and stopped him. 'Where are you going? It's early yet.'

'Yes, but it will be getting cold soon. I'm sure you don't want to spend too much time sitting around here with me.'

Oppenheimer looked genuinely surprised, or was it sceptical?

'Nonsense, Klaus. I enjoy your company. Tell you what. Why don't you and I head over to my place and knock back a few shots. Kitty's off visiting her folks on the east coast. And there's something I want to talk to you about. It's important and it might take some time.'

'Now?'

'Yes, now. Why not?' the American looked suddenly serious. 'It's not often you and I get a chance to talk alone together. This seems like a good moment.'

Fuchs's complacency evaporated instantly. All this talk had just been a way of putting him off his guard. They had known all along.

And now it had fallen to Oppenheimer to break the news to him before they arrested him. There was one chance, maybe. He could throw himself on Oppenheimer's mercy. The American understood that science couldn't operate in a vacuum. Hadn't it been Oppie who argued that trust was everything and that only by sharing information could a community of scientists really work towards big breakthroughs. But Fuchs had betrayed that trust. That was how they would see it. Only he hadn't. He had simply done the honourable thing, the right thing.

Would Oppenheimer believe him? And even if he did, what good would it do? At best, it might save him from execution. But he doubted it. Oppenheimer was already walking down the steps of the wooden veranda. He turned at the bottom. 'Come on, Klaus. What are you waiting for? Let's go. Time to face the music.'

It was the first time Fuchs had been invited to Oppenheimer's relatively splendid abode on Bathtub Row. There was an irony, he thought, in the fact that it might be his last. They walked along the dusty streets in silence. Yellow lights were coming on in the mess halls, where the GIs were sitting down to their evening meal. Here and there a mom would call out of the window of her prefab home summoning the kids in to scrub their hands and eat.

After walking up the wooden steps to Oppenheimer's porch the director simply turned the handle of the door and walked in. Crime was almost unknown on The Hill. Los Alamos was that sort of place. It depended on trust. Fuchs caught the tickle of his guilty cough in the back of his throat.

'You okay?' Oppenheimer asked.

'Of course, it is only the dust.'

The director led him into a tastefully furnished if untidy living-room. Fuchs felt himself surprised suddenly to see this other, domestic side of Oppenheimer. This was a married man's abode, with all the trappings of family life, so very different from the single men's dorm, so very different in particular from the spartan solitary existence he lived himself.

Oppenheimer went to the kitchen and came back with a bottle of Bourbon and two glasses.

'Sit down, Klaus.'

The German did as he was told. He knew what was coming.

'You're a loner, Klaus.'

It was a statement rather than a question. Fuchs was tempted to ignore it, but replied, 'I do not think so, not particularly. Perhaps I am just not very good with people.'

'But what about women, Klaus? You're friendly with Genia, lots of the wives, Kitty even, for God's sake. But you never seem to have a woman of your own.'

'There is so little time. You know how it is.'

'Don't take everything I say so seriously. It's not as if we don't have enough problems keeping our sanity up here.'

He smiled and nodded. Sometimes Fuchs felt enormously grateful that the Americans could be so distracted by platitudes in place of the truth. Yet the fencing unnerved him further. Was this going to be an accusation, or an interrogation, or neither? He downed his whiskey in one.

'You look like you needed that. Let me pour you another.'

He did. And another. And let the spirit reinforce the Chinese walls within his consciousness. He had perfected them long ago, dimly aware that he might be encouraging a latent schizophrenia, as they had diagnosed in his mother too late to stop her killing herself. When he drank, he could close off compartments of his life so that they would never leak.

But if it was an interrogation, the thought involuntarily crossed his mind, would Oppenheimer be drinking too? Seated in a battered old armchair, the director was examining the hue of the whiskey in his glass. He sipped it slowly, running his tongue around his lip after every sip. At times, he seemed far away, then the sharp eyes would suddenly refocus on Fuchs and he would begin talking again. Fuchs wondered if he would ever get to the point, if there was a point.

For a few, dangerous moments, the compartmentalization threatened to fail him and he was tempted to reveal all, to bare his soul about his meetings over the years with the man he knew only as Raymond, about his messages exchanged with the man he had never seen and whom he knew only as John. Then he remembered that this was how he was supposed to feel, remembered how the hunted man was always tempted to surrender to an irrational desire to give himself up. He began, slowly, to relax. He was not, therefore expecting the tremor of angst that ran through him when Oppenheimer asked how he felt in terms of nationality, as a member of the British team.

'Nationality is something I don't place much stock in,' he answered carefully but honestly. Any other approach, he had long decided, would be foolish. Always tell as much of the truth as possible.

'I believe science transcends nationality. In the new world that will emerge after this war, perhaps the old ideas won't matter so much.'

'Perhaps, but perhaps they still will. There are games the politicians play that the likes of you and me are not invited to participate in.'

'Perhaps that is because we would be no good at them.'

'Perhaps. Then again, they haven't done one hell of a job so far, have they?'

Fuchs smiled the grim smile required. It was another rhetorical question.

'Do you feel yourself British?'

It was an unexpectedly direct question. The answer of course was 'no'. Despite the welcome the country had given him, he no more considered himself English than the English considered him one of them. The scientific community was different. There were colonials like Rutherford, and then there were émigrés like himself. But he was, in theory at least, a British subject. He felt strangely proud of that, as though it gave him a sense of belonging. That he was routinely betraying it was something the compartmentalization coped with. He gave the only answer he could:

'I suppose so.'

Oppenheimer nodded.

'I know what you mean. Our community here transcends nationalities, as science ought to do. Yet it is war between nations that has gathered us together. We have become international politicians, in that our work will determine the triumph of one nation over another. America will emerge from this war the greatest nation on earth.'

'Yes. You must be very proud.'

'Pride is part of the problem. England, of course, will want its bomb too, providing that the damn thing works.'

'Yes, I suppose so.' Fuchs did not know what else to say.

'Sure, it took American guts and knuckle-headed managerial geniuses like Groves to get this project off the ground and even think about making it work, but the Brits have their right to equal treatment. Which is sure as hell what old Winnie is demanding.'

'Churchill is making demands?' Fuchs had always wondered just how much access Oppenheimer, as director of the project, had to political information. Now, it seemed, the man was telling him. Perhaps because he knew that very shortly there would be nothing he could do with it.

'Look at it from his point of view. Here you are, having hung on by the skin of your teeth through dark years when the rest of Europe was crumbling all around you. Then in ride the Seventh Cavalry and announce they'll finish the job after all. What's more, they've got a secret weapon that'll make sure whatever country possesses it will never ever again face as frightening a threat as Great Britain did in 1940.'

'Sounds good.'

'Yeah. But it's not his bomb. The British will leave here, when this is all over, with as much knowledge on how to build the bomb as any American, but Britain won't have one straight away. All of a sudden America is the new empire, overtakes Britain overnight, becomes some kind of – I don't know what – *super*power. Churchill knows it's inevitable. He's playing the "English-speaking peoples" card, as if we're all one great tradition, Rome taking over from Greece. He plans to ride on Uncle Sam's coat-tails, but that depends on them keeping a monopoly on our Frankenstein's monster. And you and I know that that can't last for ever. Sooner or later others are going to get there.'

'You mean Japan?'

'Come on. You know as well as I do that the war with Japan is about to end. We're going to end it, whether they actually use the thing or just show it off. And my bet is that anything that has cost them this much they'll want to use. I'm talking about our other allies . . .'

Fuchs said nothing.

'I mean Russia, Klaus. I think you know that.'

Fuchs clutched his handkerchief to his mouth, stifling a choking retch that he hoped would pass as indigestion. At any moment, he was certain, the door would burst open and the MPs would march in. He composed himself as best he could. 'Yes, I assume they must be working along similar lines.'

Oppenheimer nodded. 'Yes, I would assume that too. But they're going to have the same problem as our British friends.'

'Which is?'

'Which is, as you know, that it is one thing getting the theory of this bomb together, another getting hold of enough plutonium. Everything we've been doing over the past nine months has rammed home to us that it is something else again to make it function properly. Just duplicating some of the mechanical factors we've had to account for could take years of trial and error. Without help. I thought maybe Niels had mentioned the subject to you?'

Fuchs tried to make his face convey interest rather than understanding.

'He was worried that we were being dishonest,' Oppenheimer continued, 'worried that we would encourage Stalin's suspicions, that we ought to share technology. He had friends in the scientific community in Moscow.'

'Ah, yes. He did say something.'

'And not just to you and me. Bohr has access. He went to the top. He talked to Roosevelt. And he went to Churchill.'

Fuchs held his breath. Was that what Bohr had been hinting at all along, that afternoon of the picnic in the canyon? Or was this just another trick? Was Oppenheimer looking for a positive reaction?

'What happened?'

'What do you think? Churchill patronized Bohr like hell, told him how the free world was pleased as punch to have his services, great man and all that, towering figure in the world of science, but if he didn't mind could he bugger off back to his lab bench and leave the real business of running the world to the grown-ups. And by the way no need to say "thank you" for having been saved from the jaws of death by British bravery. The empire didn't expect gratitude, least of all from small nations, just glad to do its moral duty.

'Which is what it all comes down to in the end, isn't it, Klaus? Morality. Do you know where your moral duty lies?'

Fuchs felt faint. Oppenheimer crossed to the big mahogany desk in the corner, took a small key from his pocket and unlocked the second drawer down. A gun? But what he produced appeared to be a photograph of a document in fine print. Oppenheimer sat down again, ran his eyes down the document as if to make sure he knew what it said, and handed it over.

Fuchs adjusted his glasses, feeling the fine beads of sweat on his nose. It seemed to be a draft agreement of some sort, written partly in German. One word, printed in bold, stood out: 'Sonnenaufgang'. Sunrise.

He read the rest, then bowed his head and closed his eyes for a full five minutes before looking up to find Oppenheimer's eyes waiting for him. 'Where does this come from?' he asked.

'Geneva. Just two months ago. Signed by a man named Dulles. I wasn't supposed to see it. As you can imagine, not many people were. But I still have a few friends in Washington.'

Fuchs gulped down the remains of his whiskey. This was not what he had anticipated at all. He looked up at Oppenheimer and thought suddenly that the man looked immensely tired and drawn.

'But Bohr said the bomb could stop wars.'

'Yes,' Oppenheimer replied. 'That's what he told Churchill, too.'

'And Churchill . . .' He gestured at the piece of paper in front of him. Oppenheimer sneered.

'Churchill threw him out.'

18

Los Alamos

America. Burke rolled the word around on his tongue. It felt strange
to be 'home'. He supposed even Albuquerque was someone's home.
He had never been to the American south-west before. It was more
alien than he had expected. In the depths of winter the sun beat
down from the cloudless sky. The air was crisp, dry, warm and
filled with the noise of engines, jet, diesel and petrol – gasoline, he
corrected himself – and the parping horns of traffic pulling up in
front of the terminal building. Deep down, he knew that this, not
England, was his country. Except that it did not seem like that.

'This way for the complimentary shuttle to Hertz, gateway to
America, folks. Thank you, sir, lady. May I take your bags. Sure is a
nice day today.' The big black bull of a man with a fixed smile but
eyes that said it was phoney whisked their luggage on to the rack in
the yellow bus.

It had been Sabine who decided to follow up Nora Winter's lead
to Los Alamos itself. A quick check revealed that Hiram Carter had
been a relatively junior physicist on the Manhattan Project. But he
had almost certainly known Fuchs personally. Burke agreed,
though he wondered secretly if Nora Winter had been feeding
him a line. He had obviously irritated her. What worried him rather
more was the possibility that he and Sabine were irritating other
people too, people who had ways of showing their irritation. At
Heathrow there had been a young man in a grey suit spending an
improbably long time at Tie Rack while Sabine picked up shampoo
at the Body Shop next door. He had loitered in W.H. Smith, buying
batteries, while Burke picked up a copy of *The Times*. And then he
had turned up again in the check-in queue for the first leg of their
flight to Dallas. Burke had told himself he was being ridiculous.

Bumping into the same person three times in half an hour was almost inevitable, particularly if he was on the same flight. None the less, he had scanned the faces in the rows on a couple of trips to the toilet and had not seen him. Which meant nothing, of course. Except that if he was not on the plane, why had he been in the check-in queue? Though there was always the possibility he was travelling first-class.

He had told Sabine but she had looked at him sceptically so Burke had dismissed the idea. In any case, he had not recognized anyone on board the one-class onward flight to Albuquerque. Perhaps the Bayswater bomb had reactivated his old conspiracy-theory syndrome. Nora Winter was right. He was letting his imagination run away with him.

In the Hertz reception area Sabine took charge, as he had almost become used to her doing, producing her credit card to settle the hire car.

'Here, homeboy,' she said as they walked out on to the parking lot. 'You take the wheel.' She tossed the keys through the air, and Burke caught them with a look of surprise that obviously amused her. He didn't know why he'd assumed she would be driving. There was a curious new lightness in her mood, as if she had left a burden behind. Was that what the 'New World' did for people: liberated them from their past?

The car was a brand-new Pontiac Firebird. A convertible. Burke laughed when he saw it, and Sabine beamed back, pleased by his reaction, as if the thing was a birthday present. Left to his own devices, he would have had the knee-jerk reaction of any freelance hack on a British budget – hired something dull and spent the next two days cursing the lack of air-conditioning and leg-room. Sabine, on the other hand, he thought as he drove towards the busy Albuquerque freeway, was in it for fun. From the moment he had told her about his encounter with 'Nuclear Winter' and produced the scrap of paper with Carter's name and telephone number, she had been busy booking airline tickets, using the magic *EON* credit card that seemed to have no spending limit.

'Okay.' She looked up from the street map. 'The road to Santa Fe goes straight through the city and on to the interstate heading north. Unless, of course, you want to stay the night in a piece of history? At least what passes for history out here. Look, there. See that big building on the corner?'

Burke followed her eyes. They were, he assumed, on the edge of the city, driving through drab streets of low-rise buildings, part-industrial, part-closed commercial, walls here and there daubed with graffiti, the sort of streets that made you want to accelerate through stop-lights in case someone pulled out behind you.

'You mean that brownstone up ahead?'

'Yeah. Conrad Hilton's first hotel. Local boy made good.'

He nodded, impressed. 'That's what you got from the guide book?' She had spent hours on the plane absorbed in the Lonely Planet *New Mexico Handbook*.

'Uh huh. Want to take a look?'

Burke pulled in to the nearside lane and took a right at the hotel. A sign advertised pizzas. Clearly Conrad's roots had not moved along with his global ambitions. There was a plaque next to the old wooden door which commemorated the birth of an empire, even though the birthplace itself had been left behind.

'What do you think?'

'Are you serious?'

'Sure. I mean, we can hardly drive all the way tonight. Even Santa Fe is a good few hours on the road.'

Burke thought, why not? Somehow just being in America opened new horizons, real or imagined.

'Anyway,' she added. 'This was virtually the only hotel in town back in the forties. If Klaus Fuchs came to Albuquerque – and we have to assume he did – then the chances are that this is where he stayed.'

Burke blinked for a moment, then found himself almost laughing at the little fantasy his subconscious had been in the business of creating. Of course, she was still working.

Inside, Burke was surprisingly impressed by the style of the place. A grand piano dominated the foyer, with a couple of potted palms and a richly varnished horseshoe bar, which, judging from the rattle of cocktail shakers and the noisy banter, looked like it was already gearing up for happy hour.

Even the reception desk looked unchanged from the forties: heavy polished oak. The clerk behind it was efficient, but in a matter-of-fact way – almost English, Burke reflected – even down to the surreptitiously insolent flicker of his eyes when Sabine confirmed, as Burke had known she would, that they wanted two rooms.

Her room was on the sixth floor. His, on the eighth, was just slightly shabby, with paintwork flaked in places, hulking iron radiators and noisy, bolt-on air-conditioning units. There was a television in the corner, but not one that would have graced any hotel still belonging to the chain Conrad Hilton founded. Burke turned it on, and off. Because it was there. Then he took a shower to wash the twelve-hour flight from his pores.

Half an hour later, Burke was settling himself in at the horseshoe bar. The shabby genteel style of the hotel appealed to him and he felt he had gone into a time warp: at any moment the great revolving doors would spin to admit Sidney Greenstreet, complete with fly whisk and Peter Lorre in his wake. Or Klaus Fuchs.

'*Na!*' He had got so used to her talking English, even American-English, that German was the last language he expected to hear from Sabine Kotzke. 'See. I told you so.'

'What?' Burke was uncomprehending.

Sabine bounced up to the bar clutching a sheet of white paper. She had not changed, not even – as far as he could tell – been up to her room for a wash or a shower. She thrust it under his nose. 'Don't you just feel it, Eamonn? At last, we're really on to the trace. We're going to get there. I know.'

Burke looked down. It was a photocopy of something that looked like a list, handwritten, of names and addresses, with numbers written against them.

'Sorry, what is this exactly?'

'It's the hotel register, for God's sake. The reception clerk knew just where to find them. Old boxes in a store-cupboard.'

Burke peered at the list. The entries were for September 1945. It had been a busy time, but nothing looked like Fuchs.

'Here. Look.' Sabine's finger jabbed at a name written in a space dated 9.17.45, in that curious back-to-front American way that Burke had long since abandoned for European style.

'The seventeenth of September, 1945.' He squinted at the signature. 'Doesn't look like Fuchs, though. Surely that's a "G"?'

'Of course it is. It's "G" for Gold. Harry Gold. Fuchs's contact. The idiot even signed his own name. What's more, he didn't stay the night. Couldn't have, probably; the hotel was almost perpetually full in those days. He rented a room for the day. Just what you'd do if you wanted to meet someone in private . . .'

'And stay out of sight.' Burke completed the train of thought. She was right, of course. What it meant, though, he had not the faintest idea. They were tracking a dead man. And while dead men didn't tell lies, dead men didn't necessarily tell the truth either. In fact, dead men don't say anything at all.

High above the Thames, Dickie Boston was standing at the window of his office. His secretary Monica had left for home two hours earlier.

When the telephone rang, he looked at it for a few seconds before lifting the receiver. He answered, as always, briefly, giving nothing away. 'Hello.'

'Dickie, it's Nora.'

'My dear, what a pleasant surprise.'

'Is it?'

'What – pleasant? Or a surprise?'

'Either.'

'That depends on why you're calling. Though it's always a delight to hear your voice.'

'Hrrmph. I've had a visitor. A reporter. He was asking questions.'

'They do.'

'About Fuchs.'

'Really? I'm sure you had a lot to talk about. Reminiscences can be important in the scheme of things. Don't you agree?'

'You know I do. That's why I'm calling.'

'You weren't indiscreet, were you, Nora? Of course not. How could I even think such a thing? An old trooper like you.'

'Don't play with me, Dickie. I'm doing you a favour.'

'Some might say you were only doing your duty.'

'I sent him away.'

'To America?'

'What?'

'He and his young lady friend boarded a plane this morning for Dallas, Texas, with an onward connection to Albuquerque. Any idea why they might have done that, Nora?'

Silence.

'I'm sorry? I didn't quite catch that.'

'I might have mentioned a name. Carter. Hiram Carter. I thought it would get him out of my hair.'

'I see . . . Was that the only name you gave him?'

'What do you mean?'

'Just checking. You didn't, for example, mention Mrs K.?'

'What . . . ? No. Of course not.'

'Of course not.'

'. . . Dickie?'

'Yes?'

'It won't affect anything, will it? I mean, pension-wise. I did call.'

'Of course you did, Nora. I'm very grateful. Do keep in touch. I like to look after people, you know. It would be such a pity to lose contact.'

'Yes. Thank you.'

'Thank you, Nora. Good night.'

Eamonn Burke had set the car on cruise control at a steady sixty-five, and was lying back in his seat, relaxed, enjoying the wind on his face and in his hair. The open road stretched before them like a black line drawn in the sand. He longed to reach out his right arm and pull Sabine Kotzke's head on to his shoulder. He longed for the essence of James Dean and Peter Fonda and Tom Cruise. He thought maybe the American in him wasn't dead after all.

Sabine, beside him, had already surrendered to the hedonism. Was that how she had imagined America, he wondered, back in her teens as a member of the ironically named Free German Youth, reciting the Marxist catechism and learning that America was the devil's spawn? Had she dreamed of tossing back her fringe in the desert wind in the front seat of a speeding sportscar, high on the adrenaline of life for its own sake? He shot a glance at her. She caught his eye, as he knew she would. And winked.

They cruised into Santa Fe before they even realized it. Burke was tempted to stop, to search here for spoor of their ancient quarry too. They had reserved rooms for the night at the La Fonda Hotel: Los Alamos was still low on good-quality guest accommodation, Carter had advised. But now it was Sabine urging him on. Pointing out that their meeting was scheduled. That Hiram Carter might not wait. That he might change his mind. And there was, as ever, an urgency to her voice that overrode anything Burke could think to say.

As they continued north along the highway, Burke had to force himself to imagine how it might have been back then, more than half a century ago, heading out of a frontier town for a destination that didn't exist. The war in Europe must have seemed a long way away. In comparison this must have appeared a new world indeed, yet at the same time terribly old, primeval even, scarcely touched by man's presence. Was it the obvious place to discover the ultimate weapon, the one capable of destroying civilization?

117

'Here's the turn-off. I bet the road sign wasn't even there back in the forties.'

Burke turned the car left on to a road that widened as it climbed, giving room for faster vehicles to pass. No bad idea as heavy trucks made their way to Los Alamos. Unlike Harwell, which had lost its mission, Los Alamos remained part of the American nuclear weapons programme. The neutron bomb had been developed here, and much of the work done on the cruise missile. Burke was surprised, however, at the ease with which the modern road took them up the side of the mesa, leaving him wondering where the original track had run and where the wooden guard posts had been. It was only when they crossed a great modern bridge over a river canyon that he realized the original wartime road must have taken a very different, much more tortuous route up the mesa face.

The modern town of Los Alamos turned out to be disappointingly similar to so many other small American communities: a huddle of burger bars, Tex-Mex restaurants and gas stations. Only – and again Burke was reminded of Harwell – a few of the street-names recalled the pioneers of the atomic era. But some things had survived. Bathtub Row was obvious with its big timber houses set back from the road. The water-tower that loomed over the end of the street was presumably the same one that had dominated the ramshackle wartime settlement.

Hiram Carter's instructions to Sabine turned out to be meticulous, taking them through Los Alamos proper and out again. Having outgrown its confines and its secrecy, the complex now extended over hundreds of acres of adjoining countryside, much of it closed off behind electric fences and watchtowers as intimidating as anything Burke remembered from the bad old days of Europe in the Cold War.

Carter's house lay amid a small community of exclusive homes, where top staff from the laboratories lived. Burke spotted the house sign first, a polished wooden board with the single word 'Edge' burned into it with a hot poker. He turned in between the gateposts and stopped on rough gravel drive, behind a grey Toyota land-cruiser. The air was crisp, cool but dry. He climbed out of the car taking his hand-held tape-recorder from the glove compartment.

'You can leave that where it is, son.'

The man leaning on a walking stick on the veranda was thick-set, silver-haired, with a thin smile on his face and eyes behind tinted spectacles that might have agreed with it and might not.

'I don't like taped interviews. Makes them seem too much like interviews, if you know what I mean.'

Burke shrugged and put the machine back, though it would have been useful to have a more reliable record than his cruddy shorthand if the man actually said anything useful. But then the first priority was to get him to say anything at all.

'Professor Doctor Carter? So glad to meet you.' Sabine was on her best charm offensive. She held out her hand.

'I'm sure.' Carter turned in her direction and widened the smile but did not hold out his own hand. 'Come inside, why don't you?'

Burke followed Carter into an open-plan living area. A log fire burned in the grate of a tall grey slate chimney that took up most of one wall. Chairs were draped with Native American embroidery; the furniture was heavy and burnished to a rich deep colour. Here and there, on top of two great sideboards and a low coffee table were lumps of rock, some interestingly stratified with different coloured layers.

'Can I get you something? Coffee perhaps?'

He pronounced it in that long drawn-out western American way: kaw-fee. Personally, Burke could have murdered for a cold beer. But Sabine got there first.

'Coffee would be fine.'

Carter made his way into the adjacent kitchen slowly, using his stick, and began the business of grinding beans and setting up the percolator.

'It's all right, really,' Sabine butted in. 'Instant would do.'

'Might do you,' came the reply which managed the trick of being slow but still abrupt, Burke thought. He tried to break what he felt was a rapidly building sheet of ice.

'We're very interested in your work here, Dr Carter.'

'Glad to hear it. Seeing as you've come all this way. On Miss Winter's recommendation,' he added in a way that managed to make clear that without it he would not be seeing them at all.

'Particularly in the old days, the genesis of the programme.'

'Genesis, eh?' The old man turned to him. 'That's a good enough word for it, okay. Birth of a new world, that's what we thought it'd be. Hasn't quite turned out like that though, has it?'

Burke suspected the question was rhetorical, and decided to play safe: he smiled instead of answering. The response was a frown.

'No. I can tell you. It hasn't. Some folks'll tell you that it's safer at the moment than it has been for decades. Well they're wrong. Just 'cause there isn't an obvious enemy doesn't mean there isn't an enemy. It just means you don't know who it is.'

'How much do you remember about the programme back in the forties?' Sabine asked.

'All of it,' Carter grunted.

'The people?'

'All of them. Including your damn Fuchs. That's who you want to know about, isn't it?'

Burke and Sabine nodded simultaneously. Carter produced cups and poured the coffee. He did not ask if they wanted milk or cream.

'Let's sit down.'

For the next forty minutes they fenced around details of the early atomic bomb programme, about the atmosphere, the secrecy, the personal relations, about the characters of Oppenheimer and Groves, about people like Rabi and Kistiakowsky, Fermi and Frisch and, of course, Fuchs. To Burke's huge disappointment, Carter had known him only slightly, and had less impression of the quiet German than of some of the more colourful characters.

'I was only young, you have to understand. And I was one of Teller's boys. We were more concerned in the end with the "super" – the H-bomb – than with the little Nagasaki jobs.'

'You thought it was a good thing, did you? Dropping a second bomb?' Sabine asked

Carter's face froze into a passive mask, one Burke guessed he had worn more than once before.

'Who was counting? We were ending a war.'

'Yes, but you had already effectively ended it, hadn't you? Some of the scientists thought that even Hiroshima was too much, that a simple demonstration would have convinced Japan to surrender.'

Burke winced. To make matters worse, Carter shrugged.

'It was a war, lady. A war your people started, if you want to get moralistic. Our job was to provide the tools for the military to finish it. And to make sure we had the wherewithal to prevent some smart-assed dictator doing it again. And before you start accusing me of trying to secure one-power hegemony, I'll admit it for you. The world would be a better place today if only the United States had had the bomb. Your friend Fuchs and his gang began the rot . . .'

'His gang . . . you mean the Russians?'

'I mean what I say, lady.'

Carter drained the dregs of his coffee, then stood up, leaning heavily on his stick, and walked towards the sliding glass doors that led into his back garden, motioning to them to follow.

The sight was breathtaking. Barely twenty yards from the house, the land disappeared. Carter walked across the rough rye-grass lawn almost to the edge. The visitors followed him, and Burke immediately understood the curious house name.

Below them, a near-vertical drop of more than 2,000 feet, the young Rio Grande gushed through the bottom of the great canyon it had carved over millennia. The waters, still fed by melting snow from the mountains, were a greeny-brown. Beyond, the mountains rose, majestic as ever, just beginning to turn from russet-brown to bright vermilion in the late-afternoon sun.

'They call them the Blood of Christ, you know. Fitting somehow.'

Burke nodded silently. He knew no answer was required.

'Mr Burke, Miss uh,' he stumbled over the German name, 'Kotzke, I can see that we don't share views about the usefulness and the morality of the atomic bomb. This is not the time to argue about that, nor would there be any point in doing so. But believe me, this is not the first time the argument has been had. The first time was perhaps the fiercest. The first time was here. Then.'

'You mean there was open argument among the scientists on the Manhattan Project?'

He shrugged. 'What is open? Now or then? We were all building the gadget. We all wanted it to succeed. Scientifically. But we were not in charge of its use. There were some among us who felt they were being used. Abused even.'

'And you?'

'No. I had no qualms. I am a physicist, not a military man. Unlike some of my colleagues, I do not make the assumption that we have the right to do everything. I accept limits to my competence. Would the war have ended? Were the people who were getting so excited about it the right ones to decide? We scientists did not do much to stop it happening in the first place. And those of us who stayed on here, who gave this country the best arsenal in the world, the arsenal that stopped the Soviet dictatorship taking over your Europe, the arsenal that has put Saddam Hussein in his place, are we not worthy of a little praise too? Even if we don't claim the moral high ground?'

Burke thought it best not to answer. He closed his eyes when he heard Kotzke start. But she was not initiating an argument.

'I'm not sure what you're suggesting happened back in '45.'

Carter continued to stare out across the chasm towards the red mountains beyond.

'I'm not suggesting anything. There was treason. That's documented. That's why you're here. I'm not sure there's anything else I can tell you.'

'What about the others? What about Oppenheimer?'

Carter glanced at Burke, then turned back. 'What about him?'

'He came under suspicion, didn't he? Later.'

'That was during the McCarthy era. Who wasn't accused of Commie sympathies? He'd had contacts, of course, but he'd abandoned all those, hadn't he, for the good of his country? National hero and all that. Even Groves in the end said all his suspicions were ill-founded. So it must be true. What was that quote: "I am convinced that J. Robert Oppenheimer never consciously did anything to harm his country." What a way with words the old general could have when the moment took him.'

'Sounds suspiciously like faint praise to me.'

Carter gave a smile that reminded Burke of Nora Winter. He wondered when the pair had last met. He could imagine them getting on well together.

'You noticed those baskets on the table back in the living-room?'

'The ones with the rock samples?'

'Would you be so good as to fetch the smaller one for me?'

'Sure thing,' he said, wincing as he noticed another Americanism escape his lips.

The basket was heavier than he expected. He wondered what the old man wanted – it was hardly the time for a geology lesson, interesting as the strata of the Sangre de Cristo mountains no doubt were.

Carter thanked him, took the basket and set it on a garden table.

'How much do you know about radioactivity, Mr Burke?'

'Not as much as you, sir, that's for sure.'

'Quite.'

Carter lifted a lump of what appeared to be ordinary granite.

'Do you know what this is?'

'Looks like granite.'

'Excellent. English granite no less. From your Cornwall. You wouldn't consider it particularly harmful.'

'Not particularly. Unless you hit me with it.'

Carter laughed, a short hard laugh.

'Indeed. That is its most dangerous potential. Yet, it is, you know, radioactive. It emits radon. Everything around us is permanently interacting with radioactivity; it is the nature of the universe. There is, I've heard, a restroom in Cornwall where the dose of radioactivity obtained from relieving one's bowels is many times the permissible dose in England today. And many more times what is allowed here. But it's not fatal. You can't escape radioactivity. It is all around us. It is what men do with it that makes it dangerous. Take that other sample, the grey one.'

Burke reached out and lifted a smooth, round grey sphere, abnormally heavy for its size. It appeared to be not rock but a dull metal of some sort, and felt almost warm to the touch. Not so much like an inert object as something vaguely alive.

'Interesting. What is it?'

'Plutonium.'

Burke dropped the sphere immediately, watching in horror as it rolled to Carter's feet. He half expected it to go critical. He looked up to see the old man, still smiling, pick it up and put it back in the basket.

'You've come to no harm. Even plutonium is not as dangerous as people think. You won't die. At least, not because of what you have touched. It is not something you'd want to eat off, of course – though people did, in the fifties, you know – still eat off plates coated with mildly radioactive paint. And we hardly had a nation-wide cancer epidemic.'

Or just not one that anyone recognized, and traced, thought Burke. But he said nothing. His eyes were still fixed on the small orb of the first man-made element, lying so apparently innocuously in its wicker basket.

'I am sorry,' said Carter. 'It wasn't a fair trick. But I wanted to make a point. The plutonium bomb was the key to the nuclear deterrent – it was the only sort of nuclear device that could be produced on any scale. But even plutonium on its own was not enough. For all their brilliance, their implosive lenses, Oppie's bomb would never have worked if it had just been plutonium.'

'I know.' Sabine stepped in for the still-shocked Burke. 'There was the uranium shell as well.'

Carter sniffed audibly. 'Fat lot of use that would have been if the core hadn't exploded. The whole point about the sort of uranium they could get their hands on in any quantity was that it wasn't fissile. The U-238 isotope – you know what an isotope is, for God's sake? An atomically different variation of an element. – the common form of natural uranium, just wouldn't work. No chain reaction. It wouldn't go off.

'If it had done, there would never have been an implosion bomb. They would have used the "gun" design, Little Boy, the bomb they dropped on Hiroshima. A Danish scientist, guy called Niels Bohr, had proved U-238 didn't work and discovered the rare variant that did, U-235. Any idiot, even back then, could have made a bomb like that but there wasn't enough U-235 easily available on the planet for more than one and God knows that took enough blood, sweat and tears to extract. The fuel in that one bomb was worth billions of dollars.'

'Which was why they turned to plutonium,' said Sabine, eager to restore some vestige of intellectual credibility.

'That's right.'

'So . . .' Sabine began tentatively. But Carter needed no prompting to finish for her.

'They needed an initiator. Call it a detonator, if you like, although there was one of those too, in the conventional sense, for the high-explosive shell. They needed something that would start off the chain reaction at the heart of the bomb.'

'Polonium?'

'Yeah. Named after Poland. Fitting, eh? Discovered by Marie Curie – killed her in the end.'

'Wasn't polonium incredibly rare?'

'Was once. Not now. Not by then even. Ever since Curie discovered radium they'd been using it in cancer hospitals. Polonium is a daughter-product of radium decay. Los Alamos got its supply from a New York infirmary. They mixed it with another radioactive element, beryllium. Squeezed together by the imploding plutonium, they would fuse and release the neutrons that started the chain reaction, made the bomb go critical. Otherwise you would just have had a big conventional explosive bomb that scattered a lot of radioactive debris. The initiator turned it into an atomic weapon.

'But it still took them more than a year to get the initiator right: they conducted endless experiments, making what looked like giant ball bearings filled up with the stuff and then blowing them in on themselves to see how well they had mixed. They only needed to produce about ten neutrons in the crucial ten-millionth of a second that would matter if they were to initiate a reaction.'

Burke was lost and thought he might as well admit it. 'I'm not sure I'm following this.'

Sabine shot him a look, but Carter seemed happy to explain.

'You need neutrons to set off the chain reaction. Not many, but just enough. That was what the initiator did. You could call it a catalyst. Think of the bomb as a giant ammunition dump, if you want. Throwing a match in wouldn't be dead clever. But it probably wouldn't be catastrophic. Throwing in a Molotov cocktail on the other hand . . .'

Burke took the point.

'The trouble was,' Carter continued, 'in those days, it was almost impossible to measure neutron emissions with the degree of accuracy required. It wasn't until after the Trinity test that we knew for sure we'd succeeded.'

'We'd been experimenting with initiators for so long that we had several different models. When we found one that worked, we scrapped the rest: recycled them for the polonium and beryllium to make the new models. It wasn't as if the raw materials were particularly scarce. It was the quantities, design and manufacture that had been the problem. By the end, there were even one or two copies of each type lying around. In the euphoria over getting it right, people perhaps weren't as careful as they should have been.'

Burke wondered if that was what Nora Winter had been trying to say.

'So when the Soviets did get one to work,' Carter said, 'so relatively soon, it seemed something of a miracle. To those who believe in miracles.'

'What are you trying to say?'

'I'm not trying to say anything, Mr Burke. I am, like you and your young friend here, and indeed any good scientist, merely posing problems and looking at the theories.

'People nowadays imagine that the Manhattan Project was some sort of hyper-efficient installation. In reality, it was more like a load of bright kids trying to invent something in the garage. Like that guy who made all the money with computers back in the eighties.'

'Bill Gates?'

'Yeah, came out of nowhere and changed the world.'

'Except that the Manhattan Project made more of an immediate impact.'

Carter shrugged. 'You could say that okay. Fuchs told the Russians everything, of course. But as the technical types here had found, there was one hell of a big difference between theory and practice. An initiator's damned hard to construct. And the Soviets were working with cruddy equipment.'

'You have a theory?'

'I'm too old for theories, Mister Burke. I'm retired. I just sit here and watch the sun set over those damn mountains with a glass of Bourbon and my memories. And what I remember is just what remarkable luck those Rooskies had in the end.'

Burke looked the physicist square in the eyes, and found his stare returned. There was something the man wasn't saying.

'Tell me, Dr Carter.' If he was determined to play a roundabout game, Burke could play along. 'Just how big was this "initiator"?'

'Oh, not big. About the size of a golf ball.'

'And how do *you* think the Russians managed to copy it so quickly?'

'Ask *them* about that, them Rooskies. And ask them about Mrs K., too. They're famously generous with their records in Moscow these days, I believe. Leastways, that's what they say, even in Langley, Virginia. The sun rises in the east nowadays all right. Ask them about that, too. Ask them about the sunrise. The one that never happened.'

And with that he turned around, leaving Burke and Kotzke staring after him, open-mouthed, as he limped back towards the house.

Burke looked at Kotzke to see if she made any more than he did from a conversation that had suddenly gone off the rails. Not for the first time, he found the look on her face inscrutable.

'Excuse me, sir,' he called after Carter's retreating back. 'I think you should explain yourself.'

'Ha!' Carter didn't even bother to turn round. 'Explain myself. Who do you think you are? Who the hell ever asked Allen Dulles for explanations? They were all honourable men, honourable men all. The side gate's open. Let yourselves out.'

He stumped into the house and closed the door behind him. The interview was definitively at an end.

The dusk was falling fast as the convertible wove its way down from the high mesa into the valley of the Rio Grande and the road back to Santa Fe.

Burke was swimming in confusion. Carter had opened doors only to slam them shut, had raised ghosts without laying them. He had teased Burke's instincts and beggared his imagination.

'Jesus, I'm just glad I don't play poker with that man. He pulls wild cards from the bottom of the deck.'

'Wild cards?'

'Jokers. Whatever. Except that he wasn't joking, was he?'

'No. He wasn't. I think maybe there is nothing to joke about.'

Burke looked at her, wondering again if she had briefed him as fully as she might have done. That was the thing about journalism, he sighed. Even when you were working on a story together, there was always the possibility that someone was holding out for a better angle.

'What do you make of Mrs K, Miss K? he asked.

'Nothing at all. And what about Allen Dulles?'

'What about him? The first fucking head of the CIA, the man who coaxed Kennedy into the Bay of Pigs disaster in Cuba. Brilliant but bonkers, and probably the prototype for every insane secret service chief since.'

'Where does he fit in?'

Burke turned to Sabine, but she was gazing out over the desert to where the low lights of Indian dwellings shone a warm yellow glow. She didn't seem to need an answer.

The air had turned cold. Burke swung the Pontiac on to the Taos highway, looking forward to a hot shower and a drink at the hotel. He began to whistle.

'What's that?' Sabine had turned towards him, her face full of curiosity.

' "From Russia with Love." I figured if I have to play James Bond, then I might as well get to do the theme tune.'

She shook her head and gave an uncertain smile.

'Next stop Moscow,' she said.

19

Big Bang

Los Alamos, 15 July 1945

It was, at last, the evening before. Up on the high plateau, as they sat around over a few glasses of wine and more than a few bottles of beer in the bar at the Big House, the atmosphere crackled with mental electricity.

Like when Enrico Fermi, the short, stocky Italian, more than a little drunk, lurched over to the green baize table by the fireplace where Isidor Rabi sat chain-smoking over a pile of dollars that represented the scale of his expertise at seven-card stud.

'Anybody for a real bet?' Fermi had announced, swaying slightly.

'What do you mean?' asked Kistiakowsky, one eye still on his losses.

'On the fireworks, of course. Our little dawn *divertimento*. Will we have a big bang, or a little phut, like the fart of an old woman?' Fermi made a scornful, wet noise with his lips.

Edward Teller had been leaning on the mantelpiece, his eyes fixed on the empty grate. It was part of his job to calculate the margins of error. The dimensions of terror. Fuchs, who had made private calculations of his own, sometimes wondered if Teller inhabited the same planet as the rest of them. Already, at the Pentagon's behest, his eyes were fixed on the 'super', a 'hydrogen bomb' that would use the unimaginable blast they had yet to witness as merely a detonator.

'There are fixed parameters, Enrico. As you know,' Teller said. 'The question is how many thousand tonnes of TNT equivalent and I am conservatively estimating . . .'

'Estimates? Guesses . . . you don't really know, do you?' the

Italian interrupted him. 'You don't know for sure. None of us does. That's the point of the test. Isn't it? George here doesn't really know if his clever explosive "lenses" will work. It might all end in a wet firecracker, huh? A big bomb that just makes a mess of itself, but no nuclear, huh?'

'I'm quietly confident, Enrico,' Kistiakowsky replied in his most measured, poker player's monotone. 'But of course, you are right. We do not know anything for certain until we experiment. That is a law of physics you would agree with, I think.'

But Fermi was enjoying himself tap-dancing on their hopes and fears. 'Hey, Edward,' he called again to Teller, 'what's the betting that the whole thing's a flop. But maybe that'll be okay, you know, because it will prove it's impossible. If we can't do it, nobody can. Of course, on the other hand,' the man was almost giggling, Fuchs noted with a chill, 'maybe it'll be bigger than any of us expect.'

Kistiakowsky was getting annoyed. He had no time for the Italian's frivolity.

'For Christ's sake, Enrico, quit playing the fool,' he snapped.

But Fuchs knew better. As did Teller. Fermi was nobody's fool. It was his juggling within the very heart of matter that had brought them this far. His alternatives were not as preposterous as they sounded.

'What do you think the odds are, Izzy?' Fermi asked big, silent Isidor Rabi. 'What's the chance that we might just fry everybody in the state?'

'You mean . . .' Rabi began, but Fermi was in full flight.

'I mean the goddamn oxygen, that's what I mean. The stuff we breathe. The stuff that makes fire burn.'

'The atmosphere?' Kistiakowsky was an engineer, not a molecular chemist.

'That's right, set it alight,' Fermi's eyes were blazing. He was clearly enjoying himself, 'and who knows, we might just sizzle the entire planet.'

Fuchs had been watching the discussion from the bar where he had been keeping company with Feynmann, on whom the question weighed less heavily than the recent death of his wife. He was tempted – only momentarily – to say something. He had little time for Fermi, though he respected his brilliance. There was something too clinical in his cynicism. As if he meant it.

'Because maybe, just maybe,' Fermi was continuing, now that he had an audience to command, 'we shouldn't do it at all. Has anyone thought of that?'

The idea that they might never test the 'gadget' had not occurred to Fuchs. Too much work had gone into it. The device itself had imposed its own imperatives.

'Maybe you are right, Enrico,' said Rabi. 'There has been so much killing. It is too late now for vengeance. The Nazis are gone. We Jews who have suffered so much – so much more, it seems, than even we had feared – have we done too much, those of us who have put our energies into this weapon? Are we the same as them?'

'Like hell we are. You've seen the pictures the GIs are sending back of those concentration camps.' Fermi was not Jewish, but his wife was. 'We're just too damn late. We should have used this stuff sooner.'

'But you know it was not possible.' It was Teller who spoke now. 'You yourself have just said that even now we are not perfectly sure the gadget will work.'

'So who in hell's talkin' about the gadget? There were a thousand other ways we could've got those bastards. Dumped strontium in their water supply, for example.'

Rabi sucked in his breath. Kistiakowsky looked mildly puzzled. Fuchs sighed. He had heard, and been sickened by, the suggestion before.

'What would that have done?'

'Only killed off the populations of whole cities, that's all.' To Fuchs's surprise, Feynmann, next to him, had looked up from his glass and addressed the party in a strong, clear voice. 'Poisoned millions, condemned them to a slow, painful but very, very certain death from within as the stuff destroyed their bone tissue. Very inventive. I'm surprised no one has thought of it.'

'It is an abomination, that is what it is,' blurted Rabi.

'Worse than these gas chambers, worse than this Ossvitz place?' Fermi was challenging. The news of the camps in occupied Poland was just beginning to come in, the scale of the atrocity still defying belief.

'The place you mean is called Oswiecim in Polish, or Auschwitz in German, and yes, what you are suggesting is worse. Is this what this war has done to us all? Reduced us to the level of the Nazis?' Fuchs was surprised to hear his own voice. These were the sort of debates he usually kept out of. But then tonight was not a usual night.

'Maybe,' said Fermi crisply, twirling his wine glass in the air before raising it to his lips to down the last red drops. Fuchs suddenly felt acutely aware of his nationality, the unspoken subtext to the conversation. 'Maybe we will all find out in the morning what we are made of, and what we have made. Gentlemen, I bid you good night. We have quite a journey ahead of us in just a few hours.'

At the bar Fuchs finished his beer and turned to Feynmann, who, he noticed, was looking more animated than he had seen him in weeks.

'Do you think he meant that? About the strontium?'

'Who knows, Klaus? Maybe. Maybe not. But it would have worked all right. You know that.'

Fuchs did. And as he placed his empty beer bottle on the bar he tried to dismiss from his mind the image of all those years ago: his mother, her face contracted into a mask of agony on the kitchen floor. But into its place came a vision of Arlene Feynmann, as he had last seen her, wasting away in Albuquerque hospital.

'That's what it's all about, isn't it?' he said. 'Killing time.'

Alamogordo Desert, 16 July

No one got any real sleep, though a few, like Fermi, had retired early for a few hours' rest. The others stayed up and dozed in their seats *en route*. The journey had begun shortly after midnight in uncomfortable buses, bumping in and out of potholes on the desert track. Now, as they stood on the slopes of Compania Hill, their watches ticked towards 5.30a.m.

It was Teller who had suggested the suntan lotion. Perhaps, more than any of the others, he knew the power they were about to unleash, and the potential risks involved even in witnessing it. But he was determined not to turn away. Smearing the oily lotion on his face he told himself he would 'look the beast in the eye'. He had spent months calculating every possibility of error, weighing every chance of disaster, but in truth they were venturing into uncharted territory.

He pulled on heavy gloves and a pair of dark glasses, held a thick welder's glass visor against his face, and stared in the darkness towards the twenty-mile-distant point on which all attention was focused, the spot that the man in charge had dubbed Trinity.

The man himself was much closer. In an earth-sheltered bunker with a thick concrete roof supported by oak beams, Robert Oppenheimer scarcely dared breathe. S10000, the southern command centre, was only 10,000 yards – less than six miles – from the tall tower which supported the absurd-looking mechanical device, a man-sized sphere of steel covered in rivets, wires and bolt-on metal boxes sitting under a corrugated iron roof. The room was crowded, the atmosphere thick with nervous tension, the smell of sweat and adrenalin.

At twenty-nine minutes past the hour, the automatic timer was engaged. Forty-five seconds later the timer needle touched zero. Around the inside of the sphere of steel thirty-two detonators simultaneously fired, sending a wave of compression inwards. For a microsecond conditions at its core echoed the fiery birth of the universe itself. Had astronomers been watching the moon that July dawn they would have seen it reflect an unearthly flash.

More than twenty miles away a few of the scientists, including a youthful Hiram Carter, had assumed the recent storm had caused a postponement and were walking carefully downhill, picking their steps in the darkness. Suddenly they saw the earth before them illuminated with a light so sharp that each blade of grass cast its own individual shadow. Seconds later came the shock wave that nearly knocked them off their feet.

For Isidor Rabi it was the most omnipotent sensation of his life. Afterwards he would recall it with a sense of awe: 'It blasted; it pounced; it bored its way right through you. It was a vision which was seen with more than the eye. It was seen to last forever. You would wish it would stop; altogether it lasted about two seconds. Finally, it was over, diminishing, and we looked toward the place where the bomb had been; there was an enormous ball of fire which grew and grew and it rolled as it grew; it went up into the air, in yellow flashes and into scarlet and green. It looked menacing. It seemed to come toward one.' The atomic age was born with a bang. The whimper was yet to come.

At S10000, there was no shout of triumph. The tense silence in the shelter was broken at first by a few nervous laughs, then a few tears of released tension, and gradually a solemn apprehension of what they had witnessed. The noisy bustle seemed like a deathly hush in the wake of the apocalypse they had unleashed. Oppenheimer, the physicist who was also a Sanskrit scholar, looked into the depths of his own learning and experience for words to express the terrible enormity of their achievement and found only bleak comfort: the words of the Hindu god Vishnu in the Bhagavad-Gita scripture. 'Now I am become Death, the destroyer of worlds.'

Mainly by a pavid the while and into higher and lower strong
a will all look coming so may to send if that such that a send if
all frequent tissue a gauge a different into dumar. In all I
de-bter in smudge.

PART TWO

Fission

20

Red Eye

Eamonn Burke sat in seat 22a of British Airways flight BA224 into Moscow Sheremetyevo and surveyed, as he always did, the great expanse of forest to the north. Somewhere down there, amid the trees, were the ageing remnants of the the Cold War air-defence systems. When Ronald Reagan was in the White House, Moscow's anti-missile system had been the excuse for the Strategic Defence Initiative, known to most people as 'Star Wars'. There were advantages, the boys in the boardrooms had told themselves as they counted the cost of incoming contracts with an open-ended timetable, to having a president educated in Hollywood.

The deeper irony was that they had proved their own undoing. Most unexpected of all had been not that the Russians were so far ahead, but that even entering the race was beyond them. Mikhail Gorbachev recognized that fact, thereby ending the Cold War and with it the lucrative arms race. The balance of terror that had kept an uneasy peace since the Soviet nuclear test in 1949, had come to a seemingly sane end. Though there were still those who regretted it: men like Vladimir Zhirinovsky and other psychopaths, some of them little more than gangland bosses wrapped in flags, who nurtured dreams of a restored Russian empire achieved through an unholy alliance between Communists feeding on a cult of Soviet nostalgia and the nationalist nutters whom freedom had allowed out of the woodwork.

And the silos were still out there, somewhere. As the Boeing 757 banked for its final approach, Burke scanned the great expanse of trees, looking for another explanation for every fire-break line, examining the circles that purported to be a sewage plant, wondering about the nondescript blocks of flats clustered within dark

137

clumps of trees with only one access road. Secret installations? Or just bad planning? And between and beyond them all the little wooden houses, with their peeling paintwork, the age-old *izbas*, often without running water but always – thanks to Lenin's diktat – with electric light: village houses that still marked the ancient pattern of rural Russian life.

Sabine tightened her grip on the armrest. He noticed that she had her eyes closed.

'Don't laugh,' she said. 'You didn't spend your early years flying on Tupolevs.'

Then the wheels touched down. Welcome home to the nightmare, Burke thought. Moscow was the city he loved and loathed more than any on earth. He hoped the journey would be worth it. On the face of things, Valery Korkin had done them proud.

Since the end of Communism, Sheremetyevo had undergone a facelift, chiefly at the hands of the Irish, who now ran most of the duty-free establishments that sold caviar and Kremlin T-shirts (made in Co. Cork) to departing tourists, and camcorders and ghetto-blasters to returning natives. Their symbol was a shamrock superimposed on the Kremlin's Spassky tower. It made Burke laugh. The last great joke of the imperial age: the Irish colonization of Moscow.

The passport officials were the same as ever: spotty nineteen-year-olds in goblin-green uniforms that had once nominally marked them out as members of the KGB. The old stencilled sign on the wall was still there, Burke noticed as he and Sabine waited at passport control, the one that read: 'Please wait until emigration is free', and used to provoke the remark among resident foreigners that hell would freeze over first.

But it was the smell that reminded him most vividly of where he was: the smell of warm, wet dog. He had first remarked on it ten years ago to Valery Korkin.

'Ye-ess, maybe,' the Russian had mused in his thick guttural English. 'After all, it is only natural. My hat' – Burke recalled him gesturing to the admirable, brown-furred creation that never left his head between the beginning of November and the end of March – 'it is, of course, dog. Very good hat. Warm. And waterproof.'

Burke had gagged, but Valery had continued to defend the virtues of his headgear.

'Much better than cat . . . And you, Mr Burke, why do worry about dog when you have dead rabbit on your head?' Russians, Valery rattled on, were simply more practical about animals. This was a cold country. Fake furs were useless.

The smell, Burke had come to realize, was not just because everyone wore dead dogs on their heads. The smell was poverty in a cold climate: people wrapped up tight in old clothes, a scarcity of soap, an ignorance of underarm deodorants and a staunch belief that chewing raw garlic kept germs at bay. It was how most of Europe, Burke rationalized, had probably once smelled.

Then, finally, he and Sabine were struggling towards the airport exit. The crowd was everywhere. Pushing, jostling, touting. Men with dead dogs on their heads and what looked like dead mice along their upper lips. Swarthy faces, pale faces, eager, entreating faces, threatening faces. Only, as ever, no smiling faces. No wonder, he thought, he hated the place.

'Eamonn, here.'

Kotzke was behind him, fighting off attempts – insistently helpful – to wrest her suitcase from her grasp. One particularly persistent middle-aged man with gold teeth had hold of the handle. Burke thought he looked like a Georgian, or possibly a Chechen. He was urging her in execrable American-accented English to make use of his 'leemooseen' service.

Burke turned to help her, but Kotzke hissed something at the man in fast, fluent Russian and he withdrew rapidly.

Burke was impressed. 'What on earth did you say to him?'

'I told him he was a piece of Caucasian pigshit and could go fuck his mother. They taught us something, you know, in the Young Pioneers.'

Burke followed her, laughing, into what passed for fresh air.

'*Yamon, Yamon!*' Burke recognized the familiar distortion of his name. Within a second he was smothering in the powerful bear hug of the only Russian he could genuinely, unequivocally, state that he loved. The man to whom he owed his life.

'Enough Valery, for God's sake, you'll asphyxiate me.'

'How are you, skinny bastard as ever, while your uncle Valery fattens like pig at Easter. See I am an example of Russia's economic miracle. Everyone is returning. Even God has come back, you know, at least there are enough of his bloody priests.' Valery poured out a torrent of loud, hearty laughter.

'Come. We must go. Later we have some vodka, and you tell me all about how is London now, how the West is finally crumbling and then we find some nice whores to fuck. You have lots of dollars I hope. Christ, the price of everything is rising these days.'

'Wait a minute, you ox, let me introduce you to my friend.'

Kotzke was standing by her suitcase. 'Please, gentlemen. I would hate to disturb your plans for the evening.'

Burke would have said Valery Korkin was immune to embarrassment – but not now. Eventually the Russian stammered into speech. 'You must be Yamon's friend. He has told me he was not coming alone. I am such a pig, please forgive me. I was just making men's jokes of course. I had simply not expected a . . . a . . .'

'A woman, perhaps.' Kotzke flashed the big eyes. 'Now if you'll tell us where the car is,' she began, lifting her bags in anticipation.

'But please, allow me.' Korkin made to take them.

'That's quite okay. We girls can manage our own things. She turned to Burke as if for confirmation. '*Oder nicht, Herr Burke?*'

Korkin started back abruptly, then smiled again – a touch too deliberately, Burke thought – and gestured towards where a line of unwashed, snow- and slush-covered cars stood behind a high iron fence.

'So the beautiful young lady is really a beautiful *Fräulein*.' (Burke winced at the word, let alone Valery's pronunciation as Froleen.) 'We have much respect for our new friends from Germany,' he said, offering his hand formally.

Kotzke shook it and set off towards the car-park, turning her head only briefly towards Burke. 'Well, let's go. Business, remember?'

'Nice girl, Yamon,' Korkin nodded, eyeing Sabine's calf muscles appreciatively. 'German, huh? Very nice.'

Burke pretended not to notice him spit in the snow.

The drive from the airport to the Radisson Hotel took nearly an hour. The three of them sat in the back of Korkin's smart new Mercedes estate, driven by Slava, a shrewd-looking young man whom Korkin introduced as his bodyguard.

'Everybody in business nowadays has to have one. Slava is a good boy. Former spetsnaz,' he confided to Burke in a loud stage-whisper. 'Can kill a man with his bare hands. Very useful in the queue for cabbages, ha ha ha.' Burke noticed Slava smiled too. He obviously knew his boss's jokes.

'Also he is a good driver. Very fond of German cars. Speaks English too, and German. Such talent.' Slava nodded in polite acknowledgment of his employer's praises. In the rearview mirror, Burke could see his bright blue eyes. He looked, he thought, like one of those blond-haired, idealized portraits of 'Soviet Man' that used to adorn gable wall ends during the Communist regime: the model worker.

Moscow's traffic was as slow and dirty as he remembered it, except that now the jam of old Ladas, clapped-out buses and rusty lorries had been augmented by a sprinkling of Western cars. Mercedes, Volkswagen and BMW were the most numerous, well-maintained, obviously status symbols. Clearly the old feelings about the Germans no longer applied to the motor industry.

'You see, Yamon,' Korkin bellowed as the car bounced in and out of potholes, 'now we have lots of your smart cars in the new Russia. Most are stolen, of course. The Poles bring them in. Park a nice car in Warsaw for ten minutes these days and they say it is already on the road to Moscow with a nice new Polish number plate and a man in the passenger seat rewriting the import documents. Very efficient. I wonder why they were not when they were under socialism? You see, we have understood the basics of this entrepreneurialism – that is the right word, I think – very fast. Perhaps I should take a Polish business course. Then Slava can have a nice new car, every year. A German car, even.' He roared with laughter at the prospect.

If Sabine was listening she gave no sign, just stared out of the window at the country that had dominated her youth, as if she were sizing it up for occupation. There you go, thought Burke. When it came down to it, the Germans and Russians deserved one another.

Valery Korkin lay stretched out on the double bed in Burke's room in the Radisson, a soulless box decorated in bland international 'executive' style. Without the presence of the two Russians, Burke thought, it could have been anywhere in the world, from Manchester to Michigan. Korkin, however, gave it context. With his best Moscow manners, he had at least taken off his slush-soaked felt boots. A fine steam was rising from the socks of indeterminate colour that rested on the end of Burke's bed. Sabine had gone to her own room – the fact that she had requested one as a matter of course eliciting a nudge in Burke's kidneys from the big Russian – to shower and change, having agreed to meet them downstairs in the bar in forty minutes.

Korkin's young driver stood by the door of Burke's room, impressively rigid. Burke himself sat on the edge of the other double bed – sometimes he wondered what international hotel chain managers thought went on in their rooms – wishing the kid would sit down or something. He made him nervous, as if he was expecting an armed intrusion at any minute. Maybe he was. Korkin noticed his discomfort and said, 'Ha. Don't worry about Slava. It is just his manner. He is a good boy, well-trained, even if he daydreams a little.'

Slava, aware that he was being talked about, gave Burke a thin-lipped smile.

'So, how are you, my old friend? As slow as ever to offer drinks to your old comrades, I see.'

'Sorry. Wasn't thinking.' Burke opened the minibar.

'The usual?' he asked rhetorically, reaching for a miniature of vodka.

'You think Moscow's new sophistication has made a Campari-drinker of me, perhaps? Smirnoff, please. Anyway, Stolichnaya has a Soviet after-taste, though Slava here would not agree, would you, boy?'

Burke threw the miniature to Korkin, took one himself and looked at the driver, who was standing impassively by the door.

'Slava does not drink. At least not on duty. *Na zdorovye.* Your very good health.'

'And yours.'

Korkin unscrewed the bottle cap, clenched the neck in his teeth, then threw his head back to swallow the contents in one. Burke copied him. It was an old chums' ritual. Even so, he nearly choked as the fiery spirit dashed down his gullet. Korkin roared with laughter, Burke joined him. The Russian held out his hand for another. Burke threw it to him and took a second himself. 'So, how easy was it to find him?'

'Like looking for a pig in a shit house. If you think about it, you know where they are. Slava was very useful. He still has many contacts in the "service" and among the remnants of the old regime. There are some very bitter men out there, but even bitter men have to eat. There is nothing in Russia today that does not have a price. Information is just another commodity. But you must tell us what you want it for. You have been most unspecific, Yamon.'

Burke sighed. He could sense the concentration fixed upon him.

Even Slava seemed to have dropped his mask of professional impassivity.

'It's complicated, Valery. In fact, I'm not wholly sure I understand it. But maybe I can tell you more when I fix up a time to see Yakovlev himself.'

It was a poor answer, Burke knew. Slava looked at him suspiciously. But Korkin waved it away.

'Of course, it is not my business. You must arrange your meeting with him . . . except . . . that it is not him.'

'What? Valery. Don't do this to me.'

'I am sorry. That's life, or perhaps, in this case, the opposite.'

'But you said you'd found him.'

'I said one thing. You understood another. But do not despair, my friend.'

Korkin was lying back again, the tiny, half-empty vodka bottle held to his lower lip. Burke had the curious impression he was enjoying this.

'Valery has done what he can for you. For a start there never was any such person as your comrade Yakovlev.'

Burke had had this sort of conversation with Valery before. The only option was to let the man get on with it at his own pace, and feed him the link words when necessary.

'What do you mean?'

'It was a false name. Not a very good one, I have to say, not so very different from his own.'

'Which was?'

'Yatzkov.'

'And he is where now?'

'Kuntsovo cemetery, not far from your Kim Philby. He died in 1993. Funny, eh? He lived just long enough to see everything he'd worked for collapse in ruins.'

'Hilarious.'

'Believe me, if you were Russian, you'd laugh.'

'Where does this leave us?'

'Maybe in a good place. It depends on what you are looking for, not who.'

'It's a complicated story. I'll explain as we go along. But first I have to know if we're going anywhere at all.'

'Okay, okay. Anyhow, this is how I think: I know you. I think: always he wants the man at the top. So I do some digging. Yatzkov is dead. But even Yatzkov was only a small rat in a big maze. Who is the bigger rat. Once this was impossible to know. Today it is not so hard. Two bottles of Johnnie Walker for bribes and a spare wheel for a Mercedes – do not worry, it is on your bill.'

'My colleague's bill.'

'Really?' The Russian's eyes opened wider. 'I should have made it four wheels and an engine.'

'And the result?'

'Yatzkov's wartime controller at the KGB was a man called Yakunin.'

'Bloody hell,' interrupted Burke. 'Does everyone have to have a name that begins with "Ya"?'

'Including yourself, Yamon. But you should listen now. He was a big chief very young. Then something went wrong. Around 1948 – before the Soviet bomb. He got posted to Novocherkassk. In the Caucasus. Cherkassians, Chechens, old Cossacks. Not very nice for Russians, especially good party men. But maybe for him it was a blessing. Not to be in Moscow in the fifties, during the show trials, the purges. He survived.'

'And came back?'

'At the end of the Khrushchev era. Somebody must have felt sorry for him. Anyhow, he was pensioned off early enough to get one of the old *nomenklatura* apartments. Not high-ranking enough to get a good one, mind. Out in the fucking sticks, in the south-west of the city: Yugozapadnaya metro.' The Russian picked something sinewy from between his teeth, examined it and discarded it on the carpet.

Burke made a mental note to avoid that part of the floor, especially in socks.

'Slava here did most of the legwork, identifying the man we needed. Once we had his name, it was easy. I gave one of the girls in the records department on Smolensk Square a cock and bullock story about being Comrade Yakunin's lost cousin from Petropavlovsk-Kamchatsky. She opened the ministry address book and told me where he lived. In the old days I would have got a one-way ticket to one of the gulags just for asking.'

'Have you spoken to Yakunin himself?' Burke was apprehensive. Korkin never seemed able to draw a line between discretion and rudeness, or verbosity and offensiveness, for that matter.

'Please, Yamon. I am the soul of the secrecy. And I know these old birds. What he is wanting is peace and quiet in his old age, but also money and – most of all, I think – the idea that it was not all a waste of time. I have told him you want to write a book about America's mistakes in the Cold War, about how mother Russia was always the champion of peace. You know a lot of them really believed it.'

'A lot of our lot believed what they were told, too.'

'But tell me: why do we want to see him? If I am to be of help to you, then I must know what it is about.'

Burke considered the logic. He knew Sabine would hate letting anyone else in on her precious story. But he could see no harm in it. Korkin's money-making schemes did not extend into the media business, and Slava, despite his eagle eyes, did not exactly look like a cub reporter. As best as he could, he went through the tale that Sabine had told him, and the gobbets of information and inference he had put together from his trips to Harwell and Hiram Carter. Korkin sat spellbound. Slava picked his nose and looked distracted.

At the end the big Russian stood up and shook his head. 'So you think Yakunin may know something that this Fuchs wanted to tell the world. And the Stasi scum killed him to keep it secret?'

'Maybe. The Stasi are clearly the prime suspects. But they would have been acting on the orders of the KGB. East Germany was where Fuchs ended up, but Russia – the Soviet Union – was the country he worked for.'

'I have heard of him.'

Both Korkin and Burke turned. Up until then Slava had not even seemed to be following the conversation.

'There was a film, in the Gorbachev days. It said he was a great scientist who helped the motherland's defences. Not that we needed help from foreigners then.'

'Of course not.' Burke raised his eyebrows. 'But this isn't the only country with secrets. I have a suspicion that "our" side – the West – had something to hide too. Fuchs got a relatively light prison sentence, then disappeared behind the Iron Curtain, never to emerge. If someone wanted to keep him sweet, but out of the range of Western reporters, then they managed it very well. Right up to the end.'

'And now maybe our man will tell all. How about that, eh, Slava? Russia is the home of glasnost. Perhaps now we give lessons in openness to the British and the Yankees. Yamon, my friend, you have a brain like a bolshevik, always plotting.'

'Perhaps.' Burke smiled. 'Anything's possible. So when do we meet this Yakunin?'

'I said you would telephone this evening. I think he'll see us tomorrow. I'll come and show you. Otherwise you'll get lost. All look the fucking same, those blocks. Fucking Soviet architecture. Fucking shit country, you know. Still is.'

'Good work, Valery. You're not such a bad bastard after all. I don't know what I'd do without you.'

'You'd pay some stupid tart decent money. Still I suppose you'd get your cock sucked. Even I won't do that. How about Brunnhilde?'

Burke narrowed his eyes, raised a finger and pointed it straight at the Russian. 'Strictly business, old chum.'

'Of course, Yamon baby. I am disgusted for even having mentioned it.' Then the great crevasse that passed for a mouth cracked open and he laughed long and loud. 'Perhaps she likes it up the arse instead.'

'Christ, you are something else, comrade, come on, let's go and get pissed.'

'Not comrade, please.' For a moment the Russian looked serious, then broke into his customary grin. 'But you must make your telephone call. Then we can play find the lady?'

The telephone rang eight times before it was answered, each ring a long solid burr followed by a silence that Burke had always believed was the old Soviet communications system's attempt to encourage every caller to give up in advance. Then he heard the standard Soviet-style telephone greeting: 'Allyo?' It was aggressive, questioning, gave nothing away, not even a name or number, until the caller identified himself. Burke knew the rules; he addressed the man formally by his first name and patronymic, trying his best in limited Russian:

'*Anatoly Nikolayevich, eto Eammon Burke vas bespokoyit. Moi drug uzhé pozvonil vam.*' This is Eammon Burke troubling you. My friend has already called you. Again, no name. Again, no reason, Burke thought, for this sort of obliqueness on the telephone, not nowadays when there was – surely? – no risk of anyone listening in. But old habits died hard. That was what really constituted Moscow rules.

'*Hmmm, da, da, da.*' It was an old man's voice, tired, soft, the instinctive aggression suddenly gone. 'I guess you'd prefer if we spoke English?' The man's English was good, with an American accent, the sort learned from listening with impunity to 'Voice of America'.

'Your English is certainly very much better than my Russian, Dr Yakunin.'

'Hm, maybe. I haven't used it a whole lot over the past years. Now maybe you're gonna tell me just what it is you want us to talk about. Your Muscovite friend wasn't very helpful.'

'I think he mentioned that I was writing a book.'

'Yes, yes, but there are many types of books these days, even in Russia.' Burke thought he detected a wry chuckle. 'I need more information before I know if there is anything I can tell you. I am an old man, you know. My memory is not what it was. I would hate you guys to come all the way out here for no reason.'

Burke smiled at the vernacular, but was worried by the tone. It would be all or nothing, he realized. With an inward sigh, he took the plunge:

'It concerns the late Dr Klaus Fuchs. I believe you knew him?'

There was silence on the other end of the line. It was as if the very name of Fuchs was enough to strike dumb anyone who had ever come into contact with him. Burke pressed on, terrified that the other man was about to hang up.

'We have found some papers. They contain some very interesting material.'

Again nothing.

'We – I – thought you might like to see them. It may be nothing.' He was in danger of gabbling now, he realized. 'But they might jog your memory.' For Christ's sake, don't insult the man, and don't make him feel you want something out of him he doesn't want to give. 'I'm sure we could reach some arrangement.' Hint at money. Don't be forthright. You don't know how much Sabine's lot are willing to fork out, anyhow. You don't even know what this old bird could tell us. But by God, he's not volunteering anything.

'Dr Yakunin?' Burke waited.

'Yes. I see. Hmmm . . .'

Another silence. Then:

'I'm not sure I can help you. I'm afraid I had no direct contact with Herr Dr Fuchs. It was all a very long time ago.'

Again, a long pause, and a sigh. 'Is there anything . . . in particular . . . that you need me to comment on?'

It was the question, Burke thought, of a man who knew the answer. There was no point in holding back.

'I think so, Dr Yakunin. Dr Fuchs kept a diary. We have it. I'm

147

sure you know there was an important matter that was never disclosed. We think it is time the world knew the truth. We think you can help. The old days are behind us now. We mustn't allow any more mistakes.' He just hoped the old boy didn't think it sounded too corny. He also hoped it wasn't obvious how little they really did know.

There was another sigh, resigned this time.

'I thought it might be that. A diary, you say. A brave man, our Fuchs. And perhaps a foolish one. Perhaps you are right. I don't suppose I can do anything about it, anyway. But if you have all that, why do you need to speak to me?'

Shit. Don't blow it, Burke told himself.

'I like to do my research, Dr. There are some things I would like to check. If we are going to tell the truth at last, we ought to make sure it is accurate, don't you think?' Korkin nodded sagely, obviously approving of this appeal to higher moral values.

The voice on the end of the line had mellowed. 'Yes, I guess so. Come and see me then, tomorrow. Will your Muscovite friend be with you?'

Burke glanced up at Korkin, who shook his head vigorously.

'No, but I have a companion who is working as my research assistant,' he hastily improvised. 'A young woman. A German.'

'Ah, yes. A German. There would be. There is always a German. Very well. I live at Yugozapadnaya, south-east Moscow. I am not far from the cinema. It used to be called the Hanoi. Now, I think they have changed it. The street number is 212, not that it means very much, fourth block at that number, third staircase. Flat number 114, on the eleventh floor. I hope the lift is working. You should come about 11.00. You will excuse me if I do not offer you lunch. I live a very simple existence.'

'Certainly, Dr. And thank you very much. *Do zavtra*. Until tomorrow.'

'*Do zavtra*.'

Burke looked at Korkin and let out a sigh of relief.

'Bloody hell, Valery. I think we might have cracked it. Whatever old Fuchs-face was hiding, I think your man will spill the beans.'

'That is if he has any beans. This is still a very poor country, you know.' He roared at his own joke.

As they left the room, heading for the bar and Sabine, Slava closed the door behind them. Burke noticed he was not laughing.

*   *   *

148

Anatoly Nikolayevich Yakunin's hand shook slightly as he replaced the receiver. He crossed to the massive writing bureau that stood against the opposite wall. It was a fine piece of furniture, the sort of bureau that some nineteenth-century aristocrat would have sat at to write orders to his serfs. Its mahogany bulk was a pre-revolutionary anachronism in this typically compact example of the proletarian state's housing accommodation.

Yakunin unfolded the bureau's writing surface, its worn leather veneer scratched and scuffed with decades of use. He pressed lightly on a small section of the marquetry inlay and it sprang back to reveal a tiny keyhole. Fumbling in the pocket of his baggy trousers, he produced an old iron key ring and inserted the smallest of several keys into the lock. A panel about six inches long and three inches deep (where no doubt some nobleman once kept his mistress's jewels) clicked quietly open. Yakunin reached in and took out a package in cheap, Soviet-era brown wrapping-paper.

What it contained was not as valuable, perhaps, as diamonds or pearls. But infinitely more seductive. And a lot more dangerous to own. Now they were coming for it. As he had always known they would.

21

Fall from Grace

Snow was falling gently in thick heavy flakes as Valery Korkin's white Mercedes crossed the Great Stone Bridge over the Moska River, past the gates of Gorky Park and through the underpasses that allowed a left turn on to Lenin Prospect. Burke noted with wry amusement that that name had not been changed.

They had been delayed because Slava, uncharacteristically, had been late in arriving at the little office in Neglinnaya Street. Burke had suggested they drive themselves, but Korkin had been reluctant. Burke wondered if he was becoming used to the status of having his own driver, or if he really did think a bodyguard was essential in modern Moscow. 'He's a good lad, really. Has some dodgy friends, of course, a bit too far on the right wing for my liking. But then who isn't dodgy in this place nowadays?'

Burke noted that his enthusiasm for Slava's abilities did not prevent him giving the young man a serious dressing-down. As a consequence, Korkin was in an ill-tempered hurry.

'Fucking peasants,' he exclaimed as a couple of likely lads in woollen hats, one sporting an Adidas logo, approached the Mercedes at traffic lights, offering to clean the windscreen. Slava put his foot on the accelerator. Magically the light went green.

They crawled through Gagarin Square, with its soaring monument to the drunk hotshot MiG pilot who'd attained immortality for being stuck on top of a huge and unreliable Roman candle and managing to come back alive. It was one of the few pieces of Soviet monumental architecture that Burke could stand. At least it alleviated the unremitting gloom of the monolithic flat blocks stretching endlessly on either side. Frankfurter Allee in East Berlin had been modelled on this, he recalled, when it was rebuilt after the war and called Stalin Allee. The Stasi's headquarters had been just up a side street. Normannenstrasse. Funny that he should be reminded of the Stasi now, and their role in the fate of the late Dr Fuchs. Old shadows lingered long.

Kotzke leaned forward and unexpectedly ran a finger down behind his left ear, sending an electric tingle down his spine.

'Mmmm, I had no idea you were so sensitive. So, have you decided how to play our veteran masterspy?'

'I think all we can do is string him along, hope he actually wants to talk. Sometimes with these people, once they've made the psychological commitment to open up, it just pours out. Then again, he may decide to play difficult with us. See how much we really know. It would be better, of course, if we actually had some sort of clue to what we are looking for. Are you sure you've told me all you know?'

Kotzke sat back in her seat. 'Well, I guess I'll leave it to you and just watch. It'll be interesting to see a master interviewer at work.'

The car lurched suddenly to the left. '*Nakhui! Chort vozmi!*' Slava uttered a series of obscenities. Burke looked back to see a dumpy form sprawled at the roadside, gesturing angrily at them.

'Hey, wait. Shouldn't we see if she's hurt?' Sabine was genuinely shocked.

'This is Russian babushka,' Slava replied. 'Hard as old boots. Anyway she was drunk, almost falls in front of me. I did not hit her. Stop and we will have a policeman. And because you are foreigners he will look for dollars, a present, you understand. Russia has become more corrupt than ever. There is no law and order any more.'

Burke looked at Korkin, who just shrugged. 'I am afraid he is right. In fact, it is worse. If we had been stopped, they might have threatened Slava with a blood test, for the drink-driving, with an old needle used on Aids victims. We would have to pay to be excused. This is how they make their money.'

But Burke noticed the big man angle the wing mirror on the passenger's side to enable him to see the woman stagger back to her feet. Corruption might be alive and well, but compassion was not yet totally dead in Russia.

Soon Burke spotted the cinema Yakunin had told them to look for. He was wrong in one thing. It was still called Hanoi. Burke looked at the street numbers on the lamp posts: 200–220. They were on the right block. Slava in any case clearly knew the area. He pulled off into a parking area full of battered Zhigulis and rusty Moskviches. A single Mercedes, its roof carefully covered with tarpaulin against the ravages of the Moscow winter, testified to the new times. Clearly the fortunes of the inhabitants of this corner of Yugozapadnaya were mixed.

'Park here and stay by the car,' Korkin told Slava. 'Don't want any of these bastards pinching my wing-mirror for their handbags.'

Burke realized what was going on before either of his companions. He recognized the attributes: the clump of clucking babushkas, arms folded beneath ample bosoms, in flowery headscarves, faces like Mongolian yak-herders in a blizzard, heads shaking sombrely in reflection on mortality and its minimal blessings; the young policeman in grey uniform, his fake fur hat still bearing, *faute de mieux*, the redundant hammer and sickle symbols of authority of a dismantled state, spotty, cold, his breath condensing in clouds as he asked the few questions needed to jot down details of another demise in this sad excuse for suburbia; and on the fringes of the crowd the flowering saplings of post-Soviet manhood, a few stubble-chinned, pasty-faced youths in dog hats, blue jeans and worn sneakers, keeping the cold at bay with swigs from a half-empty vodka bottle – Smirnoff, he noted. Even here the new order held sway.

The youths stood back as they approached. The big Russian strode forwards to question the least intimidating-looking old lady. She gestured with an arm so thickly padded it barely protruded from her dumpy body. Burke looked round to find himself alone. Sabine had retreated to the edge of the car park. She clutched at the lapels of her coat, apparently to keep out the cold, but her face was blank, eyes staring into the middle distance. She looked as if she were hugging herself. As he watched the crowd, he suddenly began to feel that what was holding back the German girl was a sense of premonition.

He had witnessed the scene before. Taking Kotzke by the arm, he hurried her to the edge of the little crowd that had gathered for no obvious reason. Korkin followed, puzzled. They stopped dead when they saw the body lying in the soiled snow. The man's torso seemed unnaturally long and he appeared to have no head. Then Burke understood why. A sweater had been pulled up over his head, almost as if he had been in the act of taking it off.

Korkin was questioning an old woman. White, visibly shaken,

Sabine whispered an impromptu translation into Burke's ear. 'Fell, didn't he? Jumped maybe. Can't blame him. Not much to live for around here, is there?' The babushka crossed herself, right to left in the orthodox manner, to excuse the blasphemy of condoning suicide.

Burke looked up at the grubby concrete walls towering above them, then down again at the blood seeping into the snow. Involuntarily, he found himself counting the floors upwards to eleven.

Korkin read Burke's mind and asked the babushka who it was. The answer relayed to Burke was brusque: 'An academic. Or something. Some old fellow. Ask her.' She pointed out a particularly bulky woman who appeared to be telling a young policeman what to write in his notebook.

The policeman turned away and spoke into his crackling radio. Korkin approached the woman who had been so authoritatively dictating to him. 'Yakunin?'

'Da, da. That's him.'

She was merely confirming what Burke had known from the moment they saw the crowd: the man spreadeagled on the ice in front of him was the man they had come to visit, the man they had hoped would take them one step further on their trail into the labyrinth. Instead he was dead. It was one hell of a coincidence. Eamonn Burke didn't like it. Not one bit.

He looked back towards the little crowd, thinning now. Two more policemen had arrived and they were covering the body with a dirty sheet. Burke was suddenly struck by the meanness of it all. No doubt Yakunin had been just another Party functionary, just another little shit in his day. Now he was just another wasted life.

Korkin came towards them, shaking his head. He too was clearly shocked. He ushered them back to the car. Burke felt his anger give way to logic. His mind started racing. Slava looked at them quizzically as they climbed in.

'Dead,' Korkin told him. 'The old man's dead.' Slava asked no questions. 'Drive. Just drive.'

He started up the engine and pulled the Mercedes out of the parking lot. Korkin turned around in his seat. 'They say it happened just after ten this morning, so we can't blame Slava for being late.'

'He would already have been dead even if we'd got here on time.'

'But why?' asked Burke, of no one in particular.

'I thought you might know that.'

'It's almost as if it was planned for us to see him like that,' said Sabine.

'Like a warning,' said Burke.

'You think it was because of you this happened?' asked Korkin.

'Don't you?'

The Russian pursed his lips.

'I mean,' Burke went on, 'it's hardly a coincidence, is it? And if the thought of seeing us was enough to scare him into suicide, why did he agree in the first place. And did it look like suicide to you?' The question was loaded.

'No. It looked familiar.'

'What?' Sabine interjected. 'What do you mean, familiar?'

'Tell her the story,' Burke said.

'This business with the sweater. It brings back bad memories.'

'I don't understand.'

'It was a long time ago. In Afghanistan, where I first met Yamon here. I was in the army. Drafted, of course. We all were. In Kabul. One of our young kids. A pretty boy, from Novocherkassk. Some Chechen blood in him I think. He got drunk one night and started talking about going home. About the war being wrong. About it not being our business. One or two of the older men tried to shut him up. There was a political officer there, a lieutenant from Rostov. He told them to be quiet, said it was not the party line to stifle discussion. The young man should be encouraged to speak his mind so he could be convinced of the error of his attitude. The kid really warmed to that, said he had been worried about getting put in the brig for speaking out, said he was only saying what all the men thought anyway. There was grumbling at that, and a lot of sighing among the old lags. But the political smiled at him, said we would continue the conversation the next day, when we were all fresher, had had a chance to sleep on it. He made it clear he was bringing the camp-fire chat to an end.

'The next morning the kid was found dead in the street. Thrown himself off the roof of the barracks apparently. Pulled his tunic up over his head first. The political officer said what a pity it was, he must have been so ashamed of letting the motherland down. Sent him home to his mum in a box with a medal on it. Good for morale, he said. Pah. Stinks it does. And still this country stinks.'

In the driving seat, Slava wound down his window and spat into the road.

22

Pass the Parcel

Burke had been watching Slava's eyes in the rearview mirror when he first noticed the little red Zhiguli. Now he was certain: they were being followed. What puzzled him was the incompetence of the person doing it.

As they had turned the corner on to Lenin Prospect, heading back into town, the little car had suddenly put on a burst of speed to get through the lights behind them, then had equally suddenly slowed down. His first instinct had been to dismiss it as typically bad Muscovite driving, or maybe even the eccentricities of an erratic 'Zhig' gearbox. But even when the Mercedes pulled up early at a traffic light about to turn red, the car behind had not drawn level. If it really was a tail, it was a laughably amateurish one.

'Valery,' he said in as matter-of-fact a voice as possible. 'Don't look now. We're being followed.'

Korkin fiddled with the wing mirror so that he could see the road behind.

'The red car?'

'Obviously, I think.'

Korkin snorted. 'What do you want to do about it? We can lose him. Easily.'

'Maybe it would be a better idea if we could find out who it is that's so interested in us. And what they know about a suspected murder.'

'My thoughts exactly.' Korkin barked a quick set of instructions to Slava.

Instead of going straight on, the Mercedes took a sharp right and then a left along the embankment. Sure enough, within minutes the little red car was there again. Whoever was following would have to be very stupid to continue much longer without getting the idea that they had been spotted, Burke thought. And that was not what he wanted. Suddenly Slava swung the wheel to the right and the car turned on to the forecourt of what Burke remembered from years ago as State Petrol Station number 76, tucked out of the way, a good place to get diesel when everyone else had run out. Now it was run by the Italian firm Agip, but it was still on a road to nowhere.

Slava stopped the car short of the pumps and let Korkin out, then drove on a few metres as if to refuel. Burke watched as the Russian darted out of the car with a nimbleness that belied his size and made for the well-lit office. Instead of going in, he disappeared into the undergrowth beyond the air and water machine. Within less than a minute the red Zhiguli approached the forecourt uncertainly. I don't know who taught you your tradecraft, Burke thought, but it sure as hell wasn't the boys from the Lubyanka. Slava's eyes were equally scornful.

The car pulled off the main road, and over towards the air machine. Burke watched as Korkin emerged from the bushes to the rear of the Zhiguli, walked briskly up to the driver's door and tapped on the window, holding out a cigarette as if looking for a light. The windscreen wound down about six inches, just enough for the big man to thrust in a hand and grab a fistful of ear.

Instead of the stream of macho obscenities Burke had expected, there was a loud, unmistakably female wail. Burke was familiar with Korkin's tactic; he had seen muggers practice it. The idea was to get the other hand on the occupant's neck before any weapon could be produced. On this occasion Valery let go in shock. Burke ran to the opposite side of the little Zhiguli and, bending down, found himself staring into the tear-streaked, panic-ridden face of a woman aged about fifty.

Korkin pulled open the door, put his hand on the wheel – she instantly withdrew hers – and ordered her out. As the trembling woman stepped from the car, Burke saw she was younger than he had thought, in her late forties perhaps. She was wearing a dowdy, calf-length coat with a stitched-on astrakhan collar that had obviously been handed-down. Shabby-genteel, or what passed for it, in Moscow. Burke could see she was about to scream again. Korkin yelled at her and she fell silent, looking now as if she were about to burst into tears.

Instead she began to gabble rapidly in Russian. Korkin bundled her into the Mercedes beside a stunned-looking Sabine Kotzke. He gestured for Eamonn to get into the front. He himself remained outside, leaning through the wound-down window like a spectator at a Punch and Judy show.

'I would complete the necessary introductions,' he said, 'but I am afraid I lack some of the necessary information. Madame here has been following us. She says she needs to talk with our beautiful German.'

The woman looked lined and drawn by decades of struggling with shortages and repression under the Communists, and too set in her ways to cope with the wolf-pack mentality of embryonic capitalism. The sort of woman who formed the backbone of most Western societies, thought Burke, the sort Russia relentlessly eroded.

'Excuse me,' she began. 'You understand Russian?'

Sabine nodded.

'You are the friend of Anatoly Nikolayevich?'

'He was expecting us.'

Burke noted the sidestepping of the question.

'I am Anna Matveyevna Sukhova. I live – lived – opposite Dr Yakunin.'

Sabine nodded again, willing the woman to continue.

Burke followed the conversation as best he could with his limited Russian. Afterwards he had Sabine piece it together for him.

'It was about ten o'clock last night. I was going to bed. There was a knock at the door and it was Anatoly Nikolayevich. I was not so surprised to see him. Sometimes he will come around like that, in the evening, to ask for something. He lives – lived – on his own. He was always forgetting things. Things are still not so easy, you know, in Russia. There is everything there but who can afford it? I would lend him some tea, or perhaps a little bread. He was forgetful, he said, not very good at housekeeping since his wife died. Sometimes he would come in, just for a few minutes. For politeness' sake, I always thought. But this time, his mood was different. He seemed proccupied. Vague. As if there was something on his mind. That's when he produced the package.'

'What package?'

'This.' Burke watched her delve into the folds of her coat and produce a small paper parcel tied with string. She looked down at it in her hands, fingering it, as if it contained some last essence of Yakunin. Burke wondered if their friendship had gone beyond late-night cups of sweet tea in that bleak high-rise.

'He said he was expecting someone to call tomorrow – that is, today – and that this was for her. A woman, he said. I thought it might be a daughter; he once mentioned a girl a long time ago, but she never came. His son never visited him either. But he said she was German.'

Kotzke was watching Sukhova with what seemed to Burke a remarkably detached enthusiasm.

'But why did he give it to you?' she asked.

'That's just it. I do not know.' She was fighting back tears. 'He simply said I should keep it in case he missed her. I asked how could he miss her? Was he going out? He just shrugged and said, "These things happen. Probably there is no need, I will call about eleven and collect it from you." Then he went back to his apartment. That was the last time I saw him . . . alive.'

Sabine's hands were almost trembling at the prospect of getting hold of the shabby parcel. Sukhova was watching her with eyes that were now dry and red and searching. This woman had lost some-one. She wanted to know why. So did Burke. But if she thought she would find the solution here, she was surely mistaken.

Sabine was pressing the woman. 'What else did he say? Did he seem depressed?'

'No, why should he? Apprehensive perhaps. He was clearly worried about something. About you.' She grunted. 'But depressed? No, I don't think so. Her tone changed and she looked Sabine straight in the eye.

'Young lady. I do not know who you are or what you wanted with Anatoly Nikolayevich. But I can tell you one thing. He did not kill himself. He was murdered.' She almost spat the words out. 'For you. For this.' She thrust the package towards Sabine.

'What about this?' Sabine's eagerness seemed almost indecent. 'Did he tell you what is in here?'

'No, nothing.' Sukhova's voice was suddenly brusque. 'I know only that whatever it is caused him to be murdered. Whatever mafia you belong to, you are all as bad as each other.'

With a choked sob, she threw open the car door, hurled herself out, knocking the big Russian leaning on the window off his balance, and ran across the forecourt to the Zhiguli.

'Korkin, get her back!' Kotzke screamed.

Burke looked from one to the other. Valery stood silent and still, watching as Anna Sukhova pulled open the door of her little car and its engine spluttered into life.

'Burke, for God's sake, why don't you do something?' She had opened her own door.

'Wait!' boomed the big Russian's deep voice. 'Leave her.'

'What the hell for?'

Burke put his hand on Sabine's arm. He sensed that Korkin was right. Anna Sukhova had delivered her package.

'You have what you wanted,' Korkin continued. 'It is what the old man died for. I hope it is worth it.'

'But we can't just let her vanish like this. We don't even know what's in here yet.'

'Nor does she.' Korkin paused, letting the phrase sink in. 'In any case, where do you think she has gone? This is Russia, you forget. A very big country, with nowhere to go.'

Burke opened the mini-bar and took out two miniatures of Smirnoff for himself and Korkin, and a bottle of Pilsner Urquell for Sabine. It was not exactly a celebration; all three needed a drink to steady their nerves. Only Slava seemed, as ever, unmoved.

When Anna Sukhova had disappeared into the Moscow traffic, Sabine's first reaction had been to open the little parcel there and then in the back seat. Burke had restrained her.

'Wait. We don't know what's in there. Five minutes won't make a difference.'

So instead she had sat, like a child nursing a present delivered ahead of her birthday, with the little brown paper package on her knee.

Now, she sat chastely on the end of Burke's bed and looked up at him.

'Well, do I have your permission?'

'By all means.'

She undid the string and unfolded the paper. Inside were two sealed envelopes and two maps. Burke picked up one of them and handed it to Korkin who spread it out on the second bed.

It was a relief map, obviously in some detail although in simple black and white only, with a few heights and topographical features marked. There was no coast-line and the whole central area appeared to be a blank white space.

'What do you make of it? Recognize anything?' Burke asked the Russian.

'It is obviously a Russian military map. Old. Maybe thirty, forty years. It is hard to tell. They were so paranoid. Nothing was dated.'

'But where is it?' Kotzke pressed. 'What's that big white blank area? Some sort of military restricted area?'

'No, no. It is a natural feature. I thought at first a lake, like the Aral Sea, with shifting shoreline. You see here, there are dotted lines. But I do not think so. I think it is ice, an ice cap perhaps, where the land underneath was uncertain before modern depth-sounding machines, like some of the Siberian islands perhaps. Yes, I am certain of it. Here, this abbreviation, is for ice. But I do not recognize any of the words. It is not Russian, though some words might be, like this river name, "hvita", or here, across the ice mass: "lanyukal". It doesn't mean anything to me. It might be some Inuit or Chukchi word from north Siberia, but the scale is too close-up to be sure what it refers to.'

Burke stared at the lines, clearly marking mountains and rivers, all with incomprehensible names written in Cyrillic. The second map was, by comparison, almost featureless: apparently a great flat expanse with a river running through it. But without points of reference or scale, or the slightest indication of geographical location, it was barely worth looking at.

Sabine was shaking the small envelope, which contained something round and hard. There was writing on it, typed, in Russian: '*Za prekrashcheniya voskhoda solntsa*,' Korkin read, translating, 'For the prevention of the sunrise. What do you make of that?'

Burke shrugged.

Sabine slit open the top and extracted a round medal, still shiny, with a bright red ribbon.

'I recognize this,' she said. 'So should you, comrade.'

Korkin grimaced at the bait, looked over, then gave a low whistle.

'The old bastard himself.'

Burke recognized the familiar profile, the domed head and jutting goatee beard of Vladimir Ilyich Lenin.

'Perhaps Comrade Yakunin was more important than we thought.'

'What is it?' asked Burke.

'Only the highest military decoration of the evil empire, Hero of the Soviet Union. The medal won by Marshal Zhukov for taking Berlin and Yuri Gagarin for conquering outerspace.'

'I wonder what he did to deserve it.'

'Or why he didn't wear it, at least the ribbon,' Korkin added. 'Even these days that medal still gets some show of respect. At the very least he could have sold it to a Western collector. Stalinist relics have adapted better than human beings to the free market.'

'My dearest darling Josh . . .'

Burke spun around. Sabine had opened the second envelope and was reading from wrinkled piece of paper. It looked like the first draft of a letter, in English, but littered with crossings-out and spelling mistakes, clearly not written by a native speaker. It was brief:

'. . . This is my only way to tell you the news I had hoped to show you in person. We have a son. He is beautiful. He looks like his father. He is well. Perhaps now it will be possible for you to see him. He would like that, I know, and so would I.'

The next line began with the words: 'But I will understand if you do not . . .' crossed out heavily, as if the writer had changed her mind about expressing any doubt.

'I embrace you,' Sabine continued reading. 'I know you will act for the best. For all of us. For the whole world. I long to see you soon. Your ever loving Natalya.'

'Well, what do you make of that?' Burke said.

'I make this.' Sabine pulled a stiffer sheet from the same envelope and looked at it. She held up a black and white photograph of a good-looking young man in his early twenties, with dark eyes and a quiff of swept-back black hair. There was a number beneath him, as if it were a file photograph of a convict. Except that this had been taken for military records. The young man was in uniform.

'It's an identification number of some sort,' said Sabine. 'Finch, J. 637290 USAF.'

'I thought I recognized the uniform,' said Burke. 'United bloody States Air Force. That's his dog-tag number.'

23

Cross References

'Mabel! Will you get that darn thing?' General (retired) Abe Steiner was in no mood to answer the telephone, least of all when it was likely to be one of his wife's golf partners aiming to fix a round that would end up in another of their sessions at the nineteenth hole of the Army and Navy Club's Arlington course, slugging back vodka martinis and spitting olive pips into the ashtrays, along with the shreds of their long-suffering husbands' reputations.

Truth to tell, Abe Steiner hated the mention of golf at any time these days. He had once been down to a par 6 handicap before bad braking on a wet night coming round Rocky Creek Parkway on his way home from the Pentagon had left him with two crushed feet. The worst of it was that it had been his own fault. The driver of the Mack truck was only doing 35mph when the general's ancient and much-loved Corvette had skidded across the centre of the road, and embedded itself as far as the driver's seat in the heavy machine's undercarriage. They had had to cut Steiner out. He had spent three weeks and a small fortune in US taxpayers' money at the military hospital in Arlington. He could now get himself to the bathroom and back with the help of a stick, but mainly he was confined to a wheelchair, albeit a motorized one that had cost the US taxpayer another few dozen paypackets. At times he thought he had single-handedly sunk Bill Clinton's plans for health service reforms.

'Maaay-bell!' he hollered again, and this time got a response.

'O-kayyyyy, A-bell,' as she always called him when he got her riled. 'Just you keep your wheels on the floor. I'm there already.'

At the age of sixty-three he had become a fast-track surfer on the information superhighway. His final paycheck and a substantial proportion of the army's generous early retirement package had gone into a state-of-the-art desktop system. The only reason there was no telephone on his desk was that almost all his communications were conducted by e-mail. He had Voicenet too, of course, and as many other plug-ins as Netscape had yet devised, as well as Microsoft's competing alternatives. He could use the computer for verbal communication, if necessary, and with an onscreen image too if both parties wanted (though occasionally, unknown to Mabel, he had used the entertaining one-way only facility with a few of the premier services available for discerning gentlemen). He saw little personal advantage in answering the telephone.

So it came as something of a surprise when Mabel, in a puce trouser-suit and a gold necklace that glinted with a sheen as metallic as her hair, put her head around his door and announced, 'It's for you, dear.'

Steiner reluctantly clicked the transfer button on the handset next to the anonymous white box that housed his new twelve-gigabyte hard drive, and lifted the receiver.

'Hello, Abe Steiner here. Who the hell is that?'

'General,' came the response, in measured English tones which, despite Steiner's widely publicized anglophobia, came across as warmly familiar. 'I hope you remember me. It's been rather a long time since we last saw one another. My name is Burke, Eamonn Burke. You were a close friend of my father's. We last met at . . .'

'The hell you talking about Eamonn, boy? How the devil are you and where the hell did you get that limey accent? Hey, Mabe, guess what, it's Mickey Burke's boy,' Steiner called out, though the whine of the automatic garage door told him that Mabel was already on her way for her regular Tuesday morning appointment at Beatrice's Georgetown Coiffure and Manicure. 'So what do you know? And what can I do for you? You in town? I'm kinda guessing this isn't a purely social call after all these years.'

'No, general, it isn't.'

On the other end of the line, watching a slow steady snowfall over Moscow's Kievskaya Square, Burke remembered how Steiner, then a sturdy red-haired colonel in his prime, had put a hand on his shoulder on a similar winter's day, a quarter of a century ago, when they had buried his father in a small grey town in the west of Ireland. Steiner had taken him aside after the service, before they got into the diplomatic car that would take him to Dublin and the flight back to an England that still seemed like a foreign country.

On the edge of the graveyard, Steiner had crouched down and

looked him in the eyes. 'Eamonn, your daddy and I were buddies. The best. He did more for me than I can ever repay, or tell you. Your life is going to be different now, with your mom being English and everything. But just you remember, kid, I'm always there for you. If there's ever anything your old Uncle Abe can do for you, you just holler, y'hear.'

A year or so later, when Steiner was passing through London, he had taken Burke to the cinema, which he called the movies, and bought him popcorn and Coca-Cola and a hamburger afterwards and all the things his stepfather disapproved of. They exchanged Christmas cards, and every now and then Steiner had sent him a birthday present, usually some piece of extravagant American whimsy. Burke had been delighted to hear that Steiner had made general and dismayed by the news of his accident. But this was the first time in his life that he had ever asked him for a favour.

'I hate to trouble you but I've got a few queries about an old story. And I think you might be just the man to help me.'

'And you aren't in Washington. Right?'

'Right.'

'So you callin' all the way from London?'

'More or less.' This was no time to start explaining the complications, Burke thought. The general belonged to an older generation. If he knew Burke was calling from Moscow, he would clam up immediately. Burke gave the general a heavily censored version of events and dictated the number on the dog-tag.

'Any idea when it was allocated? Steiner asked, seizing the essentials. 'It doesn't sound recent.'

'It's not. It might even be before your time. As far back as the forties, possibly.'

Steiner breathed a deep sigh. 'Well, I'll do what I can, Eamonn. But that's one hell of a long time ago. Still, some of those serial numbers ought to check out. Just a question really of how good my access is these days. I'm not the powerhouse I used to be, you know.'

'Don't worry, general. I'm sure you'll do just fine. Anything you can help me with will be really appreciated.'

'Okay, boy. Now, why don't you give me your number so's I can ring you back, or you want I should just leave a message on your answering-machine in London? Presuming you're still on the same old number you were when you last sent me a Christmas card. And that wasn't last year, I have to tell you.'

Burke blushed involuntarily. Those were the sort of things Caroline had always dealt with. On another occasion, face to face, he might well have confided in old Abe Steiner about the decay of his marriage and the despondency he had come through. The old man, he felt sure, would have understood. As it was, he said simply, 'I've moved. But don't worry, anyhow. I'm out and about at present,' the corny old foreign correspondent's euphemism for a life lived out of a suitcase. He gave the general the number of his mobile and that of his flat in Notting Hill. If there were problems getting through, Burke said, he would check the answering machine there and call back immediately.

'Any idea when you might be able to give the matter some attention, Sir?'

'Ha! Well, let me see: I've got bridge scheduled next Thursday and my accountant's pestering me for last year's tax returns. Hell, what do you think, boy, we geriatric cripples don't get much fun out of life. I'll be straight on to it. Don't promise nothin' now, but at least you'll get a progress report within the next day or so. Maybe I'm off the active service list, but I'm still okay in the research and development department, you know.'

'I sure do,' said Burke. He hit the 'close' key and handed the phone back to Korkin.

'I couldn't tell the old boy where I was calling from.'

Korkin nodded. 'Of course not. But I am certain the satellites are secure.' He had lent Burke his satellite phone, which he argued was even safer than Burke's Eurodigital mobile.

In the Washington suburbs, Abe Steiner smiled to himself. Well, well, well. Mickey Burke's boy indeed. He hadn't ever forgotten his responsibilities towards his best friend's only son. But Burke Jnr had seemed to have little need of him over the years. But he did like the idea that he could be a friend. Particularly a useful one. And he was more useful than most people reckoned, despite his disability.

Two hours later, Eamonn Burke was sitting in Valery Korkin's Moscow office studying an atlas while Sabine looked over his shoulder. Korkin was rummaging through his shelves for other reference books.

'I still do not see,' Korkin announced. 'We have identified many of the people Fuchs mentions – Arnold, Skarkon, John in Moscow. But who is this monk?'

Burke shrugged.

'There you have us, old chum. Perhaps some orthodox priest? Maybe a nickname for some Commie intelligence honcho. Or someone in a position of power.'

'Here it is,' shouted Korkin. He had lugged a heavy tome out from under heaps of paper on the uppermost shelf and was now pointing to a line in it. Burke looked up. Korkin was holding the *Velikaya Sovyetskaya*, the Great Soviet Encyclopedia.

'I keep it,' he said in response to the unspoken question, 'if only because it is worth remembering how people used to see things. Also because apart from the bullshit, it is full of real information, albeit from a parallel universe.'

The word Korkin was pointing to was the one that had been printed across the featureless white expanse on the map: Lanyukal. But the spelling, it turned out, was less than accurate: a transliteration from the Latin letters, themselves approximations to ancient Viking runes. In the original, according to the encyclopedia, which helpfully included the Latin script, it read 'Langjökull,', which in the language of the country in which it was situated meant 'long glacier'.

'Here,' Korkin said triumphantly. 'God knows what it is you are looking for, but that's where to start: on one of the greatest glaciers in the world, on an island where they have glaciers like Siberia has forests. Iceland.'

Burke spread out the old map beside it and there was no doubt. The topography was the same, though on a much larger scale: the same curved flow of ice forcing its way between two great blobs that Burke supposed were small mountains poking up through the glacial sheet and compressing it.

'So that's where we find what happened to Operation Promifey.'

'To what?' Burke and Korkin turned to Sabine, who looked exceptionally pleased with herself.

'Promifey, at least that's what it says here.' She leaned between them and turned over Yakunin's map to reveal a scribble of Cyrillic characters in faded ink. What's a Promifey when it's at home?' She looked to Korkin.

'Not a what, a who. Promifey is some character from a Greek legend.'

'Prometheus!' exclaimed Burke, thinking not for the first time that it was odd the occasions on which his old-fashioned English public school education was called upon. 'Chained to a rock for ever, at the command of Zeus, his liver pecked at daily by vultures, but unable to die.'

'Yeeeuch,' said Kotzke. 'What was his crime?'

'The ultimate,' said Burke, his eyes suddenly focused on the map with a new intensity. 'He stole fire from the gods.'

His eyes met Sabine's.

'And here, maybe, is where he stole it from,' interjected Korkin gleefully behind them. 'Your second map was much easier. This is America. I am surprised you didn't recognise it, even written in Cyrillic. This is a close-up of one of the land-locked desert states.'

'Don't tell me,' said Burke. 'New Mexico.'

24

From Russia with Love

Moscow, 30 July 1945

The scream of the brakes, metal wheels slowing on metal rails, roused her from fitful sleep into worried wakefulness. Natalya Artyomovna Molitva was afraid. She had never even been to Moscow before. Now, as she looked out of the steamed-up window of the crowded train carriage, she realized she was nearly there. The city was already rising around her, smoky, grimy, miraculously almost untouched by the war, even though the Nazi army had come right into the suburbs.

She had been on trains for more than thirty-six hours, changing in Leningrad, where she had been shocked to see the artillery-ravaged shell of the city which had withstood the greatest siege in history. The overnight last leg to Moscow had been spent cramped in the smelly, sweaty *obschii vagon*, the general sleeping car. An old man kept squeezing past her, using the opportunity to touch her breasts, until one of the soldiers returning from the Finnish front had warned him off.

When she had been hassled, she had thought for a moment about producing the letter with the stamp of the NKVD, the Narodni Kommissariat Vnutrennikh Dyel, the People's Commissariat of Internal Affairs, and telling all of them that she had been summoned to Moscow on the command of Beria himself. Any sane person would have been terrified even to be seen in her company after that.

Natalya shivered, as she had when she kissed David, her baby son, goodbye. Her mother had looked at her with the ill-concealed sorrow born of bitter experience. There was nothing for her to be afraid of, the two men in raincoats had said as they stood at the door of her tiny flat, waiting for her. On the contrary, she was being given a rare opportunity to do the state a service. Still, she was afraid.

In a way it was no surprise. In fact, she had often wondered why they had not called on her earlier. A liaison with a foreigner was always dangerous, even when he was an ally. And now the war was over. Things would change. Yesterday's allies could overnight become deadly enemies. She remembered what had happened in 1941. When the Germans invaded.

Like everyone else she had crowded around the wireless to listen to Stalin's words at the 1945 victory parade on Red Square, and her chest swelled with patriotic pride as she heard him praise Soviet arms, enthuse about the magnificent victory to which he had led the great Soviet people, and prophesy as ever the inevitable victory of the socialist system. But then she knew, as did all the other inhabitants of arctic Murmansk who had sat listening with her, the role played by the aid that had poured in from the now-unmentioned capitalist allies, Great Britain and the United States. Up in Murmansk they knew how much Soviet prowess owed to the convoys that had braved the northern seas infested with Nazi submarines, and to the mercy flights, the bombers and cargo planes that had dodged the Messerschmitts over occupied Norway to bring in medicines, blankets and ammunition and, most importantly of all, *him*: so different from Russian men, so brave, so beautiful.

She had not meant to love an American, but she had found herself powerless not to. Every time she looked down into the blissful blue eyes of her child, so like his, her heart ached for him. And now the war was over: a blessing for some, but maybe not for her. It had been eighteen months since last she saw him. When he left, he had thought it would only be a few weeks before they met again. One day, he had said, when all this was over, he would take her away, to his home where the mountains were blue and the air was clean and they could make babies, little Russian-Americans who would grow up to see in the great new era of peace and friendship that was about to dawn. But he had never returned. She had gone on hoping for a sign of life, for a letter, though she knew it would be intercepted by the post office censors and sent to the NKVD. Was that what had happened?

Now she had been plucked from the cycle, summoned to the big building that dominated Dzherzinsky Square. The building was feared the length and breadth of Russia, from the new republics on the Baltic to distant, dreaded Magadan on the Siberian shores of the Pacific. But in the back of her mind was a tiny glimmer of hope: if a letter had been intercepted then it meant at least he was alive.

A young man in a sailor's uniform opposite asked if she was cold, and offered her his greatcoat. She smiled back. Did she know where she was going in Moscow, he asked. He knew the city well, had grown up there, could show her around. She knew a pickup line when she heard it and thanked him again, but no, she did not need assistance; she had 'friends' – her heart missed a beat at the word – who were supposed to be meeting her. The young sailor sat back. He understood, he said, but if she should change her mind . . .

The train lurched to a sudden halt. Natalya reached up for the rough canvas bag into which she had thrown a few items of clothing and pushed her way to the door.

The platform was a seething mass of people. Young men, mostly in uniform, jostled with wrinkled babushkas in widow's weeds. Swarthy Georgians and pale-faced Russian boys mingled with exotic, slant-eyed Kirghizians and Kazakhs, as well as Uzbeks and Turkmenians from the far south with their tight black ringlets and faces lined and leathern from the beating of the desert sands, all of them in the rough dirty khaki of the Red Army's battle-dress, the raggle-taggle defenders of the greatest, cruellest, most ramshackle land-based empire on earth.

How would she recognize the men meeting her, Natalya wondered. The men who had called to see her in Murmansk had said their colleagues would be there to escort her from the station. She need not have worried. Reaching the great cream marble concourse, she recognized them even before they spotted her: men with long faces in grey raincoats, even though it was a sultry summer morning. She walked instinctively towards them, and they to her.

'Comrade Molitva,' the smaller of the two said. 'We have come to escort you. The colonel is most pleased that you have been able to accept his invitation.'

She looked back at the bustling platform and the great locomotive still belching clouds of dirty white steam. The young sailor who had offered his coat was walking towards her. He smiled, then saw the two men at her side, and the expression on his face turned blank as he quickened his pace and passed by. That's it, thought Natalya, I have already become invisible.

She turned and walked with her two companions down the

station steps towards the car, a Pobyeda – Victory, she thought they were called, the very latest model. Clearly only the best would do for the men they called warriors on the invisible front.

Soon the driver was speeding through the streets towards the building that had begun life as home to the All-Russia Insurance Company but was now better known as the Lubyanka.

Outside stood the great black statue of Dzerzhinsky, founder of the Cheka, set up by Lenin to purge the socialist state of traitors. Subsequently it had been renamed, reinvigorated, purged and reorganized as the NKVD. Since 1938 it had been run by Lavrenti Beria, a chubby-looking man with wire-rimmed glasses who in his official photographs, she thought, bore a disconcerting resemblance to Heinrich Himmler, the man who, Natalya had heard, did much the same sort of job for the Nazi enemy. She shivered when she thought of him, and again as they passed into the courtyard and the iron doors slammed behind them.

The smaller of the men (Natalya had worked out that he was the higher-ranking) pushed open the door in response to the call from within. Gingerly, she walked in. Her escort made to follow her, but an arm imperiously flung out by the man standing by the window sent him back. The door closed. She found herself facing a man of medium height, no more than thirty, with still-thick brown hair, and a face lined with care. An intelligent face, she thought, to her own surprise.

'Natalya Artyomovna.' The face broke into a carefully composed smile. 'How good of you to come.' She wondered whether any of his 'guests' had declined such an invitation. 'Please, sit down.' He gestured to a simple wooden chair facing the desk.

'My name is Pavlov,' the man said, 'Ivan Mikhailovich.' He sat down opposite her and folded his arms. He could be intimidating, Natalya decided, if he wanted to be. This was obviously the face designed to placate, to reassure. She doubted he used it often.

'You are probably wondering why you have been invited here.' She nodded. Though in her heart she already knew. She would tell them that she had committed the cardinal sin of falling in love with a capitalist. She would plead foolishness and take whatever punishment was coming to her. She had done no wrong to the Soviet motherland. She had no secrets to betray. She had not betrayed Russia in her soul. And she would not betray him.

'We have information . . .' he began, watching keenly, 'to the effect that you have been having a sexual relationship with a foreigner.'

'I cannot deny it. But it was not an act of disloyalty. The man is an officer of an ally of the Soviet People.'

'That is a technicality. He is an American. That is a fact. You know that you are required to report all such contacts, for security reasons; in particular, contact with foreign military personnel.'

Natalya hung her head. Of course she knew. Everyone knew. Was this the reason they had brought her all the way to Moscow, to read her the damn rule book? Couldn't they just have sent her direct to a camp?

'In Murmansk, in war,' she mumbled, 'all the girls. There were lots of affairs. These things happen.'

'That is not an excuse. However, the state is not as strict as some people think. In the end Comrade Stalin, and Comrade Beria of course, have all our interests at heart. We would like to help you. We would like you to write a letter.'

'A letter, comrade colonel?'

'Yes, my dear. A letter. It should not be too difficult. After all, it is to the man you love. And I think you have a lot of news for him. About a little package of his that has borne fruit?'

Natalya looked flustered for a moment, then flushed. Of course, how could she have expected them not to know about David?

'But how . . . ?'

'How can you write it? Oh, I do not think that will be so difficult. We will help you. And do not worry. We will also see that it is delivered.'

Natalya's eyes opened wide. What did they want her to say? Why were they involved at all? But who cared? They were offering her the one thing she wanted more than anything else in the world: a way to get back in touch with Joshua Finch, to tell him he had a son, her son.

'Why . . . ?' she began.

'Why are we doing this? My dear girl, our great leader has always believed in doing everything possible to bring families together.'

Natalya sat back in her chair. Never in her life had she been so eager to believe an obvious lie.

'Now, what do you say,' he said brightly. 'Shall I fetch pen and paper?'

She nodded. And the man who called himself Pavlov, but whose real name was Anatoly Nikolayevich Yakunin, beamed at her.

The message he had received from Klaus Fuchs was almost beyond belief. The frightened young woman in front of him could help it become reality.

Albuquerque, New Mexico, 17 September 1945

For Harry Gold it was a trip too far. Albuquerque at the fag end of a hot summer was stifling: dry, dusty, dirty, as if the whole heat of the desert had drifted south to lie in a pall over a small city that had cracked and blistered in response. John had been categorical. Nothing, not even the risk of losing his job, was to get in the way of this trip.

Until now it had been the trips to Santa Fe that he had thought were all-important. Fuchs was the gold. Now his priority was an air force guy, some hot jock pilot attached to the big base out at Kirkland. What the heck, Harry Gold was a man who did what he was told. Besides, the pay had just gotten a damn sight better. The envelope he had collected on the steps of the Metropolitan Museum of Art the previous week had been stuffed with greenbacks of the best denomination. And what he was delivering was not exactly high-risk: a letter, it looked like, with a photograph. He was to wait for a reply. It shouldn't take long, John had said. But if it did he was still to wait, for a week if need be. Harry sure hoped like hell it wouldn't be. He'd made the meet yesterday and the kid had said he'd be back today. He sat in the leather armchair of the hotel lobby and gazed up at the rotating ceiling fan. At least this Conrad Hilton guy had a decent hotel, not at all what he expected from a New Mexico boy in a one-horse town like Albuquerque. Big ambitions too, he heard. But not as big as Harry Gold's, he thought. Yessir, Harry, he told himself, when this business is over you are going places. You have earned your reward in a socialist heaven on earth.

He did not even notice the footsteps approaching until he found his view of the ceiling fan interrupted by the dark good-looking features of the young pilot.

'Hey, Ray, how's it goin'?' Joshua Finch slapped him on the shoulder cordially. The bonhomie was part of the routine but this time, Gold could see tension on the man's face.

'Fancy a drink, kid? A beer or something?'

'You know me, Ray. If I'm not flyin', I'm flyin'. Sounds real good. But let's go head down one o' the town saloons. I could do with some air.'

Outside the swing doors, Finch dropped some of the banter. He was walking fast and Gold found himself almost running to keep up.

'I must thank you for the letter,' he said at last. 'I'm counting on what it says being true.'

Gold nodded vigorously. He had no idea what he had delivered, but he had been told that if there were any questions about its authenticity he was to dispel them as best he could.

'I have it on the "highest" authority.'

'Yeah, sure.' Finch's smile was suddenly back, genuine this time, as if the tension had dissipated. He looked down at Gold.

'The answer's "yes". But then you knew it would be.'

Gold nodded. He hadn't.

'Anyhow, thanks for the photograph. Beautiful kid, isn't he?'

Gold found himself looking, more out of idle curiosity than anything else, at a small photograph of a baby. The young woman cradling the child in her arms certainly looked attractive enough, if a little dowdy. To Harry Gold, the baby could have been any baby anywhere.

But to the young man next to him, it was the only child in the universe.

25

The Surface of the Moon

The land below was like nothing Eamonn Burke had ever seen before on earth. As the Icelandair Boeing 737 circled lower on its descent towards Keflavik airport, the barren rock beneath folded, as if in waves – a surreal stone sea, grey and shiny, surrounded by the dark winter waves of the north Atlantic.

Lava fields, Burke knew in theory, covered great swathes of Iceland. But the lava he had seen elsewhere, at Pompeii in Italy or on the Antrim plateau of Northern Ireland, had been black and rough, thousands of years old and weathered accordingly. Here molten rock had flowed as recently as the fourteenth century. Burke remembered the spectacular aerial photographs of the 1996 eruption of Grimsvötn, the volcano buried under the vast glacial ice-cap of Vatnajökull, which was larger than all the glaciers of continental Europe put together. The explosion and the heat it generated sent torrents of meltwater rushing down the scree slopes to the south, washing away the bridges on the one ring road that connected the sparsely populated west coast of the island to its bustling little capital.

Beside him Sabine Kotzke stirred and stretched in her seat. She had fallen asleep shortly after leaving Moscow. They had talked through the night about Yakunin, and the implications of his death.

One thing was certain: after a day of murder, intrigue and discovery, Sabine's claim that Klaus Fuchs had been murdered by the Stasi had suddenly seemed a lot less fantastic than it had done in the bar of the Nag's Head back in London. Despite that, the idea that the Stasi was reaching out from beyond the grave of the East German state was something Sabine seemed too horrified to even contemplate. Why? Burke asked. What experience had she had with the Stasi? Had she ever been arrested by them?

'No,' she replied, with unexpected vehemence.

'Then why the denial syndrome?'

'Denial? Eamonn Burke, believe me, you have no idea. No idea at all.' And then in a quiet, small voice, she added: 'My father.'

'He fell into their hands?'

'*Um Gotteswillen.*' She raised her eyes to the ceiling, and then lowered them again with a heart-weary sigh. 'No, no, no, no, no. He was one of them.'

Burke closed his eyes. How blind, how stupidly blind.

'I didn't know, not for a long time. I don't know if my mother did or not. But anyway they were divorced before I was a teenager.'

'It's okay. You don't have to tell me.'

'You may as well know. He wasn't even a serving officer at Normannenstrasse, oh no, not *Vati*. He was just someone who told tales on his colleagues. His whole life at the paint factory was a cover, as was his volunteer work at the youth club. In reality he was collating, cross-referencing and passing on, with recommendations for action that meant the destruction of other people's lives.'

'How did you find out?'

'Oh, not until it was too late. Way too late. I had a boyfriend: Gerd. My first, as it happened. He was a bit of an old hippy, wore a "Swords to Ploughshares" pacifist motif on the backside of his jeans, but never to work. He knew better than that. But he still lost his job. I told my father, and said how unfair it was. And he put his arm around me. And said how sorry he was. And all along it had been his doing.

'Then in the spring of 1989, when the whole sorry system was on its way to hell, Gerd was picked up on the outskirts of Dresden, him and a whole vanload of young "holiday-makers" heading for Hungary. Except that they weren't, of course. Who was in that spring? The Hungarians had opened the frontier with Austria. Budapest might as well have been the suburbs of Vienna. They were all sent to Bautzen jail and might have rotted there for a year or two if the damn Wall hadn't fallen first.

'When the mob stormed Normannenstrasse, my father's files were among the first to be found. He was damn near lynched. And do you know, I would have been the first to tie the noose.'

'Where is he now?'

'Somewhere. In the West, where they have no memories.

Working in a paint factory, I suppose. A member of the proletariat proper for the first time in his life. I don't know, and I don't really care.'

Don't you? Burke wondered. But he said nothing.

'People like my father were the tip of the iceberg, no, the scum who floated on the surface of a sick society.'

Burke nodded. But the evil, he tried to tell her, had never all been on one side. There were people in the West – people who today claimed sanctimoniously that the 'right' side had won the Cold War – who had done things that deep down were every bit as terrible as their ideological enemies. To say that the ends justified the means was no excuse, just as it hadn't been for Hitler, or for Stalin. Or Klaus Fuchs.

'Or Joshua Finch?'

'Maybe. It depends, doesn't it?'

Ever since he had seen the young man's face staring out of a photograph half a century old, and read the strange, hauntingly incomplete little letter, the spectre of Joshua Finch had dogged his imagination. And somewhere out there, if they had read the runes correctly, at the location marked on the old military map, in the inhospitable terrain rapidly rising to meet them, lay an answer: at 19 degrees, 58 minutes west, 64 degrees 39 minutes north, an ice-covered pass between two mountains on the eastern edge of a formidable crescent-shaped glacier more than fifty kilometres in length and twenty across. It had to be one of the most inaccessible spots in the world.

In contrast to the moonscape of the country's surface, however, Keflavik's modern airport terminal seemed the epitome of normality. Provided, Sabine had added, one ignored the fact that the returning natives headed straight for the inbound duty-free shop to stock up on booze to beat the draconian alcohol laws they imposed on themselves.

'Did you know,' she chirped from the pages of the airline's inflight magazine as they waited for their baggage in the customs hall, 'that beer's only been legal here since 1989?'

Korkin had warned Burke to be surprised by nothing in Iceland. Strangely, it turned out to be somewhere the Russian knew quite well. He had never been there, but he had been responsible for negotiating a business deal for an Icelandic company setting up in Moscow in the early days after the collapse of Communism.

The company directors had visited Moscow for ten days to sort out the details and, according to Korkin, they had not only spent most of the time extolling the virtues of their national culture and dismissing the Moscow mid-winter weather as 'mild' but had also drunk him under the table. He had given Burke the company's telephone number and told him to ask for Birna, who ran its communications.

'Mention my name,' Valery had said. The magnificent Birna, he insisted with a slightly disconcerting smirk, would put him in touch with the right people.

'Well, thank God beer's legal now.' Burke frowned at Kotzke as her leather suitcase came round on the conveyor belt. 'I'm gasping for a pint.'

'According to this, a pint may be your ration for the week, Mr Burke. Eon may have money to spend, but to have a serious night on this town, you would have to take out a second mortgage.'

Sabine ran to the conveyor belt to pick up her bag, gesturing to Burke's own battered suitcase rolling past. Burke watched as she hoisted the luggage clear, simultaneously tossing her head back to throw her untidy fringe out of her eyes. He could almost have mistaken her for a student backpacker, such was the strength and energy she exuded. And the enthusiasm was catching, he felt more alive than he had done in years. Burke grabbed both bags and humped them towards the exit door where a cluster of noisy Icelanders were arguing with a customs official over an improbably large quantity of Johnnie Walker whisky.

Burke and Kotzke were politely ushered through ahead of them. As, a few minutes later, was the patient man with the thick scarf about his neck who had collected only a black Samsonite case from the carousel.

Washington DC

A fresh-faced USAF cadet was beaming good-naturedly at the wrinkled visage of Abe Steiner approaching him. The smile faded when he realized the motorized wheelchair was hurtling towards the double doors at breakneck speed. Shit. Just like the old boy to challenge his disability. He dashed forward to open them just in time to prevent collision. 'Afternoon, General Steiner sir, nice to see you again. Hope we can be of help.'

The boy was one of those automatons the US services turned out too easily, the old man reckoned: polite, punctilious, patriotic and a pinhead. But he smiled back all the same. At least this was one place cripples could get into without begging, he thought as he manoeuvred his wheelchair down the ramp into the nondescript greystone building in the Arlington suburbs that housed the oldest records of the US Air Force's ramshackle archives.

In fact, Steiner had been horrified at just how chaotic the records of the supposedly most powerful strategic strike force on the face of the planet really were. Naturally, he had tried hacking his way into them using the Internet. It had seemed easier than he expected. His own old passwords (plus those of others, still in harness, which he had taken a twelve-year-old's joy in ferreting out) had got him harmlessly, and frighteningly easily, past the first electronic countermeasures.

Hell, did none of those guys watch the movies? Did none of them pay attention to the rudimentary rules of password protection? Take Willcox, for example. There was nothing more predictable than using his daughter Melanie's date of birth as a password. Steiner had been godfather at the christening.

It had been more or less the same story with Mervyn Elie, who was air force chief of staff. Steiner did not even attempt to try the man's family connections. Elie lived for his work and when he found he could no longer do it in his office – usually because no one would come to see him there on a weekend – he did it on the golf course, suborning staff to play with him, and then piling on the psychological pressure to be sure they lost.

Unhesitatingly Steiner tapped in the general's golf handicap followed by those of Jack Nicklaus and Severiano Ballesteros, Elie's two revered idols. He had gained access to the minutes of the man's last meeting with the Defense Secretary, including a discussion of air alert status in the Persian Gulf. Steiner tutted to himself. The only hope for Western civilization, he reflected, was that neither the Iranians nor the Iraqis were big golf players.

But what really riled him was that none of it had been to any avail. Sure, there had been programmes to put all of the archives on to computerized format. But what had happened was that military bureaucracy had mushroomed. The archivists were so busy recording all the day-to-day traffic, that archiving the past remained an idealistic daydream. Even the most comprehensively catalogued departments ran out around 1972, hardly surprising in the chaos of Vietnam. There were numerous cross-references to files in outhouses scattered throughout the country. Clearly there was some material available locally, but it occurred to Steiner that to do as his old friend's boy wished might even entail him heading out to Albuquerque, a thought that filled him with no enthusiasm.

The room at the Hotel Esja in Reykjavik was a twin. Sabine had made it clear that this was for practical purposes only: even German magazines' budgets were not open-ended, plus this story was beginning to call for a bit more travel than her editor had calculated, and Icelandic prices were notoriously high. Burke had held up his hands as if to say he understood perfectly, and anyway, what was she trying to imply?

The beds, however, turned out to be so far apart they might as well have been in separate rooms. Kotzke had staked out the limits in any case by declaring her intention to have the first shower. As soon as he heard the water running, Burke picked up the telephone and called the fabled Birna on the number Korkin had given him. Within minutes they had arranged a meeting with her director for that evening in a bar in downtown Reykjavik. How would they recognize each other, he asked. No problem at all, she replied. Just go to the bar and ask for Siggy.

'Quiet place, eh?' Burke ventured.

'Not exactly. It is Friday night. Is this your first time in Iceland, by any chance?'

'It is indeed,' Burke replied, warmed by the simple hospitality in the woman's voice.

'Well, have a nice night. Just keep your head down and roll with the punches.'

Which was not, he thought as he replaced the receiver, exactly what he had been expecting her to say.

26

Under the Skin

Burke and Kotzke left the hotel about nine o'clock after an excellent, if rather bland, meal of shrimp rolled in cod fillets served in a delicate dill sauce. He had, to her vocal disgust, smothered his in black pepper. They had both washed it down with a shot of brennivin, the Icelanders' extraordinary schnapps, a sort of fire-water flavoured with caraway seeds. Burke pronounced it brilliant, particularly with a chilled beer chaser, and announced that for a nation which had only recently rediscovered the art of brewing, they did not do at all badly.

Sabine had chided him for his 'English' élitism, which prompted Burke, fired by the alcohol, to redeclare his Irish-American roots. And amid much teasing banter, they had linked arms and set off in the cool night air for the brief stroll into downtown Reykjavik. The traffic was heavier than they had expected.

'Jesus Christ. Watch it!' yelled Burke as a rusty Honda Accord with four blond teenage boys hanging out of its windows almost careered out of control on to the kerb.

'So-rr-y,' came the chorused reply in exaggerated English as the lads waved like maniacs.

'Do you think there are no drink-driving laws here? I thought this would be a quiet place.'

'Eamonn, you're showing your age. And you didn't read the guide book. This is Friday. Reykjavik's big night out.'

As Sabine spoke a bar door in front of them opened, spilling out two stunningly beautiful girls, Burke could not help but notice, with long legs under the shortest mini-skirts he had seen in a decade. Holding each other up, arms around the shoulders of their matching denim jackets, the pair staggered across the pavement to slump against a parked Toyota landcruiser.

'Steady, girls.' Burke smiled encouragingly.

'Hey-ey, hello. How are you?' the taller girl replied, eyeing them up and down unsteadily. Her friend suddenly vomited noisily over the Toyota's windscreen.

'My god,' said Kotzke. 'Still fancy them?'

Burke, feeling decidedly queasy, pulled at her arm. 'What a place. Come on, the bar's only two streets from here.'

Soon they were outside a corner bar guarded by a tough-looking bouncer in a shiny black jacket. Burke could see the need for him: every two minutes the door would open and a couple of drunk teenagers would fall on to the street, pick themselves up and head for the next bar.

Burke approached. 'Good evening, sir. Have a nice night,' said the bouncer in flawless English.

Inside, electronic rock music blared through loudspeakers at maximum amperage across a red-lit mass of heaving youngsters, most with glasses in their hands, engaged in heavy petting and half-hearted attempts at on-the-spot dancing; conversation was not an option. 'Siggy' was clearly not the orthodox middle-aged business-man he had imagined.

Sabine took it all much more naturally, jiving her way through the throng. For the first time Burke began to fear they belonged to different generations. He followed her awkwardly.

The bar was long, wooden, and crowded. Burke ordered beers, in sign language, by pointing to the pump and indicating a large one with his hands, then holding up two fingers. First things first, he told himself, even *in extremis*. And these were just about as extreme drinking conditions as he had encountered since spending Saint Patrick's Night in O'Neill's bar in New York. He had been younger then, too. He was not sure he had ever been as old as he felt right now.

He exchanged a 1,000 krona note for the two beers, and was not wholly shocked when he received no change. 'Can you tell me where Siggy is?' he bawled at the barman at the top of his voice, realizing that he had not even established whether the man spoke English.

The barman smiled in a way that suggested it was what he always did when nonplussed by customers. Conditioned reflex, Burke thought. Probably not a bad one, considering.

'S-I-G-G-Y?' he repeated, doing his utmost to win the decibel war, but failing miserably.

The smile changed from neutrality to recognition. The barman leaned across, took Burke's sleeve and pointed him towards the end of the bar where a striking woman, almost as tall as himself, was standing with one foot on the bar-rail, a half-litre of beer in one hand and a long, thick cigar in the other.

'I'm not sure, but I've a funny feeling the mountainous ice-maiden there might be our man,' he bellowed into Kotzke's ear.

He inched his way towards the big blonde woman, who took her cigar from her mouth as he approached and delicately blew a cloud of thick blue smoke into the air, away from him.

'Are you Siggy?' Burke bellowed. It was just like Korkin to omit the minor detail that his contact was female. Though Burke also recalled that she had drunk the big Russian under the table. Perhaps another good reason for him not to have revealed her sex.

She nodded, grasped Burke's hand with a grip like a Valkyrie who had taken lessons in weightlifting, and gestured that he and Sabine should follow her. Lifting a hatch in the bar counter, she motioned them through.

'The back bar lacks some of the Friday night atmosphere, but perhaps you have had enough of our simple Nordic amusements for the present. It also makes talking easier,' she said, closing a barred wooden door. The noise level fell from intolerable to merely excruciating.

'At least, there's no danger of being overheard.'

Siggy smiled. 'Are you worried about that, Mr Burke?'

Burke returned the smile a little nervously. This woman had antennae.

'Perhaps we should introduce ourselves properly: Sigurdir Hafnarsdottir. But Siggy will do.'

'Eamonn Burke, and this is my colleague, Sabine Kotzke.'

Sabine nodded politely and held out her hand. Siggy bent down to take it and Burke winced. He had never before seen a woman shake another's hand like that. Sabine didn't flinch, but he saw the pupils of her eyes harden into needle-sharp pin pricks. It occurred to him that he had not understood the expression 'looking daggers' until then.

'Welcome to the Reykjavik *runtur*. I am sorry if you found it a little hectic. But then you chose your day of arrival.'

'I'm sorry? The Reykjavik what?'

Kotzke gave him the patronizing smile of a woman who had read the guidebook. Siggy explained:

'It's a ritual. Friday night. All the young people go out and get drunk and try to pick each other up, while those who are left pick fights. Primitive. But then we are a primitive people. It is part of our charm.'

Her smile revealed a mouth full of flawless white teeth. Burke had, he realized, never come across anything quite like her. Siggy Hafnarsdottir was a woman who knew her place in the world, and that place was wherever she happened to choose. For the moment, it was here and now.

'So you are friends of Valery? How is the old fox? Has he learned to drink yet?'

Burke smiled. It was a question he would relish passing on.

'Well, you know Valery.' He could see the woman sharing his amusement. 'He tries.'

The Icelander produced a laugh that was a perfect imitation of the Russian's own. He was going to like Siggy Hafnarsdottir, even if – perhaps particularly if – Sabine wasn't.

'We're working on a story about something that happened a long time ago, during the war,' he began.

'The cod war?' No Icelander could resist baiting a Briton over the way their few gunboats had stood off the might of the Royal Navy in the 1970s in its attempts to protect British fishing vessels when Reykjavik unilaterally declared a 200-mile limit.

'Actually I was thinking of the Second World War. Were there any Americans here then?'

'Ha. Are there fish in the sea? That's what brought them. Iceland has a history going back twelve hundred years and never had an army. Now it has someone else's, and their damn bombs too.'

'Atomic bombs? Out at the US base near Keflavik?'

'They deny it, of course. Plausible deniability is part of "our" Nato doctrine. Besides it would cause much unpleasantness. But everyone knows they are there. We just pretend we do not. People used to protest. A lot at first and in the sixties and seventies, they say, when no one liked the Americans. But no one wanted them to leave either. Now there are fewer and people who complain about that too, because there is less money. Such is life. But we should not be that ungrateful. If it was not for the arrival of the Americans during the war, we might never have had independence.'

'From?' Burke's Icelandic history was not brilliant.

'Denmark, of course. The Americans were only too keen to support us in 1945 against the return of any colonial power. Not that the Danes were exactly in a position to do anything about it, having been occupied by her lot,' she gave a politely jovial but clearly poisonous glance at Sabine, 'for most of the war.'

Don't mention the war, Burke thought to himself. He had never worked on a story with a German before. Christ, he wondered, was it always like this? Swimming against a tide of residual resentment, even more than half a century later? He had never thought before what it must be like to be German and carry around the weight of the world's prejudices, for the sake of an earlier generation. If Sabine was affected, she didn't show it. Perhaps you got used to it.

'Is there anyone around who knows a lot about that period, maybe someone who worked on the base, anyone who would remember any unusual events?'

'Hmm, well it was all pretty unusual, wasn't it? But Reykjavik is a small town. Everyone here over a certain age remembers – of course there are fewer of them than there were. But if you want to talk to someone first-hand, I suppose you could do worse than meet my mother. She worked in the canteen for the British soldiers.'

Why not? thought Burke. There were few better places to keep up with military news than in the chow line. 'Would she talk to us? When can we see her?'

Siggy looked at the bulky aviator's watch on her wrist.

'Too late now. Mother goes to bed early, particularly on a Friday. To miss the ruckus, you know. How about tomorrow, say lunchtime? We could meet for a coffee in town – to recover – and I'll take you there. It's not far.'

Burke agreed readily and tried to pass on his enthusiasm to Sabine, who merely nodded politely.

'And now, as they say in England, it's your round.'

She leaned forward and pounded on the door they had come in through. A moment later it opened, drowning any attempt at conversation with the mega-decibels of an old Björk hit. The barman entered carrying three more beers and set them down on the table announcing ceremoniously, '*Thrir bjóra, takk.*'

'*Takk fyrir, Erik,*' said Siggy, lifting one and draining half of it in a single mighty gulp as he closed the door.

*   *   *

185

It was late afternoon in Washington with the sun sinking slowly over the marble dome of the capitol, though Abe Steiner would not have paid it any attention even if it had been visible from the dark recesses of the archives across the Potomac in Arlington. For the past two hours his only light had been the fluorescent tubes that burned in the disconcertingly low ceiling. This was not the sort of work he enjoyed. Searching through archives on computer was one thing. He could cope with hypertext and mutually linked data pages. But it had been a long time since he had had to deal with real paperwork and even then he had had clerks to do it.

He had begun with the dog-tag serial number. In theory, every able-bodied serviceman or woman who passed through the ranks of the United States military was recorded by a serial number given them on the day of their enlistment and retained for ever. Even after return to civilian life – or death – that number said for ever that John Doe had done his bit for Uncle Sam. It was linked to medical and service records, the dry bureaucratic annotations that in the end reduced even the greatest deeds of military prowess to ticks on a register. An accounting practice in human-kind.

Joshua Finch was no exception. Up to a point. And that point was 21 October 1945. Two years earlier, the records indicated, Finch had been posted to Kirkland Air Force base, Albuquerque, as a reserve pilot on a bomber crew. He had been through basic training and had checked out way above average, both on intelligence and flying skills. It was an embryonic air force career that had all the makings of a great future, or at least a short and glorious contribution to the war effort. Except that by then the war was over. Which was what made the brief final remark on Finch's file so strange: 'Missing in action.'

Under the circumstances, when Burke first raised his head from the pillow the following morning – or rather later on the same morning after barely four hours of sleep – it was a mercy that he was still capable of rational thought at all.

'Fuck.'

'Hmm,' came the response from the bed across the room.

It did not sound like an invitation. Which was just as well, he considered. Only vaguely, on the fringes of his mind, was there a picture of Siggy waving a hearty goodnight in the black Reykjavik pre-dawn as they climbed into taxi cabs outside the umpteenth bar.

Slowly he edged his feet over the side of bed, in a search for the hotel carpet. The remainder of his body seemed reluctant to follow suit. When it did, he found himself on all fours.

'Fuck,' he said inaudibly, or so he thought until a voice came from a seemingly distant plateau:

'What a convesrsation this is.'

'Sarcasm,' Burke forced himself to reply, 'is a privilege of the healthy.'

'In that case, I give it up. Next time you decide to accompany an ice maiden through the flames, leave this poor mortal out, okay? I only hope you feel like you deserve to.'

From his position on the floor, Burke could see nothing of Sabine. She had pulled the thick goose-down quilt over her head. He stood up shakily and made his way to the wasbasin.

It was then that he noticed his mobile phone's green light blinking where he had left it on the floor, indicating that there were messages awaiting collection on his answerphone service. With his head aching as if his mental processor had been overloaded, he was seriously tempted to ignore it. After all, what was he waiting for? Nothing much. Except, of course, a message from the one man he hoped could advance their cause. Burke dialled the Notting Hill number and pressed the code he had programmed to release his messages.

There were two. The first was from George Prosset, whingeing that he had not been in touch for the past week – Burke cut him off in mid-flow and advanced to the next. He heard the unmistakable southern-American drawl of Abe Steiner.

'Hrrrumph . . .' The pause seemed to last for ever. 'Eamonn . . . it's Abe here. Boy, we've gotta talk. I don't know what you're workin' on, but it sure ain't a loser. Watch your arrrrse' – he exaggerated the letter 'r' ridiculously – 'as you fuckin' limeys say. Call me as soon as you get this message. You ain't gonna believe this.' Burke thought he could almost sense a repressed chuckle in the recorded voice, as if the old man was keeping his last line in reserve, well aware of the effect it would have:

'One of our bombers is missing.'

27

After the Party

Los Alamos, New Mexico, 17 September 1945

As the big Buick rolled down the red mesa road, Klaus Fuchs felt almost sad at the idea that it might soon be for the last time. The party was over. It was time to go home. For those who had a home.

The British mission was packing up. Rudolf and Genia Peierls were already talking about getting 'back to Brum', the abbreviation for Birmingham being part of their adopted Englishness. There was some doubt, at least in public among the scientific community, about how the nation-states would deal with the product of their labours. There was much talk about a concept called 'non-proliferation'.

James Chadwick, the head of the mission, had been particularly nice to Fuchs, talking about 'big things' in his future. He would put him in touch with Sir John Cockroft who, he had heard on the grapevine, would be setting up an establishment somewhere in England, under the aegis of the wartime Ministry of Supply. There was talk, too, about the great potential of nuclear energy as a fuel source, about harnessing the power of destruction to fuel the industry of peace. Talk, thought Fuchs, as an excuse for the absence of reasoning.

He would be staying on a while. Oppenheimer had vouched for the necessity of him remaining. Surprisingly, so had Teller. But perhaps it was not that much of a surprise. Fuchs was working on a new intitiator, a more powerful device that would detonate a more powerful bomb. Teller wanted it for his 'super'. A superbomb for a superpower. The age was making new words by the minute.

If Fuchs had thought about the future at all before now, he had done so only vaguely. Things got in the way. There were arrangements to be made if he was to continue his work – in every sense – after his return to England. He had made notes, things to pass on to Raymond. He would not miss the little man with his owl-shaped face, but he needed to know that whoever filled the role would also be reliable. The contacts would need to be regular, and he would want to be in charge.

In his heart he hoped there would be a time, not too far away, when the need for conspiracy was past. There was no doubt that the atomic bomb would change the world for ever, but how drastically and with what ultimate consequences he scarcely dared imagine. Those who worried him most were the men like Teller, who thought they already knew. Only as the Buick bumped up the ramp on to the newly repaired river bridge – now that Los Alamos was no secret any longer, things were changing fast – did it occur to him that his vision of the future might be a fantasy, the reality much more terrible. No, he told himself. It would not be. What they were doing would make sure of that. What he was doing right now was a crucial part of that.

What he was doing, according to Genia Peierls, as she cut sandwiches in Kitty Oppenheimer's well-equipped kitchen, was one of the most important tasks imaginable: fetching the drinks for the farewell party. They had decided to do it in style, with real champagne if he could get some. And she had been assured he could, from Morley's Liquor Store in Santa Fe. Her husband had looked surprised and thought they might be palmed off with some of the sparkling wine the Californians were experimenting with. But Fuchs had promised to try.

On the corner of Castillo and Alameda, where they had last met those fateful few months earlier, he spotted Raymond at the wheel of a Dodge pickup truck. Fuchs turned left, and drove down the road to the parking lot outside the liquor store. At this early hour it was empty.

Morley had been expecting him. Genia Peierls, anxious about her champagne, had been on the phone. He was a jovial man with a drinker's red nose, and was clearly pleased to be able to fulfil such a rare order.

'Here ya go,' he beamed, indicating to Fuchs a wooden case with the word Mumm and the date 1938 burned into it. 'Real champagne, all the way from France. Probably the only case in the whole damn state. Don't know as I reckoned I'd ever sell that lot after the war started. But then I guess you folks up on the hill sure got somethin' to celebrate. Watch where you pop those corks, hear?'

Fuchs smiled and the two of them took the case and carefully put it in the trunk of the Buick. He collected the rest of the order, paid cash in ten-dollar bills adding an extra one, as Genia had instructed, for Morley, who thanked him, clapping his back disconcertingly.

When he came out, the pickup was parked next to his Buick, with the hood up and a man peering amateurishly under it. 'Need some help?' he asked. Harry Gold looked up at him. Fuchs thought he detected in the little man's manner a greater, more awkward awe than before. The bomb has changed the world, he thought.

'Don't suppose you've got any tools?'

'Yes. I think I can help you,' Fuchs replied and opened the trunk of the Buick to reveal, next to the case of vintage champagne, a grey metal tool box.

'You can borrow these.'

The toolbox was heavier than it looked. Fuchs helped him carry it to the pickup. Gold wondered what it contained, but he knew better than to look. Anyhow this time, once again, he had been more than adequately paid.

'I'm in a bit of a hurry. You can hang on to them.'

'Well, that's real kind of you.'

In the dull, dry heat, the two men shook hands. It was not a farewell with any warmth to it, given the scale of their collaboration and the the probability that they would never meet again. But Gold, though he felt disappointed as he drove south along the dusty highway, knew Klaus Fuchs had never given him cause to expect more. He was just a conduit. As he mopped the dusty sweat off his brow, he wondered if that was how history would remember him: as a sad cypher. Then he realized with a jerk that, if he was lucky, history would not remember him at all.

Four miles north of Albuquerque he saw the big green military truck stationary on the side of the road, its hood raised and a young man tinkering with the engine. He pulled over.

'Hi there, you look like you could use some help.'

'Sure could, don't suppose you got any tools?'

'No problem. I've got a box in the back. Wanna help me fetch it?'

And he smiled as Joshua Finch came over and shook his hand with a hearty American grip.

190

28

Long Distance Information

Still feeling much the worse for wear, Burke and Kotzke met Siggy shortly before 10.00a.m. at a café beside Tjornin, the lake that dominates the centre of the little city. Flocks of wild ducks gathered on the surface of the melting ice. Siggy grinned broadly over the rim of her coffee cup.

'Well, Mr Burke, how about a breakfast brennivin?'

Burke groaned at the thought of further alcohol. The fact that Siggy looked, and apparently felt, fine, did not make him any happier.

'Let's go, then,' she announced, draining her coffee, just as Burke was getting round to thinking he could do with another one.

'Not to worry, I've warned mother to keep the pot on.'

Siggy drove them in her Toyota landcruiser. She said most Icelanders used four-wheeled drive vehicles outside the cities, though she spoke scathingly about the increasing number of her compatriots who never left Reykjavik and knew little about the magnificent interior of their own country.

'Well, maybe you'll get a chance to show us some of it,' said Burke, gritting his teeth as they rolled over uneven cobbles.

Her mother lived in a charming little wooden house, painted dark red. Siggy ushered them into a small, cosy sitting-room, with net curtains on the windows. A woman whom Burke judged to be in her late seventies sat on a straight-backed wooden chair next to a tiled stove.

'Please excuse me if I don't get up,' she said in faultless English that was, if anything, even better than her daughter's. 'I'm afraid it's not quite so easy as it used to be. I suffer terribly from the stiffness

191

. . . oh, what's the word? Arthritis. It is the curse of old people, particularly in a cold climate.'

'Please, Mrs Hafnarsdottir, don't bother . . .' began Sabine, only to stop short as she noticed Siggy laughing.

'Oh, now you must forgive me too,' the tall Icelandic woman said with a touch of genuine reconciliation in her voice. 'My mother's name is Helga Petersdottir. It is confusing I know for foreigners, but we do not have surnames in Iceland. Everyone takes the name of a parent. It used to be always the father of course, but nowadays we are more egalitarian.'

Burke and Kotzke perched together on the sofa while Siggy went off to make coffee.

'You worked for the British, in the NAAFI, the canteen?' Burke began. 'I hadn't realized that there were British troops here during the war.'

'They just don't teach history like they used to. Instead of the Nazis we got the Tommies and the Yankees. One after the other. You English came first. We didn't ask you, of course. Not too much is said about that these days. Hitler knew that rule: nobody asks questions of the victors. You just marched in because Mr Churchill said so. Now you know why we enjoyed winning the "cod war". We were invaded "protectively", which I think is what the Russians said when they invaded eastern Poland in 1939.

'Anyway, the big thing is: the 1940s were important times for Iceland,' the old lady continued. 'After the Germans took Norway and Denmark, we were the next obvious step. For one side or the other.'

'Why? You had no strategic resources.' Burke thought Sabine's question had the absence of tact that won her countrymen their reputation.

'Iceland may seem out of the way to you nowadays. But back then, your U-boats were trying to sink the British convoys crossing the Atlantic. They would have liked to be able to put in here. So I suppose it was important enough that the British got here first. I mean, they were merchant seamen, weren't they, on those convoys, like our lads, just trying to do a job, get food through. We could understand that all right.'

'When exactly did the Americans arrive?' Burke decided it was a good moment to steer the old lady back towards their topic.

'I can't remember exactly. The English must have been too

192

stretched. Or maybe the Americans just told them what to do. Isn't that what they always do?'

Kotzke smiled. Burke grimaced.

'I don't know. But by 1943 there were half as many Yankee servicemen here as there were of us Icelanders in Reykjavik. And I mean service*men*. Can you imagine how our local boys reacted to seeing yet another of Iceland's few vital resources used up? But the Yanks had lots of dollars and fish prices went up. So they built their airport and flew out the girls and the men went fishing and said nothing; at least not to their faces.'

'So that was when they built the American base at Keflavik?'

'No, no, no.' She said it as if rebuking a silly schoolchild. 'That came much later. No, the British built the first airfield, out into the harbour. You must have seen it. It's still Reykjavik's main airport today, for internal flights, that is. Keflavik, the new airport next to the American base out on Reykjanes, the peninsula – that's for foreign flights only. That's right, isn't it, Sigurdir?'

Her daughter called an affirmative from the depths of the kitchen.

'Of course, for us girls, it was a different matter. We were very much in demand. I settled for a local boy in the end, of course, – didn't I, dear?' Siggy had come in carrying a tray with four vast cups of strong coffee. 'But your father, God rest him, would get angry enough in his way over those Yankees, with their stockings and their chewing gum and the way they smelled of aftershave rather than dried herring. Oh dear, it was a revelation for us, I can tell you.'

Burke tried to imagine the scene as the strapping local lads, hardened by years of fighting force-nine gales in the north Atlantic to bring home a few kilos of cod, found themselves hopelessly outclassed by doughboys from Arkansas or Indiana who'd never seen the sea before they flew out across the ocean, and landed here to talk up a storm and trade nylons for dropped knickers.

'Oh, yes,' she continued, 'but that's when we found out where we really were in the world: just a convenience. Not part of America or Europe, but a halfway house in between. An unsinkable aircraft carrier, that's what they called us. But what they meant was a ready depot of girls and kerosene. Not so much a country as a refuelling stop.'

Realization dawned on Burke. Hiram Carter's cryptic remarks, the old Soviet military map, the medal, the photograph of the dashing young US air force man and the love letter, and now Steiner's vanished airplane. It all fitted together. Except that the picture made no sort of sense. A missing bomber. What sort of bomber? Was there a chance? No. But yet. If what he was thinking stood up, was it possible that Fuchs had had an unknown ally, and that together they had pulled off a coup that Western history couldn't bear thinking of?

'Eamonn, what is it?' Sabine had caught the sudden change in his mood.

'The half-way house.' What we're looking for is here because this is halfway between Europe and America. A refuelling stop. For Josh Finch.'

He turned back to the old lady. 'Was there anything in particular, any incident that stands out, any scandal, any alert at the base?'

'Heavens. Let me think. There were always alerts, at least in the early days. But it was only practice, they told us, Special fire drill, of course. Didn't want the place going up in smoke, they said. Is that the sort of thing you mean?'

'Sort of. But something more unusual. Anything to do with aircraft. An accident? A panic of some sort. A "flap", they used to call it.'

The old lady's sudden high-pitched laugh took them by surprise: 'Why, of course they did. Of course.'

'Yes?' said Burke eagerly. But it was his choice of language that had enthused the old lady.

'A flap! A flap! My goodness, I had quite forgotten. We had learned our English so seriously at school and were so keen to try it out on real Englishmen. But they all spoke so funnily, with such strange accents. And then there were the Americans, all speaking like Clark Gable in those films shown down at the picture house. Oh, the richness of the language – some of it not very repeatable, either.'

'Yes.' Burke was desperately worried that she would lose the thread he had been searching for. 'But this particular "flap", what was it about?'

'Yes, yes. Not an ear-flap, or a cat-flap, or the flap on the wing of a plane. Just a flap. Like the night the big American plane went missing.'

Burke shot a glance at Sabine.

'Tell me about it,' he said, in his best Fleet Street bedside manner.

* * *

194

Abe Steiner was not normally a man to lose sleep, not that he needed much these days. Even before the accident he and Mabel had slept in separate beds but after it, he had insisted on moving his bed into his study.

When he did finally put himself to bed, however, going through the tedious business of hauling himself from the wheelchair on to the cot that lay next to his desk, it was usually because he was ready for sleep. And then he was out like a light. Except that tonight was different. He had deliberately sat up until 4a.m. waiting for young Burke to answer his call. The boy had given the impression that it was important and, given what he had come up with, he was beginning to think that might be an understatement. By 4.15, however, he had decided enough was enough and got himself into bed.

He was certain that if he had still been on active service, he would not be passing on the information he had gleaned to an outsider. But hell, Mickey Burke's boy was scarcely an outsider. In his day his father had been so far inside, the only circle tighter than the one he belonged to was the President's asshole. Besides, it seemed the lad had found most of this stuff out for himself; Steiner was just confirming it. But confirming what? He had more questions than answers.

Then the phone rang.

'Timing, boy, timing,' he muttered to himself.

Using the grip attached to the wall, he pulled himself up to a half-sitting position and, not bothering to turn on the light, reached across for the phone on the end of the desk

'Steiner here. Who's that? Not the pope, I guess?'

At the other end of the line, Burke could not resist a grin. 'General, sir. I'm very sorry to disturb you at this hour. But I got your message. It sounded . . . ah . . . interesting, to say the least.'

'Funny, I kinda guessed you'd say that. The only trouble is, boy' – the laughter went out of the old man's voice – 'it appears to be true.' He hesitated, and Burke could hear the question in his voice. 'But then I guess you already know that.'

Burke hedged. He didn't know what to tell the old man. Steiner was an old friend of the family, but he was also – or until recently had been – part of the US military establishment. And somehow Burke had the impression that the trail they were following led on to thin ice. Playing careful was the only real option.

'We know a lot of the story, sir. But I'm really keen to know what your search turned up.'

'Okay, for starters this guy Finch was a regular ace flyer, one o' the best – a hero of the Murmansk flyin' in to Rooskyland once every coupla weeks to deliver supplies during 1943. He was a real hot dog who looked like he was headin' straight for the stars until he suddenly disappears one day back in October 1945.'

'Disappears?'

Kotzke was standing on tiptoes next to Burke, straining to catch both sides of the conversation.

'That's what I said. The note is brisk and final – "missing in action" – no details, no circumstances, nothin'.'

'Couldn't it have been some routine mission and he was shot down?'

'Who by, guy? You got cloth ears? Didn't you hear the date? 21 October 1945. We weren't fightin' a war with anybody.'

'No?' Burke probed.

'No, siree. What is interestin' is where he disappeared from.'

'Don't tell me.' Burke couldn't help himself. 'Reykjavik, Iceland?'

'Iceland? What the hell's Iceland got to do with it? This guy was based just where the squadron number you gave me suggested he'd be. You know where that was?'

There was a note of interrogation in the voice. The old man was testing him, trying to find out how much of this story Burke already knew and how much he was waiting to be told.

'You remember, don't ya?'

Desperately he scanned his mind. Finch had not disappeared in Iceland. Therefore he must have been logged as missing before he got there. Where had he come from? What was the link to Fuchs? One possibility struck him: there were only two air bases in New Mexico back then that Burke had ever heard of: Roswell and Albuquerque. The latter was, as far as he knew, the only one that Klaus Fuchs would ever have been anywhere near.

'Albuquerque.' He tried his best to make it sound like an answer rather than a question.

'Absolutely.' There was renewed confidence in the voice. Burke breathed a sigh of relief. 'Kirkland air force base, Albuquerque, New Mexico,' the general continued. Biggest backwater in the whole of the US air force establishment in 1945, except for one little thing.'

'Which was?'

'Hey, come on, you're havin' me on. Kirkland just happened to be the base where they tested and flew the modified B-29 Superfortress bombers. Your boy was one of the squadron that got left behind when the first wave left for the island.'

Burke's head was swimming. He stuck to repeating the words that left him behind.

'The island.'

'Yeah, Tinian, the island captured from the Japanese where the rest of the guys were already practising high-altitude approach runs and post-blast evasive manoeuvres. The island Enola Gay left from.'

'Enola Gay.' Burke found a line from an old pop song running through his mind: 'Enola Gay, you should have stayed at home yesterday.'

'Yup. Just about the most famous bomber of all time – or infamous, I guess, depending on your point of view. A B-29 just like your boy was flying when he disappeared. Enola Gay, the plane that dropped the bomb on Hiroshima, named after the pilot's mother, conferring on her the most dubious immortality in history. Of course, it was the Nagasaki type they were really modified to carry.'

'The Nagasaki type.' Burke was beginning to feel he had got lodged in a conversational pattern he could not escape from. Steiner had noticed it too.

'Hey, you on a tape loop or something?'

'Sorry. Just trying to make sure we don't get any misunderstandings.'

'Yeah. Though I have to tell you, I ain't at all sure what I do understand from this lot.'

'How do you mean, sir?' Burke didn't want to add that he wasn't at all sure himself, though his suspicions were growing fast amid the circumstantial evidence.

'Well, when I said your boy and a B-29 disappeared, I meant it literally. It's not in the records, not as such. But there's a gap in the squadron numbering. They moved outta Kirkland at the beginning of October that year, up to Edwards. And the numbering no longer tallies like it did during a routine inspection back in August when the others left for the Pacific. There's one plane too few. Which to my mind fits uncomfortably with the disappearance of Finch. Do you think your boy could have been joy-riding or something? You think this guy could have written off a B-29 somewhere in the New Mexico desert? Is that the idea?'

Up to a point, thought Burke on the other end of the telephone. But only to a very small point indeed.

'Eamonn?' Burke sensed a caution in the old man's voice. As if what he had said had worried him.

'Tell me, do you know what the hell you're getting into?'

'I think so, sir,' Burke replied, with more confidence than he felt.

'Hmm, what got me thinking that there might have been an accident of some sort was an oblique reference in one file. It uses the phrase "broken arrow". Finch's B-29 was called "Navajo Arrow". It's probably just coincidence, and it may mean nothing. After all, it wasn't until those unfortunate accidents in the sixties that the expression gained currency.'

'What expression?'

'Broken arrow.'

'I don't get it.'

'As of 1961, when a F-14 accidentally shed its nuclear payload over the Nevada desert, the records use the phrase "broken arrow" for a bird that fell out of the nest.'

Burke frowned. There was no getting away from it. The old man was sharp. As razors.

'Eamonn?'

'Sir.'

'You aren't trying to tell me that boy was carryin' cargo?'

'I think it has to be a possibility, sir.'

The general exhaled a long deep breath that sounded almost like a whistle.

'I had a feelin' about this. If what you're saying is true, then somebody sure as hell doesn't want the world to know. And you're gonna tell 'em? I have to say, I find it hard to believe that a plane that size could have come down anywhere in the continental United States and stayed a secret.

'Least of all,' the general continued, 'if it was carrying some sort of device. Unless he crashed in Area 51, heh heh?'

'Heh, heh,' Burke echoed the general's laugh. Hollowly. As far as he could see, the last thing New Mexico had needed back in the late 1940s was some aliens dropping in on Roswell air force base to see how things were going on. Things were complicated enough as they were.

'What sort of range did a B-29 have? Where could he have reached without refuelling?'

'Just about anywhere in the country. The B-29 was designed to be the world's first intercontinental bomber. It had the range to go four thousand miles in one hop. Could have got to Tokyo if he'd wanted.'

Or to Iceland, Burke thought. The refuelling base. Wasn't that one of the reasons the Allies had taken the island in the first place? The reason the Americans were still there. That was what had struck him as he sat in Siggy's mother's armchair.

Kotzke was mouthing at him to tell her what was going on. He nodded agreement.

'General, I have to go now. Listen, I can't begin to tell you how grateful I am.'

'Hey, for what? But listen, kid, don't go jumping to mad conclusions.'

'Sure thing, general,' he replied. Though what other conclusions were there?

'Keep me posted.'

'Will do, sir,' Burke lied. 'And thanks again.'

He closed the connection and sat down, heavily, on the bed.

Kotzke, her modesty forgotten along with the remnants of her hangover, flung her arms around his neck, her eyes glinting with excitement. 'The plane, the missing plane, that's what we're looking for, right?'

'Right.'

'The Soviets didn't just get stolen information about the bomb, did they?'

'Maybe not,' he muttered, lying back suddenly and laughing as Sabine tumbled towards him, her spiky fringe brushing his eyes, their camaraderie verging on something more sensual. 'Maybe,' he said, 'just maybe, they got the whole fucking thing.'

'And we,' she announced, to his disappointment sitting up and tossing back her hair, once again all business-like, 'are going to find it.'

Maybe, thought Burke. Unless someone stops us. Or gets there first. And his mind drifted back to the lifeless figure of Anatoly Yakunin sprawled in the dirty Moscow snow.

29

On the Wires

Burke was pacing the floor of their hotel room, his eyes moving from the mobile phone in his hand to the panorama of Mount Esja outside the window. He lifted the phone and stared at the digits, then dropped it to his side again and resumed his pacing. It was the obvious thing to do. It made all sorts of sense under the circumstances. And all sorts of nonsense. There were times when – what was the old American business school jargon? – the obvious step was counter-indicated.

'What's the matter?' asked Sabine.

'I'm worried.'

'What about?'

'About what the hell is going on here. About what the hell we're chasing. And who else might be.'

'What makes you so certain someone else is?'

Burke was close to anger. Why on earth was she being so obtuse?

'Look, the reason we're on this story in the first place is that you believe Klaus Fuchs was murdered because of something he was threatening to reveal. Anatoly Yakunin was about to do the job for him and he ended up bungee-jumping without a rope. And Christ knows how much of a coincidence that bomb in London was.'

'You don't think . . .?'

'I don't think anything. I don't know. But I am damn certain it is about time we started being careful about watching our backs, and who we trust. If there is some ex-Stasi involvement, it's dangerous enough. But if any of what we think we've pieced together is true, then there could be more players in the game than either you or I imagine. It depends how wide the circle has grown.'

'Who do you not trust? The Russian?'

'Valery? I trust him with my life. He's already saved it once.'

'He has? You didn't tell him.'

'I didn't want to embarrass me. It was a long time ago. I was a junior reporter in the war in Afghanistan, got into trouble trying to interview the Mujahideen rebels on an official Soviet press trip out of Moscow. The local Red Army captain caught two of us trying to make contact and accused us of being American spies. Threatened to have us shot on the spot. Korkin was a sergeant in his regiment, stepped in, made a fuss and took the tempo down. A year later I met him in Moscow. He'd been given a dishonourable discharge and was living hand-to-mouth as a street-sweeper. I found him a job with *The New York Times* as a translator.'

'What about your British spy, do you trust him?'

'Dickie Boston? About as far as I could throw him.'

God, he thought. Boston was logically his next call. Dickie had the access, or ought to have. But would he use it, and if he did, would he have any interest in sharing what he found? Honesty, after all, was not exactly part of his job description. But doing nothing would get them nowhere. He willed his finger out of its indecision and stabbed the keypad numbers.

'Hello.' The voice on the end of the line conveyed just the right amount of business-like briskness – a neutral tone that could easily swing into effusiveness or reprobation depending on the evolution of the conversation.

'It's me. Is that you?' Burke couldn't resist it. It was not often he had the man on the end of a string.

'Who's calling, please?' And then, after a brief silence: 'Eamonn?'

'Well it's not Jesus Christ.'

'Indeed, nor his virgin mother.'

'This is important. Maybe. I mean, I think it might be.'

'Good grief, old thing. You sound serious.' Boston passed for a second and Burke wondered if he was turning a recording device on, or off.

'I am. I mean, it is. Dickie, you remember I asked you to trawl the archives on Klaus Fuchs?'

'Like it was yesterday, old man. I thought I'd got back to you, filled in a few of the gaps. Don't tell me the story's died under you. Can't say I'd be too surprised, though. Not exactly any crackers lurking in the safes here, at least as far as I can make out.'

'That's why I'm calling. Dickie, are you sure you told me the whole of it?'

The question hung in the air. Burke pressed his ear to the speaker, cursing atmospheric interference that at this distance interfered even with digital cellphones.

'Absolutely. At least, as far as I know. It was all a bit before my time, you know. Where are you, Eamonn? This line isn't very good.'

Did that mean he really didn't know, Burke wondered. Should he tell him? Was Boston one of those who might have an interest? In a missing bomb, even an ancient one? The answer had to be yes, undoubtedly.

'I'm in Iceland.'

'How very exotic. I can't imagine our friend Fuchs ever got there. What's the connection, Eamonn?'

'I don't know. Maybe there isn't one. Listen, Dickie . . .'

'I am listening, Eamonn. Please go on. But bear in mind that I have other things to do than serve as a conduit for antique anecdotes about dead spies, even to the loyal servants of Her Majesty's Press Corps.' He uttered the stock phrase in a way that managed to emphasize the mock-respectful capital letters.

Burke took the plunge. 'What would you say if I told you that in 1945 someone stole an atomic bomb right out from under the Americans' noses in Los Alamos, and then lost it?'

There was a moment's silence on the other end of the line, and then Burke heard Boston's voice, as self-assured and cynical as ever. 'I do hope that's not what you are going to tell me? Because if it is, I'm going to have to tell you that I think you are stark staring mad.'

As Burke put the phone down with exasperation, Sabine looked up at him, her dark brown eyes focused narrowly on his:

'Not convinced, hmm?'

'No. But can you blame him? This half-baked hack rings up to tell him that there's a nice line going in previously owned atomic devices, that Iceland has joined the nuclear club unintentionally, that the CIA and the FBI and MI5 and MI6 and the KGB and God knows who else accidentally mislaid one of the most dangerous eggs in the global nest half a century ago and nobody has bothered to pick it up.'

'No. But it's not a question of belief, is it? We have evidence.'

'Oh no, we don't. I'll tell you what we have. We have a cryptic diary left by a confessed traitor going gaga; a dead Russian's map of "Treasure Island"; and a piece of yarn-spinning by an incapacitated geriatric Cold War warrior with an overactive imagination backed up by nothing more concrete than an Icelandic granny's reminiscence?'

'Perhaps we should think it through.'

'Okay. Let's just imagine that this whole thing is true, that an American airman really did smuggle a bomb out of New Mexico in 1945. It begs a few questions, doesn't it? Such as: where is it going and why does it stop in Iceland?'

'The second part we've done: it had to refuel somewhere.'

'So why not somewhere on the eastern seaboard, in the continental United States?'

'I don't know, unless the presence of a B-29 would have aroused too much speculation at one of the big east coast bases.'

'So where was he taking it?'

'There's only one real answer, isn't there? Where do you think?'

'Moscow?'

'Where else? Or at least Murmansk. That's the route our boy knew. It avoids going over most of inhabited Europe. The question is: did he get there?'

'Well, if he didn't we have to face the fact that Finch and his cargo may still be out there. And that that is what someone is willing to kill for.'

'To get hold of an atomic bomb.'

'Maybe. Except something's wrong somewhere. Apart from anything else, it would be a very old atomic bomb. Still lethal, no doubt, but of more real interest to a museum than a would-be superpower. Since the collapse of the Soviet Union there has been more atomic technology floating around on the open market than pig meat in a hot-dog factory.'

'Terrorists?'

'Same thing applies. It's easier to buy raw material for a bomb these days than to start a global chase for one that's half a century old. Of course, back in 1988, when our friend Fuchs was offed, things were different, weren't they? What if the Stasi killed Fuchs not just to keep him quiet, but because he had revealed to them the possibility of getting their hands on a bomb of their own?'

Sabine looked perplexed. 'But East Germany was an arsenal of nuclear weapons. Why would they have been interested in a vintage model preserved in the ice?'

'Think about it.' Burke was warming to his theory. 'All the nuclear weaponry in the DDR was under Russian control. The last thing they wanted was a German finger on a nuclear button. And even before Fuchs died, it was fairly clear that the Kremlin could no longer be relied upon to support the straw men in Berlin. So when the Stasi finds out that Herr Doktor Fuchs, of all people, knows the whereabouts of a vintage, but presumably still functional, atomic device, it must have seemed like a golden opportunity.'

'For what?'

'For insurance.' The more he thought about it, the more plausible it seemed. 'To preserve Erich Honecker's tinpot dictatorship. Imagine how the world would have changed if East Germany, back in the spring of 1989 with the winds of revolution whistling around the corridors of power everywhere from Warsaw to Budapest, acquired a unilateral nuclear deterrent.'

'To deter against what?'

'Against reunification, for Christ's sake. What other threat did Honecker face?'

'The real threat was from within, from people like me.'

'Yes, but with a bomb, they would have had a free hand to do what they liked internally. They could have sent tanks into the streets and declared martial law.

'And who would have been the saviour of the politburo, the heir apparent? Mielke, of course.'

'Erich Mielke, the Stasi minister? But he was even older than Honecker.'

'Sure he was, but those old bastards believed they were immortal. Besides, everyone knew by then that Honecker had cancer. His days were numbered. Mielke must have believed he could be Europe's equivalent of Kim Il-Sung, last defender of the Stalinist system.'

Burke was getting carried away. Kotzke shook her head slightly.

'But all that is gone, Eamonn. Long gone.' She took a deep breath and looked at him sceptically, as if she was sure there was a better explanation. Burke had seen the expression before, from unimaginative editors doubting a tortuous but disarmingly comprehensive story he had painstakingly pieced together to fit the facts. But wasn't conspiracy theory what Kotzke had hired him for?

30

The Insecurity Man

Several dozen arctic tern rose from the icy surface of the lake, turning a lazy circle in the air before descending once again, like a squadron of fighters returning to base. Burke was impressed by their sense of formation. Envied it even. Formation was what he longed to see imposed on the tumble of conflicting ideas in his brain.

For the second morning in a row they were sitting around a window table in the cosy café beside Tjornin pond. Yakunin's map and an Icelandic equivalent lay on the table. Siggy was entranced and admonitory in equal measure.

'This is simply not the time. You must wait. A few weeks at least.'

Any journey to the 'interior' required serious preparation, especially in winter. Two months earlier, she insisted, she would have turned down the expedition altogether. With temperatures that never climbed above freezing, and a sun that barely climbed above the horizon, the world of ice and snow and semi-permanent darkness was a prospect that only a fool would have considered. The problem was not the cold but the heat: the volcanoes, in many cases still active, that lay under the ice caps.

'The danger is that when travelling on glaciers at any time – and particularly in such geologically unstable conditions – there is a real risk of a crack opening up, or of finding a huge chasm blocking your way. And detours themselves are dangerous; there is no effective way to map the shifting ice. It's better in summer: at least it's clear where the glacier starts and stops. I'd recommend you postpone this until the end of June.'

'I don't think we have the time,' said Burke. One thing was clear:

they were not acting in a vacuum. A circle was closing around them. And a circle always reminded Burke uncomfortably of a noose.

'The initial route is fairly simple,' Siggy sighed and continued. 'Up towards Kjölur in the central highlands. At this time of year, it's easiest to fly there. Just a few kilometres south-west there is a hut, at a place called Thojafell – it is used as an emergency shelter, but we also keep snowcats there. We will be able to use a four-wheel drive that far, but after that the cats are the only option. You have used one before?'

Burke and Kotzke looked blank.

'Don't worry. It is just like riding a motorbike, only not so painful if you fall off. Most of the time.' And she did another imitation of Korkin's loud laugh.

Burke cast a make-the-best-of-it smile at Kotzke. He thought her grin looked distinctly phoney.

'Okay, I am probably mad. But I agree,' said Siggy. 'When do you want to start?'

'As soon as possible, really. How long will it take you to set things up?'

'A day or two at most.' Despite the attempts to put them off, Burke was impressed now by the cool confidence of the Icelander. 'I will call one of my colleagues up in Kjölur. It is useful to have someone who really knows the territory. I suggest we take the 4.30 p.m. flight the day after tomorrow. That will give us a good night's rest. It will be important to start early when we set off for Langjökul itself.'

'Sure, whatever you say. But what are we going to do here for the next forty-eight hours or so?'

'Go swimming,' the big blonde said, as if it were the most natural thing in the world.

The man at a window table in the restaurant across the lake from the café in which Burke and his friends were seated was also thinking of birds. He cut another pink slice of the local delicacy which he had decided – to make best use of his time – to enjoy as an early lunch: roast puffin. It tasted slightly fishy.

He wondered about the state of mind of his quarry, so seemingly safe and secure in their warm café. People took security for granted. But it was not the natural order. It was something forced upon an unruly world. It was people like him who made the difference: the troops who patrolled the front line between security and insecurity.

Once, in a very different context, people like him had been labelled 'fighters on the invisible front'. It was not such an inappropriate description, he thought.

The old man in Yugozapadnaya had once stood on that front line too; that was why he had been reluctant to open the door, so early in the morning. He had peered timorously through the crack he opened, putting his faith in the flimsy metal chain. But a second's violence had ripped the little screws from the woodwork. The man had not been as scared as he had hoped, or imagined, despite the knife held at his throat. Instead there was steely resentment lurking beneath the surface of the watery old eyes. He had revealed nothing. The security man had felt no remorse as he pulled the old man's sweater over his head and manhandled him towards the window: it was an old KGB trick, and he relished the irony.

A movement at the corner of his vision refocused his attention. The doorway of the café opposite opened. He summoned the waitress quickly, asked for the bill and paid in cash, assuring her that the unfinished plate of puffin breast had been delicious, but that he had a plane to catch. Slipping into his dark blue anorak, and pulling the hood up, he walked out into the cool sunshine and strode as briskly as any Icelander out for a morning constitutional. He watched as Burke and Kotzke climbed into a Jeep Cherokee with hire plates, while Siggy headed up the hill towards the Toyota he already knew was her's. That was awkward, he thought; but then again maybe not that awkward. Maybe they were just forcing his hand.

31

Blue Blood

Burke pulled the Cherokee on to the black tarmac strip that ran through the thick blanket of snow and on to the moonscape of Reykjanes peninsula.

It was barely twenty minutes' drive to the Blue Lagoon, one of the country's most famous – and most easily accessible – tourist attractions. Burke swung the wheel to turn the jeep off the smooth tarmac and on to the rough and ready stretch of asphalt that led to the bath-house.

· At first sight it looked more like an oil refinery. Huge silver domes and intricate coils of blue-painted piping emerged from a thick white ground mist: warm water turned to steam on contact with the freezing air. The lagoon was a by-product of the Svartsengi power station, siphoning up superboiled water from one and a half miles beneath the earth's crust.

'Looks like something out of Star Wars,' Burke remarked.

'More like the devil's brewery,' responded Sabine.

'Time for your afternoon dip, Ms Kotzke.'

'Eammon,' she exclaimed in a voice that exuded not so much enthusiasm as queasiness, 'have you seen the water? It's turquoise, like someone's imported it straight from the cover of one of those Caribbean holiday magazines, only boiled it first.'

It did, too, Burke thought. The colour was not a reflection of an azure sky, but the product of the copper oxide in the spring's mineral content. The Blue Lagoon's waters were touted as a cure for anything from impotence to angina. But most people came for the thrill of it.

In the little tourist shop Burke bought the house speciality, a disposable waterproof camera. When else might he get a picture of

Sabine in a bikini? A few minutes later, he emerged from the men's changing rooms and took in the unlikely scene framed in the viewfinder: a landscape of snow dominated by a vast, brightly coloured industrial installation forming the backdrop to a rowdy gang of hulking semi-naked men splashing two blonde ice maidens in black swimsuits carrying trays of iridescent cocktails, clearly designed to match the hue of the steaming water. At that moment Sabine emerged from the women's changing rooms, but not – he noticed with disappointment – in a bikini. Instead she wore a silvery snakeskin-design one-piece.

'Eammon, what the hell's going on? This looks like something from Fellini's *Satyricon*.'

'According to Siggy, it happens every couple of weeks. Oil workers from one of the Norwegian rigs. So as soon as they get the chance they book a helicopter and a hotel and paint Reykjavik red. Or blue, it looks like tonight.'

'Naaa, haaalloo.' A bearded bear of a man, with a figure like Luciano Pavarotti, approached them, beaming, his eyes at Sabine's thigh-level.

'English? Come on in, the water's lovely.' He held up one of the bright blue drinks for Eammon. Burke took it, sniffed and threw it back in one. Curaçao and brennivin with a twist of lime, he guessed. Who said fire and ice didn't go together. He plunged beneath the gently bubbling bath-water of the lagoon.

A second later, Sabine surfaced inches in front of him, rising like a sultry, slick-haired sea goddess, silver and gold, eyes closed, dark hair dripping.

'Christ, that's wonderful,' she gasped. 'It has to be bad for you.'

'Hey, Englishman,' came the cry from across the lagoon. Burke looked over and saw the nordic Pavarotti raise yet another iridescent cocktail to him while simultaneously raising a stocky hairy leg between the lithe pair of one of the ice maidens. She screamed, sending a tray of empty plastic glasses over her head to mixed cries of shock and hilarity.

The blonde valkyrie's swimsuit had slipped off one shoulder exposing a perfect platinum breast with pert nipple which she seemed in no hurry to cover up. Pavarotti, half-submerged and advancing upon her like a surfacing whale, had it clearly in his sights. Suddenly he rose from the water as if about to break into an aria.

'Aaaaargh . . .'

It was always the same, a high-pitched wail that Burke had heard a thousand times, in the backstreets of Belfast, the deserts of the Gulf, Sarajevo's sniper's alley. The truncated cry rose and snapped with the detonation, a whiplash crack that burned through the arctic air even as it filled with screams.

Burke fell forwards instinctively into the red-stained water, pushing Sabine down, submerging her head. Half-naked bodies scrambled for the pool edge or cowered like frightened frogs. Through the clamour Burke heard the roar and squeal of a car engine gunned into life and retreating at speed. Then the shouts, sobs and screams subsided, eerily, into the silence of horror.

On the surface of the water floated a great inanimate mass: Pavarotti, a whale now in the gunsights of the hunter, a wasted mass of blubber oozing blood and guts. The bullet, Burke noted, with the war correspondent's eye of experience, had blown a hole the size of a child's head in his belly.

Sabine was pulling herself out of the water on to one of the rocks. Burke, already out, stretched out a hand to her.

He noticed he was still holding the disposable camera in his other hand. The old freelancer's instinct, he thought grimly: never drop anything that has a chance of making you money. It must have been from about here that the shot was fired. Burke lifted the camera to his eye as he had done a thousand times at scenes of devastation. The lens confirmed what he had known instinctively the moment the shot exploded in his ears: from here it was clear he and Sabine must have been the target.

The circle had indeed become a noose. And they had only just escaped the executioner.

32

God's Kindergarten

The turbo-prop engines of the little Icelandair commuter plane throbbed noisily. Eammon Burke was worried, but he was also very, very happy. He looked at Sabine's tousled hair and felt her breath warm on his neck, then turned his face and kissed the top of her head, breathing deep her faint, slightly musky, sweet scent, like fresh hay drying in the sun. It had taken murder to bring them together.

They had fled the Blue Lagoon like guilty thieves and driven out to Keflavik rather than back into the city. Whoever was responsible might have been waiting for a second shot. From a café they had telephoned Siggy. Her first reaction had been incredulity, her second caution. She advised them to leave the hire car at the airport and take a cab to the little harbour of Grindavik, a few kilometres away. There was a guesthouse there; she would call ahead and tell them they were coming. In the meantime, she said, she would call her contacts and make sure that everything was ready. With luck they would be able to leave the next morning, half a day earlier than planned.

At Grindavik they checked in and then walked out on to the jetty that protected the town's fishing boats from the arctic squalls. A cold salty breeze was gusting in and Sabine had taken Burke's arm instinctively, as one does for warmth, and he had held it tightly, both of them aware now, for the first time, as they watched the light fade and deep ochre, blues and gold stretch briefly across the northern sky, that they faced something more sinister than either had imagined: not just the echo of an old evil, but a very present one. She had hunched her shoulders and suggested they return to the warmth of the little guest house. He had looked down into her eyes, fancied he saw an entreaty of another order and kissed her hard on the lips.

In their small twin-bedded room they had fallen upon each other hungrily, peeling clothes like the loose skin of ripe fruit as they fell into the embracing warmth of the goosedown duvet on Sabine's bed. His hand unzipped her tight jeans and burrowed into the damp warmth between her legs. Sabine sighed and raised her buttocks as he eased the denim, stiff and damp from the rain, over her thighs, tracing a warm wet line with his tongue down the inside of one, his mop of unruly hair brushing between her legs until he came back up to roll his tongue around the tight little bud of erogenous flesh, swollen already by her excitement. He felt her shiver with desire and his own erection swell almost painfully in response.

She clawed at his back, pulling the open shirt over his head and hers, enclosing them as if in a tent while his lips, still wet with her own juices, fastened upon hers. She came before he penetrated her, aroused by the moist firm pressure of his penis as he held her arms above her head and rubbed his hard chest against her small soft breasts, and then again as he thrust himself inside her, inspired by her orgasm, and whimpering with lust as he slid his big firm hands down the length of her body.

'That,' she said afterwards, as he lay spent across her, suddenly so much smaller and more vulnerable, 'was fucking brilliant!' He laughed, and she laughed too. But it hadn't been, he told himself later, drifting off into a troubled sleep; it had been more like making love.

The flight to Kjölur took barely thirty minutes. The place reminded Burke of the grey villages in the west of Ireland, small, homely and functional. From the air Siggy had pointed out the Langjökul glacier in the distance: a great lake of ice spilling over barren rocky crags. He tried to imagine what it would have been like, flying over this terrain in bad conditions in an aircraft equipped with only the primitive navigation equipment of the 1940s. The thought made him shudder. Sabine had stared out of the window for almost the whole trip. He feared for a moment that the night before might have become a morning-after embarrassment. But then she squeezed his hand. And held on to it.

On the ground their welcoming party was an automatic boost to morale: a striking, tall, suntanned man with hair the colour of white gold. He came striding out of the tiny terminal building behind

Siggy, who ran across the snowy tarmac to embrace them. They looked to Burke like a different species: arctic animals frolicking in the landscape that only they could consider home.

'This is Magnus Haraldson. I call him my polar bear.'

The tall man grinned, displaying a dazzling array of white teeth, and held out a hand to grasp Burke.

'Nice to meet you,' he said in English as flawless as Siggy's.

'*Und Sie auch, gnädiges Fräulein.*' His German sounded to Burke as archaic as it was immaculate, and the gestures matched, inclining his head as he held out his hand to Sabine.

'*Es freut mich sehr,*' she replied, with a remarkably ready smile that made Burke feel jealous.

'So, I think everything is in order,' said Magnus as they clambered into his Japanese four-wheel drive.

'I have thought the best thing is to go straight to the hut at Thojafell,' Magnus said, looking at Siggy with an implicit question in his voice.

'Yes. How is the heating?'

'I have been there already this morning and lighted the stove. It should be warm as a sauna. The scooters are ready and fuelled. I have also checked out the GPS. Everything as it should be.'

'What's the GPS?' asked Sabine.

Burke looked ironically askance at her. Surely in Germany even gung-ho girl reporters were more techno-savvy than that.

'Ah, it is the great American toy,' replied Magnus. 'Global Positioning System. It works with the satellites. An aerial on each scooter bounces up a signal to the sky and back comes a map reading. Or even better, if you live in a part of a world that has good maps, it can feed in on to it.'

'Like this,' said Magnus, adjusting a few trackpad controls on the clip-on unit, until the digital numerical co-ordinates disappeared to be replaced by a grid that to Burke's eyes appeared empty, until he recognized the name Kjölur in one corner and a flickering hairline sight a few millimetres to the south-west.

'It has changed lives up here,' said Siggy. 'For the first time people can have a definite idea of where they are, even if the icefog comes down.'

'Pahh!' went Magnus. 'My father's people always knew where they were. They could tell from the winds, from the light in the sky.'

Burke leaned against Sabine and was rewarded by a tongue darted into his ear. The world wasn't such a bad place after all.

In fact, he thought, as he looked out through the frost on the vehicle's side windows, the world was extraordinarily beautiful. Already the sun was beginning to go down, casting a glow over the snowscape that mixed baby-blue and rose-pink. God's colours for kindergarten, he thought. It seemed incredible, as they crunched their way along a trail that led up on to a high plateau limited by the tinted peaks of the ice-capped mountains beyond, that this frozen paradise had been tainted.

The little hut appeared out of nowhere as the four-wheel drive lurched over an escarpment. The roof was low, gently sloped and weighted down with thick snow packed in successive layers since the beginning of winter, some six months earlier.

Magnus was already out of the vehicle, unloading their bags on to the ground. Siggy had gone up and opened the door which, to Burke's surprise, was unlocked even though it contained valuable supplies.

'There's no theft around here,' Siggy had explained. 'How could there be? Everyone knows everyone else. A stranger in Kjölur would stick out like a tree. Still, given the unwelcome interest in our expedition, perhaps it was rash.'

Inside, the hut was illuminated by a fluorescent strip which showed up the concrete of the walls and the spartan metal furniture. It was not at all the homely place Burke had imagined. He had seen too much Switzerland.

Siggy told them the place was part of a network funded by the government but maintained by local people as a shelter in case of a sudden storm. Out on the ice it was important to have a fixed point of reference, somewhere that offered at least a degree of protection if the weather turned against you. They were marked on every map.

Sleeping accommodation was communal – four sets of bunk beds, Burke noted with some disappointment. Magnus was busy in the corner lighting a fire in the stove. The fuel was anthracite and took a lot of heat to ignite. At last the coals began to glow and he left the little iron door open to allow the warm air to circulate. Siggy, meanwhile, had put together a rough-and-ready meal of hot soup and dumplings from their supplies.

'Here, try this.' Magnus produced a bottle of clear liquid and began to pour measures into tumblers.

'No thanks,' Burke countered. His night on the town had left him with a psychological resistance to the burned caraway seed flavour of the local poison.

Siggy laid a hand on his arm. 'It's not brennivin.'

'I should think not,' boomed her compatriot. 'Birna would never forgive the suggestion even.'

'Who is Birna?' asked Sabine.

'My friend,' Magnus replied in a voice that implied everyone knew who his friends were.

'She also makes this,' put in Siggy.

'Which is?'

'Only the best aquavit in the world,' Magnus answered Burke's query proudly. He leaned across the table conspiratorially. 'Up here, we make it from local grain and the water of the glaciers. Pure. Water that fell as rain a thousand years before the first Viking set foot on Iceland. Skøl, cheers, prost, my friends.'

He lifted his glass across the table. Eamonn, Sabine and Siggy clinked their own against his, then followed suit as their host downed the alcohol in one. Burke felt the warmth course through him, but to his surprise felt no burning in his throat, though his brain immediately registered the kick.

'Impressive.'

The Icelander smiled appreciatively and refilled their glasses.

'Wait just one minute,' said Sabine. 'Maybe it is not such a good idea we all get very drunk.' She turned to Siggy.

'Have you told Magnus?'

'About what happened at the Blue Lagoon? Of course, I imagine all Iceland knows by now.'

Magnus nodded. 'You think someone was trying to kill you because of what you are looking for in the ice. Do you think whoever it was is still after you?'

Burke glanced at Sabine. She nodded.

'I'm afraid, yes. But we don't know why.'

It was Burke's turn to frown.

The two Icelanders looked at him. It was Siggy who spoke:

'That's not strictly true, is it, Eamonn?'

Magnus leaned forward across the table.

'Perhaps you might at least enlighten us as to what exactly we are looking for?'

'What we believe to be out there is a plane, a plane that we think might be carrying . . .' Burke hesitated a second, 'radioactive material.'

'Radioactive material?' Magnus repeated. 'You mean a nuclear missile? From Keflavik? The Americans' base?' He banged his fist suddenly on the table. The empty glasses jumped. 'I knew it. I always knew they were not to be trusted.' He went to get up.

Siggy put a hand on his arm. 'Wait, my big bear, you jump to too many conclusions. Let us hear the man out.'

Eamonn took a deep breath. 'We don't know exactly but it may be something like that, though it may go back even before Keflavik. But whatever it is, we think someone desperately wants to stop us getting to it, telling the world about it.'

'Then we will help,' the Icelander declared, as if delivering a government statement, while replenishing their glasses. 'Iceland is not just a puppet any more. We may be a small nation but we have our pride. Do you think that these people who tried to kill you at the Blue Lagoon, they are from the CIA?'

Burke was taken aback. Funny, it took someone else, someone fresh to crystallize the worry that had been forming in Burke's mind. The CIA meant Allen Dulles, the man Hiram Carter had mentioned. But Dulles had been dead for decades, his interventionist policy cast on the rubbish heap of history even before the Cold War had ended. But what about his legacy? Were there still those who might be endorsing it? What else had Carter said? 'Ask them about that an' all, them Rooskies.' They had done that. And the man who could have given the answers had paid with his life. However, there had been something else, too. It had almost flashed into his head the evening before when he had stood with Sabine on the jetty at Grindavik, watching the sun set. Sunset. Sunrise. That was what Carter had said just before he mentioned Dulles: 'Ask them about Mrs K, too. Ask them about the sunrise. The one that never happened.' The words scrawled in Russian, by Yakunin, on the envelope containing the letter and the photo of the airman: 'For the prevention of the coming up of the sun.' In other words, stopping the sunrise. Was there a link?

He sifted through the evidence again. A scrap of a diary from the man who gave Moscow the secret of the bomb, suggesting that he had done much more than that. The link to Yakunin, and the murdered Russian's legacy which had, thanks to Abe Steiner, unearthed the unresolved story of Joshua Finch. But what was Nora Winter hinting at, and what had Hiram Carter meant with cryptic comments about the other Los Alamos scientists? Was it possible that Fuchs was not the only spy?

No wonder he had got short shrift from Dickie Boston. Though that had been before the Blue Lagoon nightmare, just as when he had first spoken to him in London, the explosion on the Bayswater Road had not yet happened . . .

Magnus was looking at him intently as if trying to read his mind.

'If you think there is some sort of nuclear device out there, is it not dangerous?'

'It might well be. This thing has been out there a long time. It almost certainly crashed to begin with. We have no idea what condition it's in. It could be fractured, even leaking radioactivity. What is certain is that there is someone out here who either wants to prevent us reaching it or, probably more importantly, wants to get there first.'

'Wait,' Magnus said. 'If you are correct, then they might kill others also who know about this.'

'Certainly.' Sabine, obviously relieved that Burke had not told the whole story, was not going to be left out of whatever spin-doctoring he planned. 'Why?'

'I don't know. It is just that . . . Well, you remember old Gundar Peterson?'

'Yes, of course.' Siggy turned to him and for a moment Burke thought they were going to have a cosy chat about mutual acquaintances. 'I heard he committed suicide. About a month ago.'

'That's what people said.'

'But you think something different?'

'It is just his death was so unexpected. For him to have killed himself, you see. Gundar used to be a bit of a heathen. Named all his ponies after the old Norse gods. But he had caught religion recently, taken to going to seeing the pastor. We had a bit of a laugh about it down in the village, thought he just fancied her. At the funeral she was pretty cut up. But she allowed him to be buried on consecrated ground, even though it was assumed he was a suicide.

'And there was something else. Something that ties in uncomfortably with your story.'

'Gundar had a little farmhouse not far from here. He kept ponies, good old Icelandic ponies, like your Shetlands,' he nodded to Burke. 'Gundar loved his beasts, looked after them like a father. Some said he was the father of a couple.' He laughed, a short brief laugh. 'Then they all started to die. It was what depressed him.'

Sabine grimaced. 'How awful. What was the reason?'

'No one knew. Least of all old Gundar. He thought it was divine retribution for his past misdeeds. He had been at sea, and led a pretty racy life.' He smiled at the old man's memory. 'In the end it got to him. At least that's what we thought. He shot Freya, his favourite old mare, then blew his own brains out.'

'Yeech,' went Sabine.

'Except that . . . ?' Burke was watching the man's eyes. They seemed troubled.

'I don't know. There just seemed something wrong about it. I took a look at a few of the other animals and asked the vet to carry out an autopsy on the remains of the mare Gundar shot. What he found was cancer, a deep-seated bone cancer. It baffled him because it was a sort normally associated with long-term absorption of radioactive material.'

Silently, the big Icelander got to his feet, lifted the bottle of aquavit. Burke thought for a moment he was going to drain the rest in one gulp. Instead, he walked over to the sink and quietly poured it out.

'Magnus, what's the matter?' Siggy asked, then stopped herself, as if she had suddenly realized what else was troubling him.

He turned back to the table. 'The ponies didn't just graze on the grass near the glacier. They drank from the meltwater. The same water that Birna uses to make her aquavit.'

33

Cracked Ice

When Burke opened his eyes it was already after dawn, and a pallid grey glow tinged with pink was filtering through the small, heavily misted window. Sabine stirred beside him, curled inside the thick down sleeping-bag. She had climbed down from the top bunk shortly after they had turned the lights out. They had made love quietly, but without guilt, passion almost intensified by the modest necessity of containment, after a little rearrangement zipping together their two sleeping-bags. She told him afterwards she remembered doing the same at Communist youth organization weekends in the Saxony hills. He had sulked at her for awakening his jealousy. She had kissed him on the nose and snuggled down, falling asleep in the crook of his arm. He had lain a while revelling in a togetherness he had thought banished from his life. But he could not stop his mind working on the tale they had heard over supper, until eventually the alcohol worked its insidious magic and he succumbed to tiredness.

Awake now, and filled with the apprehension that comes with dawn in a strange climate, he realized that Magnus and Siggy were nowhere to be seen.

For a fleeting moment, he panicked.

Then the door crashed open and Siggy stormed back into the room, her breath trailing clouds of steam behind her.

'Come on. Magnus has everything nearly ready. We would do well to be on the move as soon as possible. You can never tell how long a journey's going to take.'

Burke stirred himself, shaking Sabine gently by the shoulder.

'Hey, mousey. Time to end the hibernation. Spring's nearly here.'

Siggy smiled. 'You should wash if you want to. There is hot

water. We are quite civilized, you know, even up here. I will go and tell Magnus we are ready to go soon. Half an hour at most, please. There are special coveralls in that cupboard.' She pointed to a wooden chest in the corner. 'Put them on. They are insulated and also stop snow getting inside the clothing.'

Sabine hauled herself to her feet and stumbled towards the sink in the corner. Burke stretched and made his way to the door. He closed it again rapidly.

'Brrr. Wrap up warm like the lady said. You could catch your death out there.'

Sabine turned and looked at him.

'Sorry, that was an unfortunate turn of phrase.'

'Taste isn't exactly our profession, is it?'

Magnus was standing alone uttering what sounded like old Norse imprecations when Burke emerged from the warmth of the hut, dressed in his tomato-red overall.

'Good morning. You look troubled?'

'It is nothing too terrible. Just that the weather is not as friendly as I'd hoped.'

Burke looked around him. Apart from the cold, it seemed a beautiful morning. Visibility was excellent and the sky was the palest blue. Magnus noticed him looking up at it approvingly.

'Hah, you like our light? It is one of my country's best features. But not today. Behind that blue is a white you do not see, yet. It is coming down.'

Burke looked at him quizzically. 'A storm of some sort?'

'The very opposite my friend: a stillness, a great whiteness that sometimes descends over the glaciers. It cuts the light, or rather the reflections. Suddenly everything is as one colour. At times like that distance and height become very hard to judge. And on a glacier those are the things that matter.'

'Should we wait until it looks more settled?'

The Icelander shrugged. 'Maybe. Maybe not. This is a very obvious place to wait. Perhaps too obvious. Also, I might be wrong.' He grinned.

'Even we folk up here are only human, you know, although we do not like to admit it. Come along, it is best we get started.'

Burke looked back to the door of the hut to see Sabine emerge. Her skin shone in the pale sunlight and her eyes sparkled.

'Look at me,' she shouted, pirouetting in her scarlet overall.

'Am I cool or what? And get a load of these!' She fished in her pocket and produced a pair of deep blue-lensed wraparound sunglasses. 'Maybe I look like some fifties Italian movie star on a skiing holiday.' She posed as if for the cameras, and then ran up to him.

They walked arm in arm across the crunchy fresh snow to where Siggy was already removing sheets of tarpaulin from what appeared to be motorbike sidecars on tank treads and skis.

'Snow scooters,' Magnus said with evident relish in his voice, like a motorcycle enthusiast showing off a collection of vintage Harley Davison. 'The best mode of transport on earth.'

Burke did a quick count and realized that there had to be almost a dozen of the hybrid vehicles. Siggy was firing up the engine of the lead scooter, a gaudily painted red and yellow machine. Clearly visibility rather than camouflage was the prime consideration.

'You have not ridden one before?' asked Magnus.

Both Burke and Kotzke shook their heads.

'Do not worry, it is very easy. Watch.'

The Icelander threw his leg easily over the nearest machine and turned a key in the ignition. All of a sudden the preternatural silence of the winter landscape was shattered by a Hell's Angel on a moped.

Magnus grasped the throttle with his right hand and revved the engine, then demonstrated the clutch and gear change. Without warning, he disengaged the clutch and the machine slid off, accelerating rapidly across the snow, propelled by its treads. The Icelander cut into a sharp U-turn a hundred yards away, leaning into the curve like a motocross master, then coming back towards them, standing up in an obvious feat of bravado. Faster and faster. Burke wondered what the vehicle's top speed was.

The Icelander brought the machine to a stop only feet in front of them and leaped off, leaving the scooter still chugging away.

'Now it is your turn.'

Sabine checked the zip on her overall and climbed astride a scooter.

'Like this?' she asked, as Magnus leaned over her to demonstrate the gear change.

'Hey, Eamonn, yours is over here.' Siggy had stopped tinkering with her own scooter and had started up another. Burke walked across to it, looking back just in time to see Sabine bolt off across the snow. For a novice, she was obviously a very quick learner.

'Your friend is good.' Siggy nodded appreciatively in her direction.

'She is, isn't she.' Burke was considerably more apprehensive, but after a few false starts and firm but tolerant instruction he too managed to get the machine going. The sensation of speed was exhilarating although he noticed from the speedometer that he was barely doing 40kph. As he crested a small snow drift, he saw Sabine and Magnus hurtling towards him.

'Whoa,' he called as they drew alongside.

'Well, what do you think?' said Magnus. 'Are we ready for an expedition?'

Sabine was radiant. 'Aren't they exciting? I'm going to give up all other jobs and become an arctic explorer, no, polar racer.'

Soon Magnus and Siggy were loading supplies on to a small trailer on skis that was attached to the back of his scooter.

'Not too much. But our chances of getting to the spot marked on your map and back again before the light fails are only fifty-fifty,' Siggy explained. 'This is a four-man tent with good insulation. Also we have some heating equipment, lights and a little food. With luck we will need none of it, but out here only a fool travels in the dark and it would be unwise to go without it.'

'Hey, no need to convince me,' said Burke. The thought of spending a night out on the glacier was scary enough even without someone with a gun looking for them.

'Normally we would have left a detailed itinerary with the town services in Kjölur, but in the circumstances . . .'

'I understand. It would have been too easy to trace us.'

'Yes, though Magnus is not entirely happy. He thinks whoever is trying to harm you already knows where you are headed. If he was hoping we would lead him to this thing, then he would not have tried to kill you at the lagoon.'

'Yes,' said Burke. 'That had occurred to me too.'

Magnus looked up and beckoned them over.

'I wanted to show you this. It is important. I hope none of us will get separated but in case something stupid should happen, this is your lifeline.'

He was indicating a small device that looked to Burke absurdly like a lap counter, just behind the handlebars on each scooter.

'This is the GPS, the global positioning system I was talking about earlier. Up here there isn't a sensible man or woman now who'd go out on the glacier without it. This antenna,' he pointed to a small plastic wand on the rear of the scooter, 'transmits continuously to the nearest American communications satellite, which then triangulates it with others in a network all around the planet. It beams back to you the precise co-ordinates on the map and the direction you are currently taking. You cannot get lost. Ever. At least in theory.'

'Ever?' Sabine looked doubtful.

'I said you cannot get lost. I did not say the ground could not open up in front of you. It is small consolation knowing your exact latitude and longitude if you are stuck thirty metres down at the bottom of an ice crevasse.'

'Thanks.'

'But the most important thing is that this should allow us to establish when we are at the precise co-ordinates indicated on your old Russian map. Not that we have any guarantee, of course, that those are accurate.'

'Of course.' Sabine smiled. 'But we also have this.' She removed from her shoulder bag a hand-held device in black plastic with a dial and a speaker.

'What is it?' asked Siggy. Burke suspected he knew already.

'A Geiger counter,' replied Kotzke.

Burke looked down at the physically unimpressive liquid crystal display of the GPS. It seemed simple but it was a perfect guide only if you had a good grasp of latitude and longitude, along with a detailed knowledge of Icelandic geography. He suddenly wished he'd taken that orienteering course back in school.

It was agreed that Magnus should take the lead. His bright orange snow scooter and fluorescent green coverall set against the white snow made him look like a day-glo version of the Irish Republic's flag. Sabine followed close behind, with Burke on her tail and Siggy bringing up the rear. Burke resisted the temptation to catch up with Sabine and try to carry out a conversation which would in any case have scarcely been possible, given the noise of the scooters. It was just that there was so much they had not yet talked about. Their plans when this escapade was over. Both of them, he thought, might become minor media celebrities after the story broke. Then there would be a book, certainly. With a bit of luck, it might even be a success. He fantasized that it might bring them in enough money to buy a small property somewhere he fondly thought of as 'away from it all'.

He looked around him. Iceland maybe? Only joking, he told himself, though on a day like this, crisp, cold with a clearing sky above them, he could almost imagine it. He could certainly see what magic Magnus's bleak homeland held for its inhabitants.

Bavaria came to him in a flash: somewhere in the foothills of the Alps, with Austria only a skip and Italy a jump away. He was tired of London, but, Dr Johnson's maxim notwithstanding, he was by no means tired of life. Not any longer. Not when a new life might be just around the corner.

How far Sabine shared his attitude was something he preferred not to think about. Little more than a one-night stand, Burkey boy, and already you're a mug for the woman, he could imagine George Prosset telling him in El Vino's. Daydreams are one thing, he thought, but what mattered was never again to let a woman become the the be-all and end-all. There were other things that mattered more in life. Or then again – as Sabine dropped back and took one hand free off the handlebars to blow him a kiss on the rushing icy wind – maybe there weren't.

The sun was high now, or at least as high as it would go this far north of the equator at this time of the year. The insipid sky of early morning had given way to a pastel blue and now deepened to an almost turquoise shade. Magnus turned around in his seat and gave them a thumbs-up sign, indicating the sky. Clearly his concerns about the weather had been somewhat allayed. The GPS, Burke was glad to note, appeared to be functioning perfectly, with the liquid crystal display indicating both their position and heading. Only one thought gave him momentary cause for concern: if he could fix his own location so accurately, then so perhaps could someone else? Were they in a quest after a missing artefact, or the prey in a winter hunt?

According to the readings on his GPS they were only a few dozen kilometres from the co-ordinates on the map he now mentally referred to as 'John's legacy'. The timing was good. With luck they would be at the site well before midday. Who knew how long they might have to search, or whether there was anything to find? Even in late March there was little light left in the sky much beyond 3.00p.m.

Neither Burke nor Kotzke noticed when they left terra firma and began travelling over the last slowly shifting ice mass that was Langjökull. The snow provided a seamless cover. After about an hour's travelling, Magnus braked to dawdling speed and held up a hand to signal to the others that they should draw level, carefully. As soon as they had done so, Burke realized why. Just beyond the

Icelander's scooter was a chasm almost two metres wide, big enough to have swallowed any of the snow scooters. He could not see the bottom, at least not without venturing a lot closer to the edge than he felt would be wise.

'Be careful,' warned Magnus, 'you must always remember this is ice, not land. It is always possible for a whole section to sheer away and widen the crack.'

Burke suddenly appreciated with what skill their 'polar bear' was negotiating the seemingly featureless landscape. The terrain they were traversing was a natural minefield.

'How deep is it?' asked Sabine.

'From the appearance, I would guess some twenty metres here, but maybe further along it could be up to fifty or sixty metres. The icecap here is thick, and it makes its own laws.'

'But the direction we want to go in,' Kotzke said, indicating the GPS, 'is that way.' She pointed straight across the crevasse.

Magnus shrugged again in the way, Burke guessed, that had become his habit with foreigners who tried to deny the forces of the elements.

'Here, you can see, nature is often master. We must do as she says. We cannot go across, therefore we will go around. It will take time. We must simply hope it will not take too much.'

Sabine turned and looked at Burke as if he might somehow have a solution.

'What do you think, Eamonn?'

'I think', he replied, looking at the great blue-white shards of ice, 'that it reminds me of Superman's fortress of solitude,' he replied, slipping his scooter into gear and starting off after Magnus who was already making tracks in front of them, keeping at least ten metres from the edge of the crack.

For what seemed like a wasted eternity they coasted alongside the ice chasm, while their GPS indicators showed clearly that they were moving diagonally back on themselves and away from their destination. Then, just when Burke had begun to think they would end up camping for the night on this glacial wilderness without even having reached their target, the crack disappeared, sealing itself up as if they had reached the end of a giant zip-fastener in the ice. Magnus turned and set off on a new heading, straight for the twin peaks of the hills that channelled Langjökull's frozen water towards now-distant Kjölur.

*   *   *

The sun was no longer clearly visible by the time they reached the first outcrop of rock that indicated the great glacier was being squeezed by the earth underneath. By now even Burke and Sabine were handling the snow scooters confidently, and had taken to swopping places in the convoy or occasionally drawing level to exchange a few shouted words of conversation.

The change in the landscape, however, worried Burke. He had noticed Magnus also scan the horizon from time to time for any sign of human presence. On the stark emptiness of the glacier any colour other than white would have stood out sharply. They themselves he thought disconsolately, must have been visible from miles away, little specks of brightness in an empty landscape that was turning more monochrome by the minute. But he had been reassured that anything else moving would have been equally visible. Now, however, as they approached the rocky excrescences, he realized that either would provide excellent concealment for a watcher, or even a whole team of watchers, if they were in camouflage gear.

When the sun began to fade, Burke had pulled his scooter up beside Magnus and pointed his head at the whitening heavens above them. The Icelander had simply nodded, not exactly glumly, but not exactly enthusiastically either. As he had predicted, the sky was fading to a flat eggshell that in turn dulled the surface of the snow beneath, killing reflections. It was as if colour had been slowly stripped from the world. Burke thought it must have been days like this that inspired the old Norse legends about the end of the world, when the great wolf would eventually catch up with the sun and swallow it.

So he scarcely noticed when Magnus stopped his machine dead in front of them, until the Icelander cut off the engine. Burke eased his throttle back and came to a stop alongside.

'To save petrol,' the Icelander replied to the unspoken question. 'This is it. We're here . . . wherever here is.'

Burke felt a burst of adrenalin, looked around triumphantly at Siggy, then down at his GPS which, almost to his surprise, gave the reading that until now had been no more than a legend on a faded military map. He lifted his head again and looked around him, and saw . . . nothing.

Sabine came up to him. He saw the look in her eyes too: blankness.

'Well,' he ventured, 'what did we expect? Smouldering wreckage? A big yellow radiation warning sign?'

As if he had prompted her, Sabine reached down into her pannier and produced the Geiger counter. She turned it on and they all heard the familiar ticking, soft, barely perceptible at first, and then, as she moved her snowmobile forwards, markedly louder.

'That's it, that's a trace.' Burke almost shouted the phrase.

'Sorry, that was just me playing with the volume. This is a sensitive device but the signal here is extremely faint, indicating little more than a high level of background radiation.'

'That's it, then. Wild goose-chase.'

'The map co-ordinates were hardly going to be spot-on, Eamonn, were they?'

'No, but this is obviously the place. In the sort of storm we're talking about that night, those two mountains over there, small as they are, could have been a fatal obstacle.'

'Particularly to a pilot flying low to avoid radar.'

'Which you British had only just invented, and would almost certainly have been installed at Reykjavik airstrip.'

'So let's go closer.'

'Yeah, but we have to presume that that's what the search parties they sent out must have done.'

'Then and for how many years afterwards.'

'Eamonn, that's it. That's what we have to consider. Why did they not find the plane?'

'I don't know. Remember, up until two days ago I didn't really believe it existed. Since then, I've been assuming it either disintegrated or got buried in snow.'

'Snow melts, not all of it, not here on the glacier, but enough to reveal something as big as a crashed bomber. It couldn't have completely disintegrated. At any rate, we have reason to believe its cargo didn't, so how could it suddenly disappear?'

It was Siggy who spoke. She had been listening to their conversation with a wry smile. 'I think you have just seen the answer to that question.'

'Uh? Of course, the crevasse. You think it got trapped in there?'

'No.' Siggy was trying not to be condescending. 'Not in there, it was not big enough to swallow a plane, although it could have taken large parts of it. But that is a new crack, not an old one. You see how they change. Next year the ice will press together again in winter and the crack will close up, much of it. Then we will get spring and the thaw and the tensions change. Maybe it will open wide again, wider even, or maybe another will take its place. There are many such fissures in a glacier like this. That is why it is such a dangerous place.'

Sabine turned to her. For almost the first time, Burke could detect not the slightest hostility towards Siggy.

'I understand. She's right, Eamonn. But what do we do? Could this thing be trapped in the ice underneath our feet?'

Magnus looked at her in surprise. 'Maybe, but it is unlikely, even if your plane crashed on this exact spot. This is a glacier, and glaciers move. Right now, the ice we are standing on is heading – slowly but surely – for Kjölur. It would take many thousand years for it to get there and, unless a new ice age occurs, it will melt before it does, but we still know the direction we are going in: through the peaks and down to the lowland.'

'So all we have to do is follow the flow of the ice?'

'It is not that easy; the glacier is big, and we do not know exactly where we should start from. Glaciers do not move fast. It is unlikely that anything would have drifted in the ice more than a few hundred metres at the very most, even over the course of half a century. It is not possible to tell where a fissure might have been more than fifty years ago. But there is another option. I should have thought of it yesterday.'

'What is it?'

'Follow me.'

Magnus turned the key in his snowmobile's ignition again and set off towards the nearest of the rocky peaks jutting through the ice.

'Look,' he said as they stopped close to the snow line. 'Follow the line of my finger, down there; about eight kilometres away is Gundar Peterson's cottage.' Burke could just about make out a speck that at this distance might have been a house or a rock. But both he and Sabine nodded.

'Look above it and you will see a black line.' This time both of them could clearly see it.

'That is a volcanic lake; the one I told you about. It is kept warm from beneath, but it is also fed water from Langjökull, up here where we are now. The meltwater starts about a kilometre or so higher up. If I am right about Gundar's ponies then that is where we could pick up a trace.'

'Come on,' said Sabine, her face brightening, 'what are we waiting for?'

Burke shrugged and, with only a half-glance at the greying sky, followed them.

From his own vantage point the security man watched the little procession of snow scooters make its way down the rock. He was secretly impressed. He had never believed they would get there. He lowered the telescopic sight on the M40A1 and stroked his moustache. The rifle could hit a target a kilometre away with an accuracy of inches, magnified ten times through the Unertl sniperscope mounted on the barrel. He had acquired a liking for it during his service with the United Nations forces in Bosnia. He had practised with it, cynically, playing the crosshairs over men, women and children as they moved in the streets of Sarajevo, forever worried, but unaware that one of their 'guardian angels' was also the angel of death.

The rifle was only a last resort. He had already made arrangements for the main firework display. He thought his masters would approve. The evidence would be gone. For ever. He set down the gun and used a small pair of field binoculars to track their progress. He had not used them earlier when the sun was high. He had known too many good men in the thick forests of the hills around Sarajevo shot in the head because the sunlight had caught the reflection of their polished lenses (and a few macho Balkan dickheads, too, killed because they insisted going to war in Ray-Bans). But now there was not enough sun in the sky even to cast a shadow. He was not sure, of course, if anyone in this group was armed, although he had watched the big blond native in the ridiculous lime-green outfit scan the hills like a hunter as they approached. But he was confident that he had not been spotted. His white with dappled grey battle camouflage, from the winter war in Bosnia, blended perfectly with the snow and rock terrain.

Now, as they set off in the direction of the distant volcanic lake, he eased himself out of the rocky niche from which he had been watching them and clambered quickly over the black basalt towards the hollow where he had left his own snow scooter.

'Stop! There's something here,' shouted Sabine suddenly.

Burke turned around. She had fallen back about 100 yards behind the rest of the party. They had descended a quarter of a mile from the pass between the two stunted mountains, and were now at a part of the glacier where they could see large snow-free patches where the ice itself was clearly visible, a vibrant blue even under such a featureless, insipid sky. Not far from here, Magnus had explained, there was still volcanic activity beneath the glacier itself. As a result, a river of meltwater, still at temperatures just above freezing, ran under the ice cap towards the lake in the valley below. Sabine had jumped off her scooter and was kneeling by the side of the ice holding out the Geiger counter. It was ticking loudly.

'The reading just took off. It's clearly limited to the snow-free area.'

The radiation level was mounting, though still well short of anything that might be considered dangerous. Though not so for the ponies that Peterson had kept: if they had been drinking water with this degree of contamination for any length of time, it was no wonder they had got sick.

'Then let's follow it upwards,' Burke said. 'Nothing trapped in the ice is likely to have made it down this far.'

There was suddenly enthusiasm in the air. Despite himself, Burke found he was twisting back the throttle to get a little extra speed out of the vehicle as they climbed. Sabine, however, had thrown off her earlier caution and was driving as fast as the machine would go on the slope, hurtling past Magnus who shook his head.

'Careful,' Burke called after her.

He looked ahead to see Sabine accelerating ever faster. Then with a sudden shock he saw her scarlet scooter throw its caterpillar treads into the air in a flurry of snow and vanish from view.

'Sabine!' he yelled at the top of his lungs, his cry drowning out any scream from her.

Magnus too had watched in horror, then pushed his throttle to full and headed for the spot.

Siggy and Burke followed, Burke driving erratically, his eyes glued to the empty space where he had last seen the girl he now knew with a bitter certainty he loved, as they covered the few hundred yards to where the 'bear' had stopped.

Magnus had halted his scooter about ten metres away from the edge, dismounted and scrambled up the slope, his feet in their felt-soled boots crunching on the thin layer of compacted fine dry snow. There was a familiar smell in the air, one that did not belong here, the smell of spilled diesel. Sabine had disappeared at a point where the slope evened off so it was impossible to see beyond what she had obviously assumed was a plateau in the icefield, but which now revealed itself to be the edge of a precipice. The question was: did it drop six feet, or 600?

It was with a dry mouth that Eamonn Burke rushed past Magnus, and stopped on the edge.

34

Meltwater

The North Atlantic, off the east coast of Iceland, October 1945

Artyomy Nosov was feeling sicker than any dog he had ever seen. Over the heaving gunwales of the survey vessel the waves pitched, dark green-black and sinister. He clasped his stomach and once again retched into the dark water. Never again, never ever again, he promised himself, would he take up an assignment at sea. But even as he thought it, he knew it was a hollow boast: when orders came direct from Dzerzhinsky Square, it was a brave man who said 'No'. Or a dead one.

'Comrade lieutenant, a radio signal. Come quickly, please.'

Nosov staggered towards the door that led to the bridge. Icy sleet whipped by the furious wind stung his face. Jerking open the door, he glanced up briefly at the blackness above. No night to be on the high seas in a small ship; no night at all to be trying to fly.

Inside, the lights gave an artificial impression of cosiness, reinforced by the haze and aroma of strong Russian tobacco smoke. It was muggy even. Warm from the engines below. The heavy smell of hot diesel mingled with the smoke and the acrid scent of sailors' sweat on well-worn clothing. Nosov could see the captain sneering at him. He was a loyal Communist but like most hardened seamen, he had little time for political officers, especially some Muscovite who had no experience of the sea.

Oleg Baranov, the pale, timid-looking radio operator who to Nosov seemed little more than a child, was looking up from his desk, one hand holding his headphones, the other poised with a pencil above a sheet of damp paper. Nosov looked at him questioningly. The boy nodded urgently.

'Yes, yes, it's what you said. I have been monitoring the frequency all evening.'

Nosov frowned. It was too early. But then, even Yakunin had been unsure just how and when the man would make contact. A call sign, that was all. Repeated once or twice at most, to make sure it was picked up. A sign that he was on his way. With cargo. A short signal transmitted on a short-distance frequency. A signal that Nosov would then translate into a different codeword, one that they could send out on the ship's shortwave without fear of interception because it would be meaningless, one that would reach Murmansk, where Yakunin would be pacing the floor of the freezing control tower, still believing his Greek heroes would deliver: Prometheus, who stole fire from the gods, and Perseus, the slayer of the Gorgon. Nosov had looked them up, these funny codewords, in the great Soviet Encyclopedia, but he was damned if he understood what relevance they had.

But it was academic, in more ways than one. It was obvious that the boy was not hearing what they had been expecting.

'Perseus?' Nosov prompted him. 'In Morse, Latin script, remember, not Cyrillic.'

The boy nodded but his face was still drawn. His hand worked on the paper with the pencil. They had assured Nosov that despite his youth he was one of the best 'listeners' in the Soviet navy.

'It's fast, repeated. But not Perseus. I think it's a position, a heading . . . this.' He pointed to the marks he had made on the paper; a precise, neat hand.

Nosov bit his lip. The boy was right. This was a map reading, the last thing in the world he had expected. The man – if it was him – was broadcasting his position. It was insane. Unless . . . he was in trouble. He looked through the smeared windows at the featureless sleet-streaked blackness outside.

'Now, repetition,' the boy was saying. 'The same letters, over and over . . . SOS.'

Nosov closed his eyes.

The boy was looking down now as if afraid to face the world.

'It's stopped,' he said.

35

Fate's Fickle Finger

Eamonn Burke looked down into the abyss with half-dead eyes that dreaded what they might see. The sight that confronted him took his breath away. It was not at all what he had expected.

Instead of Sabine's body lying like a discarded doll on jagged shards in a deep ravine, he saw a virtual rift valley extend beneath him, a great canyon of ice and snow, as if a fault line had opened up in the glacier. And against the far wall, more than twenty metres away, where the ice again rose vertically, lay a chunk of torn grey metal bearing the silver star roundel of the United States Air Force. A cry from far below tugged him back to reality.

'So for God's sake, stop admiring the view and come down and help me.'

Beside him, Magnus broke into a loud belly laugh and pointed down almost vertically to where the ice fell away before their feet. Sabine was lying face-down in a drift, more than a dozen yards away from the crumpled wreckage of her scooter. The handlebars were twisted round 180 degrees, and a thin trail of blue vapour escaped from the ruptured fuel tank.

That she was at least still alive was demonstrated by the number of German obscenities. '*Verdammtes Arschloch*. See, what did I tell you? Aoow, *Scheisse*. And you didn't believe me. *Verdammt noch mal*. Will someone help me; I think I've broken my damn leg.'

Magnus returned to Burke's side with a length of thick nylon twine, and proceeded to construct a cat's cradle which he then told Burke how to use.

'Wait until I give the signal.'

With that he walked to the nearest scooter and attached the twine to the frame, just above the caterpillar treads. He turned on the ignition.

'Now,' he said.

Burke stepped into the cradle, waited until Magnus had taken the strain of his weight on the scooter, and began to lower himself over the precipice.

'Okay, I'm there,' he called, as his feet touched the snow layered on the surface of the sunken glacier. Christ, he thought, she must have hit this hard. He made faltering progress, even though Sabine lay only a dozen or so yards away. All the time he found his eyes wandering from her to the great hunk of silvery metal on the other side of the chasm.

Burke kneeled down, stroking her hair. 'Can you move?'

'It depends which bits. I'm afraid I'm going to be even more flat-chested than ever. God knows how much of me was crushed by the impact. I felt like so much air had been expelled from my lungs I'd never breathe again.'

'You were lucky.'

'We were lucky.' She turned on to her side, the effort causing her pain. 'Look, Eamonn, there it is. The diaries were right. They really did do it.'

'Or at least had a go at it. This hardly looks like a success story, in anyone's terms. Where does it hurt?'

'Just about everywhere. But I'll live.'

Burke rolled up the leg of her scarlet snowsuit.

'It doesn't look good.'

'It doesn't feel good.'

From the knee down, her leg was a mass of purple bruising, with an ominous, almost black mark about halfway down the shin.

'It's probably broken.'

Kotzke grimaced. 'What next?'

Burke glanced up at the walls of ice that surrounded them and the darkening sky above. Already there was little light left in the pale northern heavens.

'Don't even think about it.'

'I'm trying not to. But Eamonn, it's all true. There really was a crash.'

'Yes, but I still have to be convinced of what it proves.'

'It proves at the very least that a Russian master spy half a century ago knew about the crash of an American bomber that the Pentagon itself has never admitted.'

That, Burke had to admit, was pretty undeniable.

'And,' she added grimly, 'that he was probably murdered for that knowledge. As was Klaus Fuchs for threatening to reveal it.'

In the drama of the past half-hour, Burke had pushed the other danger that threatened him to the back of his mind. For the moment it was enough to deal with the situation they were in.

'We're going to have to call in a helicopter to get you out of here.'

'Like hell you will. Are you serious? We have just landed – in my case almost literally – on the scoop of the century, and you want to call in the flying doctor with the camera teams that will follow. Not on my budget, Mr Burke.'

'But you're hurt, for God's sake. A story's just a story.'

'But some stories are bigger than others. I've done my leg in, not broken my neck.' She smiled the engaging big-eyed smile that Burke had found irresistible at their first meeting. 'And I'm damned if I'm going to let it, or you, spoil the sensation.'

'He-lloo. Room for a little one?' It was Siggy, he saw, coming down the sheer ice face the same way he had.

'Magnus has decided to pitch camp for the night.'

Burke looked at her, horror-stricken.

'We have to get her out of here.' He ignored Sabine's renewed protests.

'I agree,' said Siggy, examining Sabine's bruising. The internal bleeding was obviously bad, although it seemed unlikely to lead to a serious haemorrhage; the broken leg would need setting. There was no possibility of her using a snow scooter – even if hers had not been written off. She could ride on Magnus's ski-tow, but it would hardly be very comfortable.

'In any case, there is nothing we can do now until the morning. They do not send out the helicopter from Reykjavik after dusk unless it is a real emergency and it would be dark now by the time they reached us. Magnus is calling to Kjölur on the radio telephone to advise them that we have had an accident.'

Sabine sat up, her face contorted occasionally as a flash of pain shot through her. 'Eamonn, as we're stuck here, why don't you at least see if there's any sign of the rest of the thing, before what's left of the light fades.'

He looked at her with a mix of frustration, exasperation and admiration. Even in these circumstances, he knew she was right.

Burke trudged off across the ice towards the remains of Joshua Finch's B-29. Here it was – the physical proof that Fuchs had been talking about in those cryptic diary entries: '*the material evidence remains frozen. But one day there will be a thaw . . . nothing stays hidden for ever.*' Burke almost laughed. They had thought the thaw he referred to was metaphorical, the end of the Cold War. But the dour scientist, with his literal, empirical mind, had not been indulging in poetic licence. He had quite simply meant what he said.

Awe overcame him as he approached the the severed aircraft tail section. The thing was enormous, he realized, far bigger than he had imagined, a colossal feat of aircraft engineering for its generation: a huge aluminium sail almost as big as a three-storey building. The left horizontal section that had obviously hit the ice wall had buckled beyond recognition, but the right side protruded still at an angle of almost ninety degrees to the vertical. Burke took off his insulated ski gloves and bent down to touch an aileron. The metal felt, unsurprisingly, as cold as the ice it was all but imbedded in.

He found himself wondering about the last moments of Joshua Finch. Was he alone? Had he realized the risk he was taking? He would have known the route, of course, the long flight through dark skies over icy waters around the North Cape and down on to the Kola peninsula and the forbidding arctic city of Murmansk. That was what he had planned, Burke was sure. That was Klaus Fuchs's secret. What Burke was less certain of was the links between them. Who else had been involved? Was it possible that Joshua Finch was just the lynchpin for some wider conspiracy?

The plane had broken up in the crash. Perhaps Finch had been flying low to avoid detection and in the apalling weather had clipped the hills, plummeting down on to the glacier. Whether the fissure had existed then was impossible to tell. Perhaps it had been caused by the impact. The plane's disappearance into it and the heavy snow which had fallen for days afterwards went some way towards explaining why the search parties had never found it.

But then they would not even have known where to start. Thermal-imaging was science fiction in the forties. There would have been no helicopters equipped with high-tech heat-sensitive equipment scouring the country, as there would be if something similar happened today. They probably thought Finch had crashed into the sea. Or even imagined he had succeeded. They must have deduced soon afterwards, surely by the time of Fuchs's arrest and trial four years later, the extent to which the West had been betrayed, just how far American atomic supremacy had been compromised. For all they knew, back in the cold winter of

1945, the atom bomb might already have been in Stalin's hands. Was the history of the immediate post-war years based on that false premise? And would history have been different if it had been true?

But where was the main body of the plane? In the falling light, Burke's eye followed the trajectory that the angle of the tail section indicated. It meant nothing, of course. There was no guarantee that the rest of the fuselage had not been snapped off at an angle. It depended whether the plane had broken apart on crashing. Or whether, for some reason or other, it had cracked up in mid-air, although that seemed unlikely.

With a glance back to where Siggy was ministering to Sabine's leg, he began cautiously to make his way along the ice wall. The running water that Magnus had heard was somewhere in front of him. For more than 200 yards he continued. Then the landscape altered dramatically. The rift in the glacier had widened to a point where the opposing ice walls were nearly 400 yards apart. Now, in front of him, the 'ground', as he could not stop himself thinking of it, fell away again.

Burke watched as the running water flowed between the cracks in the ice, falling through the fissures, slowing as it lost heat. Here and there strange shapes like frozen fingers emerged from the body of the glacier where the running water had joined with it. Around them the flow slowed until the water seemed sluggish, as if its very molecules were slowing, tempted by the solidity around them to settle down.

Burke clambered carefully downwards, watching as he did so to make sure of a way back. When he got to the base of the nearest 'finger', he realized that it towered above him, more than twice his height. He reached the edge and looked, not without trepidation, around the corner to where the chasm plunged away even further, and a distant rumble and fine spray suggested a real waterfall of considerable magnitude.

It was then that he saw it. Indeed, it was as if it had been suddenly dropped on him. The sundered fuselage of the bomber – its colossal wings still attached but each snapped upwards in the middle at a preposterous angle – lay like a maimed eagle, wedged in between walls of ice, the great engines like fledglings sheltering underneath, their vast propellor blades twisted and broken. The flow of water descending from the flaw in the glacier ran through the broken fuselage as if it were a feature in an ornamental garden. Inside, Burke was certain, were the answers to their questions.

But now was not the time to go further. Within twenty minutes it would be dark. The flat colour of the sky suggested maximum cloud cover. There would be no moon, and Burke did not fancy trying to make his way up through the maze of ice in darkness. By the time he got back, in fact, it was already dark.

Siggy was waiting for him at the bottom of the precipice where a tent had now been set up.

'I've found it,' he managed breathlessly. Then, remembering his priorities, said, 'How's Sabine?'

'She is fine. She is lying down in the tent. It would be too risky to try to move her in the dark.'

'Where is Magnus?'

She gestured upwards. 'He is up there. He will sleep with the equipment. We have all we need down here. Also it will be more sheltered here if there is a wind.'

Burke was horror-struck. 'He'll freeze to death up there without protection.'

Siggy smiled, a firm smile that Burke thought was more generous than genuine. 'He will be okay. He has a good sleeping-bag. He will sleep on the supply trailer, under the tarpaulin. It will not be comfortable, but he is an Icelander. He is used to worse. It would be much more dangerous to leave the equipment – and the vehicles – unattended.'

Something about her tone made Burke realize that there had been a change in their situation while he had been gone.

'Has something happened? Any sign of "company"?'

She knew what he meant. 'Not as such. It is just that when Magnus tried to radio to Kjölur, he couldn't get through. All there was on the airwaves was static.'

'Is that unusual?'

'I don't know enough about it. Sometimes, I know, there can be interference when there are electrical storms. But this is not that sort of weather.'

'What does Magnus think?'

'He is not happy. He says it is "white noise". It happens out here. There is electricity in the air. When there is the aurora borealis, the lights in the sky, then it is impossible even to try to radio. Sometimes phones work up here. Sometimes not.'

36

The Heart of the Matter

Much to his own surprise, Burke found the atmosphere in the tent convivial. But the thought of Magnus doing the real macho bit, braving the elements up on the surface of the glacier took the sheen off the occasion, that and the gnawing worry over the lack of radio communication. In the back of Burke's mind was the uncomfortable idea that their signal might be being jammed. They had contemplated taking turns at keeping watch during the night, but in the end decided against it. The insulated tent was black and almost invisible in the moonless night.

Sabine had been almost beside herself with excitement when Burke revealed that they were so close to the main body of the wreck's fuselage. He could not be sure, he said, but from what he had seen it seemed the plane had simply cracked in two, probably on impact with the glacier.

'If there ever really was a "Fat Man" bomb in there, we're about to find it.'

'What I don't understand,' said Siggy, 'is that if this plane was carrying any sort of bomb, why didn't it explode when he crashed? Why wasn't half of Iceland evaporated?'

'An atomic bomb was never designed to explode on impact,' Burke explained. 'In fact, the biggest problem they had in designing the first ones was in getting the things to explode at all, in a nuclear explosion that is.'

'I still don't follow.'

'The sort of bomb they dropped on Hiroshima was dead simple, a sort of gun assembly that fired one piece of uranium into another. But they were too expensive. They simply didn't have enough uranium of the right grade. The type of bomb we have here, if

240

we have one at all – the type used on Nagasaki and the one that was the prototype for all immediate post-war production-line atomic weapons – depended on a complicated controlled "implosion". A whole shell of explosives arranged to blast inwards and compress the radioactive core to beyond critical point. In fact, the core itself was one of the most difficult parts of the whole assembly . . .'

'Hey, you were actually listening to what that mad American told us, weren't you?' Sabine interrupted.

'Anyway, not only did they have to have this very precisely tooled initiator made up of highly radioactive materials, but in order for it to work, the explosives in the shell all had to be set off simultaneously; which meant the detonators all had to fire at exactly the same time, and that meant wiring them up to an electric trigger device set on a timer, which in turn, of course, had to be primed. When the people from Los Alamos set off the first one at the Trinity test site in the New Mexico desert, it was all wired up to the command centre. They just threw the switch and an automatic timer took over.'

'Fine on a test site. But how do you do that when you're dropping the thing on a target?'

'Ever heard of batteries?'

Siggy's face cracked up. 'You're kidding me. You mean the reason that thing could crash at whatever the hell speed it did and not go off was . . .'

'Yep,' confirmed Burke. 'Batteries not included.'

Shortly after first light the next morning, Magnus woke them. The big Icelander was putting a brave face on his night out, but it was clear he was freezing cold. Siggy brewed up coffee using the fuel cells he had brought down from the supply trailer.

'What worries me most is that I still can't get through on the radio. It's not as if the weather could be responsible. You can see from the sky that it's clearing. It'll be perfect flying weather within the hour. We could call in a helicopter and be out of here in no time.'

'Are you crazy?' said Sabine, inevitably. 'I for one am not leaving here without the proof we came for. This is no time to give up.'

'You're in no condition to move anywhere much, let alone start hiking over the ice,' Siggy told her.

'Look, I understand what you've done for us here, but don't play the schoolmistress. I know what the situation is. I've a broken leg, probably, though it might be just a crack. But if Eamonn's right, then the wreckage of this damn plane is only a few hundred metres away. Surely you two big strong men can support a little girl like me as far as the beginning of the second crevasse, at least to where I can catch a glimpse of the thing.'

Burke looked across at Magnus, who shrugged and sighed, a gesture Burke took to mean that they had already exceeded safety parameters beyond any common sense.

'There's another consideration,' Burke said. 'We could be walking into trouble.'

'Did you see any sign of life yesterday?' inquired Sabine.

'No, but . . .'

'No, but nothing. What was the point of even getting this far if we give up now?'

And that was it. Somehow they had agreed that Eamonn and Magnus between them would support her as far as the 'rollover', from where she would be able to see into the crevasse where the wrecked B-29 lay. Then they would think again. Siggy had rescued the camera from the pannier of the written-off snow scooter. They would leave the makeshift camp as it was, but Magnus insisted on taking his radio phone along; they would try at ten-minute intervals to get a message through. As soon as they established contact, he insisted, they would ask for help, whatever ideas about exclusivity Sabine might have. If they had no luck in getting through by noon, they would pull out anyway. It was not ideal but they could always winch her up to where the remaining scooters were and load her on to the trailer for the trip back to Kjölur.

The sun had already begun to creep up towards its low zenith by the time they reached the point where the fault in the ice-cap split. In front of them, the crumpled wreck of the aircraft's shattered fuselage lay like the broken silver toy of some primeval giant.

Sabine gasped involuntarily. 'Oh, Eamonn, it's beautiful.'

He gave her a sideways look. 'I bet you enjoy road accidents too.'

'No.' She feigned annoyance. 'But it is, isn't it? There's a sort of tragic poetry to it, like coming across Scott's camp in Antarctica or the wreck of the Titanic, still untouched after all those years.'

'I know what you mean,' Burke admitted reluctantly. There was something unexpectedly moving about the vision in front of them. This huge, deadly artefact had been neutralized by its surroundings, a weapon of death with a potentially lethal cargo brought down to size by the merciless inhospitable landscape around it: an instrument of destruction reduced to the status of incidental decoration. Except, he reminded himself, that it was still leaking poison.

'I'm coming down with you.'

'What? Don't be ridiculous.'

For an instant her eyes flashed at him with the cold fire of a wounded animal. Burke looked at Magnus, who nodded. Despite the glint of victory in it, her smile seemed like a reward.

'Come on then, but keep hold of the radio phone. It's up to you to keep trying to get through. Believe me, you'll prefer it if Magnus here doesn't have to strap you sideways across his scooter for that long ride back to base.'

Sabine made a face. But even so, Burke could sense the satisfaction as he and Magnus took her by the arms again and began the slow, tricky descent down the broken ice.

'We have to have pictures, you know,' she said. 'Once it gets out that this is here, there'll be cordons all over the place; the US military will go bananas, and that'll be the last we ever see of it. You have to find the papers. There's bound to be something: orders or documentation, the original flight schedule maybe. Something that'll prove that this flight was what we know it was. Make sure you check. They'd be in the cockpit, next to the pilot, I mean . . .' Her voice tailed off.

'Yes,' said Burke. 'He's going to be in a hell of a condition after all these years.'

'It only just occurred to me. I hadn't thought, really. That there'd be bodies.'

'We don't know that. We don't know anything much, do we?'

'I guess not. Be careful.'

But they did know, Burke thought, as they picked their way gingerly, like competitors in a strange three-legged slow-motion obstacle race, down through the ice boulders towards the wreckage.

Siggy had descended ahead of them, armed with Sabine's weatherproof Nikon. Eamonn and Magnus called over to her from the entrance to the shattered fuselage.

'Smile for the cameras, boys,' she shouted to them.

They waved back, and Siggy clambered to join them.

'Hand me the camera,' Burke called, as he and Magnus let Sabine down on to an ice boulder by the side of the aircraft. 'We're going to want some shots of the interior of this thing.'

There was something surreal about stepping inside the broken fuselage of any aircraft, let alone one that had crashed half a century ago. Almost immediately the world outside disappeared. He was inside a tunnel, a vast open tunnel made of metal but cluttered with the paraphernalia of wartime and a dead generation: webbing, steel compartments bolted on to the inside of the airframe containing emergency equipment that had turned out to be useless when the end had come. Burke put out his hand to steady himself against the superstructure only to find he was clutching paper. He withdrew his hand and saw a faded black-and-white photograph of a young girl with platinum blonde hair fall to the floor and turn to slush as it soaked up the condensed moisture from the volcanic stream that trickled through the compartment.

Burke looked down and saw water lapping around the thick soles of his insulated boots. The warm water that flowed down from the heat source under the ice and continued over an escalating series of cascades down to Hvitarvatn lake below, trickled here through the cavernous empty hull of the plane. Empty. Burke stopped, and looked around him as if uncertain of the evidence before his eyes. Or rather, the lack of evidence. The bomb bay doors were enormous, clearly modified for the possibility of dropping an early atomic device. But of the device itself, there was no sign. He cursed under his breath, and then laughed at the irony.

'What the hell . . . ?' Helped by Magnus, Sabine had limped into the doorway, and stared, as he did, at nothing. 'I don't understand . . .' she began.

'Nor do I,' replied Burke. He knew how desperately she had wanted this to be the scoop of a lifetime. 'We've found it okay, and then again, maybe we haven't.'

'They've been, haven't they? We're too late. It's been stolen.'

'Hardly.' Burke was letting her down gently. 'Look: this plane may be ripped open but there isn't a hole big enough to get a 1945 "Fat Boy" out of, except for the bomb bay doors and they're on the ground. There never was a bomb in here, at least certainly not when it came down. We have to face it.'

'I just don't understand.'

'So what was it all about? What was this guy doing if not stealing a bomb?'

'Maybe there's something in there that'll tell us.' She gestured forward, towards the flight deck, where the door lay open, thrown carelessly back as if one of the crew had just passed through it.

He picked his way towards the open door and put his head through. Burke had seen corpses before, only too recently. The vision of the fat Norwegian swimming in his own blood and intestines in the Blue Lagoon rose unbidden to his eyes. But he had also seen the bodies of those long dead and still unburied: in Afghanistan particularly, where the ancient belief that carrion should be allowed to pick clean the bones of the dead had fitted in only too well with the ebb and flow of civil war.

This was different. The glass of the cockpit windscreen was, inevitably, shattered. But no wind blew through it. The air was still, cold, like the air inside a butcher's walk-in freezer. For a moment he wondered if the body that lay slumped forward over the instrument panel might conceivably have been preserved, like a lump of meat in a chill cabinet. There was no smell of decomposition. Then he came to his senses. It had been more than half a century since there had been life in the corpse before him, half a century of winters and summers, even here, half-buried in a glacier on the edge of the arctic. He braced himself, and touched the cracked leather flying jacket. Almost at once, the body that had been Joshua Finch toppled to one side like a broken puppet. Burke found himself staring into the empty sockets of a yellowed skull, black holes in bone to which vestiges of shrunken skin still clung, like rotted leather, their only colour that of corruption. He started back involuntarily, restraining the impulse to gag. The figure slumped to the cockpit floor, landing with a sickening crack as the exposed skull hit metal.

Beneath it, Burke noticed for the first time, lay a hard black briefcase. Papers? Documents? He bent down to pull it out from under the body.

'Eamonn, quick, look at this.' Back in the main body of the aircraft Magnus and Sabine were squatting as she held out her Geiger counter, which was going wild, only a few feet away from what appeared to be an old metal toolbox, lying broken and rusty in the stream that flowed through the fuselage. 'I had forgotten to turn the Geiger on.'

Thanks, thought Burke, though he said nothing.

'The question is,' Magnus was saying in his annoyingly ponderous way, 'what is inside?'

'Be careful,' Burke warned.

But the big Icelander had already managed to use an ice-pick to prise open the corroded lid. Inside the box was another one – Burke was reminded of Russian matryoshka dolls – this time made of heavy, soft grey metal, probably lead, similarly fractured, presumably by the impact of the crash. Sabine's Geiger counter was thundering in their ears.

'I'm not sure this is at all safe,' she said. Burke winced at the understatement. His first instinct was to get out of there as quickly as possible. But his experience at Hiram Carter's hands had persuaded him to risk a few minutes' exposure.

Magnus was working on the lead box with the pick. It opened easily. Burke had no idea what he was expecting to see, until the moment he saw it, when he realized it was what he should have been looking for all along: in a dull grey metallic casing lay a sphere of shiny metal of an unearthly hue, somewhere between grey-green and silver, the size of a golf ball. With a chill of recognition he realized he was looking at a mixture of polonium and beryllium embedded in plutonium, exactly as Hiram Carter had described it: an initiator, the perfectly machined heart of an atomic weapon.

He looked up, unable to prevent just a hint of triumph creeping into his voice. 'Maybe we weren't so very far wrong, after all.'

Back outside in the clear light of the winter sun, Burke took the ice-pick and used it to break open the combination lock on the document case. He had begun to suspect what he might find inside. With trembling fingers he pulled out a thick sealed manila envelope. He glanced at Sabine.

'What do you think?'

'I think we open it. We're journalists, not archaeologists.'

Burke used his thumb to rip open the envelope from the corner. Inside was a letter, typed on lined foolscap paper. Burke caught his breath. In the top lefthand corner, it bore only a one-line address: 'PO Box 1663, Santa Fe, New Mexico.'

The letter was brief. It was addressed to Igor Kurchatov, care of the Soviet Academy of Sciences, Moscow.

'Dear colleague,' Burke read. 'In deep and troubled awareness of the new era that has dawned upon the world, we send you a gift. It is a dangerous present and we are acting dangerously, many would say, in sending it to you. But we know that your own research has led you in the same direction. And we believe that only by providing this token of our belief in the need for openness in the scientific community can we prevent calamity overtaking us. There is no future *in* conflict; there can now be no future *for* conflict. The hope of humanity lies in achieving an equitable balance. We trust you will understand this, and that you can persuade the men of political power to understand also. Yours in science.' There were sixteen signatures. Burke read them with a sense of awe. At the top of the list was Niels Bohr, followed by Isidor Rabi and Klaus Fuchs. Near the bottom came the name that he had secretly been hoping to see: 'J. Robert Oppenheimer, Director, The Manhattan Project'.

But the one below that was a bonus. A bonus that would shake the world. A signature so immediately recognizable that the name typed alongside was redundant: 'Albert Einstein'.

37

Farewell, My Lovely

Burke threw back his head and laughed. All of a sudden he could see nothing but the picture that swam in front of his eyes: a grainy black and white photograph that stared down from the bedroom walls of a million science students – an old man with an unruly shock of white hair and twinkling eyes sticking his tongue out at the camera and the world. At last Burke understood what Albert Einstein had been laughing about.

'Do you know what this means?' Burke demanded. 'This is the biggest story of the decade. It cracks the Western establishment's mythology wide open. Fuchs was just the fall guy. The top half of the Los Alamos team – the best brains on the planet – was willing to give the bomb to Moscow rather than allow American hegemony. With fucking Einstein thrown in. We'll make every front page in the world. This calls for a celebration. Wait here.'

Burke's mind was dancing as he scrambled back towards the little tent he now thought of as their 'base camp'. His emotions had done as much see-sawing as they could cope with in a single day. The idea that Fuchs had had high-level support had been creeping into his mind more and more. He saw now that the idea of stealing a bomb had been fantasy from the start. He had missed the scientific approach: send the Russians the one bit they really needed. But he had never imagined that Einstein might be involved. It made perfect sense, of course. Even though the great physicist had never been involved personally in the work at Los Alamos, it had been his inspiration. His letter to Roosevelt back in 1942, pointing out how close German research could be to achieving an atomic weapon had been crucial in persuading him to back the Manhattan Project. But Einstein's purpose then had also been to ensure a balance of terror, a balance that would make it impossible ever to use the weapon and survive. There could be no repeat of Nagasaki.

But what the story needed, it occurred to Burke, was a photograph that would win over editors and back up the Einstein signature: a long view of the bomber, with its shattered cockpit and the faded paintwork of a red Indian brave above the legend 'Navajo Arrow', in its grave in the glacial ice. He eyed the landscape through Sabine's Nikon in the hope that it would give him the perspective he needed. In the centre of the viewfinder was a rocky outcrop, where the stone once again squeezed the river of ice. It was not far, about two hundred yards. From there, he guessed, looking back up at the plane, he would get the right sort of vista. Treading carefully, he began to climb.

Tucked into a nook on the stone slope above the glacier on the other side of the aircraft, the man in the camouflage suit panned the fuselage with his Unertl gun-sight. He had seen Burke enter the shattered silver tube. The German girl, unfortunately, was not with them. He focused on her separately, wondering if it was worth trying a single shot, but even as he considered the possibility he saw Kotzke move forward. She too was clearly going towards the plane. The trouble was, from his vantage point he could not quite see the entrance to the fuselage. Too bad, he mused. As long as he didn't see her emerge back into his field of vision, he could assume she would go down with the rest. He put down the rifle and took out a small radio transmitter from his rucksack. He did not see Eamonn Burke leave the fuselage. By the time he looked up again, Burke was out of sight behind the wall of ice that hemmed in the plane's nose section.

He pressed the frequency button, sending the LCD display rocketing through the numbers. He watched it spellbound; having come to it later than most, he never ceased to be amazed by modern technology. For the past twenty-four hours the little gadget had been set to block the standard radio telephone frequencies. Now it was going to send a signal of its own to the little radio-activated detonator he had implanted at one end of the Semtex plastic explosive fixed along half the length of the bomber.

Funny, he thought as he hit the 'send' key; he had always wanted to know what it would be like to bring down an aircraft.

The explosion threw Burke forward almost before he heard it, jarring his knee painfully against the exposed rock at the edge of the ice sheet. He turned in horror at the long, slow roll of thunder that followed. The scene was unimaginable.

Instead of a great silver cigar lying in a trench of blue-white ice, there was a pall of grey-black smoke. For a second he wondered if there really had been a bomb on the plane that they had not noticed. He scrambled to his feet as the ominous rumble continued. The ice was cracking. With a noise like the sudden snapping of lightning-struck oak, the entire landscape seemed to give way. He glanced in panic back towards where Sabine, Magnus and Siggy had been sitting on the ice. None of them was to be seen. The whole 'roll-over', where the ice descended from one layer to the next, was in motion, like a frozen waterfall in a sudden thaw. He watched in horror as the crescendo built. Burke staggered, slipped, and then he too was on the ice – ice that was moving. His footing gave way beneath him. Then the lights went out.

38

The Wages of Sin

Brixton Prison, south London, December 1949

When they finally came for Klaus Fuchs, they did not knock at the hour before dawn, the apocryphal favourite time of the secret policeman, but in very English fashion, around tea-time on a Monday afternoon.

He knew already when he saw the black Rover saloon pull up outside the prefab house on Ninth Street, which he had been so recently allocated. And now here was Henry Arnold, Harwell's security man who had become his friend over the past few months, even as Fuchs had begun to suspect he was really his interrogator. He was rattling the door knocker, politely, patiently. With two plainclothes officers, probably not from the local constabulary, he thought, waiting calmly by the car.

The journey to London was pleasant, in the circumstances, the conversation almost affable, as if there was an eagerness on both sides to avoid any embarassment. What mattered – to both – was that it was over now. His arraignment in a closed court at Bow Street was quickly conducted in an atmosphere of terse formality, before he was taken in another car, handcuffed to a very ordinary, if extremely burly policeman, to the bleak Victorian fastness in south London they called Brixton Prison.

It was on the second day there, spent in a solitary cell that seemed surprisingly adequate accommodation to a man who had endured four long years of the privations of the high desert, that he met William Skardon, though he introduced himself only as 'Jones'. Skardon told him that he represented 'another branch' of the security services. He was the man who had made his reputation within the ranks of MI6 by interrogating William Joyce, the notorious 'Lord Haw-Haw' who had broadcast for Hitler. Skardon had extracted the confession that had led to Joyce's execution – something Klaus Fuchs did not need to know.

Ever since seismologists back in September had detected the tremor that was the unmistakable signature of an atomic device, detonated somewhere in the vast deserts of Kazakhstan, it had only been a matter of time before they moved on Fuchs, Skardon told him. The newly constituted Central Intelligence Agency, under a man called Allen Dulles, had worked with the FBI on some old transcripts out of the Soviet consulate in New York. Armed with a newly deciphered code book, they picked up a trail that was not hard to follow. But there were gaps. It would help him if he filled in the details for them. He knew the penalty for his crime, did he not?

'Yes,' Fuchs replied calmly. He had been resigned to it, ever since it was made clear to him that as a British subject, one who had taken the oath of allegiance to His Majesty King George VI, he was guilty of treason. 'Death,' he said simply.

Skardon said nothing.

And in the end, with no hope of clemency suggested, Fuchs painted a picture of the early days of his espionage. In that he was unstinting. He sacrificed everything he considered of little worth, including details of a pudgy, owl-faced man he knew only as 'Raymond', enough corroboration for the FBI of the evidence already pointing to Harry Gold.

But on other matters, he proved more resistant. Were there others of his level, Skardon probed, who had perhaps shown more sympathy with the idea of nuclear proliferation than was considered correct? Fuchs was enigmatic, preferring to sidetrack the conversation into abstract areas, though he insisted they were strictly relevant.

'Words are so very emotive. "Proliferation" would be a bad thing. "Balance" is not. The illusion of omnipotence is.'

Only once did the conversation verge on what might be termed politics, when Skardon challenged Fuchs about his reason for selling his knowledge to a foreign power.

'First of all, I sold nothing. That implies a transaction of some sort. None occurred. Second, let me ask you a question: if you were a horticulturalist and had discovered a new strain of wheat that was far more productive than any other known to man. What would you do? It would be very profitable, would it not?'

'I suppose so. Yes.'

'And to share it would be folly?'

'Maybe.'

Fuchs smiled. 'Even if by so doing, you could avert the disaster of famine?'

'Dr Fuchs, that is not what we are talking about here. We are talking about weapons.'

'Ah, of course, I thought we were talking about principles.'

When asked directly about his relationship with Oppenheimer, all Fuchs said was: 'A brilliant scientist; an estimable man. But he is an American. I am not. You must not equate us.'

And when Skardon brought the conversation down to the issue of atomic initiators, Fuchs was genuinely shocked.

'First you must persuade me, Mr "Jones", that your own security clearance is adequate for me to discuss such details with you.'

Skardon found him exasperating. 'We know what happened,' he bullied, 'back in 1945.'

'Yes,' replied Fuchs. 'I thought you would, sooner or later. That is probably a good thing, don't you think?'

Only once did Skardon get more out of him than the confession that was eventually published:

'Dr Fuchs, I believe you could tell us more about the object that landed at the base of Army Group 509 in New Mexico in July 1947.'

Fuchs allowed himself a rare smile. 'Ah, yes, Roswell. I'm afraid that was a bit of a prank. But it was necessary, you know. As necessary as anything else.'

In the end Skardon was resigned to the fact that Fuchs had told him all he ever would. Even the threat of death seemed to have no terror for him. Skardon left it to the officially appointed lawyer, however, to tell him that, as Britain had been an ally, rather than an enemy, of the Soviet Union at the time of his offence, the maximum penalty was only fourteen years. He never knew if Fuchs registered any relief.

39

Quiet Time

Burke opened one swollen eyelid a fraction and tried to close it again. He saw nothing but white. Then he tried again, and made out shapes in the white. His hands, he realized, were freezing. He tried to raise his head off the blissfully numbing surface that he now understood was ice. A world filled with threatening noise had suddenly been replaced by one of total silence. Somehow it was even more threatening. He forced himself up to his knees, painfully, and looked around at a landscape of almost spectral beauty.

There was no aircraft, not even a deep glacial trench where it had lain. The sheet ice had closed over it: as definitively as a bank vault slamming on its treasure. But no combination on earth could open this closed door.

He stumbled forwards uncomprehendingly, calling out a single name, the name of a woman who ten days earlier had meant nothing to him, but now meant the world. A lost world. 'Sabine! Sa-bi-ne!'

Panic fought with shock and despair for command of his logic and emotions. Rescue. He would radio for rescue. But the radio didn't work, he remembered. And in any case he didn't have it. And there was nothing to rescue. They had been in the plane, all three. And the plane had gone. Gone for ever. Cold, bitter tears coursed down his cheeks. There was no point in doing anything. Ever again. There was nothing out there but silence. The silence of the tomb.

PART THREE

Fallout

40

The False Dawn

Lager 65771 Gosudarstvennoye Upravleniye Lageryei.
Trans-Ural jurisdiction. Magnitogorsk, April 1955

The old man spoke through cracked lips, his face lined and weathered by the frost, his eyes almost opaque, the effects of the encroaching cataracts compounded by snowblindness.

'Rudi,' he breathed, his voice coming in harsh rasps. 'You know what is happening.'

'Yes, my general,' the younger man replied, 'you are dying.'

The old man nodded. He was glad that his friend had told the truth. His brother officer, he reflected, but now also – above all, perhaps – his friend.

Rudiger Aschenheim watched with cold eyes. They would have been filled with tears, had he any left to shed. But crying was not something he could even remember how to do. Tears were for other men, and women too. So many women, and their children. Tears were a luxury. They had all learned that, in the end. Blood was the fluid that mattered: the fluid that was spilt most copiously in their profession. Tears were part of the mopping-up operation.

The general turned his head painfully. He looked at the cracked window that failed miserably to let light penetrate the freezing wooden hut they inhabited along with forty-eight other prisoners. But in any case the general could no longer see anything more than a vague patch, a lighter rectangle in the pervasive gloom. And that was only now, for the few short weeks of the year when they were permitted to quit their back-breaking labour before the pale light faded from the sky. Soon the spring would come. In Bavaria, he thought, it would have arrived weeks ago, brought girls out into the

257

English Garden, young men swigging from litre steins of frothy beer by the Chinese pagoda. They had passed through Munich briefly, in the spring of '45, seen the charred remains of the pagoda, after an RAF attack. He had wondered at the time if the young Englishmen who had blown this oasis of conviviality to hell had known it was named in honour of their country. Not that it mattered. Not that anything mattered. Not now.

The Siberian spring was an altogether different case: no gentle blossoming of snowdrops and crocuses followed by the translucent green of the linden trees in new leaf. Here spring was a torrent of meltwater, an eruption of new life out of the arctic tundra, most of it malevolent: swarms of mosquitoes rising from the fetid swamps as the frozen earth melted on top of the permafrost; and the water, with nowhere to go, turned the soil into slush. The temperature would soar and then, none too soon, drop again, freezing the sweat on their backs as they laboured on the dictator's mad plans to carve factories into this inaccessible wilderness. The general would not regret his failure to see another summer. He would labour no more. Another dictator had plans for him. Death.

'R-R-Rudi,' he began, his feeble voice almost failing him. The other inmates had crowded to the far end of the hut, not just because the few coals they were allowed glowed miserably in the rusted brazier. They respected the privacy of old comrades at the final hour. Their own discipline had gone, long ago. But they had not all become animals. The Russians saw that, and resented it. It had given them the strength to achieve the onerous tasks set them each morning. Some, perhaps, still hoped, even now, to return home. To what, none of them knew.

'R-R-Rudi.'

'Hush. There is no need. There is nothing to say. Nothing that needs to be said.' A trace of a smile crossed Aschenheim's cracked lips. He would have made more of it, but it had been so long. The only smiles that passed between men in the camp were faint expressions that said, 'Yes, you and I face the same fate, each day.'

That was all anyone could expect. Survival was what mattered, or didn't, depending on the individual. No one questioned anyone else's decision, not any more. One day, they had all said, one day. But that was once upon a time. Today there was only today; tomorrow, there might be today also. But not necessarily.

He put his left hand – gnarled, horny and dirty, the hand of a man of sixty who had spent all his life in manual labour, rather than that of a forty-year-old who had once trained to be a lawyer – on top of the general's. The old man's flesh felt like little more than strips of scrawny meat hanging on cold bones beneath shrivelled chicken skin.

General Hermann Freiherr von Rulenstein closed his almost useless eyes. He could see more in the darkness that lay within. More of the things that he wanted to see. As well as those he would rather have forgotten.

'Yes, Rudi, there are some things that should be said.' His words came out as a croaked whisper. 'Things that someone, someday, should know, for the history books, if they still write them.'

Aschenheim looked back at him, his face expressionless.

They had been through it all together, from the glory days in France in 1940, when they rolled through the fertile countryside like young gods with the world at their feet, and nubile French goddesses in their beds. Resentment was fleeting, resistance a joke, more an invention of the beleaguered British. In the summer of 1941, he had watched the young Frenchmen of the division Charlemagne sign up to serve the Führer in the crusade against Bolshevism. The new world order, that's what they had called it.

Europe was being remade. Yes, there were problems. The black uniform of the Waffen-SS was regarded with respect but also with fear, not only by the local population but by the regular Wehrmacht. Though he knew that most would have given almost anything for a transfer, to join the élite, to wear the 'Death's head' badge that signified they were ready to make the ultimate sacrifice for their country, if needs be. He had even laughed at those who had suggested their 'skull and crossbones' made them look like pirates.

Yes, of course, he had heard the rumours that unpleasant things had happened, that the Reich division had been involved in ugly scenes, had done things that even in wartime were not supposed to be tolerated. But he put most of it down to enemy propaganda. And some of it to the excess that he knew was inevitable when men were frightened and fighting for their life, and then, in spite of their fears and against their own expectations, ended up in a position of invincible power. There would be apologies needed, later. But he was in von Rulenstein's division, and they were one thing and one thing only: the best damn army in Europe, possibly in the world.

And he was the general's adjutant, far from some of the fighting perhaps, but always there, where it mattered, when it mattered. As he had been at the end, after the ugliness of Croatia, after the disaster of Greece, then the reverses in Italy, there in the closing chapters when the young gods were turned into messenger boys – the moment, ironically, when fate hung heaviest on their shoulders – there when they could have fled the cruel future hiding in wait for them, when they failed history, and history failed them.

When the general spoke, therefore, the words came as little surprise to him. 'Do you remember Switzerland? The hotel by the lake in Geneva?'

As if he could ever forget. How long ago was it? Only ten years, almost exactly. But it seemed like a lifetime. Or two.

Geneva, March 1945

'*Herein.*' As soon as he had uttered the command to enter, General von Rulenstein regretted it. The tone had been too imperious for a Zurich businessman. It had been such a long time since he had worn civilian clothes that he had forgotten some of the mannerisms that went with them. He looked down at the lapels of his suit as if to remind himself. Rather nice, he thought, a fine, dark blue woollen herringbone, almost English in cut. Not inappropriate, under the circumstances.

'Two gentlemen downstairs to see you, sir,' the maid announced, bobbing respectfully. Von Rulenstein was immensely relieved that she spoke the local French patois, which he had little trouble understanding, rather than the Swiss-German dialect he found both incomprehensible and comic. The idea of mimicking it himself had been the only aspect of the mission that worried him.

'Ah, the Americans.' He smiled. 'Send them upstairs, please, and ask them to wait a few moments in the sitting-room. We shall be with them shortly. See to it that we are not disturbed. We have business to discuss.'

Turning to the younger man standing by the window, he added in German, 'This will be the importers from New York, Rudi. Please check that the documents for the chocolate contract are ready.'

One could not be too careful. There were few Swiss in Geneva, even in the lower ranks of the hotel trade, who did not have at least one other language. The maid bobbed again and left.

'Shall I go next door, sir, to greet them, while you change?' the younger man asked, coming almost to attention as he spoke.

'Yes. I suppose I ought to. It will be what they expect. Creates more of an impression. And this is, after all, an important occasion. Come to think of it, perhaps you should change too.'

'Sir.'

Major Rudiger Aschenheim, equally ill at ease in his tweed jacket and baggy dark flannels, brought his heels together, a movement of subconscious habit, bowed slightly from the waist and walked to the door of the adjoining bedroom where his own uniform hung. They had unpacked them this morning, from the bottom of their business luggage. He had taken the precaution of pressing both, not a job he appreciated, but on a mission such as this, bringing a batman would have been unwise. And there was obviously no question of entrusting that particular chore to the hotel laundry service. Their uniforms would be needed for only a short spell, but useful, to impress on their visitors that, despite everything, they were still a force to be reckoned with: a fighting force, and one that had shown itself, before the odds were stacked so heavily against them, to be without equal in the world.

Von Rulenstein breathed out, feeling more himself as he pulled on the familiar high-coloured tunic of his uniform. It had been a good idea to take a suite, he reflected. In any cases, a hotel sitting-room was no doubt where many of the business deals that took place in Geneva were conducted. The Hotel Walliserhof had been a good choice, too. Friulani, the Italian intermediary who had arranged the meeting, had suggested it. Respectable. Expensive, of course. Formal. Its distinguished nineteenth-century frontage was modest in comparison to some of the grander hotels which had sprung up along the lakeside in the 1920s and 30s. The interior was all dark mahogany and antique Persian rugs scattered on polished parquet; the staff were polite, efficient and apparently wholly uninquisitive. Herr Zwüngli, the owner, was the soul of Swiss confidentiality, he assured them.

The two men were already seated in the heavy brocaded arm-chairs in front of a fireplace of almost baroque magnificence when Aschenheim opened the door and entered the adjoining sitting-room. He saw them stiffen slightly at the sight of his black uniform. It was a reaction he had become used to, although he had never before come face to face with a ranking enemy officer who was in civilian clothes, or one who was not his prisoner.

The chemistry in the room was awkward. Both men had risen from their chairs as he entered. But neither had exactly stepped forward to shake his hand. It was as if they were hanging back, embarrassed somehow by the fact of their presence in the same room. As well they might have been, of course. Out there in the wider world, only a few dozen miles to the south and to the north, soldiers of the great alliance they represented were engaged in mortal conflict with his countrymen: killing and being killed for a few feet of territory. The war was not over yet. Except that in reality, of course, it was. The only question was whether or not the result was a foregone conclusion. That was why they were here.

The awkwardness was dispelled, however, by the entry behind him of von Rulenstein, resplendent in his black Waffen-SS general's uniform with the knight's cross and oak leaves at his neck, a man who even when staring defeat in the face knew the worth of displaying his honours. Von Rulenstein could be hearty when he felt the occasion demanded it. Before either of the other two could react, he had moved quickly around the octagonal table that separated them and grasped the hand of the thinner of the two, a tall, gangly man with an aquiline nose whom Aschenheim took from his demeanour to be English, though he could not prevent himself from wondering if he might be Jewish. How odd it must have been, he thought obliquely, back in the days when no one noticed or cared about such things. If there ever really had been such a time.

The Englishman seemed taken aback. But instinct had won out and he had gripped the SS-general's hand. The American, he noticed, had taken the opportunity to move towards his own side of the table and had busied himself with his briefcase, taking from it a bound folder of documents which he laid face-down. Aschenheim studied him. He had no doubt that this was the senior partner. The man was older than he had expected, about fifty he would have guessed from the greying of his hair and the little moustache which, had the man been German, he would have said was a tribute to the Führer's own upper lip. It was not quite as square-cut, of course, and on this American, allied with the gold-rimmed glasses and the darting, intelligent eyes under beetling brows, made him look more like a member of an American comedy troupe he had vaguely heard of, bizarrely named Marx.

It was the American who, still not having shaken hands, took the initiative, speaking in clear German with just a hint of Viennese dialect. 'Good to see you, gentlemen. My name is Harper, and my colleague here is Colonel White, from British Intelligence.' Aschenheim was certain that they were cover names, and resented a situation that required him and his superior to prove their identities while they were forced to take the enemy's word on trust. But that was a factor of the position forced upon them.

'May I suggest we get down to work,' the man who called himself Harper said. 'We do not have much time. As you know things are moving quite fast, both on the Rhine and in Italy, and of course on the Russian front.'

The SS-general nodded. He had no need to hear more allied gloating. It was only a matter of time.

'I must congratulate you on your forces' capture of the bridge at Remagen. It was a very well executed military operation.'

'As planned. Thank you for your co-operation, General. Unfortunately, it has caused one or two problems with the Russians.'

'Problems?' Von Rulenstein sounded apprehensive. Remagen, Aschenheim knew, was part of the package. But the others had negotiated that, at enormous personal risk. It was the gambit; now it was time to examine the consequences. There could not be problems at this stage. It was too late.

It was the Englishman who spoke next, his German equally impressive, if rather correct and uncolloquial:

'We have had a missive from the Soviet foreign ministry. They have suspicous minds. They were surprised that one bridge on the Rhine had been left intact, and suspect, I believe, that German capitalists would prefer their industrial heartland to be captured by Allied capitalists rather than Communists.'

Von Rulenstein snorted.

'They have also, I am afraid, heard rumours of the meeting in Lugano two weeks ago.'

Aschenheim could not keep the shock from his face. The brief encounter in a small chalet on the outskirts of the lakeside resort had been set up only after the most complex manoeuvres to which he himself had been party. It had been negotiated through Italian intermediaries who, he had been assured, were wholly trustworthy. He should, of course, have known better.

'Is this a problem?' Von Rulenstein had asked the question with a remarkably straight face. He made a mental note never to play poker with the general. As if they would ever be in a bigger game.

The American smiled, the eyes half-closed behind his gleamingly polished spectacles.' 'I don't think so, general. We have decided that, given this unfortunate leakage of information, we can no longer rely on keeping the project referred to as Operation Sunrise secret from our Soviet allies.'

Aschenheim almost fell off his seat. The general, he noticed, had gone white, but remained otherwise outwardly calm.

The American continued. 'We have therefore let it be known that we are negotiating a separate surrender of the German forces in Italy, without reference to the high command in Berlin. Obviously this is a highly classified matter and there is every need for the utmost discretion, which is why Moscow was not informed.'

'And their reaction?'

'They have asked for two Soviet generals to be present at the talks.'

Aschenheim sat dumbstruck. The conversation was spiralling out of his comprehension.

'But I do not see them. I trust you have not kept them waiting downstairs. Herr Zwüngli would not like that. Most untidy.'

The American smiled. He knew this game. 'No. We did not wish to trouble them too much. They have been informed that we will let them know the precise date and time of the surrender ceremony as soon as we ourselves are aware of it.'

'An excellent choice of words, Mr Harper.'

'Thank you, general. May we then proceed to the details? I would like to convey to you and your associates, once again, our appreciation of the measures already undertaken, but also the need for a speedy resolution. I have with me, as requested, a status report – severely curtailed, I'm afraid, for reasons which I have no doubt you will understand – on a development which we expect in the near future to radically alter the situation. I am instructed to let you see this but not, I regret, to take it away with you. I am, however, empowered to present you with an already drawn-up version of the protocol already discussed. We will expect an answer within the shortest period of time. I am willing to go through it now with you and answer any questions.'

'I have one, first of all. Is it signed?'

'It is signed, general. At the highest level. For that reason I can allow you to take one carbon flimsy copy only, which will of course not bear the signatures. You can imagine the ramifications if this got into the wrong hands. The originals will stay with us, until everything is settled.'

'I understand.'

For the remaining two hours, as the pale spring sunshine faded from the sky over Geneva, a scene of tranquillity untouched by the carnage in the rest of Europe, they sat in that room and pored over the piece of paper as if destiny itself depended on it.

'Rudi.' The old man's breath was coming in short rasps now. 'They betrayed us.'

'Maybe, Hermann. Maybe history betrayed us.'

'But they promised. The world could have been so different.'

But would it have been better? Aschenheim had long wondered. The thought of how things might have been had weighed heavily over the years, like a leech draining blood from the source. Only here, in the camp, was life reduced to its bare essentials, to life in the face of death, to a genuine appreciation of what constituted kindness and the quality of mercy in the sure and certain knowledge that the world was full of unforgiving cruelty.

'Rudi, you will go back, one day, to Germany. Maybe someday soon.'

He was stroking the clammy parchment of the dying man's skin. It occurred to him that he did not know what he was dying of. Medical care was non-existent, even for the guards, as far as he could see. Cancer, perhaps, he had lost so much weight; malnourishment, of course, though that went without saying; the loss of hope, undoubtedly, perhaps the worst thing of all: a slow steady atrophy of the soul.

'You must take this with you when you go. Hide it. Show them. Tell them all.'

Rudi looked down. From within the rags wrapped around his waist, the old general was fumbling at the piece of rope which served as his belt. He tried to help him without really knowing what he was trying to do. The belt undone, the old man dug his skeletal hand inside his soiled underclothes. For a few seconds it seemed as if he was panicking, then his breathing slowed again and his hand emerged from a tear in the grubby grey material with a tiny oilskin pouch, grey too, the colour Rudi recognized immediately as the old Wehrmacht waterproof material used to cover ammunition. It had been cut down and crudely sewn together.

'This.' The general held it towards him. 'Take it, keep it. They never found it, never took it.'

He was unsurprised. When they were brought to the first camp, they had been stripped of everything from their uniforms to their boots, but they had never been strip-searched. Their old Wehrmacht underwear was left to them as a sole reminder of their fatherland. Ten years later, they were still thankful for it. There had never been any replacements.

'*Fertig, fertig.*' The words were little more than a whisper. Finished, he seemed to be saying. His last business done. But it also meant 'ready'. Was he saying that he was ready to meet his maker? There had always been a religious element beneath the general's once-tough, unshakeable exterior, some relic of his Catholic childhood. Was that where he was now, in some sunlit foothill of the Alps? Far from the horror to come; the horror that was now behind him for ever. Rudi made the sign of the cross over his forehead. But it was another four hours before he was dead.

Afterwards, when they had carted the body outside to be covered in an old tarpaulin, left by the side of the hut, with the others, an effective deep freeze until the earth would be soft enough to bury it, Rudi took the oilskin and opened it, although he knew already what it contained. The thin flimsy paper with its blurred carbon copy printing was still surprisingly legible. A testimony to German oilskins, he thought. There was no point in opening it out. He knew what it said. He just had no idea what the old man expected him to do with it. History had already been written.

41

Head Filled with Straw

The days after his return from Iceland were hollow pages in the life of Eamonn Burke. He wandered through them aimlessly, his mind without focus, mostly in a vague alcoholic daze. He was rarely drunk, but never really sober. He developed a routine that revolved around the opening hours of The Parson's Nose, an unremarkable, relatively anonymous public house on the corner of a side street off Notting Hill Gate, frequented by market traders from the Portobello Road, a small clique of locals and a large number of occasional drinkers; trendy folk, Burke might have called them if he had been in a mood to notice. Mostly he sat in the corner, quietly, over one pint after another. He usually took a newspaper, though he rarely read it. He took it because he had found it discouraged conversation. He hid behind it. From the world. From himself. In the afternoons, he took long, slow walks around the houses, oblivious to his surroundings, often unnoticing of the weather which remained inclement. It was one of those years in which spring would come late to England, when summer frocks would emerge optimistically from winter wardrobes, and then be covered up again under long raincoats as common sense once more took precedence over sensibility. Burke paid little attention.

After the 'event', as he still referred to it in a protective impulse, a way of avoiding the detail of the memory, he had scrambled his way back towards the top of where the original ice rift had been. The tent and all the supplies that they had let down into the glacial chasm had vanished as the great masses of ice had lurched together. But to his surprise, if he had still been capable of such an emotion, the three undamaged snow scooters had remained essentially in one place, carried along on the top of the tidal wave of frozen water.

Acting on blind instinct, he had managed somehow to gun one of them into life and clamber on board, setting it chugging across the ice, guided – very roughly – by his memory of what their original GPS co-ordinates had been, uncaring if some uncharted chasm swallowed him up. Chance – he could scarcely call it luck – preserved him, even when night fell. By the time he saw the few lights he took to be Kjölur he was on the verge of total exhaustion, and stumbled into the small town only to collapse on the step of the incongruous brightly lit burger bar that was its solitary eating establishment. The last thing he heard was the sound of an over-amplified Oasis hit blaring out of the door opened by two giggling teenagers who fell over him screaming.

The following morning he had wakened in soft sheets in the small town's only guesthouse and told the owners an abbreviated version of his tale – minus the plane, minus the history; all these people were interested in was any possibility of saving lives. But they had shaken their heads, and muttered among themselves. He caught the name 'Magnus' and thought he read in their stern compassion a with-holding of blame, partly out of politeness and partly because this was a self-reliant land and Magnus should have known better. He gave them the map co-ordinates, as best he could remember, but if they organized an expedition, he was not asked along. Transport back to Reykjavik was arranged; the road was now already passable. And in his pocket he still had the only thing that gave him any grasp on reality: a ticket back to London.

There had been fourteen calls on his answering machine when he came back. He left it switched on. Over the first few days, he noticed involuntarily, the number continued to mount up, but now the phone had ceased ringing. Life was like that. After a while people gave up on you. Quite rightly, he thought. He had not even bothered to listen to them. Once, when he was on his way out to the pub, he heard George Prosset's voice wondering where he had got to, and suggesting lunch at The Vineyard. For half a second, or probably less, he thought afterwards, he had almost considered taking him up. He knew Prosset would urge him to resume his life, to start taking journalism seriously again, to forget the strange German girl, to write up the story, even as a feature – a magazine piece of course, not something for the foreign pages of *The Times* really – but someone would take it, as an act of exorcism really. It would be good for him. Lots of things would be good for him, Burke knew. It was just that he wasn't interested in any of them.

He had even sacked Mrs Konopka. By default. He had simply forgotten to leave her money out and as he was seldom in when she called there had been no possibility to sort things out. She had left him a series of notes, polite at first, then curt and finally angry. She had a family to support, money to send back home to Krakow. She knew he was not well, she said – he wondered why, or how? – but she really could not work for charity. He meant to pay her, but increasingly felt he could not face the embarrassment, worse still her solicitous care. She would want to talk things through, make him nice cups of tea or her own, special, Polish remedy, the one she resorted to when her husband (an almost mythical figure to Burke) disappeared on one of his regular benders: strong hot coffee laced with Wyborowa vodka. An antidote, she called it, to reality. In the end he sent her a cheque for three weeks' pay, apologized for his inattention and said he would be going away again. He would be in touch when he got back, if she still cared to work for him. Since then, however, he had seen her in the street, leaving another house where she worked on Tuesdays, and crossed the road to avoid discussion. He knew she had seen him too, seen the lie, and taken umbrage.

With Mrs Konopka's departure, the habitual chaos in his flat had multiplied. He found himself kicking things into heaps in corners in order to find space to walk across the floor. Only the newspapers were tidier than normal; Burke lifted the pile each morning and set it on top of the previous day's, unopened. It would have made sense, he knew, to call in at the newsagent's and cancel them. But that would have been another psychological admission.

He avoided other journalists' haunts, watched little television, didn't go to the cinema, couldn't even pick up a book. It was as if distractions were a betrayal. Though he knew that there was nothing to betray. The dead didn't care.

At times, the Fuchs business troubled him, but not enough for him to do anything about it. Whatever it had all been about was over. It didn't matter any more. Nor did he. Nor did she. Life, he realized, had changed tack and was moving on again, leaving the incidental casualties behind. Burke had been thrown overboard, like surplus ballast, and he had no intention of swimming along futilely in the wake. If sinking was the only alternative, well that was okay by him. There was no burning desire for vengeance, no itching, unslaked curiosity, just a dull emptiness that could not be cured, only suffered.

Occasionally, sitting awake late at night listening to the noise of the wet tyres on the tarmac in Ladbroke Grove, he would pass the time by playing himself at chess. It was, it amused him to think, a suitably sterile occupation. The chess set was expensive: a British Mueseum copy of the old Lewis chessmen, with carved figures of Norse warriors. He found himself staring at the figure of the black queen. Each game ended in stalemate, or a draw. It was not even that he was bored by the lack of an opponent, rather that he saw the dance of the pieces on the board as a suitable expression of his life: a frenetic, pointless jousting, manoeuvring for position, without any meaningful conclusion. The idea of either side pushing into a winning position seemed ridiculous. It amused him to play without taking pieces, watching the confusion multiply in the centre of the board. But without casualties, the game was more pointless still.

He left the board permanently set up on the one corner of the dining-room table that was unoccupied by piles of paper or empty bottles. Most of the flat was strewn with shed clothes, unwashed. He had recently summoned the effort to take some to the launderette after he noticed people sniffing at him in the pub. For all his lack of self-respect, he had no desire to be barred as a vagrant.

But there were still piles of clothing everywhere, particularly on the bed. Two nights in a row he had simply fallen asleep on the living-room carpet. On the second occasion he woke up in the small hours to find the light still on and the carpet beside his face wet. He told himself he must have spilled some beer, though for once there was no bottle beside him. He had not been crying. To have done so would have been self-pity and even he was not that pathetic. But as a result he remade the bed and slept in it.

The next night Valery Korkin called.

Burke was in the kitchen when the telephone rang. The sharp, electronic brrr startled him. His domestic world had become one of predictable silence. He ignored it and let the answering machine take over while he continued applying rough-hewn hunks of cheese to a stale slice of bread, ready to grill. He smothered it in black pepper. Even his taste-buds were jaded.

Korkin's voice was remarkably clear for a line from Moscow.

'Yamon, how are you?' the Russian declared, obviously half-expecting an answer. 'Why are you never there when I want you, you useless piece of batshit? Your uncle Valery must as always do all the work.

'Also, best of all, I have your monk.' The voice waited, as if still not believing that there was only a machine at the other end. But it was also what Valery did in conversation, waiting to see what impression his pronouncements made. He thought about picking up the phone, clearing things up straight away, but his heart was not in it. He would send Korkin's office a fax, something he could compose when he had more time to think about it, a formula of words that would let him down gently without getting involved in explanations.

The Russian's voice continued, talking to the tape as if he now, reluctantly, accepted it was the only listener. In fact he was not even talking to the tape. It had long ago filled up with all the messages Burke had ignored. 'Hmmmha? You see. I have been working like you said. And it is very interesting. But I will tell you in person. You must come here. To Munich. Ahhha? You see. You are thinking I am Soviet man still, bound to the gulags. But no, here I am enjoying German luxury. I am not leaving an address or number. It is too complicated, too dangerous. Too many people might be interested. You will understand. Come here and we will go to see the monk together. He knows everything, why they killed my Siggy, the filthy secret they are hiding. I see you Tuesday, midday, at the Veesun, hmm? Your little German girl said you knew where that was.

'Oh, by the way, she will be coming too.'

The phone went dead just as Burke reached for it.

42

Bavaria, Bavaria

Margarethe Kröning arrived late for work on the last day of her life. By the time she got out at Messegelände U-bahn station, a fine, steady spring drizzle was falling. She pulled up her coat collar as she stumped the few hundred yards to the base of the Bavaria monument. As she hauled the heavy iron key out of her handbag and walked up the stone steps, she took no notice of the young man sitting in the BMW parked on the other side of the road.

Less than five minutes later the car's occupant, having glanced at the heavy Rolex oyster on his wrist, put down the Munich guide book he had been reading. He found the neo-classical pseudo-goddess ugly, but the book praised the monument for the fine view from the top, which was all that mattered. He put on his 'working' jacket, climbed the steps slowly and approached the open door in the base of the pediment.

'*Guten Morgen*,' he addressed the dumpy woman seated beside a little desk inside.

'Too cold for the time of year.'

'Am I your first customer?' he said, watching for any reaction to his accent. He hated that.

She nodded. 'Won't be many today. Not the weather for sight-seeing.' He handed over his two Marks. She thanked him perfunctorily and, for form's sake, gave a thin smile and wished him a good rest of the day. He smiled back, stepped inside and then strangled her from behind with a length of piano wire.

Cursing at the old lady's unexpected weight, he dragged her body into the corner. He took from his pocket a neatly printed sign and hung it on the outside door-handle. It read simply: '*Geschlossen, wegen Personalmangel.*' Closed because of staff shortages. He had copied it from one in the window of a restaurant downtown. Quite apt, really. He shut the door, took a key from the desk drawer and locked it behind him. Quietly, calmly, he began climbing the circular stairs. In his other hand he carried a neat nylon padded bag, in a pocket of which he had stored the piano wire, close to the other tools of his trade, and a freshly-made salami sandwich. He had an hour or so to wait.

Eamonn Burke got out of the Munich U-bahn at Theresienwiese station, and was struck by the desolation that confronted him as he came up the escalator to street level. It had taken him a while to grasp that Korkin's 'Veesun' was actually *die Wiesen*: the meadows, short for Theresienwiese, the site of Munich's annual beer festival, the Oktoberfest. The last time he had been here, it had been hard to move for the crowds.

Burke realized he was seeing the fabled 'Wiesen' for the first time as they must be for most of the year: a great plain of gravel and tarmac that looked more like a bomb clearance site than any sort of meadow. The only structures were a couple of drab grey portaka-bins, a few dozen yards from the U-bahn entrance, serving no obvious purpose, with blinds drawn over the windows. He scanned the drab expanse for any sign of the bulky Russian's figure.

His nerves were agitated. From the instant Korkin had put the phone down on his answering machine, it was as if caffeine had been injected undiluted into his veins. Sabine was alive. That was what the Russian had clearly implied. No matter how he turned it around in his head, there was no other easy interpretation to be put on that final sentence. He replayed the message in his mind, cursing the fact that the full tape meant he had no way of hearing Korkin's actual words again. He looked for ways of telling himself he had misheard. He had seen her die, hadn't he, along with Siggy and Magnus, when the ice cracked and the damn plane disappeared into the bowels of Iceland? And why had she not contacted him if she was really still alive? The questions tormented him, robbed him of sleep. There was no alternative: he would make Korkin's rendez-vous. But what had the man discovered. Was he really going to get to the bottom of this? Did he want to? Yes, if it meant he was really going to see her again.

Burke glanced at his watch. Still five minutes until noon. Not that he expected Korkin to be strictly punctual. Not unless he had changed his habits. Here and there a few dog-walkers strolled with their pets, stopping for them to answer the call of nature, scrabbling in the gravel. One of the city's prime sites was nothing more than a giant dachshunds' toilet. In the distance, towards the great statue that dominated the skyline, there were one or two couples, walking arm in arm like lovers out on a spring day despite the drizzle. Burke thought he could have imagined more romantic venues.

He looked up at the Bavaria statue, a jolly green giantess standing in front of the stone neo-classical portico that reminded Burke of the British Museum. Munich's Hall of Fame, a mini-state's mid-nineteenth-century folly modelled on the Panthéon in Paris, dedicated to busts of great and famous Bavarians, an ambition that made even the old joke about famous Belgians seem good. And this ridiculous statue: a hulking female figure – modelled perhaps on one of the Oktoberfest waitresses who could carry a dozen steins of beer at once – standing by the side of a lion, a sword in her belt and a laurel wreath clutched in her raised arm: Bavaria personified watched over the empty arena of debauchery like a tutelary deity, with sightless eyes.

At that precise moment, however, Bavaria was not as blind as Burke imagined. Inside the hollow head, the man smiled as he identified the solitary figure ambling down the central tarmac pathway. There were three apertures, designed for tourists to gain a panoramic view over the city's spires. Through the one to the left he caught a glimpse of the great neo-Gothic pinnacle of St Paul's with the giant gold clock hands pointing almost vertically to indicate midday.

He settled into position in front of the central aperture, amused to notice the almost perfect resting-place for his right knee provided by the concave contours of the inside of Ms Bavaria's nose. He levelled the telescopic sight and centred the cross-hairs on Eamonn Burke's forehead.

Burke saw them only when they were almost upon him, the old couple, huddled together against the damp, cool weather. For a moment he thought they must be short-sighted, advancing upon him as if he wasn't there, she with her wicker shopping-basket over one arm, stooped slightly against her husband, a big man with a typical Bavarian hat pulled down over his eyes. He too was bent over and walked with the aid of a stick. Only the speed of their awkward gait was surprising.

Burke moved aside, off the tarmac path on to the gravel, to let them past, then flinched suddenly, thrown off-balance, when the bulky old man stretched out one arm to grab him. At the same time he threw back his head to stare into Burke's eyes and cackle.

'So you do not recognize your old friends?'

With astonishment Burke found himself staring into the unmistakable ogre-like grin of Valery Korkin.

'Or even little old ladies.' The voice was instantly familiar.

'Sabine.' Burke turned in wide-eyed wonder to see her wink up at him, her spiky fringe sticking out from under the grandmother's headscarf.

'I thought you were . . '

'Yes. I know. Me too.' She squeezed his arm, beaming at him, holding yet restraining him. 'Not here. Quick. Valery fears you may be being watched.'

Korkin had taken his other arm and was steering him gently but firmly towards the Bavaria statue.

'Let's go, my friend. We have a lot to talk about.'

Burke felt suddenly light-headed. Surely, none of this could really be happening.

And then it wasn't.

Plucked by a giant hand, Korkin leaped backwards, falling, pulling Burke with him, throwing him and Sabine together. Sabine screamed. From somewhere in front of them came a flat crack, echoed, like a car backfiring in a cul-de-sac.

'What the . . .'

'Run, Eamonn, run. Come with me.' Sabine was shouting at him, terror in her voice. 'Come, Eamonn, please. He'll fire again.'

Burke looked down at the great bulk of Korkin, flat on the ground, astonished eyes staring into space. A dark, seared hole was punched in his forehead and thick scarlet rivulets formed amid the gravel behind his hair.

Eamonn Burke sat hunched in a trance over the body of his friend, his hands soaked in blood, his slow, almost silent sobs swallowed by the hubbub. Sabine Kotzke kneeled beside him, hugging him, every now and then still staring around her apprehensively as if she, too, believed that at any moment black lightning might strike.

The paramedics from the Krankenhaus arrived with the bustle of authority, ready to remove mourners by force if need be to deal with the injured. But one look at Korkin's staring eyes and the dark hole drilled in his forehead was more than enough to persuade them to leave Burke alone with his grief.

Uniformed police officers in their distinctive bottle-green trousers and mustard shirts were fanning out in all directions. Several were instantly deployed in the streets, hurrying traffic along with whistles and gestures. A young sergeant, constantly conferring with a crackling voice on his radio, attempted to take details from Sabine. No, she had told him, she had seen nothing. One moment they were walking together, the next he was dead. The shot came from up there, in front. She waved wildly towards the huge neo-classical monument. A detachment was sent at the double. The policeman was talking trajectory, turning to his radio. There was talk of roadblocks, arguments about traffic flow. No, she lied, she could think of no reason why anyone would want to kill the victim. An old friend, of Herr Burke's. No, he was not Irish. A journalist, from London. The dead man? No, also not from Munich, a visitor, Russian. Ah, the policeman nodded as if everything had suddenly become clear. Russians were everywhere, the new Sicilians.

And all the while, Eamonn Burke remained there, staring into eyes that stared back, but not at him. The medical orderly kneeled opposite him, on the other side of the body, and reached across to take his hand. He gave it to her, unthinking, and she moved it down, watching his face as she did, gently, testing his reaction, and with Burke's fingers closed Valery Korkin's eyes.

'*Komm schon*,' she said softly. He did as he was told, allowed her to raise him to his feet. Instinctively, the ambulancemen moved in, lifting the not-inconsiderable bulk of the dead man on to the green canvas stretcher. A blanket was pulled up over his face.

Without waiting for instructions, they carried him away. Untidy, thought Burke, that's what it would have been. Untidy to have corpses littering the Wiesen. Two women police officers were escorting Eamonn and Sabine to the car. They knew it was difficult at a time like this. But there would have to be statements, details, forms, next of kin . . . Burke thought of the big Russian's unfettered existence. No, no next of kin, just some sad faces and empty beds from Minsk to Magadan.

43

Death and Resurrection

The morning after Valery Korkin's death, Eamonn Burke awoke to the sound of persistent pattering rain on the wooden windowsill of the Hotel Am See. Sabine Kotzke, resurrected from the dead, lay next to him, leaning on her elbow, her dark eyes watching his. He wanted to reach out, to kiss her, to tell her it was all okay. Except that he wasn't sure that it was. She had come back into his life when it was at its emptiest, but she had brought murder with her.

It had been late by the time they got to the hotel in Starnberg, on the edge of the great lake south of Munich. Not far from here, on the nearby Ammersee, Sabine had told him, Bavaria's mad King Ludwig II, the one who built all those crazy palaces, had been found drowned. She had planned it as a romantic destination, a place that reminded her of the little guesthouse on the Icelandic coast at Grindavik. She had not counted on them bringing a ghost into their bed.

It had not helped either that Frau Kruger, the manageress, had clucked like an old hen, welcoming the young couple and tittering salaciously how she'd saved them the best room, with the view over the lake. And all because the *junge Dame* had said it was a special reunion. And what a pity the *junger Herr* was looking so pale, but it was probably the weather.

Most of the day had been spent at the police station, both grateful for the numbing effect of ritual and bureaucracy: statements delivered, arrangements set in force for cremation. Burke had seen no point in having the body shipped back to Moscow; it was an indulgence Korkin would have laughed at. 'What, like Vladimir llyich, pickled and placed in a mausoleum, there's a thought, ha ha ha ha,' he remembered the Russian once cackling with black humour at the thought of his own funeral. The police had said they would be in touch. They were – somewhat obviously, Burke had just refrained from saying aloud – treating it as murder. There was a lot of trouble with the Russian community. Burke had said nothing, merely acquiesced when Captain Wegener had asked him not to leave the Munich area without letting him know. Not that there would be any problem, of course, but they could be needed as witnesses, if – he meant 'when' – the murderer was apprehended. Then they had left, arm-in-arm, not so much as young lovers, but an old couple united by an unexpected bereavement.

Later, at the hotel, Burke had held her close. Squeezing her to him as if the action might prevent her from being ripped away from him again. They had made love almost guiltily, with a fierce passion. And then he had rolled away from her, leaving a suddenly cold empty space between them, until she had stretched out a hand to touch his, and he had held it tightly, coming back to kiss her on the lips, softly, tenderly, before they both fell asleep.

Now, with the rain drumming on the glass pane, Burke was struggling to come to terms with what had happened. Numbed by the shock, Sabine and he had still managed to pull together the pieces of the weeks they had spent apart, the weeks of her death, as Burke insisted on putting it, as if this was some sort of afterlife.

After the explosion that had sent the Navajo Arrow, Magnus, Siggy and all proof of the 'Einstein conspiracy' hurting into a hole in the earth's crust, she had lain unconscious for longer than she knew. At least several hours, they told her later. When she came to, she found herself lying in a wide deep crevasse, and freezing cold. As night approached she thought she was finished. Only then, turning painfully, had she found in her pocket Magnus's radio phone. Unsurprisingly, in retrospect, the signal was clear. She had hit the 'send' button, homed in on his pre-set frequency and, against the odds and her own expectations, a helicopter out of Reykjavik had picked her up within hours. She was suffering from frostbite and her leg was broken in three places.

They had sent a search party back to look for Magnus and Siggy. The offical report said that the whole ice shelf had cracked and shifted, closing together over a new fissure that stretched for more than a mile. There was no hope that anyone who had fallen into it could have survived. These things happened, occasionally, towards the end of winter, when the temperature changed. They were surprised to find anyone venturing out on to the glacier at this time of year. Especially an experienced guide such as Magnus Haraldson. But everyone could make mistakes.

The magazine, she said, had medevacked her back to Berlin where she had lain in the Charité Hospital for three weeks and had learned how to walk again. The plaster had only just come off when Korkin rang from Moscow.

'Why the hell didn't you call?' Burke cut in.

'Why didn't you call me?'

'I thought you were dead. I'd seen you die, for God's sake.'

'Had you? How well did you search?'

The protest died in Burke's mouth. In the end, the only possible answer had to be: not hard enough.

'I was in shock,' he said finally, lamely.

'I know. Now,' she said, and brushed his hair with her hand.

Had she really thought that he cared so little? But what had he done to prove otherwise?

He turned his head away on the pillow. Sabine turned it back. All that mattered, she insisted, was that they were together again, and the death of Valery made it more important than ever that they finish what they had set out to do.

'You seriously want to go on with this? Now? This stupid bloody business has nearly cost both of us our lives. And has undoubtedly caused the death of one of my oldest, dearest friends. Brutally, stupidly, meaninglessly. Isn't it about time we called it a day, quit while we're ahead, or at least still alive? No bloody story is worth martyrdom, let alone dying at the hands of some psychopathic hitman with an agenda that, in the end, I don't give a flying fuck for.'

'Don't you?'

'No!' He was almost shouting.

'Then you're not the Eamonn Burke I remember.'

'No.' His voice had dropped, was quiet now. 'No, maybe I'm not. And maybe I don't want to be.'

'And it's all meaningless?'

'Yes . . . At least it is to me.'

'Even if it wasn't to Valery? Even if he knew the risk he was taking. If he thought that there was something here worth telling the world about. Whether or not his death was meaningless depends on you.'

Christ, thought Burke. Let this cup be taken from me.

'He did more than just identify the "monk", you know. He found "Mrs K".'

'Who?'

'Mrs K. Or I should say Comrade K. Hiram Carter mentioned her. Told us to ask the "Rooskies" about her. Turns out it took a "Roosky" to unearth her.'

'And . . . ?'

'Her name was Konenkova, Margarita. She lived in America with her husband Sergei, a sculptor, from the mid-1930s until the end of the war. In 1935 a young woman called Margot introduced her to her stepfather, Albert Einstein. She was fifteen years younger than him, but that did not stop them having an affair which ended only when she was dragged back to Moscow in 1945.'

'So . . . ?' Burke swallowed his feelings, suppressed his choking admiration for what Valery Korkin had done for him. He was reluctant to let her draw him back into this with some stupid cat-and-mouse guessing game.

'She was also a spy for the NKVD, reporting straight to Lavrenti Beria in the Lubyanka.'

Burke closed his eyes and wished the world away.

An hour later, Eamonn Burke found himself driving Sabine Kotzke's red convertible through sunlit spring woods along the shores of the Starnberger See.

The 'monk', she had explained, was real. He lived in a monastery. Korkin had arranged for them to meet him at 11.00, after mass. Easter mass. Burke had jolted. It had not occurred to him that today was Easter Sunday. Yet somehow the news failed to uplift his heart. The road ran from the Stanberger shores through dark pine woods which parted to allow a glimpse of the sparkling blue waters of the Ammersee.

'Breathtaking, isn't it?'

'Umhumm,' Burke acknowledged tersely. But it was, he admitted, despite himself, undeniably beautiful: well-tended countryside, neat and ordered, a harmony of man and nature. Each village they passed through had a blue-and-white maypole decorated with spring flowers. Here and there a brightly painted onion dome poking over the trees would indicate the presence of a church. Wherever one was visible, a trickle of people could be found making their way to the Easter morning mass. Still a godfearing folk in spite of everything.

At Herrsching they took a left turn by the maypole. Burke kept one eye on the rearview mirror. The road rose and then descended into another village. He swung the car right again and another onion dome appeared in front of them, green, wooden, set high on top of a tall square tower painted white and pastel pink: a church made out of coconut ice, he thought absurdly.

'*Die Wallfahrtskirche.* We're here. The Pilgrimage Church, on the holy hill of Andechs. That's where the monastery is.'

'Monastery? It looks more like the entrance to a failed theme park.' He turned the car into a huge, packed carpark with a banner above proclaiming it was reserved for guests of the monastery. Apart from the church tower on the hill behind them, the main thing he could see was a rather down-at-heel mini golf course.

'This is a working monastery.'

They had crossed the road from the car park and were climbing a steep cobbled path that wound up the side of the hill towards the church. He could now see the more substantial, fortress-like buildings of the monastery itself. They passed a white stone building painted in the inevitable Bavarian blue and white. A sign declared it was the Monastic Brewery Gaststätte. Two middle-aged men sitting on a bench holding litre pots of frothing dark beer smiled at them.

'Do a good pint, do they?'

'Andechs is also a farm, famous for cheese and butter. And yes, they brew one of the best beers in Bavaria,' she said.

The place seemed more given over to commerciality than godliness. On the right was a children's playground, an ice cream stall and a booth where a character with a wizened face was sticking mackerel on wooden sticks and arranging them around a brazier. Only the poster in a glass case advertised the more sacred aspect: '*Ostersonntag. Heilige Messe zur Auferstehung unseres Herrn Jesus Christus.*' Easter Sunday, holy mass for the resurrection of our Lord Jesus Christ.

'It is a big day, Easter. They will be very busy, especially later. Right now most people are at mass.'

Though not all of them. As they reached the top of the hill the monastic buildings opened out into a great enclosed square of tables and chairs with views over the green fields below. Parents clinked beer glasses together and soaked up the morning sunshine while children argued over big salty pretzels and boiled eggs, brightly coloured in greens, oranges, reds and blues. But over the clatter of plates and the noise of profane conversation, Burke could hear the soft, almost ethereal piping of plainsong, a high melodic arhythmic chanting unchanged since the Middle Ages.

'I forgot to ask. What order are they?'

'*Benediktiner.*'

'At least we won't have a vow of silence to contend with.'

Sabine went ahead and edged open the main door to the church. The volume of the singing had risen: a strange melody, ancient yet unfamiliar, the high perfect plainsong of the chanter answered only slightly less musically by the congregation. Burke followed her and stepped inside, into a world of high baroque splendour he had almost forgotten existed: grand swirls of gold on pastel blue, incense and cherubs, candelabra, candles and statues of the virgin. Burke stood, pressed amid the crowd facing the altar, and wondered. Sabine, close to him, whispered in his ear as the organ surged into Mozart's 'Credo'.

'They have a lot of treasures. Old things. Relics.'

He gave her a quizzical glance.

'The sceptre of Maximilian of Austria. It contains a bit of the rod with which Christ was beaten. And twigs from the crown of thorns itself.'

He turned to look at her, the theatrically sceptical look on his face a mute question. She shrugged in reply.

An old wooden rod, some dried twigs. People had gone to war over such things. Old ironies, wars over memorabilia of the God of Love. Perhaps some day a cult would preserve with equal humbug and adoration a lock of Michael Jackson's hair, a pair of the Spice Girls' pants. Perhaps they already did.

He was brought down to earth by, of all things, the Lord's Prayer, chanted in alternate lines by the priest at the altar – a monk, Burke supposed, perhaps even the abbot himself – and the ranks of people standing before him. The words, so familiar as to have lost most of their meaning in English, reimpressed themselves upon Burke now in the German, as if the language alone altered their context. Forgive us our sins, the audience repeated, as we forgive those who have sinned against us, '*und erlöse uns von dem Bösen*'. Deliver us from evil.

Burke saw again Valery's body hurled between them, heard the precise distant crack, saw the hole in his head, the astonishment in his eyes, the mess of the exit wound, dark blood and matted hair.

'Come on, let's go.' He pulled Sabine's arm.

'No, this way.' She looked at him, alarmed by the tone of his voice. He followed her to the side door across the body of the chapel. She pushed him through.

'I'm sorry.'

'You don't have to say anything.'

They had emerged into a courtyard, roofed over with glass, between the church and the main part of the monastery. In front of them, against the whitewashed wall, a row of crosses was fixed: large wooden crosses, five or six feet high. There was writing on them. A couple with obviously bored children pushed past them. Burke could hear the man complaining:

'Hurry up, Trude, or all the seats will have gone.'

'*Ja, ja*, Ernst. I know what you are like. And I suppose you think I'm driving us home.'

The older boy, a sulky looking youth of about fourteen, took a blob of chewing gum from his mouth and stuck it on one of the crosses as he passed.

Burke thought of calling after him, after his father, but thought better of it. He walked up to the cross and flicked off the offensive material. He looked at the inscription.

'*Magnitogorsk. Ural. Danke für den gesunden Heimkehr,*' he read aloud. With thanks for safe return.

'Former POWs, captured on the eastern front. Some of them spent a decade and more in captivity. Lucky to have survived,' Sabine said. 'Some of them brought crosses here, on pilgrimage, as a gesture of thanks.'

'And atonement?'

'Sometimes. But not all of them were criminals, you know.'

'No, not all,' said a voice behind them.

Both of them turned round, surprised at the interruption, and found themselves looking into the open, calm face of an elderly monk in a black cassock, tied with a simple white rope belt. 'But many of them sought atonement even so. There is much to atone for in the world; that is why we have the chapel over there.'

He gestured to a small glass door in the wall at the other end of the courtyard, leading into a dark room lit by candles.

'The Chapel of Reconciliation,' the monk explained. His face was deeply lined, weather-beaten, the look of a man who had spent much of his life outdoors, in manual labour perhaps, a careworn face, but not a sad one, as if years of reflection had conquered ancient grief. The little hair that remained in sparse clumps at his temples was white. Burke thought he had to be at least eighty years old, maybe more.

'You are tourists, perhaps pilgrims?' It was said with a smile, a courtesy implicit in the suggestion of any sort of religious motive rather than just the festival of eating and drinking going on below.

'Not exactly,' Sabine answered. 'We are here to meet someone.'

'Brother Klement, perhaps?'

'Yes,' replied Sabine in surprise.

'I am he. I noticed you arrive. I have a room above, with a view,' he said in answer to Burke's obvious, unspoken question.

'We need to talk,' Sabine said.

'So I understand. Let us go for a walk in the gardens.'

He led them through the courtyard round the side of the church where they had come in, a benign old figure, nodding to the tourists and making the sign of the cross over the worshippers now beginning to flow out of the church down towards the beer hall.

In the garden, however, the monk's tone changed. He asked the first question: 'Your Russian friend. He was so very persuasive in asking me to see you. He did not come with you?'

Burke answered brusquely, the only way he could. 'Valery was murdered, last night in Munich.'

'Ah, yes.' He nodded, as if he had somehow been expecting it. 'On the Wiesen. I feared it might be him. You look surprised. Andechs is a place of sanctuary, but it is not so very unworldly. I saw the television news. The police are linking it to the Russian mafia. Obviously that is not what you believe.'

They walked slowly – the old man was no longer very nimble – Burke and Kotzke on either side of him. Inevitably it was she who went straight to the subject.

'Brother Klement. Valery Korkin was a good man. He should not have died, certainly not in vain. He had already lost someone dear to him because of this business. He said you could explain.'

'This business?'

'I don't know where to begin,' Sabine was rattling on. 'It goes back to 1945. Before he died, Valery said it was the context that mattered. He said that you knew.'

'What, may I ask, set you off on this dangerous "wild goose chase"?'

Burke thought it was time he made a contribution. 'A diary, *apparently*' – he saw Sabine flinch at the qualification – 'written by Klaus Fuchs, the atom spy.'

'Hmmph.' The old monk almost chuckled. 'So he did write it after all, good for Klaus.'

44

Old Books and Old Faces

Burke stared at the monk, hardly able to believe what he had just heard. 'You knew Fuchs?'

'Of course. In Dresden. I was his driver. That is why you are here.'

'Are you going to explain?'

The old man sighed, as if he was dredging up troubled memories buried deep under years of contemplation and tranquillity.

'Yes. That is what I agreed with your friend. And I do not break promises, especially not promises made to dead men.'

They had reached the end of the path. The monk turned around and began pacing back along the path.

'To start with, I should tell you that I was not always known as Brother Klement. My real name is Rudiger Aschenheim. Bavarian by birth, Berliner by adoption, veteran of the bad old days.'

'The war.' Sabine filled in the blank.

'Yes, the war. And before. And after. But for the years that you think of, I served in the Waffen-SS.'

Burke recoiled.

'Oh, do not get sanctimonious. The SS were not all concentration camp guards. We did not all bayonet babies for sport.' His face was serious. 'Some of us murdered men our own size, and bigger, men who were trying to kill us, though as a rule we killed more of them. At the time that was considered a virtue rather than a crime. It was called war, and we were good soldiers, in a rotten cause.

'I know about atonement, believe me. The cross you looked at in the courtyard, it was mine. I carried it here when I decided to take a different sort of orders. On my shoulder. Today, looking back, it seems a foolish gesture, but at the time it seemed worthwhile. But then perhaps we make gestures largely for our own sake.'

'I don't understand,' Sabine interrupted. 'When was this?'

He looked at her with those dark eyes that seemed to Burke to take in more than just outer appearance, eyes that went deep, confessor's eyes, searching the soul.

'Don't you, young lady? Are you sure? I wonder.' Burke could see Sabine shift from foot to foot, as if something in the tone of the old man's voice had made her uneasy.

'If you want to know the story, you will have to be patient with me. I came here in the summer of 1961, via Berlin. I walked into West Berlin only two days before they built the Wall. But in one way or another I had been away from home almost all my life.'

'You were a prisoner of war?'

'Yes, I was a prisoner. Not like those who were taken in the West. You Westerners forget that sometimes. You think we were all released in 1945, to enjoy the *Wirtschaftswunder*, launched by American cash while you, the loyal allies, were still paying America interest on your war debt. Hardly fair? I quite agree. But it was not like that for all of us. Fate in 1945 was a particularly arbitrary mistress: twelve long years in the gulags I spent, for being in the wrong place at the wrong time. From April 1945 until June 1957. When they let me go, they sent me to the "zone", to their puppet state, to Dresden. They gave me work as a driver – ah, the things I had driven, even tanks – and attached me to the local scientific institute. That's where I met Klaus Fuchs.'

'He was already there?'

'No, it was nearly two years before he arrived. Even then I did not know that he had come almost straight from an English jail. He was a quiet man, very much the typical professor, ostensibly glad to be "home" although it must have been a quarter of a century since he had lived in Germany. His father was still alive, nearby in Leipzig. And anyway, for him, work was home. He lived for his science more than for politics. I don't think it took him long to realize that life in a Russian colony wasn't exactly the free socialist paradise some of the old Communists had dreamed of, even though he didn't have to queue like the rest of us. He could go to the special shops. It was useful for me too. I had a wife at last. *Spätes Glück*, we say in German, Mr Burke, late happiness. Ach, short happiness.'

'What happened?'

'She died. Cancer. In 1960. They said it was natural causes. Klaus told me the truth – we were on first-name terms by then. He said it was pollution, from the chemical factories, and worse, in the air and in the water of the housing complex where we lived on the outskirts of Dresden. I was lucky to escape the same fate, if that is what you call luck. That was when I decided to leave, to discover if there was anything left for me in the home of my childhood. I found this.' He gestured at their surroundings.

'But this is not why you have come. You have come, as the general always believed someday someone would, for the piece of paper that he left with me. A piece of paper that I believed no longer mattered. But what do I know?'

Burke looked questioningly at Kotzke. But her eyes were on the monk. He turned to the old man.

'What piece of paper?'

'You do not know? Funny, the Russian knew. It is a draft treaty, an agreement if you like, between two warring parties.'

'A surrender document.'

The monk smiled enigmatically and looked into Burke's eyes.

'Not exactly. In fact, quite the contrary. More like a draft declaration of war.'

Burke was as impatient as Sabine now, willing the old man to get on with it.

'I have told you I was in the Waffen-SS – I place great store by the prefix "Waffen", you understand . . . ?'

Burke nodded again. Perhaps sanctimoniousness was only to be expected from an ex-Nazi in holy orders.

'I must take you back to the closing stages of that terrible war . . .'

He closed his eyes, as if turning back time behind the shut lids.

'In the late spring of 1945, the war was over for Germany. Allied forces were in Italy and on the left bank of the Rhine. The Russians were driving a spearhead through East Prussia and Pomerania towards Berlin.'

Burke nodded impatiently. He was not looking for a history lesson. Yet all of a sudden those distant events came back to life, except that it was a different life, seen through the eyes of a man who had been there, fighting, on the losing side, seeing his world vanish into rubble around him.

'I was stationed in northern Italy under the command of General von Rulenstein.' His eyes misted over. 'A strange man; charismatic is the word you would use nowadays. A good soldier, but his real talent was people. He knew how to play them, from the foot soldier

287

to the power brokers in Berlin. We had served together in France, tasted the fruits of victory, entertained Heinrich Himmler himself, head of the SS. Von Rulenstein laid Paris at his feet.

'Himmler was impressed. Von Rulenstein, with me at his side, became a trusted envoy throughout the senior ranks of the SS and the Wehrmacht. We heard the rumblings, at all levels, the first real prophesies of doom after von Paulus's Sixth Army was destroyed at Stalingrad. After that, we knew we could no longer win the war. The Führer still believed in miracles. But for those with any military sense, damage-limitation was the only strategy that made sense. Hitler believed in a "wonder weapon". For a while it seemed there might even be one: the V-2 rockets launched against England, the jet fighter aircraft. Who knows what might have happened if there had been time. But there was nothing to stop the Russian steam-roller. Everyone but Hitler could see it. The Allies too. And they were almost as unhappy as we were.

'The countries in eastern Europe, for whose sake the Western powers had entered the war, saw victory stolen away from them: the replacement of one occupying power by another. The Poles, in particular. They knew from April 1943, when Berlin announced the discovery of mass graves containing the bodies of ten thousand Polish officers at Katyn and claimed it was the work of Stalin's NKVD, that for once the Nazis were speaking the truth. The Allies pretended not to believe it, but it was only a sham. As so often in warfare, pragmatism won out over morality. Even then, you see, you thought in terms of "West" and "East", "us" and "them". Even before the phrase was invented, the Poles knew an iron curtain was being built and they were on the wrong side of it.

'You know who invented the phrase?'

'Of course,' Burke said. 'Churchill.'

'Pah.' The monk's eyes were sparkling. 'He only borrowed it. The real master of rhetoric coined it first: Joseph Goebbels, in February '45. Hitler was right about one thing: the winners write history.'

'How does your piece of paper come into it?'

'Ah yes, our little piece of paper that meant "peace in our time", in the phrase of your Mr Neville Chamberlain. How easily we fool ourselves.

'You have to understand that at its end the Nazi state was not as totalitarian as it had been. Hitler was finished. The fact that he did not see it and was determined to go down in the flames, pulling Germany with him, did not sit well with the rest of the gang. After the purge in July 1944, following the bomb plot, things went quiet. But from the spring of 1945, when even a blind man could see that everything was lost, others – SS-chief Himmler in particular – were putting out feelers for peace.'

'But no one would have listened to Himmler,' Burke interjected.

'In the end, no one did. But the full horror of the camps had not yet been revealed. Atrocities were a matter of scale. Good and evil are prejudiced terms in wartime. After Katyn, you already knew the truth about Stalin. And did it matter? In March, through the intermediary of some highly placed Swiss-Italian businessmen, contact was made between Von Rulenstein and intelligence officers of the United States and Great Britain. We were looking for a way out. To our surprise, they offered one.'

Burke was speechless. Sabine hung on every word.

'They said they were acting on the highest authority. There were fears that Stalin would not stop, even at Berlin; that the Red Army's goal was the Rhine, if not the English Channel, or worse. Sooner or later, there would be a confrontation. They wanted it on their terms. They said they had a wonder weapon, but it was not yet ready. It had been designed for use against Germany, but few of us now believed that Germany would last that long. There was another option; but it depended on us. They wanted proof of co-operation. If the Allies were bogged down on the Rhine, then all would be lost. But if a way could be found for the Allied forces to cross, then the Red Army's advance could at least be equalled.

'Once that had happened, on the right terms, an armistice in the West would be declared: an unconditional surrender in theory but not in fact. Crack Waffen-SS divisions would be transferred to the eastern front; the Allies would proceed to Berlin, and beyond. The Poles would retake Warsaw. No one imagined that Stalin would live with it, but by then they hoped, the wonder weapon would be ready. The Soviets would not be given the option. The Americans would have the power to destroy Moscow with a single bomb.

'The map of Europe would be redrawn according to America's and England's plans. Germany would lose land, but not as much as Stalin intended. The country would still exist, even if there could be no guarantees for members of the present government. We were being offered a lifeline and an ultimatum: refuse, and annihilation was inevitable, with war crimes trials to follow. They called it "Operation Sunrise", a new dawn for Europe.'

'My God,' Burke breathed rather than exclaimed. Sunrise. Men like Hiram Carter had known all along what the atomic bomb had nearly been used to seal: a pact with the devil.

'What went wrong?' Sabine pressed.

'History. Von Rulenstein circulated the ideas secretly through the network. Himmler was unhappy, for obvious reasons, worried that his role in ordering the executions in the camps would come out; worried that the deal would not spare him. But others took the initiative. The division on the Rhine did their bit and "forgot" to destroy the bridge at Remagen. The Western allies got the bridgehead they wanted. A few days later, Von Rulenstein and I travelled incognito to Geneva. There we met with two intelligence men, one representing the British and the other, the one who was really in command, the Americans. He later became quite powerful.'

'Allen Dulles,' Burke filled in, wondering how he had taken so long to see the connection.

'Precisely: the first director of the CIA. We left with a document, the original of which had been signed by both Roosevelt and Churchill, a piece of paper that could have changed world history.'

'Except that it didn't happen.'

'No.' He gave a wry smile. 'When we returned to division headquarters outside Milan, there was an urgent message from Himmler ordering von Rulenstein to report personally to Berlin. There was an aircraft waiting. By the time we got there, everything was in a state of chaos. Himmler was no longer making sense. The Führer had had one of his fits when he learned about Remagen, accused everyone of treachery. Von Rulenstein decided that even to show Himmler the paper was to invite a firing squad. We speculated how to get it to the rest of the network, but even if we had, there was no longer any easy way to get out of Berlin. We tried to drive east, to see how near the Russians were. On the road outside Frankfurt-on-Oder our staff car was overturned by an artillery shell. The driver was killed. We were unconscious. When we came to, the Red Army had passed us by. We swopped officers' uniforms for those on the corpses of ordinary soldiers and surrendered. There was no option.'

'And von Rulenstein still had the copy of the Allied offer?'

'Yes. The Russians never thought to search ordinary ranks for papers. We lost our boots and our overshirts and were shipped to Siberia. We didn't even know the war was finally over until we reached the Urals in July, and were joined by troops who had been taken in Berlin during the last days in May.'

'And now you have the paper.' Sabine was making a statement, not asking a question.

'Von Rulenstein held on to it like a talisman; he had this idea that some day it ought to be published, so that future generations could judge whether or not what had happened had been for the best. Before he died, he gave it to me.'

'But you disagreed?'

'To be quite honest, I didn't care. I kept it because he asked me to. It was only when I met Klaus, all those years later, that we realized we had both played parts in the same drama. His was the greater, of course. But for what he and the other scientists had done, they might have gone ahead anyway.'

'And used the atom bomb on Moscow.' Christ, thought Burke.

'But they didn't dare, because by then they weren't sure the Russians didn't have a bomb of their own.'

Burke saw what Hiram Carter had been hinting at. 'They'd found out they had one fewer initiators than they thought.'

'Precisely. Moscow didn't get the initiator, of course. We know that now. But the Americans didn't know that then.'

'No, they wouldn't have. But they knew that one was missing, along with a B-29 which was last seen making an unscheduled refuelling stop in Iceland. And that was enough for the men in the Pentagon to put two and two together and make five. Especially if anyone bothered to look up Joshua Finch's service record.'

The monk waved the comment away. 'In any case, the Russians decided to make sure. Moscow sent a message back to the Americans. A sort of practical joke, Klaus called it. But then he had a strange sense of humour. I suppose the right word for it was a dummy. Constructed with the help of Klaus's instructions and the brilliance of the Soviets' chief nuclear expert, a man called Igor Kurchatov . . .'

To whom the Einstein letter had been addressed, thought Burke.

'. . . They built a flawed replica. It still took nearly two years, and would never have worked, of course. But it was never intended to. To disguise the fact, it was already cracked when they sent it on its one-way trip to America . . .'

'To Roswell, New Mexico,' said Burke, the final piece of the puzzle falling into place.

'You may know better than I. All Klaus told me was that it was contained in a low-altitude ballistic missle, based on the German V-2, fired from an offshore warship and designed to fall in the

291

vicinity of some important army base. He said it was a brilliant decoy that averted war. I do not know if it was true.'

You bet, though Burke. No wonder there had been such a fuss about the 'Roswell incident'. No wonder the first spokesman to talk to the media had said it was a UFO. Anything must have seemed safer than the truth at the time. Roswell was the new home of the 509th Bomb Group, Finch's old unit.

All of a sudden, the worst fears of the US military establishment must have appeared to be confirmed. Instead of a pre-emptive strike against a state with no comeback, the nuclear stalemate had been born overnight. There would have been doubters, of course, hawks and doves, as always. But the governments in Washington and London had changed. Roosevelt was dead; Churchill was out. Enough for a serious case of cold feet: a hiatus of nearly four years until 1949. By which time Kurchatov and co. had got their act together for real, as the whole world knew. Burke saw abruptly what the combined effect of the Einstein letter and the 'Sunrise Protocol' would be: first-hand evidence of infidelity. Together they would overturn the prevailing myth of the Western world.

That myth held that the men of knowledge and the men of war, the scientists and the politicians, had acted as one to face down evil. They had developed a terrible weapon but used it in the cause of peace, and then no more. They had been united in purpose and sense of responsibility: white knights wielding a mighty sword, dispensing both judgment and mercy. And they had been stabbed in the back. Only ignominious betrayal had let down the powers of light and ushered in the dark age of the Cold War and the arms race. Klaus Fuchs had been cast as the Judas of our era.

Except that it was all a lie. Far from being united, they had all along been riven by doubt and distrust. With good reason. The scientists had distrusted both the morals and motives of their leaders, and stepped outside them to take their own fateful decision. And the men of war had proved as dangerous as the scientists had feared, practising not restraint but further aggression. It had not been mercy or magnanimity or simple humanity that in the end had held back their hand from unleashing further horror on the world, but older, more familiar deterrents. Doubt. And fear.

'Can you show us this document, this treaty offered to the Nazis?' Sabine was breathless, gripping Burke's arm though he hardly seemed to feel it.

'Yes, of course. Didn't I say? I don't break promises. But it is in the library. Come.'

It was like waking from a dream but finding the real world harder to focus on. As they walked, from within the ancient stone walls of the church Burke could hear calm clear voices, thin on the cool April air, sacred music dedicated to the Saviour's resurrection, unheeded by the revelling crowd of beer drinkers below. All human life is here, thought Burke. Lies and legends. Piss and wind.

The monk took from his rope belt a heavy iron key and turned it in the massive oak door before them. It swung open, admitting them to a magnificent room nearly three storeys high, lined with bound volumes and illuminated gently by light falling through panes of old glass that rose from the top of the bookstacks into the great Gothic arches.

It was just as the monk turned to close the door behind them that they heard a voice which set Burke's nerves on edge:

'*Entschuldigung, darf ich aber mitkommen?*' Excuse me, might I join you. German, spoken with a matchless English accent, one that Eamonn Burke recognized only too well, even if the context was one that confused him.

'Eamonn, old man, begorrah. Good to see you.'

45

Sunday, Bloody Sunday

He stood there, smiling, an expectant look on his face like a
pregnant pig, an expression of infinite politeness and self-confident
superiority. He might have been jumping the queue for taxis at
Charing Cross. You don't mind, do you, old boy? his manner said,
my business is so much more important than yours.

'Boston,' Burke said the name with contempt in his voice. 'I
suppose we should have been expecting you.'

'He stepped through the library door, leaving Brother Klement
holding it in his wake, like a college porter ministering to one of the
'young gentlemen' Boston had always affected to despise.

'Jolly well done. And this, I presume,' turning towards Sabine,
'must be your delightful young partner-in-crime, if you'll pardon
the expression. So glad to see you're unharmed by your recent
dreadful experiences. I believe we have mutual acquaintances.'

Burke shot Sabine a quick glance only to find her staring at him
with an outraged 'Who on earth is this and what is he doing here?'
expression on her face.

Behind them the monk had closed the door and turned the key.

'*Ein unerwarteter Gast*?' An unexpected guest, he was asking.

'Oh, surely not. Hardly unexpected, as I think Mr Burke here was
trying to say in his inimitable way.'

'You bastard.'

'Tch, tch, tch. Breeding will out. So much for that expensive
public school education. Didn't quite make an Englishman of you in
the end, old thing, did it. Or maybe it did, hmm? An Englishman in
the mould of Philby, Maclean, Burgess and Blunt, eh? Shirtlifters
and traitors unlimited.'

'I haven't betrayed my country.'

'No, maybe not, but then that's because you don't have one. Or perhaps you're rediscovering your roots. I'm afraid it's not exactly what Uncle Sam wants either, the sort of muck-raking you're up to.'

'Americans have a respect for the truth that matters more than upholding myths.' But Burke hated the words for their naïvety even as he heard them coming out of his mouth.

'Yes, but only Nixon could go to China. I'm afraid the world's a much more complicated place than that, as you very well know. My job's not as terrible as you seem to think, Eamonn. I just clean up the mess other people make, or in this case before they make it.'

'That's what you call it, is it? Making people sick and then cleaning up the vomit?'

'Let's just say that in Hollywood terms, I'm the continuity boy. One of those charged with making sure the sins of the fathers *aren't* visited upon the next generation. Certain things, you see, have to be dealt with outside the normal framework of operations.

'This'll make the biggest story since Philby and Watergate rolled into one. They'll swallow you and your stupid service.'

The smirk faded. 'That's what they want, of course.' He turned to Sabine. 'I was intending to ask you to pass on my regards to Hermann Dickel at the end of all this. How is my friend?'

'Dickel?' Burke shot a sideways glance at Sabine. The name was familiar. Dickel had been the commissioning editor at *EON* who had signed the letter giving him the assignment. What had he got to do with Dickie Boston?

But Sabine was not looking at him. She stood clutching her bag so tightly, Burke could see her knuckles whiten. Brother Klement had moved back against a bookcase and was watching, intently, carefully. He had spoken no English. Burke wondered if he understood what was being said. How much did he himself, come to think of it, really understand? Except one thing.

He spat it out. 'I knew it had to be you. One of your thugs pulled the trigger, but you did it. Siggy, Magnus, Valery, all of them, even some poor bloody Norwegian oilman and a London cabbie. Why?'

'To scare you off your story. That's what you think isn't it?'

'Because it's bloody well true, that's why. All to save your version of the past, to protect the great legend of the Cold War warriors. "Preserving history", that's what Nora Winter meant, except that it took me such a bloody long time to realize what she was hinting at. That's why you didn't want me to see her, isn't it? So how come Nora survived? Why didn't she get her Majesty's Government's short sharp terminal shock treatment too? Or is she too much inside, still one of the boys; didn't leak too much and ran back to teacher to report what she'd let slip out of school. Is that it?'

'My God, you've really swallowed it, haven't you?' Boston looked at Kotzke. 'Congratulations, my dear. But then he never was very bright, not half as bright as his reputation.'

Burke was not going to be distracted. 'You're pathetic, Boston. Worse, you're defending a rotten system and you don't even see it. Might is right, eh? Except that half the best brains in the Western world saw what you were up to and tried to stop it . . .'

'. . . and started the Cold War instead! What's that to be proud of? A bunch of naïve idealistic fools who thought that just because they knew numbers and theorems they knew how to direct the future of humanity. How much did it cost to save their consciences, in terms of the thousands killed, the tens of thousands jailed, the millions oppressed over forty years in Soviet-occupied Eastern Europe? Not to mention how close we nearly came to blowing the planet apart? All because Moscow got a bomb ten years earlier than it would have done without help, and because we thought they had one even earlier.'

But Burke still had the vision of Valery Korkin's bloodied corpse lying in his arms. He wanted to wipe the smug supercilious sneer off Boston's face and grind it into the ancient library's floor. Except that Boston was making a strange sort of sense.

'We didn't know the plane never got there until you found the damn thing for us. We fell for their stupid trick.'

'Roswell.'

'You are well informed.'

'Well enough informed about the bloody murderous game you've been playing to cover up.'

'Stop it, Eamonn.' Boston took a step backwards. 'Don't be a bloody fool. None of this is your fault. You've been used. Don't make it worse on yourself.'

It was not the voice Burke was used to. Gone were all the effete cadences, the mocking wordplay. This was Dickie Boston with his Midlands vowels talking business.

'He's lying,' Sabine burst out, an angry edge to her voice. 'It has to have been his men, killing to cover up their foul-smelling little secrets.'

'I think you know the boot's on the other foot. I've a feeling your honesty credentials aren't going to impress our friend here very much. I'm surprised at you, Eamonn, going along so happily as the krauts' patsy.'

'What the fuck are you on about, Boston?'

'Oh, you don't mean she didn't tell you? Tch, tch, that was naughty. Still I can see how she might not. No guarantee, was there, really, that you'd be keen to do the bidding of the BND?'

'The what? Shut the fuck up, Dickie . . .'

'Oh, come on, Eamonn, for God's sake, you've been around. BND, *Bundesnachrichtendienst*? German intelligence? Don't tell me you really didn't guess? I thought you journalists were supposed to be on the ball.'

'You're scum, Mr Boston,' Sabine spat out. 'You and your kind always have been. Claim the moral high ground, the great white Anglo-Saxon democracies, can do no wrong, don't you? Or is it just that you don't get found out? All we wanted was to tell the world the truth. And is it so very terrible, to say that Germany does not have the monopoly on skeletons in the closet? None that we're going to kill to protect half a century later. Unlike you, you murderous bastard.'

'She's right.' Burke was staring at her, infected by her passionate indignation, even if the words weren't quite what he was expecting. And Boston was talking nonsense, lying to turn him against her.

But Boston seemed unperturbed, his eyes riveted on Sabine, though he was talking to Burke. 'Listen to her, Eamonn. Oh yes, I wanted to stop you all right. Just what good do you think you'll do with this tale? You'll blow a bloody great hole in the Atlantic alliance. And whatever you might think, whatever excesses we might have committed – and I stress *might* – it's still been a sight better than any of the alternatives in this godforsaken century. But it was her side that did the killing. I wasn't prepared to murder you, or anyone else for that matter, just to kill off a newspaper story. There are other ways, you know.'

Burke looked to Sabine and registered with a queasy stomach the look of uncertainty in her lowered eyes. Boston was unrelenting.

'Wise up, for Christ's sake. You were meant to think I was behind those assassination attempts. They knew that was the one way to convince you this was the exclusive of a lifetime. Spooks kill to keep secrets. Just a little too enthusiastic in their execution – if you'll pardon the pun – but then it wouldn't be the first time Jerry's gone over the top, would it? I always knew old Dickel could be a ruthless bastard. But even I was impressed. Nothing like real blood to give the illusion of authenticity, eh?'

Sabine was shaking her head. Violently, as if hearing something she refused to believe.

'It's not true, I swear. Hermann can be impetuous, but he is not a cold-blooded killer. He would not have given those orders.'

'What's not true . . . ?' Burke began. 'Hermann? Your editor, right?'

A harsh little laugh erupted from Boston. 'Editor? *Herr Chefredakteur* Dickel? What a good name for the head of BND disinformation. A creative job if ever there was one.'

Burke watched with horror the cold light die in Sabine Kotzke's eyes. In the church across the courtyard, the voices swelled. The glass in the library window exploded into fragments. Burke dived under the thick oak reading table as a hail of bullets raked the room, hurling splinters of wood and fragments of ancient bookbindings into the air.

For a second he held his breath. From his position underneath the table, Burke could see Sabine's legs and the monk's black robes, where they had thrown themselves to the floor about ten yards away, next to the wall. Their upper halves were blocked from his vision by a long, glass-topped display case. Of Boston, he could see no sign. He wondered if he had been hit. That sort of fire was meant to kill. It could cut a man in half. Or woman.

There was no doubt about who was firing. Korkin's killer had come back to finish the job. But who was he working for? Boston's little speech had raised a terrible doubt in his mind, one the gunman's first words did nothing to dispel:

'*Raus, alle,*' he called in German. But then he repeated it in English. 'Out, all of you.'

The gun opened up again. A short staccato burst.

The reply was a single round that Burke heard ricochet off a wall. He edged towards the rear of the heavy table. Only a few feet away, he realized with a start, Dickie Boston was standing up, behind one of the Gothic pillars. From inside his smart navy blazer he had produced a gun which he was now clutching with both hands, more like a Los Angeles cop than a denizen of London's clubland. Fuck me, thought Burke: bloody James Bond after all.

Another round winged into the architecture, sending a spray of white plaster dust like a miniature snowfall on to the library's floor.

'Please. The documents please. Then no more killing.'

Boston dropped, and rolled over, to end up under the table beside Burke, breathing heavily. A single shot slammed off the edge of the heavy oak. It had to be four inches thick. Burke wondered if a direct shot from a high-velocity weapon could pierce it, and decided, uncomfortably, that it probably could.

'The traitors are dead. *Vechna Rus* requires no more blood.'

'Jesus Christ. *Vechna*. Not the Krauts after all,' muttered Boston. Burke stared at him perplexed.

'Eternal Russia,' Boston whispered. 'A band of nationalists well to the right of Zhirinovsky. Based in St Petersburg. Most of them ex-special forces. Mad as hatters. And I thought it was her lot.'

'We thought it was you.' But even as he said it, Burke wondered what he meant. 'Her lot': was he accepting Boston's preposterous allegations? The whining ricochet of a bullet off the masonry behind them brought him back to the matter of the moment.

'Please. The documents. But now.'

There was something familiar about the voice. A tone, a timbre, an inflection, an accent. With a tingle that ran the length of his spine, Burke recognized the voice of Slava Rusakov. Korkin had been killed by his own bodyguard.

A bullet zinged through the empty space above them and embedded itself in the wall behind. From the real world outside, the great bells of the pilgrimage church erupted into their booming, joyful carillon, pealing the glad tidings of the Resurrection. Loud enough to waken the dead.

Thunk, thunk, thunk. Three single rounds thudded into the pillar behind which Boston had been hiding. The man was playing with them. But how long would his patience last?

'Slava,' Burke called out. Boston stared at him as if he had gone mad. 'Slava, why did you do it? You killed Valery, for God's sake?'

Crouching beside him, Boston mouthed in astonishment, 'You know him?' then nodded in encouragement. The more the nutcase was distracted, the better their chances.

'Ah, Yamon.' Slava was calm, worryingly so. It made Burke sick to hear the killer mispronounce his name so familiarly. 'You are so very right: for God's sake, indeed.' The voice turned harsh. 'He was a traitor. He had to die. You were not the target. He was. He would have sold Russia for a moment of fame.'

No. But for the lives of his friends, Burke was tempted to say. He said nothing.

'Like the old man. He was a traitor too. He should have known better. But he was a Soviet. He cared nothing for the real Russia.'

'And Siggy and Magnus, in Iceland. And the Norwegian. And the taxi driver in London.'

'For the Norwegian, I am sorry, but even good marksmen cannot avoid the fool who leaps into the bullet. Of your taxi driver, I know nothing. Your mad bombers, they are not ours.'

Burke closed his eyes and groaned at the irony. His imagination had taken him one step too far.

'But the others, Magnus and Siggy.'

'Regrettable. But necessary. We do not want the status quo damaged any more than your British secret service does, whatever the treachery of the West towards Russia in the past. Your cause and ours is identical, Mr Boston. Give us this document and we will make sure it never sees the light of day.'

Burke turned to Boston, who sneered. 'Like hell they won't. Vechna are dedicated to restoring an orthodox Christian version of the Soviet Empire, probably with a fucking Tsar, for all I know.'

But it was Sabine who was doing the shouting now, from somewhere on the other side of the long bookcases that ran down the left-hand side of the library.

'You're lying, Slava. Admit it. You destroyed the plane and the evidence of how the scientists of the West helped Russia back in 1945 because you don't want your people to know about it. That's why you tried to stop us. You don't ever want to admit that there might be people in the West who aren't dedicated to destroying Russia.'

Of course, thought Burke. Suddenly it made sense. But if she had seen it like that all along, why had he been so blind? Or had he simply failed to understand what made Sabine Kotzke tick. And then he stopped thinking and started worrying. About the sudden silence. About the effect her words were having on Slava.

But Sabine hadn't finished. She was speaking again, a loud, measured tone, a very German tone, Burke thought, that was meant to be calculatedly calm, but he worried that the Russian might find it smug, even goading. 'That's why you want the Sunrise Protocol, isn't it, so that you can use it as and when you want to show that the West has been plotting against Russia for ever? That's your version of the truth. *Pravda*, eh? Like in the newspaper.'

A hail of automatic fire raked the room. She had hit a nerve. An exceedingly raw one, too.

The next instant, Burke was thrown back as Boston sprang out from under the table, letting off four shots at the Russian, before again darting behind the stone pillar. From the balcony Slava Rusakov could probably see almost the whole of the room. The balcony ran in a U-shape along both sides and straddled the width of the library at the end opposite the main entrance. Access to the gallery level was by a single spiral staircase in the centre at his end. Simply by moving along the 'U', the Russian had a clear shot at almost any angle. He could wait, Burke thought, but not indefinitely.

As it turned out, the decision was not wholly up to the Russian. Suddenly he was hurled backwards by a shot from below. The bullet that tore through the wooden floor he was standing on seared the arm of his leather jacket and left him winded against the wall. But he sprang back to his feet, sprinted across to the far corner of the balcony, leaned over and fired repeatedly across the floor below.

Burke heard a shot, a shout, and a female cry above the explosive roar. Two sharp reports slammed into his brain. The harsh hot reek of cordite singed the musty air. He squinted at the pillar where Boston had taken cover. He was not there.

Burke edged to the left-hand side of the table, hoping it was outside Slava's line of fire. On the other side of the library, beneath the balcony, Sabine lay on the floor, crawling slowly towards her lost weapon. Burke realized what had happened. Sabine Kotzke had had a gun and had used it. She had counted on surprise, marksmanship and luck. But too much of the latter. She must have known she would only get one shot. And she had blown it. Her weapon lay in open view of the gunman. Inaccessible. Except that, for some unknown reason, he had stopped firing.

'Scum.' The voice was unmistakably English, albeit without a trace of its usual affected plumminess. It was followed by a single, muffled report.

In the brief moment that Kotzke had distracted the Russian's attention, Dickie Boston had summoned up all the adrenalin and the instinct he had once honed on the firing ranges of southern England and spun round the pillar, both hands forward in the classic firing position, and pumped two rounds straight into the godsent target of Slava Rusakov blazing over the edge of the balcony.

Eamonn Burke raised his head cautiously above the table to see Boston standing by the foot of the spiral staircase, gun still smoking from the final shot he had put into the back of the head of the corpse that slumped like a seasick sailor over the edge of the gallery.

Burke's heart was pounding as he emerged from his shelter, noting the charred gouges in the old oak. Glass lay on the floor in glinting multicoloured shards. The air reeked of gunsmoke. Burke breathed it deep into his lungs as he sighed with relief.

'Well done, Dickie. Bloody well done.'

He looked for Sabine, eager to take her into his arms, the doubts that Boston had sown forgotten.

'Don't touch it.' Boston snapped. He had spun round to face Sabine who was crawling slowly towards her lost weapon, his pistol trained on her.

'Stand. Now.'

She did as she was told, one hand clutching her bleeding shoulder.

'Thank you. Over there, please, next to old Eamonn.' Sabine, her eyes flickering between them, moved slowly across the room. Like a reprise of a nightmare, the whole grotesque conversation of a few minutes earlier came back to Burke. He stared at her, willing truth out of her blank expression.

'Stop,' Boston commanded bluntly, when she was only a few feet from Burke. He had both of them covered.

'Right, let's have no more fucking about. Just hand over the "*dokumyenti*",' he parodied Slava's accent, 'and we'll get the history books nicely closed again, all right?'

'You think it's that easy, don't you?' Sabine spat out.

'I know it's that easy. This silly little episode is almost over, and I intend to finish it. Now be a good girl, and I won't blow your silly fucking head off. Because I could, you know. I can always blame it on him.' He jerked his head in the direction of the Russian's corpse. 'And believe me, no one is going to be asking me any questions. So don't piss about. Let's just get on with it, hmmm?'

Burke watched with horror. Boston, just seconds ago their saviour, was now the threat. And he wasn't joking.

'Dickie?' His voice was imploring, appealing to the man's humanity. Surely the madness was over now.

'I'm sorry, Eamonn, but this is important. Your friend here's little lot have broken the school rules. We're out of bounds now.'

'But she doesn't have it.'

'I'm well aware of that. But there would be no point in threatening Brother Klement now, would there? He's become far too unworldly to care for his own life.'

The monk was hovering timidly, his face ashen, his arms folded within the sleeves of his cassock, his eyes closed as if in penitence, a vain prayer that a burden he had never asked for be lifted from him.

'But he might just care for hers. Or yours. So what do you say, *Bruder*, I'm not going to waste time. Let's make it a count of three, shall we?' He levelled the pistol at Sabine's head and squeezed the trigger. 'One . . . two . . . three . . .'

The detonation came like a blow to the head with a cricket bat. Burke felt the force physically, his eyes squeezing shut, his ears protesting at the pain. He looked up to see Dickie Boston slumped on the ground at his feet, a black burn mark on the side of his head oozing red, the gun still smoking in his hand. A few feet from him, Sabine Kotzke stood wide-eyed as if glued to the plasterwork, gaping at the hole in the wall beside her. Then her head turned, slowly, as did Burke's, to stare in amazement at the old black-robed figure standing by the library wall holding Sabine's pistol in his hand, an expression of almost incalculable grief on his face.

'It may seem a strange thing,' the monk said in impeccable English. 'But that is the first time I have ever killed an Englishman,' and he dropped the gun with a clatter on to the parquet floor.

46

Götterdämmerung

Burke looked at her, then down at the body of Dickie Boston, and at the monk who now kneeled on the blood-spattered parquet, his eyes closed in prayer, or perhaps just to blot out the world around him. Sabine Kotzke stared at the ground, then lifted her head and stared back. Burke thought that for a moment she looked grateful. He was almost laughing, trying not to cry.

'Listen to me, Eamonn.' She was angry now. 'The CIA thought they'd hidden all traces of the Sunrise Protocol when they bought up the Stasi files. Most were destroyed, not by some Communist praetorian guard determined to go down with the secrets of the old regime but by the boys from Langley, the computer kids with their electronic erasers.'

Burke watched her lips move, his face blank.

'Why?' he asked. 'What the hell was it all about? What's in it for you?'

'You wouldn't understand, would you? I grew up in a world that rewrote history to order. My schoolteachers pretended Hitler and Stalin had never been allies. They told us Berliners welcomed Soviet troops with open arms in 1945 – when my grandmother and her sisters were hiding in the coal cellar with blackened faces in the vain hope of avoiding gang rape. For all I know, my grandfather was some Ukrainian peasant who used his prick like a bayonet. I could go on and on, you know: Berlin 1953, Budapest 1956, Prague 1968, Warsaw 1981 – all the lies that made evil acts of cynical repression seem justifiable for the greater good. Instead, here we had a different story, a legacy left by one of the demons of the Cold War, Klaus Fuchs. A story of a few scientists getting together to do the wrong thing, but for the right reasons, individuals who could make a difference, while the bloody governments went about their bloody business as usual.

'Okay, so Boston knew it was Dickel's idea, not the politicians'. Ours are as bad as yours. Worse maybe, ever since the move back to Berlin. But a few of us, in the service, a few of us who'd been victims already of a state abusing its power, we thought we could make a difference. Were we so bloody wrong to try?'

But Burke was shaking his head, eyes closed now.

'All right, Eamonn. Hear no evil, see no evil. Is that your attitude? Well what's the difference between that and your precious Winston bloody Churchill and the saintly FDR plotting to switch sides at the last moment to secure their global ambitions. Nothing, except that they were on the winning side.

'Okay, so it didn't happen. But just because they think they won the Cold War too, even yesterday's questions are not to be asked. Is that it? Maybe it is only some nutcases who're prepared to kill to stop the truth coming out, but maybe not. So what will you do now? Join the cover-up?'

Burke was silent. 'Look,' she said. 'We didn't know it would end like this, didn't know about Vechna, about Slava and his mates. Or at least, I didn't. Dickel didn't. Or just didn't think. I don't know. Oh, for Christ's sake, Eamonn, don't you see. We knew most of it. Fuchs's diary was relatively complete, but we didn't have the evidence. We knew you could find it. And it would all be so much better coming from you.'

'Fuchs. Who killed him?'

Sabine gave an exasperated shrug, as if nothing mattered less. 'Oh, Eamonn. God. The devil. I don't know. He was an old man.'

'There was no murder, was there?'

'We had to get you interested, involved. You needed a conspiracy. But we couldn't just feed you the big one. We needed you to find out, for yourself, as well as for us.'

'Dickie was right. You thought I'd be your patsy. The mad conspiracy theorist who'd be delighted to learn that his own side were the bad boys after all. Oh yes. And what's more it damn near worked.'

The torrent dried up as quickly as it had begun. She had tried to get him angry, he thought, to force some emotion into him. She had got him angry all right, but not in a way she would ever know. Not now. He shook his head. And looked back at her, wondering what she saw.

All Eamonn Burke could see the was futile vanity of the whole vainglorious endeavour. He could see it as plainly as he saw Brother Klement, kneeling by Sabine's weapon, tears trickling down his cheeks, tears of regret for the necessity of taking a life in order to save a life – the age-old dilemma of the Christian soldier, faced even by ex-Nazis. He saw it as plainly as he saw Sabine Kotzke standing there, convinced of her own righteousness, yet shaking with uncertainty. He turned his head and walked quietly towards the library door, turned the key in the lock, and stepped out into the pale spring sunshine. Away from the stupidity of it all. Away from the slaughterhouse. Away from her.

Outside, he saw nothing. Not the laughing beer-drinkers. Not the shocked faces of those who had gathered in a tipsy group, frightened and astonished by the commotion. He didn't know what he was going to do. Didn't know who would believe him, or what they would do if they did. He didn't know what he believed in any more. But then nothing really had changed; he had never really known. Only for a moment, he had made the mistake of deluding himself. He had grasped hold of a string in a hurricane only to find out it, too, was blowing in the wind. Now the ground he stood on had turned to dust, dust with blood in it. Behind him he heard a woman's voice cry out. He thought it called a name. He didn't notice whose. The red convertible sat there brazenly with its hood down in the spring sunshine. He walked past it to where the buses brought the strangers and took them away again. The last thing he wanted to do was look back. He resisted the temptation.

Appendix

From the spring of 1945 Heinrich Himmler began to put out peace feelers to the West. Official history says he was rebuffed. In March 1945, to the Russians' surprise and envy, the Western Allies found the Rhine bridge at Remagen undefended. Allen Dulles, then working for the OSS in Bern, met on several occasions in Geneva with 'top-level contacts', including SS representatives, to discuss a separate surrender of German forces in Italy. The plan, known as 'Operation Sunrise' became known to Moscow and provoked protests from Stalin. It was overtaken by events on the eastern front.

◆

By June 1946, nine months into the programme to develop the hydrogen bomb, the atomic arsenal of the world consisted of nine American 'Fat Boy' weapons of the type dropped on Nagasaki. Of these only seven could be made operational. The reason was a lack of the crucial initiator devices.

◆

On 29 June 1954, after hearing evidence from Edward Teller, among others, the United States Atomic Energy Commission concluded: 'Dr Oppenheimer is not entitled to the continued confidence of the Government and of this Commission because of the proof of fundamental defects in his character.' His security clearance was withdrawn. He died of cancer of the throat in 1967, at the comparatively young age of sixty-two.

◆

Secret material from Albert Einstein's private archives, only released in 1998, revealed that from 1935 to 1945 he had an affair with Margarita Konenkova, the wife of a Soviet sculptor. She was, in fact, an agent of Moscow Centre.

◆

Anatoly Yatzkov, also known as Yakovlev, code name 'John', was the NKVD's 'rezident' in New York throughout the Second World War. He died in Moscow in 1993. To the end, he maintained that his successful espionage owed a debt of gratitude to an unnamed agent, known only as 'Perseus', based in Albuquerque.

◆

United States intelligence services have never identified Perseus, nor pinpointed his treason. As a result, the most authoritative government publications insist, in spite of the evidence from Moscow, that this agent was either 'mythical or a composite'.

A Note on the Author

Peter Millar was born in Northern Ireland and educated at Magdalen College, Oxford. He is an award-winning foreign correspondent, critic and columnist who has covered Central and Eastern Europe for the *Sunday Times* and now also writes for the *Financial Times*, the *Daily Mail* and the *London Evening Standard*. He has lived in Berlin, Moscow, Paris and Brussels, and speaks four languages fluently. He is married and has two children.